*The Golden Silence*

'[A] compelling crime novel which speeds along, never faltering in pace, to a gripping showdown.'                                        *Scotsman*

'Crime aficionados have particular cause to be grateful to the talented Paul Johnston: apart from the much-acclaimed series of Quintin Dalrymple, Scottish-set novels, Johnston has created another, equally distinctive series. The Alex Mavros books are set in Greece (where the author now lives), and this half-Greek, half-Scots private eye is a memorable creation; resourceful, quixotic and sympathetic. *A Deeper Shade of Blue* was a powerful outing for Mavros; *The Golden Silence* is, if anything, even better. This time, Alex is assigned to track down a missing teenager. As Alex searches, he is aware of a host of savage deaths in Athens. Then Alex begins to notice connections, and as he enters a dangerous criminal underworld, the remnants of the civil war begin to figure in a lethal scenario. Mavros is a more straightforward character than the eccentric Dalrymple, but this new series is proving to be Paul Johnston's most trenchant work yet.'                    *Good Book Guide*

'With this gripping, vicious thriller, Paul Johnston proves yet again why he deserves his place on the crime-writing pedestal beside Ian Rankin and Quintin Jardine'                                        *Daily Record*

'Good characterisation and exciting moments in this very readable thriller'                                        *Sunday Telegraph*

'Paul Johnston is, in my opinion, one of the most underrated crime writers . . . This book is original and high-paced . . . Johnston deserves to be a bestseller with this one.'                    *Shots Magazine*

'Paul Johnston reveals the Athens that the Greek Tourist Board don't want us to know about. Dark, terrifying and still shadowed by its past, this is a city that nurses its secrets until the tenacious Alex Mavros rips the curtain aside. This is a gripp

'As in all the best thrillers, bullets
follows the trail to the missing girl
the agonising fires of Greece's aw

PAUL JOHNSTON

# The Golden Silence

HODDER

First published in Great Britain in 2004 by Hodder and Stoughton
First published in paperback in Great Britain in 2005 by Hodder and Stoughton
A division of Hodder Headline

The right of Paul Johnston to be identified as the Author
of the Work has been asserted by him in accordance
with the Copyright, Designs and Patents Act 1988.

A Hodder paperback

2

A CIP catalogue record for this title
is available from the British Library

ISBN 0 340 82564 2

Typeset in Monotype Plantin Light by
Hewer Text Limited, Edinburgh

Printed and bound by
Clays Ltd, St Ives plc

Hodder Headline's policy is to use papers that are natural,
renewable and recyclable products and made from wood
grown in sustainable forests. The logging and manufacturing
processes are expected to conform to the environmental
regulations of the country of origin.

Hodder and Stoughton Ltd
A division of Hodder Headline
338 Euston Road
London NW1 3BH

Readers will save themselves headaches by noting that:

1) Greek masculine names ending in -is, -os and -as lose the final -s in the vocative case: 'Damis, Panos and Nondas are watching the news.' But, 'Watch the news, Dami, Pano and Nonda.'

2) Feminine surnames are formed differently from masculine ones: Alex Mavros, but Anna Mavrou; Stratos Chiotis, but Rea Chioti.

*The Free News*, Athens, April 18th 2002

# BRUTAL MURDER IN THE NORTHERN SUBURBS!

by Lambis Bitsos, Crime Correspondent

Construction worker Petros Aslanis had the shock of his life on Monday morning when he arrived on site in Metamorfosi. Lying at the bottom of a foundation trench for the new motorway was a naked male body!

'At first I thought it was a heap of rubbish,' said Mr Aslanis, 44, a local resident and father of three. 'People are always tossing junk into the trenches and the poor guy's skin wasn't white, it was covered in bruises. Then I saw the blood on his head and ran for my supervisor.'

Units of the Greek Police arrived promptly and cordoned off the scene, causing heavy traffic congestion in the area. Commander Nikos Kriaras, recently appointed head of the organised crime division, stated that a murder investigation was underway. 'The severity of the injuries and the absence of clothing rule out accident and suicide,' he said. 'There is evidence to suggest that this is yet another in the spate of gangland killings that has plagued the city over the last two months. Citizens can rest assured that all necessary steps will be taken to apprehend the vicious criminals behind this scourge.'

The commander did not specify the nature of the evidence linking this death to earlier ones, but sources indicate that the as yet unidentified victim underwent torture. The fact that little attempt was made to conceal the body suggests that it was left as a warning or an example. The northern suburbs of Athens have become a battlefield for criminal organisations fighting over lucrative drugs, protection and prostitution rackets.

'It's a disgrace,' said Mr Aslanis. 'This place used to be peaceful, but now I fear for my daughters every time they leave the house. When is the government going to do something about the violence?'

The body of the unfortunate man has been taken to the morgue for forensic examination. In the meantime, work on the desperately needed motorway has been suspended while police comb the scene, traffic in the area is at a standstill, and residents of the capital walk the streets with fear in their hearts.

# I

'And another thing,' said the Fat Man, leaning over the only occupied table in his café in the Flea Market area of central Athens. 'They can take the stinking Euro and ram it up their—'

'Cut it out, Yiorgo,' Alex Mavros interrupted, the miniature cup of unsweetened coffee halfway to his lips. 'I don't need to hear this first thing in the morning.'

'First thing in the morning?' the heavy figure scoffed. 'Some of us have been up since five-thirty. Some of us have a real job to do.'

Mavros couldn't stop himself from rising to the challenge. 'You have a real job, do you? Making coffee for rapacious market traders is enough to justify your existence, I suppose. Karl Marx would be very impressed.' The Fat Man was still nominally a Communist, even though his membership of the Party had brought him more trouble than joy.

'At least I'm not a lackey of the rich. There won't be any private detectives after the revolution, you can bet on that.'

'Bet money on that?' Mavros shook strands of his long black hair from his face and smiled. 'Like the players at your illegal card table every evening? I don't think the comrades will be sanctioning those in the perfect state either.'

Yiorgos gave a grimace. 'You think you're so smart, you poxy half-breed. Just because women swoon over your weird eye . . .' He lumbered off towards the kitchen area. The chill cabinet was clanking to cope with the spring warmth.

Mavros finished his coffee and took a bite of *galaktoboureko*.

Life would be unbearable without the Fat Man's coffee, known among his select band of customers as the best in Athens, and his aged mother's pastries. This morning's tray of the custard-filled filo was yet another masterpiece. Fortified, he returned to the field of combat.

'It's not my fault that, unlike yours, my character is made up of the best of two nations,' he said over his shoulder. His long-dead father Spyros had been a leading Greek Communist, while his mother Dorothy, who still lived in the city, was Scottish. 'And as for my eye, well, I'm not complaining.' Although Mavros's right eye was the bright blue he had inherited from his father, the left was speckled with his mother's brown. It was true that some women seemed to find that flaw a source of fascination.

The Fat Man grunted, his head bowed over the piece of goat's cheese that he was slicing. 'That would explain the way the delightful Niki dotes over you, eh, Alex?'

Mavros gave his friend a sharp look at the reference to his girlfriend. He got up and went over to the enclosed courtyard at the rear. New leaves were beginning to appear on the extensive branches of the vine that had woven itself around a buckling pergola. The stacked chairs and tables were covered in grime.

'Any chance of you cleaning up out here?' he called. 'You know I use this place for business.' He invited potential clients to the Fat Man's to vet them. He'd never felt the need of an office and it kept people out of his home. If they disapproved of the run-down café, he didn't want their custom. He wasn't a Party member. He wasn't politically committed at all – it seemed that he hadn't inherited that gene – but he liked to confront his customarily well-off employers with life on the street.

'Clean up yourself,' came the reply. 'I'm busy.'

'Busy filling your belly?' Mavros spread his arms wide.

'Come on, Yiorgo, at least give me a hand. Don't I bring you customers?'

The Fat Man came out reluctantly, a couple of grubby cloths in his hand. He was still chewing, the pouched cheeks and bald head giving him the look of an oversized, tonsured chipmunk. 'How many of the capitalists' Euros do you think I make out of the customers you bring me?' he muttered, tossing a cloth to Mavros. 'You've hardly worked at all the last few months.'

Mavros started wiping a table. The Fat Man was right. He hadn't been busy since the turn of the year, when he'd been involved in a major case involving terrorism that had ended badly. Since then he hadn't felt like going back to his normal work, tracking down missing teenagers who'd had enough of home or people who'd been sucked in by the capital's numerous temptations – drugs, prostitution, gambling. He'd have to find a client soon, though. The bills were mounting.

'The bastard Euro,' the Fat Man said, when Mavros didn't reply.

'Christ, don't start again.' Ever since the drachma had disappeared at the start of the year, Yiorgos had been on the Euro's case. He had a point. There had been widespread unsanctioned price rises in Greece as in other countries, and the new currency wasn't popular. 'Anyway, what are you so down in the mouth about?' Mavros demanded, glancing up through the pergola into the strong sunlight. A northerly wind was dispersing the pollution cloud. 'It'll soon be Easter and you'll be shutting up shop to spend even more time with your nutritional requirements.'

The Fat Man dropped a chair on to the gravel. 'Screw you, you long-haired sack of shit. Can't you take anything seriously?' This was one of his standard tactics. As soon as the abuse got too personal – that is, his weight came up – he started to play the earnest citizen. 'Haven't you noticed,

Mr Head-in-the-Sand Private Investigator? This country is going to the dogs.'

'What, more than usual?' Mavros stepped back and admired his handiwork. At least one table was in commission now. 'Anyway, I thought the Party was supposed to have an internationalist outlook.'

The Fat Man flicked his cloth at a fly that was buzzing around them. 'All right, smartass, the whole of Europe's going to the dogs.' He snorted. 'Thanks to the Euro. But it's worse here than anywhere else. I mean, the gangsters are torturing people and tossing their bodies into building sites now.' He glared through the dust that had risen between them. 'Of course, that's a different kind of crime from what you work with.'

'It is,' Mavros replied, giving his friend the eye. 'As you well know, I'm a missing persons specialist, not a homicide detective.'

'Oh, well, that's all right then,' the Fat Man said ironically. 'So what do I do when some scumbag with a gun in his pocket comes by and asks for a monthly contribution if I don't want my place to go up in smoke? What do I do when they find out where we live and put the frighteners on my mother? Christ and the Holy Mother, Alex, your father and brother wouldn't have ignored the shit that's happening.'

Mavros was scrubbing a chair, his eyes down. Yiorgos knew how to get to him. His father had dedicated himself to improving people's lives, while his brother had been a leader of the student resistance to the dictatorship. He blinked at a sudden memory of Andonis's smiling face and wide blue eyes. Although he'd devoted all the time he could to finding his brother, there had been no trace of him since he'd disappeared after a secret meeting in 1972.

'Not fair, Yiorgo.'

The Fat Man wasn't mollified. 'Anyway, aren't the people who have been committing all these murders missing?'

'I suppose they are, my friend. But no one's offered to pay me to find them.'

The café owner's eyes widened. 'Is that all it takes, you mercenary?' he shouted, jamming thick fingers into a pocket beneath his stained apron. 'Here,' he said, throwing coins on to the table. 'Interested now?'

'Jesus, Yiorgo, calm down.' He picked up a two-Euro piece that had fallen to the ground. 'You know I'll help if anyone hassles you.' He handed back the coin.

The Fat Man gradually got his breathing under control. 'I know that,' he said, his tone less agitated. 'But what's happening in the city is wrong. You know it as well as I do. Someone's got to do something.'

Mavros nodded. 'Someone plural. The cops, the politicians. There isn't much that individuals can do.'

'Bullshit, Alex. That's the easy way out. You did plenty in the winter.' The Fat Man knew about the terrorism case, had even played his own reluctant part in it, though he'd been sworn to secrecy. 'You said it yourself, it's spring. There's no excuse to stay inside now. Get out there and do your thing.'

Shortly afterwards, Mavros headed for the door. Yiorgos was right. It was time he started work. But where were the clients?

It was a morning made for killing.

The reed beds on the shore by Kastoria in the far north of Greece were resounding with the calls of aquatic birds, the newly arrived pelicans resplendent in white and pink. The Father sat at the bow, the Son stood at the oars of the blue-painted boat. The younger man eyed the ridges of the mountains that surrounded the expanse of water. Albania lay not far to the west. They were six hundred metres above sea level and there were patches of snow on the peaks, despite the strong sunlight. The wind from the north still had more than a hint of winter's teeth about it.

The Son, tall and bulky, pushed forward on the heavy lengths of wood to bring the boat into position over the place where perch were to be found. He controlled the craft with its high prow and stern without conscious thought. The red-tiled roofs of the town on the promontory were glowing in the sun, the last of the morning mists having disappeared on the wind.

'It's the shape of a kidney,' the Son said.

'Eh?' The Father, now crouching at the bow with his net at the ready, had a rough voice.

'The lake. It's shaped like a human kidney.'

'In the name of God, what are you babbling about, boy?' The silver skein reared up in the air and came down over the rippling water. 'I'm trying to catch these fish and you've suddenly become a medical expert.' He leaned forward and started manipulating the net with strong fingers. His face beneath the cap that he wore low over his eyes was weather-beaten and deeply furrowed.

'There was a time when you were interested in the organs of the body,' said the man at the oars. His voice was soft and even, his face smooth. His dense curls and easy smile would have made him good-looking if it hadn't been for his eyes. They were icy blue and piercing, as ungenerous as a tax official's.

'What makes you think that time has gone?' the older man said, glancing over his shoulder. His eyes were dark-brown and bloodshot, even colder than his son's, and the grizzled moustache, stained by nicotine, cut across his face like a scar. He started to haul the net in, his gaze now on the surface of the water. Flashes of silver came from fish that were struggling frantically. 'What do you know about . . . fuck!' He jerked his head and shoulders back. 'It's the pike!'

The Son dropped to one knee, keeping his left hand on the oar to steady the boat. His eyes narrowed, focusing on the shadowy green shape that was driving the perch in the net to even greater frenzy. His right hand quickly located the spear that lay on the floor planks.

'Move to the other side,' he said, his voice betraying no emotion. 'Slowly.'

When the Father had complied, the Son stepped forward carefully, keeping the keel level. The net, secured to the bow, was now bulging above the surface as the small fish tried to evade the jaws of the predator. There was a brief glimpse of the pike's broad flank the instant that the Son struck. He drove the shining weapon into the water with a loud effusion of air. Immediately after the blow, he grabbed the shaft of the weapon with his other hand and hung on.

'Gaff it,' he said, legs splayed to keep his balance. 'Gaff it and keep clear of its jaws when we get it out of the water. Those teeth will take off your hand.'

The older man smiled as he picked up the long implement. 'You'd like that, wouldn't you, boy?' He stretched forward and hooked the pike by its gills.

Trying not to rock the boat too much, the pair dragged the creature over the side and dumped it on the floor. Its uneven jaws lined with needle-sharp teeth were snapping together continuously, a large and glassy orange eye staring up at them.

'Kill it,' the Son said, letting go of the spear and stepping back to the oars. He grinned as the pike's tail slapped against his lower leg. The birds in the reeds, disturbed by the commotion, were sending up volleys of raucous cries.

The Father looked up at him, one boot pressing down on the fish's head as its metre-long body continued to writhe between them. 'What the matter? Haven't you got the stomach for it?'

'You know I have. But you're getting old. You need to keep your eye in.'

The Father shrugged and drew a long, serrated blade from

the sheath on his belt. With a swift cut he almost severed the pike's head, watching as its dark blood spattered over his waterproof trousers.

'Not bad,' the Son said as he moved the oars to steady the boat. 'Don't forget the net.'

The Father was already pulling in the catch. When the net was on board, he opened it and started to toss the gasping perch into a bucket next to the motionless predator. 'A good haul,' he said, when he finished.

'But it isn't time to go in yet,' the Son said, leaning on the oars.

The older man twisted his head towards him. 'You've heard from her?' Their long-established practice was that messages from their employer were only discussed on the lake or in the stone-lined garage beneath the house. The likelihood of surveillance was minimal, but they weren't the kind who left anything to chance.

The Son nodded, his eyes scanning the lake. There were no other boats near them. 'One of the family's musclemen was taken out last night. He turned up in a construction site this morning, naked and beaten to a pulp.'

'Tortured like the others?'

'Tortured after a fashion, so the insiders say.' He laughed. 'Not expertly.'

The Father ran his bloody fingers over his moustache. 'So we're wanted in the big city, are we? When?'

'We need to leave today.' The Son started to propel the boat towards the harbour, his arms moving in effortless strokes. He was wearing the tattered roll-neck he always used on the lake and there was stubble on his face. The clothes would be changed and he would be clean-shaven before they started on the long drive to Athens. Among the many things he had learned from the Father was to be well turned out for a job. 'I can go on my own, you know.'

The older man's jaw jutted forward. 'No, you can't, boy. I'm not ready to retire yet.'

The Father looked away, hearing the bells from the town's numerous churches. The faithful were observing the latest rite in the lead-up to Easter. The sound eased his mind. He'd been brought up to respect the Church. It was an integral part of Greece. As a young man, he and his fellow soldiers had fought for the nation. His subsequent career in the Military Police had been dedicated to saving it from Communist traitors. He took in the white walls of Kastoria's old houses and their reflection in the blue-grey water. It was as if there were a shadow town in the lake, inhabited by the silent ghosts of the criminals he had destroyed. But he had no fear of them.

'Hey, wake up.' The Son's mocking voice cut into his thoughts. 'Didn't you always tell me to keep my wits about me at all times?'

The Father stared at him. 'You walk a tightrope,' he said slowly. 'You live in an enclosed world where only you matter. That way, only that way, can you prepare yourself for the business in hand.'

The Son laughed again, this time louder. 'The business in hand. Why can't you say it? We're—'

'Silence!' the Father shouted. 'We don't talk about what we do, boy. We don't talk about what we feel.'

The man at the oars was silent. Although there was still a smile on his lips, his eyes were emptier than before. He looked down at the lifeless pike, its smooth green side disfigured by the mark of the spear.

'I served my country to the best of my abilities,' the Father said, disregarding his own order. 'I punished the godless enemies of the state. And how was I repaid? I had to come up here to the back of beyond with nothing more than the clothes I was wearing.'

'You soon made good.' The Son was familiar with the old

man's black moods. The only way was to humour him and wait for them to pass.

'Yes, I did. After your mother . . . your mother died, I started on the production line at the fur factory. I decapitated the animals, I skinned them with my own hands . . .'

You were just the man for that line of work, the Son thought, keeping the boat away from the shore till the tirade ran its course. The Father was losing his grip. He would soon be a hindrance on the trips south.

'. . . had to burst my balls at that accursed factory,' the old man continued, spittle on his moustache. 'Eventually I ran it, I made it a success. And I was smart enough to sell up before women stopped buying furs and the business went down the drain.' He glared at his son. 'I paid for your extra school lessons, I paid for your motorbike and your first car. And I taught you everything about the work we do.' He pushed the cap back on his forehead. 'So don't mock me, boy. There's more than enough life in me yet.'

The Son nodded and rowed towards the harbour. The old man was calm again, the storm had passed. Now it was time to concentrate on the preparations for the trip.

There was a shout from the wall.

'Holy Mother, look what the old man and his boy have brought in,' said a bald-headed man in dungarees to his companions, pointing at the carcass of the pike. 'Nothing escapes them!'

The Father looked at the Son. For the first time he smiled back at his heir and successor, his eyes mirroring the chill water of the mountain lake.

Mavros walked towards the ancient temple, thinking about what the Fat Man had said. In the past he would have got on the phone and chased his contacts for clients. That prospect made him groan. He should have gone straight back to work after the big case at the end of the year, but he'd been shaken by the fact that he'd brought his family into danger.

He stopped at the kiosk by the station and looked at the midday newspapers that had been hung about it. Most of them featured the latest gangland killing. He stood beneath *The Free News*, the country's leading independent paper, and scanned the article by a journalist he knew. A fuzzy colour photograph of a naked corpse in a pit was displayed between the headline and the first paragraph of text.

'Disgusting.'

Mavros turned to find an old woman in a moth-eaten fur coat standing beside him. Her hair was immaculately arranged and a small dog was sniffing the ground at her feet.

'Don't you think, young man?'

'Terrible.'

'Of course, the dead man will be an Albanian, you can be sure of that. They come here and steal our property, our young people's jobs—'

Mavros gave her a disapproving look. He bought the paper, then walked quickly away. He had no time for the common prejudice against the immigrant workers who kept the nation's economy running. Besides, he reckoned from the little he'd read that the victim was as likely to be Greek as any other nationality. Despite the incursions of Russian and Serbian gangs, the majority of criminals were home-grown. He looked up at the Acropolis from the newly pedestrianised street. The buildings on the rock were resisting the wind, their glorious lines giving a tantalising hint of a more perfect world. Then he heard the roar of buses and cars from the streets below, their engines tainting the air and their drivers hurling abuse. Modern-day Athens was about as far from perfection as you could get.

His mobile phone rang.

'Alex, is that you? For God's sake, speak!'

'Niki, hi. Sorry. I didn't recognise the number.' Since the terrorism case, Mavros had been cautious about identifying himself. He suspected that his phones were still being monitored and he didn't want to make the security operatives' lives any easier. His girlfriend Niki Glezou, unaware of that, had been growing more and more infuriated.

'Ah, he speaks. Sorry, Alex. You're right. I'm at a colleague's desk.'

'Good morning.'

'Yes, I suppose it is morning for you. You've only just got up, haven't you? Are you at that revolting café?' Niki and the Fat Man had a relationship based on mutual loathing.

'No, I'm not. I'm . . . working.'

'That sounds convincing. What are you doing? Reading the paper?'

'I call it researching contemporary crime trends.'

She gave a sardonic laugh. 'Really?'

'Niki, are you by any chance having a bad day?'

'No, I'm not actually. You're in luck. I'm in the city centre and I'm in need of an early lunch.'

'Okay.' He gave the name of a nearby restaurant.

'Good idea. I'll be there in twenty minutes.'

Mavros put his phone in the pocket of his leather jacket and retraced his steps past the ancient marketplace. He turned on to his street and passed his apartment building. At least no new graffiti had been added to the wall so far. There wasn't much room for more, given the political slogans ('The Government Sucks American Dick'), football supporters' ribaldry ('Olympiakos Do It With Pigs') and social comment ('You Are What You Shop'), but that didn't usually stop the spray-can artists.

The restaurant was on a narrow street that ascended from the Roman market. Breathing heavily, Mavros stopped and looked back down. The new grass in the open space below was glowing in the midday sun. The area on the northern flank of the Acropolis had gone upmarket in recent years, old houses being bought and refurbished by the Athenian elite. Some of them even had swimming-pools on their roofs, the rectangles of blue standing out like brilliant mosaic-pieces.

Mavros went into the vine-clad arbour in front of the restaurant. He and Niki had been regulars since they got together a year back. A smiling waiter ushered him to their usual table in the corner of the terrace. Mavros relaxed into a comfortable chair – none of the Fat Man's backbreaking kind here – and ordered a beer and a plate of appetisers. Before he'd swallowed his first piece of octopus, he heard Niki's voice.

'Beer, Alex? How much work are you going to do this afternoon? Actually, I'll have some too.'

He stood up and kissed the cheek she presented. She was wearing a white blouse and short pink skirt that displayed her full figure and slim legs. Her hair, brown with blonde highlights, was as untidy as ever, and there was an unusually warm smile on her lips.

'How much work are you going to do?' he enquired, pouring beer into a glass for her.

'Less than this morning, I hope.' She dropped a leather satchel replete with files on to a chair and sat down opposite him. 'I spent most of the morning trying to get my superiors to agree to new community facilities in the northern suburbs for my Russian-Greek immigrants.'

'Successfully?'

She took a long drink. 'I think so.' Her dark brown eyes locked on to his. 'You know how good I am.'

He nodded, smiling. 'At your job as a social worker, yes.'

'At everything,' she said, pouting.

'At everything, of course,' Mavros said, backpedalling. Niki was often insecure and she compensated with a notorious temper. It could be useful with recalcitrant officials, but it made her unpredictable.

'Shall we have some red mullet and mountain greens?' Niki asked as the waiter appeared.

Mavros nodded. The fish were expensive, but they were worth it.

'So,' Niki said when they were alone again, 'has any work turned up?'

'I can't tell you that. Haven't you ever heard of client confidentiality?'

She laughed. 'This is Greece in case you've forgotten, you half-Scots fool. People talk about everything here.'

Mavros looked away. If anyone talked about the terrorism case he'd been involved in, heads – including his – would roll.

'All right, Alex, you don't fool me. You aren't working, are you?'

Mavros was fiddling with a piece of bread. He met her gaze and shrugged.

'Don't you think it's time you did something to justify your existence?'

He raised his eyes to the sky. First the Fat Man, now Niki. 'I'm heading that way,' he mumbled.

'Well, let me help you.' She pulled a cardboard folder from her satchel. 'The Tratsou family, formerly Tratsov. Father Dmitri, mother Maria and eighteen-year-old daughter Katia. Ethnic Greeks from the former Soviet Union. I looked after them in the months after their arrival – arranged housing, medical care, you know the sort of thing.'

'Yes. And?'

Niki speared a piece of feta with her fork. 'And they're one of my success stories. Dmitri got work on the new motorway – he's an experienced foreman – and Katia was doing well at school.'

Mavros watched the waiter lay a platter of fish on the table. 'Was doing well at school?'

Niki opened the folder and rummaged through it. 'Out of the blue, she vanished a month ago. And she hasn't been in touch since.'

'Why are you telling me this?' he asked suspiciously.

'Look at her photograph. She's a pretty girl.' Niki's face hardened. 'Ideal fodder for those filthy nightclub owners.'

Mavros examined the image in front of him. This Katia wasn't just pretty, she was stunning. Her hair was strawberry-blonde and she had high cheekbones that gave her an exotic air. 'Why do you say that?'

'Well, it's obvious, isn't it? She has a body to match her face. You can imagine how much Greek men would lust after her. It's common knowledge that the gangs lure innocent girls with offers of work that turns out to be enforced prostitution.' Niki seized a fish and broke its head off. 'The bastards.'

'I'm not clear why you're telling me this,' Mavros said disingenuously.

'Yes, you are,' she said, her mouth full.

He gave up the pretence. 'You're inveigling me into taking on this case.'

'Inveigling you?' Niki said, with a laugh. 'Nothing could be farther from my mind.' Her bare foot suddenly started working its way up his leg. 'Though I promise to make it worth your while if you look into where she's got to.'

'I don't know,' he said. He never showed much interest initially to avoid people taking advantage. In this case, it looked like it was too late.

'The police just added Katia's name to their missing persons list and did nothing,' Niki said, picking up another fish. 'I'm not asking you to work for free. Dmitri has money. Just don't charge him your rich people's rate.'

Mavros grunted. 'Give me more details.'

The expression of a hunter who'd snared a particularly large rabbit spread over Niki's features. 'What a good man you are,' she said, keeping her foot where it was and taking a sheet of paper from a file on the chair next to her. 'I wrote it all down. Address, phone – you'll find that the mother doesn't speak much Greek, but Dmitri gets by.'

He recognised the postcode of a residential area north of the city centre. 'You wrote this in advance,' he said, glaring at her. 'You knew I was going to say yes.'

Niki bowed her head, but failed to conceal a smile.

'You think you can get me to do anything. You think I'm your puppet.'

'No, I don't.' Niki's face was serious again. 'Katia's parents are distraught. She wants to go to university. She's not the kind to disappear and certainly not the kind to stay out of touch. Something's very wrong here.' She kicked him, not very hard. 'She's vulnerable, for Christ's sake. Don't you want to help?'

The truth was that the family's plight had moved Mavros, even though from experience he knew the likeliest explanation was that Katia had gone off with a boyfriend. He was holding back because he always tried to avoid mixing business with his private life. The terrorism case had made him even more unwilling to do that.

'All right,' he said, reaching for his glass. 'I'll look into it. But I want you to promise that you'll keep your distance. I have to do this my way.'

She raised her own glass and clinked it against his. 'Done, Alex. Oh, there's . . . there's one more thing.'

Her reticence made him suspicious. 'What?'

'The father, Dmitri. He's a bit . . . well, a bit impulsive. You'll have to keep an eye on him.'

Mavros sat back and let out a sigh. He was a sucker for people who went missing, but he knew well enough that they often did so because the ones they left behind had driven them to it. The odds were that her father had done that with the beautiful Katia.

The house on the hillside was quiet, the clamour of the city twenty-five kilometres away to the north. The wind was coming through the line of cypresses that barricaded the estate, making the tops of the trees bend like restless fingertips. Far below, the white-capped waves pushed out from the rocky coastline towards the islands in the gulf.

'Very well,' said Rea Chioti, turning from the bullet-proof window to dismiss the nurse. 'I'll be over to see my husband shortly.'

The woman in white tunic and blue trousers bowed her head and retreated on rubber soles.

Rea watched her go and then walked over to the large mahogany desk in the corner of the room. Before Parkinson's disease had confined Stratos to his bed, he'd run the family enterprises from that desk, preferring the villa to his numerous other properties. He would go to one of the offices when business required, but he was always happier in the house he'd built after their marriage in the mid-seventies, when he was fifty-five and she wasn't yet thirty.

'You never thought it would come to this, did you, Strato?' she said under her breath. 'A woman running your life's work.'

One of the phones rang, the red light flashing to show that the line was secure.

'Good afternoon.'

She recognised the voice and returned the greeting, not using the interlocutor's name. In the early days her husband had taught her the basic tenets of security and she still applied them despite the advances in technology.

'We have the targets under surveillance as instructed.' The man's tone was respectful, though not as much as she'd have liked. Like many of his colleagues, he'd been troubled when she took over the family business, even though her ailing husband gave his blessing.

'Good. I'll advise you which one to move on tomorrow.'

'They're coming?' It was understood that the Father and Son were never referred to openly.

'Yes, they're coming.'

'One more thing. The shipment we discussed yesterday. It'll be on the street tonight.'

'Good. And the problem at the club?'

'Resolved. We brought in three Lithuanian women. Two of them can actually dance.'

Rea made no reaction to her subordinate's irony. She had no qualms about any of the family's operations, but she could imagine what it must be like for the women who worked in the clubs and brothels.

'Make sure we're not left short again,' she ordered.

'I've already taken steps.'

She terminated the call and moved away from the desk. Above the marble fireplace there was a portrait of one of Stratos's ancestors – a glowering warrior in a brightly coloured tunic, his belt stuffed with pistols and his long moustaches twisted. She pressed a catch at the bottom of the ornate frame and swung the painting away from the wall. Behind it was a stainless-steel door. Before she pressed out the code on the panel she caught sight of her reflection. As ever, her appearance pained her. Her auburn hair, perfectly styled, set off the smooth skin of her face, the long, straight nose and the bright red of her lips. She knew that many women in their fifties would have begged for such a face. The problem was that it wasn't her own.

The steel door opened. There it was, the most prized of her possessions. She'd bought it from a tame antiquities dealer and no one else knew about it, not even her husband. The funeral mask dated to the fifteenth century BC and it had been found in a secretly excavated Mycenaean tomb. Standing in front of the artefact at the same level, she looked into the eyes. The person they belonged to would have been alive not long before this likeness in gold had been placed over the features – veins pulsing, eyes moving between long lashes, lips speaking honeyed words. Yes, she was sure the mask was a woman's, whatever the experts might say to the contrary – a woman who had seen much of life, its joy and its pain. A woman like herself.

Rea stepped back a few paces, her eyes still locked on the golden face. Its power attracted her, but at the same time she was repelled. She understood too well. There was a magical quality to the hammered metal, as if the person beneath had been a sorceress, a conqueror of men. The mask was bent and twisted, the left side out of kilter. Although the nose had been crushed in the collapsed tomb, she could see that it had been long and imperious. The ears, stylised loops, were delicate and feminine, despite the curious perspective. But it was the lips that sealed the gender for her. They were formed into a pout, but not one that was coquettish – rather, it was a display of indomitable will. And they had been stitched together, the lines of thread and the puncture marks made by a master craftsman. What man would have been memorialised after death like that? A warrior was buried with his swords and spears, his strength celebrated beyond death. But a woman? As now, the female of the species had only her wits and her tongue to save her from the bestiality of men. What had this woman said, what words of love or deception had she spoken?

Rea caught her breath and steadied herself against a chair. She couldn't block out the thought that the mask hadn't only been bent out of shape by the pressure of the earth. Perhaps it represented the woman as she was before she died – in agony, her lips sewn tightly together, her features damaged by beating, the left eye bulging. What torture had she undergone before her spirit failed?

Stepping forward quickly, she slammed the safe door and pushed the painting back over it. The mask, the golden mask. She should have left it undisturbed, but that was never an option. It had too much to say to her, even though the woman it once covered had been silent for thousands of years.

Rea went back to the desk and looked at the figures her numbers men had produced. The profits made in the previous month by the family's legitimate and criminal businesses were down. But all she could think of was the mask of a woman who had remained true to herself in the face of death itself.

# 2

After lunch Mavros walked back to his flat and stretched out on the sofa. Niki had gone off to another meeting, happy that he'd agreed to take on the search for the missing girl. He felt less lively. It was often like this at the beginning of a case. Before he got involved, he struggled to raise an interest. He slid the photo of the young woman from the envelope Niki had given him and examined it again. A smile, dimples under the prominent cheekbones, but more than a hint of uncertainty. Niki was right. Katia was definitely vulnerable.

He picked up the phone and dialled her home number.

'Yes?' came a gruff male voice.

'Mr Tratsou?'

'Who is this?' The man's Greek was fluent enough, but there was a heavy Russian accent. He sounded very tense.

'My name's Mavros, Alex Mavros. Your social worker Niki—'

'Yes, yes, I know who you are. This morning Niki told me you help us.'

Mavros shook his head. She had set him up completely.

'You are private investigator, yes? You find my Katia?'

'I'm going to try. Can we meet?'

'Come to house, nine o'clock. You have address?'

Mavros confirmed that he did and rang off. Dmitri Tratsou hadn't given him the impression of an impulsive man, more one whose world had been shaken to the core by the disappearance of his daughter. He hoped that this wasn't going to be one of those cases that ended with him giving parents the worst kind of news – infatuation with a grasping partner, drug addiction, prostitution. It happened often enough.

Reaching over to his jacket, he took the newspaper from the pocket and read through the story on the front page. The author Lambis Bitsos, a lanky, perpetually hungry and pornography-obsessed journalist, was a long-standing contact of his. They'd traded information in the past, though he hadn't seen Bitsos recently. He'd kept his mouth shut about the terrorism case and the reporter hadn't been impressed.

He read on and swore under his breath. The story referred to the police commander Nikos Kriaras, now head of the organised crime division. Kriaras was another old contact, one who'd provided him with several clients. He'd been deeply involved in the terrorism case too, but they were no longer in touch.

'What do you know about the criminal underworld, Niko?' he said to himself. Then he remembered how well-connected Kriaras was. He probably had a different gang boss round to dinner every weekend.

Feeling the weight of the food and alcohol, Mavros drifted into an uneasy doze. He found himself running after a blonde woman through dark and deserted streets, the name Katia issuing from his lips. Then she was in a building site, no workers around, the bulldozers and drilling machines motionless. And then she disappeared, as if she'd been grabbed from below. He reached the edge of a pit and made out a body face down at the bottom, naked and still. But the hair was no longer fair, it was brown, and the skin was covered in bruises and weals. Mavros watched in horror as the head began to move. The features were blurred, but they gradually came into focus like a photographic image being fixed in the tray. It was his brother Andonis's face, a soft smile on his lips.

Mavros woke with a start, his whole body taut. In recent

months Andonis had been more distant, but suddenly he was back. He had to do something about it. There was only one person who could help. Grabbing his jacket and phone, he headed for the door.

The nearby square was packed with people, the building works at the underground station making the chaos even worse than usual. Souvenir shop owners were touting the new season's wares. Mavros wiped his brow. There were still a couple of weeks to Easter and it was already hot in the city.

As he moved up the steep slope towards his mother's apartment building, he felt his calves complain. She lived on the side of the inner city's highest hill, but she was all right – she took taxis everywhere. He walked to keep fit, and because two- and four-wheeled transport was more trouble than it was worth in Athens. That policy had its drawbacks, one being that he never felt like going anywhere after a large lunch. He stopped to catch his breath in the open space of a square with a Roman reservoir. Boys playing football had hung their jackets on the statue of a poet, giving him the look of an overdressed tramp.

Mavros normally used the stairs, but this time he succumbed and took the lift to his mother's apartment on the sixth floor.

'It's me,' he said, knocking on the door. He had a key, but he knew she would have the chain on.

'Alex.' Dorothy Cochrane-Mavrou leaned forward and kissed her second son. 'You should have rung. I'm on my way out.'

'Oh.'

'It's all right, dear, you can come in for a minute.' Dorothy looked at him. 'Is something wrong?'

'No, nothing,' he said, following her in. She was wearing a smart woollen suit, a string of pearls round her neck. 'I can't stay long anyway. Where are you going?'

'To a book launch.' Although she'd been in Greece since the

late-forties, Dorothy's accent retained a Scottish burr. After her husband's death in 1967, she'd built up her own publishing company.

'You look great, Mother.'

'Och, I'm fading and you know it. White hair and a limp. I feel like an old granny.'

'You are an old granny,' he said, sitting down at the end of the sofa nearest the bookcase with the family photos.

Dorothy laughed. 'Thank you, my son. Though I have no grandchildren from you. How's Niki?'

'God, Mother, don't put any pressure on me, will you? Niki's all right. I had lunch with her today.'

'I'm glad you two seem to be getting on better these days.'

'Yeah, well,' he said, remembering the problems they'd been through. 'Maybe things will work out. I don't know.'

'You sound pessimistic,' Dorothy said, sitting down beside him. 'Don't be.'

Mavros had turned to the black-and-white photos – his father Spyros with his thick moustache and penetrating gaze; the youthful Andonis smiling as he had so often. 'I didn't inherit that from either of them, did I?'

His mother took his hand. 'They both had their dark times, Spyros especially. But he got over them.' She nudged him. 'At the risk of repeating myself for the thousandth time, you have to let Andonis go. You've been looking for him since you came back from university and it's ruining your life.'

Mavros swallowed hard. 'Searching for him has made me what I am.'

'I know, Alex. And you're very good at finding people. But now you have to concentrate on those you can help. Andonis isn't coming back.' Her voice broke as she spoke the last sentence, but she gave a brave smile. Over the years, she and Mavros's sister Anna had come to terms with the disappearance. Only he had kept fighting it.

Mavros thought back to the dream he'd had of Andonis. It seemed he couldn't even read a newspaper story without seeing his long-lost brother. 'I know, Mother,' he said, blinking. 'I'm going to let go. I can't . . . I can't hold on to him any longer.' He was expecting Andonis to appear again, but this time there was nothing. He wondered if, by making the resolution, he'd finally sent him into the void.

Dorothy squeezed his hand and they sat in silence for a while.

'I must be going, Alex,' she said gently, looking at her watch.

'Right.' Mavros got up and helped her to her feet.

'Are you sure you're all right, dear?'

'I'm fine.' And, in truth, he was. He felt better than he had for a long time. But he didn't risk a last look at the family photographs.

Damis Naskos, his pumped-up biceps sheathed in a dark suit jacket and his short brown hair spiked with gel, tightened the lace of his shoe and stood up. He was in a room at the rear of the Silver Lady Club on the coast road with the other security personnel, as they were called ironically by Lakis the Boss. Bouncers was what they were. Not that Lakis was much better. He was only a low-level arselicker who answered to the club manager Mr Ricardo, a hard man with no hair but plenty of attitude. Even though the Chiotis family controlled eleven other clubs and thirty-seven bars, Mr Ricardo reckoned he was something really special. Damis never got more than a scowl from him.

'Have you seen the new girls?' asked Yannis the Driver. He chauffeured Lakis around when there were drugs to be off-loaded. 'One of them's got an amazin' pair of jugs on her. They say she's from Lithuania. I've never had one of them.'

Damis shrugged. 'Me neither. I had a Latvian once.'

'What the fuck's a Latvian?' Yannis burst into raucous

laughter. 'You sure she wasn't one of those slags from the Ukraine in disguise?'

'Yeah, those stinking cows get everywhere,' put in Peasant Panos, dropping the knuckle-duster he'd been polishing into his jacket pocket. 'One of them gave me a terrible dose of—'

'Gentlemen, that will do,' Lakis the Boss interrupted, his greased-back hair gleaming in the strong light. He surveyed them with an icy smile. 'Our customers will be arriving shortly. Get to work.'

The three of them nodded obediently. Damis followed the others out, straightening his tie. Panos, a country boy from the wilds of central Greece with less brain power than an ox, was always first on any job – not because he wanted to impress the Boss, but because he enjoyed putting himself about. Yannis the Driver, on the other hand, was very keen on showing the Boss how smart he was. Damis let them take the lead. He'd been keeping his head down, making sure he was well set.

'Evening, ladies,' Yannis called to the gaggle of scantily dressed dancers on the Silver Lady's stage. Although the lighting and the music systems were top-quality, the tables and chairs were flimsy, recycled from one of the family's other clubs that had been burned out in the last turf wars.

The women ignored them. Not that Yannis and Panos cared. The bouncers were assigned a dancer at the end of each night unless a customer took priority. When that happened, there were always plenty of hookers who'd oblige for free. Most were from the old Eastern Block, illegals who had no choice about what they did. Damis felt sorry for them. He'd often seen them dabbing away tears and he was sure that, given the chance, they'd go back home like a shot. But he'd been careful never to make his sympathy obvious.

He took up his position by the door, under the five-times life-size figure of the naked silver woman. The family must have paid off plenty of local officials for her. Yannis was at the end of the red carpet and Panos was out in the car park. There weren't many punters around yet. It was early, but Lakis the Boss liked to get them out as soon as the doors were open. Just in case any rival headbangers had a go.

He slid a hand round his back and checked that the automatic pistol was in position. He'd never had to fire it yet, but he'd pulled it out a few times. The ways things were going – the families kidnapping each other's men and beating the shit out of them, then dumping them in the open to make a point – he didn't think it would be long till he had to use his firearms skills. He just hoped the action wouldn't get too hot before he had a chance to better himself. Then again, maybe a good bit of inter-gang violence would be the thing to put him in the spotlight.

Damis watched as Panos ushered a car into a parking space with exaggerated arm movements. The fool looked like he was herding goats back home in the mountains. Screw Lakis, Damis thought, and screw Ricardo. The family was what counted. They were the key to everything, Stratos Chiotis and his cold-eyed looker of a wife Rea. Now that the old man was nothing but a bedridden wreck, the wife was in charge. Since there were no siblings or children and the other relatives were working in the legitimate businesses, she was the one for him. But in the nine months he'd been a bouncer and general provider of muscle, he'd only seen the woman a couple of times when she came to inspect the operation. He had to find a way of getting to her.

'Are you concentrating?' Lakis's voice was low, his breath a mixture of cigarettes and mouthwash. 'I wouldn't like to think any man of mine let his mind wander.'

'I'm concentrating, Boss,' Damis replied, sounding as keen as he could.

'Good.' Lakis moved his mouth closer. 'Because I've been watching you and I don't like everything I see.'

Damis kept his eyes on the customers who were being

greeted by Yannis. 'You can depend on me,' he said between his teeth.

'Make sure I can.' The Boss went back inside.

For a few seconds Damis thought he'd blown it.

No chance, he told himself. He was far too good for that.

Mavros walked down the slope and took the number eight trolley-bus from outside the university's illuminated façade. The roads were packed, as was the trolley. The shops were open late and people were stocking up for Easter – gifts for relatives back home in the provinces, new clothes for them-selves and their kids, anything to display how prosperous they were. It was natural that an atheist like Mavros would dislike Easter, but the religious ceremonies weren't what got him down. He found the build-up to the explosions of grief and joy on the big weekend quite moving, at least from a distance. The pretext that the occasion gave the faithful to show off was what he despised.

He got off halfway up the incline of Alexandhras Avenue, helping off an old woman weighed down with plastic bags.

'Bless you, my boy,' she said with a toothless grin. 'May your family have joy of you.'

He smiled back at her, wondering how much joy he gave Dorothy and his sister Anna. His mother had never really come to terms with the job he had chosen, even though she knew that the urge to find Andonis was behind it. And Anna? In recent years they'd got closer, but for a long time he'd resented the happy life she'd made for herself with her husband and children, as if Andonis's disappearance was no longer impor-tant. No doubt she'd approve of his decision to give up on their brother.

Crossing the wide thoroughfare at the lights, Mavros walked into a grid of narrow streets. The area of Gyzi lay back from the avenue on a slope that steepened rapidly. There were flights of steps between some levels, cars and motorbikes parked precariously. What struck him most was the compressed nature of the place. Streetlights lit the lower levels of the apartment blocks, but the upper floors loomed over him. He felt like a traveller fighting through a dense forest of monstrous stone trees. People shrank into insignificance, their presence marked more by the vehicles they drove than by their own physical substance. He was in a realm of shadows, a set from a German Expressionist film that used skewed angles and perspectives to hint at mankind's twisted heart.

The noise emanating from a bar on the corner ahead dispelled the fanciful thoughts. Motorbikes were blocking the pavement, their riders lounging against graffiti-covered walls. The drinking-hole's name, Bonzo's, was proclaimed by a crudely painted sign. Mavros stepped on to the road to get past, smiling as he recognised the music. One of the leather-clad youths attempted a tough guy's stare as he approached.

'Something funny?'

Mavros locked eyes with him. 'I was listening to Led Zeppelin when you were at your mother's tit, my friend.'

There was a pause as the guy glanced at his companions, then they started to laugh.

'Looking forward to collecting your pension then, are you, Grandad?' one of them asked. 'You're wearing a wig, aren't you?'

Mavros walked on, the smile still playing on his lips. They looked pretty harmless and they'd soon find out that life wasn't all guitar solos and power riffs. There wasn't any point in spoiling their fun. Besides, they outnumbered him four to one.

Crossing the road, he found the street door of the missing girl's block and rang the bell marked 'Tratsou'. He spoke his name into the microphone when the father's voice came through and walked into the unlit hall after the lock disengaged automatically.

'Second floor,' the Russian-Greek shouted down the stair-well. 'The lift doesn't work.'

Mavros went up and was met by a stocky figure with a thick beard.

'Idiot caretaker,' the man said. 'Soon building will fall down.'

Mavros looked around the dingy landing. 'At least you're not in a tent any more.' He'd seen from Niki's file that the family spent their first two months in Greece in a reception centre with limited facilities. He took the hand that was extended and felt its strong grip.

'You are investigator, eh?' Tratsou said sceptically, running an eye over him. 'You look like pop star.'

Mavros shrugged. 'You look like a gorilla, but I don't mind.'

There was a pause and then the man laughed, but only briefly. 'You find my Katia, I give you everything I have.'

Mavros heard the longing in his voice. The burly construc-tion worker was struggling to keep a grip on his emotions. 'I'll do everything I can, Mr Tratsou.'

'You call me Dmitri,' the Russian-Greek said, leading him to the open door of his apartment. 'I call you Alex, yes?'

A pale, thin woman came down the stuffy corridor, wiping her hands on a cloth. She looked at Mavros beseechingly, her eyes red and damp. A stream of indistinguishable sounds came from her chapped lips.

'This my wife Maria,' Tratsou said, saying a few words in Russian. 'I tell her you find Katia.'

Mavros touched her arm and smiled. She bowed her head as if she was praying.

'Come, Alex, we can talk in here.' Tratsou led him into a sitting-room that was even hotter than the hallway. The walls were hung with icons and photographs of elderly men and women. 'Maria, she remembers the old country and the family we leave behind. Me, I love Greece and I want to get rich. This not possible in former Soviet Union.'

'Unless you're a businessman.' Mavros accepted a glass of tea from the woman, who gave him another imploring look. 'Or a criminal.'

'And I am not,' Dmitri said, signalling to his wife to leave.

Mavros nodded. 'You're working on the new motorway from the airport, aren't you?'

Dmitri slurped his tea. 'That's right.'

'How did you get the job?'

The Russian-Greek raised his shoulders. 'Friend of a friend.'

'You mean someone else from the former Soviet Union?'

'No, Alex, I mean my social worker, your Niki.' He gave a restrained laugh. 'She make introduction to boss. I have experience, I know what I do.'

'They just found a body up there, didn't they?'

'About a kilometre from my site.' Dmitri ran his stubby fingers through his beard. 'I thought I get away from such things when I leave Soviet Union, but no, they are everywhere.'

'They are everywhere,' Mavros agreed. He'd been wondering if his new client could have any connection with the Russian gangs who'd been building up their presence in Greece. There might be a link there with his daughter's disappearance.

The bearded man leaned forward on the sofa, his hands on his knees. 'So, how we find my Katia?'

'We start by you giving me as much information as you can about your daughter and everyone she came into contact with. Friends, relatives, teachers, people she spoke to in the local shops . . . it doesn't matter how insignificant. It's a pity your wife doesn't speak Greek. I'd like to hear what she has to say.'

The Russian-Greek met his gaze. 'Maria is good woman. She tell me everything. I not hide anything from you.'

'I'm sure you won't, Dmitri. Here's what I want you to do. Write down the names of the people Katia knows and any phone numbers and addresses. I'll go through it with you later.'

'What you going to do?'

'I want to see Katia's room. No, you stay here. I prefer to go on my own, if that's all right. Which one is it?'

Dmitri got to his feet. 'First on left. I tell Maria what you do.'

Mavros watched from the corridor as the Russian-Greek comforted his wife, who was weeping and wringing her hands. Mavros knew he was intruding, but it was important to examine the room alone. He'd often found that he learned more about a person from the space they lived in than from the people they lived with.

But how much would he discover about the young woman a month after she'd last been there?

During the afternoon, the Father and Son packed their gear into the BMW in the garage beneath the house. It was a typical mid-nineteenth-century merchant's mansion. The tall white walls were pierced by narrow windows, those on the lower floors barred, and the red-tiled roof steeply pitched. The balconies on the top floor sat on stone supports. Storks were nesting on one of the chimneys, but they didn't cause a problem. The old man had installed central heating when he bought the house fifteen years earlier. At the same time he'd cleared out the disused storeroom in the basement and converted it into a garage. That enabled them to keep the car off the street, as well as giving them privacy when it came to loading and unloading.

The Son prepared a meal before the long drive, standing at the marble sink to clean salad vegetables. The Father was at the window that looked out across the lake. He was smoking a strong-smelling cigarette.

'You've packed your tools?' the Son asked over his shoulder.

'You really think I'm going senile, don't you, boy?'

The Son laughed softly. 'Like it or not, you're getting old.'

The Father stared out over the lake's now placid water. The mountains beyond it were shimmering in the sunlight, the watercourses and stone chutes cutting into their sides like wounds. 'There are still things I can do better than you.'

'You think so?' the Son said under his breath. 'We need to eat.' He carried a cabbage and carrot salad to the table where he had already set out bread, cheese and olives. He watched as the old man stepped across the wooden boards, his gait stiffer than it used to be.

'What's this?' the Father demanded as he sat down. 'Rabbit food? Your mother always gave me meat.'

'Even during Lent?'

The Father's hand came down hard on the tabletop. 'Yes, even during Lent. Your mother always gave me what I wanted.'

That was why she always looked old, the Son thought. The bastard had treated her like a slave with his shouts and slaps. Not that it mattered. The Son had never cared for his mother. He'd never cared for anyone. That was the legacy of the Father.

'Wipe that stupid smile off your face,' the old man said, tearing a piece of bread apart. 'Tell me what she said. In detail, you hear? I put you in charge of communicating with the employer so that I could concentrate on my handiwork, not so you could keep things from me.'

Your handiwork, thought the Son. Why can't you call it by its real name? 'You know how it works,' he said, when he'd finished chewing. 'We go down to Athens and wait for them to contact us.'

'Don't play games,' the Father growled. 'She told you what kind of job it's going to be.'

The Son nodded. 'You heard the news, didn't you? That body they found at the motorway site was one of the family's people. The opposition beat the man to death, no doubt after extracting every useful piece of information from him.'

'So we reciprocate on the family's behalf.' The Father finished eating and lit another cigarette, exhaling across the table. 'I take it we'll be paid the normal rate.'

'Of course.' The Son waved the smoke away. 'And there may be more work in the offing.'

'Why didn't you tell me that before?' the Father asked with a glare. 'I'll need extra clothes.'

There are plenty of clothes shops in Athens, old fool, the Son thought. 'I wanted to keep it for a surprise. And now you've made me blab it out.'

The Father gave a bitter laugh. 'Haven't you learned, boy? No one can keep secrets from me.'

The Son got up and started collecting the plates. What the old man said had always been true. Silence was not an option when he went to work on people. But the Father wasn't the only expert. It was time the younger generation prevailed. Maybe this trip to Athens would give him the opportunity he'd been waiting for.

He turned on the tap and ran water over the plates, his eyes fixed on the magnetic strip he'd attached to the wall a few days before. Five stainless steel knives were glistening in the light from the shadeless bulb, their edges honed.

Closing the door behind him, Mavros looked around the small bedroom. As he did, he tried to project himself into the mind of its occupant. It seemed that Katia was a typical high-school student. The walls were covered with posters of popular actresses and singers, the bedspread adorned with pink hearts. There were photos of girls and boys, probably school-friends, pinned to a board. He took some. Her desk was piled high with school texts and exercise books, arranged more tidily than most teenagers managed. There was no computer, so Katia hadn't been involved with any suspicious chat-rooms, at least not from home. The only other pieces of furniture were a cheap wardrobe and a matching chest of drawers.

He sat down at the desk and flicked through the school books. Most were heavily annotated, with no doodles. It looked like she was a keen pupil, as Niki said. The drawers contained nothing except stationery and old texts. He got up and pulled open the drawers of the chest. Nothing except clothes, all neatly folded. The wardrobe was filled with surprisingly good quality dresses and coats. Her father hadn't stinted on her appearance and it seemed that she hadn't taken much with her.

Mavros sat down on the bed and ran his eye around the room again. There was a small icon on the wall, her mother's doing, he was sure. It was almost covered by a purple scarf that hung from a hook above. On the chest stood a small music centre, a pile of Greek pop CDs beside it. It could have been the room of any Athenian schoolgirl. Katia had apparently taken steps to shake off her Russian background and conform to her new homeland's standards. But there was something missing. He couldn't grasp the personality of the young woman.

He stood in the middle of the room and tried to think like an eighteen year old. There must be a hiding place, somewhere that Katia kept her secret possessions – the make-up her father wouldn't approve of, the flashy jewellery she'd have bought herself and, if Mavros was lucky, the letters written to her by boys. It was impossible that such a stunning young woman wouldn't have had admirers. But where was the hiding place? The space beneath the bed was taken up by empty suitcases and the bottom of the wardrobe contained only a rack of shoes, all of them packed with newspaper to keep their shape. He took the stuffing out of a couple of shoes and there it was – evidence that Katia was a normal young woman. The lipstick and mascara were wrapped in plastic bags, as were a pair of earrings and a silver bracelet. But she hadn't taken them with her. It seemed that she'd left unprepared. Did that mean she hadn't gone willingly?

He heard movement outside and put his finds back, not wishing to alarm the parents with that idea.

Dmitri's head appeared round the door. 'You find any-thing?'

Mavros shook his head. 'Your daughter is very tidy.'

'My wife is very tidy. I ask her if she find anything strange in here and she say no.'

They went back into the main room. Dmitri presented him with a list of names in surprisingly good writing.

'My grandfather teach me Greek letters when I was boy,' he said.

'That's a help.' Mavros took out the photos he'd removed from Katia's pin board. 'Tell me, does your daughter have a boyfriend?'

The Russian-Greek averted his eyes. 'No.'

'You don't expect me to believe that a pretty girl like Katia didn't attract the attention of the boys in her class.'

'What you saying?' Dmitri said angrily. 'My daughter is slut?'

'Calm down,' Mavros said, opening his arms. 'I'm trying to find her and I can only do that if you help me.'

'All right. There was a boy . . . a young man. But not any more.'

Mavros saw that the bearded man was reluctant to speak further. 'What happened, Dmitri?'

'He was bad for her. I tell him to go away.'

'When was this?'

'About two months ago.'

Mavros looked at the list. 'Is he on here?'

'No.'

'What was his name?'

'Katia is not with him, I am sure. She promise me.'

'Okay, but you can see I have to talk to him.'

The Russian-Greek didn't look convinced. 'His first name is Sifis. I don't know the other.'

'Was he at school with her?'

'No. Older. Maybe twenty-five. That was problem for me.'

Mavros pointed to the photos he'd spread out on the coffee table. 'Is he there?'

Dmitri touched one of the prints. It showed a handsome young man with long hair and a carefully trimmed goatee beard. He was sitting on a motorbike.

'Where did Katia meet this Sifis?'

Dmitri got up and went to the window. 'Down there, at the bar. She never go in, I tell her not to, but this bastard, he see her passing when she come back from evening classes.'

'Have you seen him since Katia disappeared?'

'He not come round here any more.'

Mavros heard the certainty in his voice. 'What did you do?' he asked in a low voice. 'Don't worry, I won't run to the police.'

'Nothing bad. I just tell him what will happen if he see Katia again. He believe me.' The Russian-Greek smiled briefly. 'His motorbike need to go to the repair shop.'

'Have you been down to the bar asking for him?'

'Yes. They not tell me anything. But, Alex, listen to me. Katia cannot be with this fool. She swear to me she want university, not boyfriend from bar. She swear to me.'

'All right. You don't know where Sifis lives?'

'No. Is lazy bastard who does not work. Katia know that. She will not be with him.'

Mavros went over to the window and looked down at Bonzo's. The young men he had spoken to were still hanging around on the corner. 'Did you tell the police about Sifis when you reported Katia's disappearance?'

The Russian-Greek grunted. 'Greek police? Worse than Soviet pigs. They treat us like criminals. Don't give shit about Katia. They do nothing to find her.'

Mavros knew he was right. Thousands of people went missing every year in the city and the police had other priorities, especially if the subject was over eighteen like Katia. It was also the case that repatriated Greeks were often viewed as second-class citizens.

'Here,' Dmitri said, 'have vodka.' His wife had brought in a bottle.

Mavros accepted a glass and knocked it against his host's. 'Good health.'

'And to my daughter.' The sturdy man's voice broke.

Mavros gave him time to calm himself. 'What did Katia have with her on the day she didn't come home?'

'I write this down also.' Dmitri turned over the piece of paper. 'Normal clothes. Jeans, pink blouse, yellow anorak. And satchel. She go straight to evening class after school, Friday March twenty-second.'

Mavros pointed to a city-centre address. 'At this place?'

'Yes. They say she was at lesson normally. And other students see her leave.'

Mavros would be checking that. 'Does she have a mobile phone?'

'Yes, I gave her last Christmas and she always take with her. I try every day, but is always switched off.'

'Tell me about Katia. I haven't got much of an impression of her so far.' He glanced at the list. 'She doesn't seem to have many friends.'

'No close friends, I think. Is difficult for her, coming from former Soviet Union.' Dmitri shrugged. 'And maybe I push her too hard to study. But she wants it herself, she wants to be doctor.'

'What about interests outside school? What does she do in her free time?'

The Russian-Greek gave a melancholy laugh and filled their glasses again. 'What free time? She study, she sleep. Finish.'

Mavros thought back to the bedroom. 'She listens to music and she has posters of pop stars on her walls.'

'All kids have this, yes?' He raised his glass. 'Good health.'

Mavros sat back, the vodka tingling in his throat. The missing Katia was proving to be a hard one to fathom. And now he had to ask her wounded and overprotective father if she'd ever had anything to do with drugs. Sometimes he wished he was in another line of work.

# 3

Silence. All around was silence.

Then Stratos Chiotis heard the faint rattle of his own breathing.

Where were they? Not the cretinous nurse who thought the fact that he couldn't speak meant his mind had turned to mush. She was in her chair. Not the guards with the bulges in their jackets and the earpieces. He caught glimpses of them when he was wheeled out on to the terrace on good days. What good were they to him now? It would have been better if the opposition had got to him. No, where were the ones he had worked with, the ones he had spent his life with? All gone before him into the darkness and still he lingered on the surface of the earth, bent and twisted like an earthquake victim, his chin pressing into his chest and his back curved like a bow. If he'd been a Christian like his long-departed mother, he'd have believed he was being punished for his numerous sins. But he hadn't been to a church in years, he wasn't enough of a hypocrite to profess belief. He wondered if some malevolent god was laughing at him. All his life he'd carried a weapon and now, when he needed to end his life, he couldn't ask for one. He couldn't even raise a finger.

At least the television and radio were switched off. Rea – cold, decisive Rea – told the nurse that he couldn't follow them. She was wrong, but he'd lost interest anyway. There was nothing but politicians shouting at each other, tuneless music, and fatuous advertising. The world was inhabited by idiots, he knew that better than anyone.

Now that he was alone, locked inside the body that had betrayed him, he combed through his life continuously. His parents came across from Turkey with the exchange of populations in 1922, only to work themselves to death in the slums of Piraeus. He started to organise his brothers and cousins when he was ten. They stole anything they could get their hands on, standing up to the bigger boys and the vicious policemen with their batons. Then the country was occupied by the foreigners. There were countless opportunities for black-market dealing, for collaborating with the Germans and Italians, for selling out the idealistic fools in the resistance. By the fifties he'd established the Chiotis family as a force in the criminal underworld. They ran nightclubs and brothels, smuggled drugs and other contraband through the port, and took the shopkeepers for all they were worth. He took personal charge of the most important angle – paying off the policemen and politicians who were greedier than any thief.

Then the game got harder. His brothers were shot down one by one in the sixties as the rival gangs toughened themselves up. It looked like the Chiotis family's operations were doomed. But the Colonels' coup in '67 changed everything. He already knew the men who counted, he'd been working with them for years. Suddenly it was possible to run officially sanctioned businesses as well as the established lines of gambling, drugs, prostitution and protection. That was what saved the family. He made sure they were so well-connected, his nephews and nieces completely clean, that no policeman or official could move against them after the dictatorship fell.

Rea had been the final surprise. He'd recognised her ambition the first time he saw her, he'd been told what she was capable of. She'd been loyal to him throughout their marriage, helping him as he became less capable. Still, he hadn't imagined that she could take over the business, never thought she could be so ruthless. It was as well that she was. The local competition was eating into the family's share of the market, and the new boys – Fyodor's Russians, the Serbs – were making things worse.

But, for all her virtues, Stratos felt sorry for his wife. She was even harder than he'd been in his heyday, but she'd yet to appreciate the lesson that he'd needed all his life and the horror of a failing body to learn. You could live for yourself, you could sacrifice everything and everyone to your own ends, but you'd finish up empty inside, a husk of a human being. For him, it was too late to change anything. He'd killed too many people, destroyed too many innocent lives, but maybe Rea still had a chance. Could she look beneath the mask and save herself? Could she break the silence and speak to the ones she'd betrayed? If not, her life would be as worthless as a cockroach's.

Like his.

Mavros went down the stairs to the darkened entrance hall in Dmitri's block. As he suspected, his question about Katia and drugs had been greeted with indignation and a voluble denial from her father. Mavros believed Dmitri knew nothing, but his experience told him that parents rarely had a clue about their children's experiments with illicit substances. As far as he could tell, Katia was a pretty straight kid. Except that she had an ex-boyfriend with long hair and a motorbike, who was several years older than she was. It was time to check out the bar that Sifis had frequented before the Russian-Greek saw him off.

Mavros crossed the street. The young guys he'd spoken to were no longer on the corner, but their bikes were there. He went up the steps to the entrance of Bonzo's. The two-storey building would originally have been a wealthy Athenian's house, the dilapidated neoclassical portico and carvings suggesting that it was at least a hundred years old. It was dwarfed by the modern apartment blocks that had grown up around it. There would have been plenty of money on offer from developers to clear the site and produce another modern monstrosity. Obviously the owner was making more from booze and whatever else was trafficked in the bar.

Inside the street door there was a bouncer wearing a tight black T-shirt that emphasised his inflated biceps.

'Hair OK, age not so good,' he said with a loose grin. 'You sure you're into this scene?'

'You sure you're into it?' Mavros asked, raising an eye at the muscleman's shaved head. He decided to try his luck. 'I'm a friend of Sifis.'

'Oh, Sifis.' The bouncer laughed. 'You're the wrong sex for him.' His brow furrowed. 'Haven't seen him around for a while. Probably found himself another squeeze.'

So Sifis was a lady's man, Mavros thought. Maybe his client had been right to be hostile. 'I'll see if anyone else I know is in,' he said, pushing open the inner door. He was immediately buffeted by a wave of guitars. Having a conversation here wasn't going to be easy. He saw the young men from the street at the bar, bottles of beer in their hands and heads nodding to the beat. Homing in on the one who had made the crack about his hair, he tapped him on the shoulder.

The guy turned quickly, a flash of alarm on his chiselled features. When he recognised Mavros, he relaxed and nudged the nearest of his friends. 'It's the Grandfather,' he shouted above the din.

Mavros leaned close and put his mouth to the young man's ear. 'I want to talk to you. Outside. It'll be worth your while.' Dmitri had told him that he'd cover reasonable expenses.

There was suspicion in the young man's eyes. Then he shrugged and started towards the door, beckoning to one of his friends. Mavros went after them, narrowly avoiding the elbows of a spaced out girl who was jerking about to the music.

The two guys were waiting for him on the pavement, their hands on their hips and their faces set hard.

'Relax,' Mavros said, with a smile. 'This won't take long. But I'm only talking to one of you.' He knew they'd close ranks if they outnumbered him.

'All right,' said the guy he wanted to speak to. 'But my mate's staying in view.'

Mavros nodded and led him down to the corner. 'What's the problem? I'm not a cop.'

'Never thought you were. Those fuckers don't come into Bonzo's.'

No doubt they were paid to keep clear, Mavros thought. 'What's your name, my friend?'

The young man hesitated. 'Zak. What's yours?'

'Alex. Listen, Zak, I'm not interested in what goes on in the bar and I don't give a shit what you and your friends get up to. I'm going to ask you one question and I'll give you a twenty for the answer, okay?'

'A twenty?' Zak said with a sardonic laugh. 'Such generosity.'

'I might be prepared to up that, depending on how we go.'

'All right, try me.'

'How can I get in touch with Sifis?'

Zak's eyes widened. 'Sifis? Who the hell's Sifis?' he asked innocently.

'Come on, you and your pals are regulars here, aren't you? The slob on the door knows Sifis, so I'm betting you do too.' Mavros took out his wallet.

'Put that away, man,' Zak said, glancing around. 'People will think I'm dealing.'

'Just tell me where to find Sifis and I'll let you get back to the music.' He gave an encouraging smile. Underneath the patina of bravado, Zak was a standard nervy kid.

'Why do you want to find him?'

Mavros decided to come clean. 'Do you know a girl called Katia?'

Zak's expression softened. 'Katia? The Russian one? She's a real looker. I don't exactly know her, but I saw Sifis with her a couple of times.'

'Here?'

'Yes, but then they started going to his place. Her old man was giving them grief.'

Mavros stepped closer. 'And where is his place?'

Zak's head moved back. 'Who are you, man?'

'I told you, the name's Alex.'

'But what do you do?'

'I look for missing people,' Mavros said, looking into the young man's eyes. 'Did you know that Katia's been missing for a month? Did you know that her parents are climbing the walls?'

Zak glanced towards his friend. 'No, I didn't know that. I haven't seen Sifis for weeks.'

'How many weeks?'

'I don't know. A month, maybe two.' Zak looked down. 'He lives at Schina Street, number four. His surname's Skourtis.'

'Anything else you want to tell me about him?'

The young man jerked his head back in a negative gesture.

'All right, here's your money.'

'No, man, keep it. Use it to find the girl. She was a sweet one.'

Mavros nodded. 'And, Zak? I'd appreciate it if you didn't tell him I'm coming.'

The young man raised a hand and turned away.

Mavros watched him and his friend go up the steps to the bar. Buttoning his jacket, he noticed a movement at a window in the block across the street. The bearded Dmitri was staring down at him.

Mavros returned his gaze and then moved away. He'd made it clear to his client that he wasn't to interfere. As yet there was nothing he could tell the worried father. Nothing that would ease the pain that was consuming him and his forlorn wife.

Rea Chioti went into the master bedroom, dismissing the nurse who got up as soon as her employer came in. Stratos was in the hospital bed that had been brought in when he started to slide out of the king-size one that they hadn't shared for five years. There he was, curled in on himself like a foetus in the womb, confined by the rails at the side. He'd never served time in jail, but he was in solitary confinement now.

'I'm going out, Strato,' she said, noticing that his eyes were half-open. The doctors had told her that it was important to maintain normal communication with the patient. She was sure that his mind had been destroyed by his condition – he never reacted to words directed at him – but she felt she had to perform this last conjugal duty, if only for a few minutes each day. 'I have a meeting at the Silver Lady.' She stepped closer and leaned over him, wondering if he could see her or smell the scent of her perfume, perhaps hear the rustle of the silk she was wearing. 'Go into the darkness, old man,' she said, touching the shrivelled skin on his wrist.

Rea turned away, thinking that there had never been anything akin to love between them, only mutual usefulness. Stratos wanted a young bride to show his associates and the competition that he was still vigorous, while she needed the fresh start he'd given her. The best thing about her husband was that he didn't ask questions. He probably already knew the answers, but at least he didn't hark back to the disaster that was her old life.

Before Rea left the villa, she went into the study and checked the various phones. No messages had been left on the land lines and nothing had come through on her mobiles. That meant the Father and Son were on their way. She allowed no one else to communicate with them, for security and for reasons of her own. Only Stratos knew about those and he wouldn't be telling anyone now.

After she'd walked across to the portrait above the fireplace, her heels ringing on the tiled floor, she stood still for a time. Even though the golden mask was behind the steel door, even though it was concealed as it had been by the weight of the earth across the centuries, she could still feel its power – as if it was calling to her, as if the woman whose face it recorded was reaching out from the other side. But there were others, more recently dead, who were trying to find her as well.

Rea blinked and stepped away. Picking up the small bag that held her cigarettes and phone, she went into the hall. The guard on the door nodded to her and spoke into the microphone on his lapel. After a brief pause he opened the heavy door and escorted her to the Mercedes. The men by the gate had snub-nosed machine-pistols in their hands. The driver raised his hand to his cap and waited for her to slide into the leather seat beside him. After her husband was confined to his bed, she'd taken to travelling in the front. It made her feel more in control.

'Where to, Mrs Chioti?' the man asked, keeping his eyes off hers.

'The Silver Lady.' The rule was that destinations were never given out in advance. Stratos was once driven into an ambush by a chauffeur who'd been got at by the opposition. He escaped uninjured; the traitor ended up in the foundations of a new apartment block.

There were few lights on the single-track road down the hillside, but that changed as soon as they approached the main coastal highway. Rea sat back and took in the cars flashing by – people heading for the fish restaurants and clubs, young couples trying to find a deserted spot to make out, an endless procession of vans and trucks. She glanced over her shoulder and saw the lights of the second Mercedes close behind. Her husband had never moved anywhere without back-up and she saw no reason to change the system. But she wished that, just once, she could drive herself, unaccompanied by guards and minders.

The club was about ten kilometres south of Athens, near the yacht marina where Stratos kept the larger of his cabin cruisers. She saw the huge, spotlit form of the silver woman some time before they reached the car park. It was almost full, the security man initially failing to recognise her car and directing them to a customer parking place.

'Moron,' the driver said as he made rapid hand movements. 'I'm pulling up by the red carpet for you, Mrs Chioti.'

Rea waited until the Mercedes glided to a halt and one of the guards from the second car had opened her door. She swung her legs round and got out of the car, blinking momentarily in the flash of a camera. A photographer from one of the scandal-sheets was grabbed by one of the guards and manhandled away. Then, as she stepped on to the carpet, she slipped into another dimension.

The first thing she heard was a single shot. There was a gasp from the security man next to her. She turned and saw his shirt flower crimson, his arms flailing as he went down. Then she heard a series of cries, saw the men around her drop to one knee, their weapons in their hands, pointing in different directions around her. There was another shot and she heard the high-pitched ricochet of a bullet from the Mercedes's armoured shell. Then another shot, this one clearer, as if her ears were growing accustomed to the frequency. The driver crouching by the front of the car fell back, his head an explosion of red and grey.

Rea's senses started to function normally again. She heard screams and yells, the dull pounding of music from the Silver Lady, the noise of cars and lorries in the background. She stood motionless, her bag still under her arm. The guards, unclear where the shots were coming from, had started loosing off their machine-pistols blindly. Even though she felt no fear, she was unable to move, her arms and legs frozen.

Then she saw a man running towards her down the red carpet, his arms pumping and his knees high. An earpiece slipped out into the airstream he was creating. His chest was heaving and his eyes were wide, fixed on her. For some reason she noticed that he'd put too much gel on his short brown hair.

'Get down!' he shouted. 'Get down!'

In an instant he was on her, crushing her to the ground and smothering her with his body. She smelled his mint-flavoured breath. There was more gunfire from close at hand and then it began to peter out. The screaming continued, getting louder as people raised their heads and saw the blood-drenched bodies of the two men by the Mercedes.

'Mrs Chioti, Mrs Chioti,' came an agonised voice, 'are you all right?' She recognised it as one of her guards'.

'Stand back,' said the man who was shielding her. 'I've got her.'

'Who the fuck are you?' demanded the guard.

'Never mind that, have you secured the area?' Her protector sounded calm. 'It was a sniper. On a roof across the road.'

'Do as he says,' Rea ordered, keeping still despite the discomfort.

The weight came off her. 'I take it you weren't hit,' the man said. 'I don't see any wound.'

'I'm not injured,' she replied, 'but you almost suffocated me.'

'Rather that than what happened to the men standing next to you.' Her rescuer rocked back on his knees. 'Yanni?' he shouted. 'Get Panos and stand on either side of us when we get up.'

'What's going on?' Rea asked.

'I'm going to take you inside. You'll be safe there.'

She waited as two men she didn't recognise came up.

'Mrs Chioti?' said one of her guards from further away.

'It's all right,' she said acidly. 'This bouncer seems to know more about what he's doing than you people.'

The young man with the gelled hair smiled. 'I'm going to get you up now. I'll be behind you and my colleagues on either side. We'll take the shots if there are any more.'

'What?' one of the others gasped.

'Come on, Yanni, it'll only take a few seconds. Ready? What about you, Pano?'

'Let's go, Dami.'

'Right, Mrs Chioti. One, two, three.' The young man put his arms round her and lifted her up, positioning himself between her and the Mercedes. 'Walk quickly. Now!'

The four of them managed to get into step and before she knew it, they were inside the Silver Lady. There was a line of staff keeping the customers back, allowing them to get into the rooms at the rear without delay.

The door closed behind them and the trio in dark suits stepped back. Rea took them in. One with a sharp face, another who looked like an all-in wrestler, and the tall man who had saved her. He was brushing dirt from his knees as if he'd slipped on the street rather than risked his life for someone he'd never met.

'Well,' she said, waving away the bald-headed club manager. 'I have to thank you gentlemen.'

'What you have to do is improve your security,' said her saviour, now rubbing the elbows of his jacket.

Rea smiled. 'And I suppose you're the man to help me do that, are you? What's your name?'

The young man stopped fiddling with his suit and looked at her, a smile spreading across his lips. 'My name's Damis Naskos. And yes, I am the man for you.'

There was a tense silence. Then the woman who controlled the most extensive criminal organisation in the city laughed out loud.

Mavros headed down the uneven paving stones of a street parallel to the main avenue. It was nearly midnight, only the occasional neighbourhood grocery store still open. The orange trees that lined the pavements were sweet-smelling, the blossom at its height, but the reek of exhaust-fumes was prevalent even in this residential area.

As he walked, Mavros mulled over the start to the case. He'd found a lead immediately, but he wasn't congratulating himself yet. If Katia had run off with her boyfriend, there wasn't much he could do. She was eighteen and she could choose for herself, whatever her father thought. But he had the feeling things weren't that simple. The man she'd been involved with lived only a kilometre from the family. If Katia was the loving daughter that her father portrayed her to be, surely she'd have been in touch.

He found the street without difficulty – it led on to the avenue – and stood outside number four. It was a nondescript post-war block with four storeys, some of the apartments lit up. The balconies were festooned with vines and other plants, water dripping on to the pavement from the first floor where somebody had been hosing down their miniature garden. Mavros stepped round the river that had formed under the steps and went up to the street door. There was the standard row of buttons, most of them with names written in scripts of varying legibility. But there was no Skourtis. Shit, he thought. Had Zak sent him off with a false address? He thought about that. It didn't seem too likely, given that he could easily go back and put the squeeze on the young man.

He heard unsteady footsteps behind him and turned, to be

confronted by an overweight middle-aged man with sunken shoulders. He smelled like he'd taken a bath in ouzo.

'Does Sifis Skourtis live here?'

The drinker was fumbling with his keys. 'Uh.'

'Uh, what?'

'Uh . . . yes,' the man said, blinking at him as he slid the key into the lock. 'Third floor. The one with the holes in the door.' He gagged and Mavros stepped back. 'Fucking druggie.'

Mavros followed him into the building. 'Have you seen a girl with him?'

'Uh?'

'A girl,' he repeated. 'Blonde, very pretty.'

The man was stumbling towards a ground-floor door. 'Uh, blonde . . . very pretty? I wish . . . I wish I had.'

Mavros watched him struggle with his keys again and left him to it. There were fewer piss artists in Greece than in most countries, but the ones who chose that road went down it with Olympian virtuosity. Even if Katia had been around this apartment building, the guy probably wouldn't have made her out through the alcohol-induced haze.

He went up to the third floor, making as little noise as possible. The fact that Sifis Skourtis was known as a dopehead meant he was potentially a handful. People who left their names off the entry phone usually had a reason. He pressed the light switch when he reached the landing and saw what the drunk meant about holes in the door. The bottom section looked like a heavy-calibre machine-gun had been directed at it. There was no name on the doorbell here either.

Mavros reckoned that a gentle knock would get the best results. He tapped the door and then stood back so that the occupant could see him through the spy-hole.

'Who is it?' came a faint male voice.

'The name's Alex. Is that Sifis? I need to see you.'

There was the sound of coughing. 'You got money?'

Mavros took out his wallet and held up some banknotes. 'I've got money.'

A chain rattled and then the door swung open. A thin young man with rat's-tail hair and sunken cheeks was leaning against the wall. There was no sign of the goatee from the photograph. His face was now covered in heavy stubble.

'You're on your own, yes?' he said weakly. He looked to both sides of his visitor.

'Sure.'

'Then get inside.'

Mavros did as he was told and took a blast of fetid air. The small apartment was dimly lit, the shutters closed. The main room was littered with plates and aluminium containers, the remains of the food covered in mould. Techno music was coming from the speakers of a cheap system, the volume inappropriately low.

'Nice place you've got here.'

'Fuck you,' the young man said with a gasp, staggering past Mavros and collapsing on to the ragged sofa. On the table in front of it were a syringe, teaspoon and twists of foil. 'How much d'you want to score?'

Mavros was still holding the banknotes. 'Who decorated your front door?'

Sifis looked up at him blearily. 'Sometimes people get desperate, you know?'

Mavros went closer and leaned over him. 'How desperate are you?' He caught sight of photos strewn on the cushions and floor. They were all of Katia, some of her with Sifis. She was smiling or laughing in most.

'Aw, fuck, man, I'm desperate enough. Let's get this finished so we can both get high.'

Mavros picked up the photos and sat next to the sprawling young man. 'Okay, here's how we're going to do this. I'm going to ask you some questions, you're going to answer them, and then I'm going to pay you. Clear?'

Sifis's eyes were less bleary now. He tried to raise himself, but didn't have the strength. 'Who the fuck are you?'

'The name's Alex. Don't worry, this won't take long.' Mavros held up one of the photos. 'Katia Tratsou. Where is she?'

Sifis blinked and then slumped forward. 'Katia?' he said, his voice cracking. 'Why . . . why do you want to know?'

Mavros got up quickly and went back through into the hall. There was no one in the tiny kitchen or in the stinking bathroom. He pushed open the door to the bedroom. There was a heap of stained sheets on the bed and the wardrobe doors were open, revealing a few shirts. There was no sign of a female presence, and no school satchel or any of the clothes Katia had been wearing the day she left home for the last time.

He went back to the main room. Sifis was where he had been, his chin on his chest. It took Mavros a few seconds to work out that the noise coming from the young man was sobbing. He sat down beside him again.

'Where is she?' he asked gently.

'I wish . . . I wish I knew,' Sifis said, raising a hand to his eyes. 'I really wish I knew.'

'When was the last time you saw her?'

The young man swallowed and wiped his hand across his eyes. 'I don't fucking know. Must be a month.' He glanced down at the equipment on the table. 'Since she went, I've been . . . I've been sampling the goods.'

Mavros looked at the numerous pieces of foil. The rate Sifis was going, his supply would soon be cut off. The scumbags in the gangs who controlled distribution wouldn't let a dealer turned junkie consume their profits for long.

'Were you still seeing her after her old man warned you off?'

Sifis didn't seem to be disturbed by the question. His head

was down again, his breathing shallow. 'Yes, of course. We were just more careful. I used to pick her up a couple of streets away from her place.'

'And you brought her here?' Mavros ran his eyes around the wreck of a room.

Sifis gave him an angry look. 'It wasn't always like this, you know. I've only let it go recently.'

'I believe you.' Mavros leaned closer, his expression hardening. 'Did you give Katia any dope?'

Sifis's head jerked back. 'No way. I didn't do it myself until . . . until she went. Only grass.'

'So what happened? You and Katia were carrying on as usual and then, on Friday March the twenty-second, she didn't show up?'

'That's exactly the way it was,' the young man agreed, staring at Mavros. 'I arranged to meet her after her evening class, but I was a bit late. They'd already finished.'

'This is the place in Kanningos Square?'

'Yes.' Sifis's eyes narrowed. 'How do you know? Who the fuck are you?'

'Never mind that. She'd been at the class?'

'She said she was going,' the young man said sullenly. 'I thought she'd ring me, I thought she'd come here. But she never did. I tried her mobile, but it was switched off.' He burst into a loud sob. 'It's never come on again. That bastard, he moved her away, I'm sure of it.'

'You mean her father?' Mavros shook his head. 'He doesn't know where she is either, I promise you.'

Sifis roused himself. 'The Russian lunatic doesn't know?' He stared at Mavros. 'You mean Katia's gone missing?'

'Officially. You haven't had the cops round?'

The young man shrugged. 'I keep my head down.'

Mavros decided to turn the screw. 'And you were such a chicken that you never went back to Bonzo's?'

'I . . . Christ, that guy's a fucking headcase. He . . .' Sifis broke off and glanced at his right wrist. 'He almost broke my arm. And he did some damage to my bike. No way did I want any more of that. I've got customers in other bars.'

'Can you think of any place she could have gone?'

Sifis gave that some thought. 'No. Katia's a smart kid. She works hard. It was difficult enough to get her to spend time with me.' His voice broke again. 'I want her. I miss her. I fucking love her.' He wiped tears away. 'Why are you looking for her? Do you know her?'

'Friend of the family,' Mavros said, handing him a twenty-Euro note. He wrote his mobile phone number on the back of a photo of Katia and asked for the young man's. 'There's more where that came from. Call me if you hear anything.'

Sifis rubbed his eyes. 'So no one knows where Katia is? Jesus Christ.'

Mavros got up. 'Someone knows. And you can be sure I'm going to find out who.' He turned away and headed for the door. Katia's boyfriend was scrabbling for another hit before he got there.

The Father and Son spent most of the night on the motorway. The BMW took them past the trucks easily enough, apart from the frequent sections where traffic had built up. The Father insisted on doing the initial stretch, which wasn't as quick as the north-south highway. The Son let him have his way. The old man's reactions were still good enough, the only slight deviations from the lane occurring when he lit one of his numerous cigarettes. The Son put his seat back and lost himself in his thoughts. The Father didn't approve of what he called 'woolly thinking', so the Son closed his eyes and pretended to be asleep. But, all the time, he was weighing his options.

The Father was still useful to him, there was no doubting that. He was the one who had the connection with the family, their sole source of income. The old man had first met Stratos Chiotis in the early-sixties when he was in the Military Police. He'd helped the crime boss with some unspecified work – selling him arms from military bases, the Son was pretty sure. One of Chiotis's lines of work had been supplying weapons to opposition groups in the Middle East – terrorists in the common tongue. During the dictatorship, the Father had grown even closer to the family. The Son didn't know exactly how, but he was sure it had something to do with what the Father was best at – torture. He'd started the business they were still involved in – getting information out of criminals, carrying out reprisals and generally scaring hell out of the family's rivals. The old man had done that in his time off from his work as an interrogator.

The Father had taught him everything he knew: how to make people shit themselves and spill their guts without a hand being laid on them, how to beat them for the right amount of time to ensure that what they said was the unadulterated truth, how to use the tools that he'd checked three times before packing them. The Father and Son had become a made-to-measure enforcement and persecution agency. Stratos Chiotis stated his requirements and they produced the results. The money was good and they were protected because the head of the family dealt with them himself.

Except that now Stratos Chiotis wasn't the one giving the orders. Even before the old man's condition had deteriorated, his wife had been communicating with the Father. The Son could remember the first time the woman had called the old man – back then, he still handled communication with the family himself. Something about Rea Chioti had spooked the Father. He'd taken the call in the kitchen and the Son had watched a sick smile spread over his face. At the same time, he seemed to find the conversation awkward. Soon afterwards he told the Son to talk to the family in future, saying it was time for him to take on more responsibility. But the Son wasn't fooled. There was something about Rea Chioti, and it wasn't just that she had once been a seriously attractive woman – still was if your taste was for mature flesh.

The Son drove the rest of the way to Athens with the Father snoring in the seat beside him. The old man had stopped the car to empty his bladder, his voice harsh when the Son spent a minute longer in the petrol station than he deemed necessary. The bad-tempered old bastard. When would he retire into drooling incontinence like other men of his age?

The radio was on, low enough not to disturb the Father. As he drove past Thermopylae, the Son heard a breathless reporter talking about what he called 'a machine-gun battle' outside a nightclub on the coast road. Elements of the criminal underworld were said to be involved.

It looked like the stakes were being raised every night. That made the Son lick his lips.

# 4

It was late when Mavros got back to his flat. He opened the door as quietly as he could because Niki had said she might spend the night. Checking the bedroom, he saw that the bed was undisturbed. He went into the main room and fumbled for the light switch above the TV, then pressed the button on the remote control. Simultaneously, he heard the voices of Niki and of his reporter friend Bitsos. He jerked his head round.

'What time is it?' Niki said sleepily, sitting up on the settee. Her hair was in a state of chaos and her eyes were gummed up.

Mavros glanced at his watch. 'Just after two.' He took in the scene on the screen. Policemen were cordoning off a car park outside a nightclub. 'What's going on?'

'I saw it earlier,' Niki said with a yawn. 'Some lunatics firing off their popguns at one of the clubs.' She patted the surface beside her. 'Sit down, Alex. Don't I get a kiss?'

Mavros complied, his nostrils filling with Niki's sweet scent. On the TV, Bitsos, his cadaverous face and bald head not looking their best in the glare of the lights, was midway through an account of what had happened.

'. . . here at the Silver Lady. The two dead men are believed to have been security personnel. Fortunately no one else was hit in the crossfire, but there was considerable damage to customers' cars.'

'Morons,' Niki said, leaning against Mavros. 'Can't they find a way of ripping off the public without killing each other?'

'Sh,' he said, leaning forward.

'According to eyewitnesses,' Bitsos was saying, 'the shooting started shortly after ten-thirty when this Mercedes –' the reporter pointed at the luxury car behind him, its windscreen cobwebbed with cracks '– in which well-known businesswoman Mrs Rea Chioti and her driver were travelling, pulled up outside the club. It is owned by one of her family's companies.'

Niki stood up, holding her unzipped skirt with one hand. 'How come those Chiotis people aren't behind bars? Everyone knows they're behind half the crime in the city.'

'Because they have very good lawyers.'

'And because they know the right politicians.' Niki walked past him. 'I'm going to bed. Maybe you'll join me when there's something less fascinating on the TV.'

'I won't be long,' Mavros said, ignoring her irony.

Lambis Bitsos was now interviewing a policeman, who was displaying the standard mixture of mock horror at the iniquity of contemporary society and blithe confidence that the wrongdoers would soon be apprehended.

'And what will the new head of the organised crime division be doing about this latest outburst of violence on the streets of the nation's capital?' Bitsos asked.

'Well done, my friend,' Mavros said. 'Nail them to the spot.'

'Commander Kriaras will be making a statement tomorrow morning,' the officer responded robotically.

Mavros shook his head. 'Commander Kriaras hasn't got a clue.'

He watched as Bitsos signed off with a typically downbeat assessment: 'Unless the authorities can control this latest outburst of violence, the prospects for a safe and successful Olympic Games are faint.' Even though there were more than two years to the games, journalists couldn't resist tying them to any story.

'Goodnight, Lambi,' Mavros said, hitting the off button.

'And sweet dreams.' The reporter was by a long way the most pessimistic person he knew. Being called to murder scenes in the middle of the night had that effect.

As he took his clothes off in the bedroom, Niki rolled over. 'Where have you been tonight? Was Dmitri plying you with vodka?'

'I had a couple,' he said, sitting down with his back to her.

'What's the matter?' Niki moved closer and put a hand on his thigh.

'Nothing. I'm just tired.'

The sheets rustled as she sat up. 'What have you discovered?' she asked, suddenly awake.

'Nothing,' he mumbled. He didn't want to alarm her.

'You're not fooling anyone, Alex. Turn round.' Her hand was tighter now, the fingers pressing into his flesh. 'Have you got something on Katia?'

He removed Niki's hand and slid under the covers. 'I shouldn't be telling you. Dmitri's the client and I haven't advised him yet.'

'Don't give me that procedural bullshit. Tell me what you've found.'

'All right. It doesn't look too good. I managed to track down Katia's boyfriend. He's a dope dealer, would you believe?'

'Christ and the Holy Mother! Dmitri will go crazy.'

'It's not a conversation I'm looking forward to. The guy seems to have hit his own goods big time since Katia disappeared.'

'You mean he hasn't seen her?'

'So he says. I believe him. He seems genuinely cut up about her. He thought that her father had taken steps to separate Katia from him.' He frowned.

'What is it?'

'Dmitri hurt him before Katia disappeared. Now I see what you meant about him being impulsive.'

'He has a temper. When the family was in the camp, he got into more than one fight.'

Mavros turned to her. 'And it didn't occur to you to mention that to me? Thanks a lot, Niki.'

She pursed her lips as she did when she went into battle, then seemed to think better of it. 'Sorry. I didn't want you to turn down the case.' She came closer and hooked a bare leg over his. 'So, what do you think?'

'A beautiful young woman like that? She's a prize catch for all sorts of miscreants. She never talked about leaving home or wanting to travel?'

'No, she seemed content with her parents in their new country. Christ, Alex, what are you going to do?'

'The usual thing. Talk to all her friends and contacts – neighbours, school, night classes.'

'You don't sound very optimistic.'

He shrugged. 'There were photos of her in the boyfriend's flat. She looked happy with him. If he doesn't know where she is, it's not too likely that anyone else will.'

'What can you do?'

'What I always do. Use my intuition.'

Niki studied him for a while, then lay down and turned over.

Mavros turned out the light and let the darkness smother him. Sleep wasn't quick to come. He was haunted by the image of the lovely young Russian-Greek and the distraught faces of her parents. Not for the first time, he was in danger of letting a case get too much of a grip on his emotions. He didn't know any other way to do his job. Then, as he felt himself sinking at last, it struck him that his long-lost brother had been absent from his thoughts all evening.

He wasn't sure how pleased he should be about that.

Damis was wide-awake, the snores of the other bouncers reverberating through the thin walls of the flat. It was provided by their employers, in a shitty apartment block a couple of streets back from the coast road. The Silver Lady was nearby, but that was all it had going for it. The furniture was old, the heating operated either on sauna level or not at all, and the traffic noise was constant. Living with Yannis the Driver and Peasant Panos would have been bad enough without the slimeball Lakis keeping back part of their pay as rent.

Damis could have closed the window, but he needed the breeze. Growing up beneath the mountain on the island of Evia had given him a feeling for nature. Even after years in the city, he still thought of the fields on the lower slopes, the barley rippling in the breeze and the stony heights where eagles circled. But he never went back. His parents were old and confused, looked after by his sister. She didn't talk to him because of the work he'd chosen, though she accepted the money he sent every month. He found himself wishing he was back in the island's open spaces, but he clenched his fists and concentrated on the real world. The one populated by animals like his colleagues.

'Fuckin' hell, Dami,' Yannis had said after Mrs Chioti had swept from the office at the back of the club. 'You could have got us all killed.'

Panos didn't look too aggrieved but he followed Yannis's lead. 'Yeah, why did you make me stand next to her? I wanted to fire back at the bastards.'

'Boys, boys,' Damis said, his arms outstretched. 'I just made your careers. She's got her eye on us now. Didn't she say she'd be in touch?'

Yannis gave an ironic laugh. 'And you believed her? You arsehole. Grow up.'

'Yes, you'd be well advised to do that,' said Lakis the Boss, coming in the rear door. His face was white and his tone even sharper than usual. He didn't like being upstaged by his bouncers. 'Mrs Chioti has more on her mind than you idiots.'

Damis had raised his shoulders and smiled at him, unperturbed.

But now, in the narrow room in the apartment, he wondered. Lakis was probably right. How likely was it that La Chioti, as they called her in the popular press, would concern herself with an impulsive hired hand, even if he had protected her from a sniper? Was he condemned to years of frisking scumbags with more money than brains before he got another break? He didn't know if he could stand it. And even if he was lucky, where would that leave him? He'd heard of a guy at one of the family's other clubs who'd been singled out for a special job. He was found in a back street with his neck broken and no one thought it was an accident.

Sure that sleep wouldn't come, Damis started doing his exercises – multiple sets of stomach crunches and press-ups. He only stopped when the burning in his limbs was unbearable, even though his breathing was still under control. He'd wait as long as he had to. This was what he'd been working towards for years, this had been his motivation ever since Martha's agony had started. He bowed his head as he thought of his first girlfriend – her large brown eyes with the fine lashes, her smile, the way she would run her fingers through the hairs on his arms. They used to go up the hillsides back home, Martha's arms wrapped round his torso as he forced his underpowered motorbike up the dirt roads. They used to lie in the new grass at springtime, the poppies nodding in the wind off the sea far below. But she'd gone from him a long time ago, her features ravaged and the flesh shrunk from her limbs. She lived but she was dead to every world but her own, and that one made her writhe and babble, her eyes bulging as if she was being strangled. Martha had gone to hell.

Damis let his muscles slacken. He would win the fight, he

told himself. He would win for Martha. He lay down on his bed and waited for dawn.

Mavros was back at his client's apartment block by ten in the morning. Some of the neighbouring flats were empty, but others contained people to question. A middle-aged man with heavily powdered cheeks and enough mascara to crack an egg was unsympathetic to Katia's disappearance – 'Silly girl, she was too pretty for her own good' – but Mavros put that down to jealousy rather than any involvement. The other residents, mainly mothers with pre-school children and old people, were concerned for the young woman and her parents, particularly the stricken mother. But none had any knowledge of her activities, or of any friends she might have had.

Sitting on the stairs, Mavros ran his eye down the list of names he'd copied from the entry buttons outside the street door. There were two flats closed for the duration. According to the neighbours, one was occupied by a couple who spent the tourist season working in a hotel on Crete and the other was a sailor's – he hadn't been seen for over a year. Neither of the doors showed any sign of being forced, so he discounted those names. That left only Mrs P. Arpazoglou. Given that he hadn't yet come across anyone who'd struck him as the building's gossip-merchant, he hoped he was about to strike lucky.

He rang the bell and stood back from the door.

After a few moments, a strident voice rang out. 'Who is it?' Scuffles behind the polished wooden surface suggested that the occupant was observing him through the spy-hole.

'I'm a friend of the Tratsou family,' he said in a reassuring voice. 'The name's Mavros.'

'Is it about Katia?' said the overweight old woman in house-coat and slippers who opened the door. She could scarcely contain her excitement, eyes glinting above puffy cheeks. 'Oh, the poor mother. The young of today have no—'

'Could I ask you some questions?' Mavros interrupted, sure that he'd found the block's busybody. The old woman's flat faced to the front, her first-floor windows and balcony giving a good view of the street and the bar on the corner.

'Of course, my boy,' she said, smiling coquettishly as she peered at his business card. 'You're a private investigator? Oh, dear, that means it's serious.' With people, especially women, of the older generation, the card was often more use than a bribe. It made them feel that being nosy was a virtue. 'Well, I can tell you some things about that girl. Let me make us some coffee.' She bustled towards the kitchen.

'No, thank you,' Mavros called. 'I'm afraid my time is limited.'

The old woman turned. 'Of course.' She came back and waved him to a sofa that was covered in clear plastic. The flat was spotless. There were flowers on the table and family photographs on most of the surfaces. 'My husband,' she said, catching the direction of his gaze. 'He's deceased.'

'My condolences,' Mavros said, taking in the man's care-worn face. 'You knew Katia, then?' he said, taking out his notebook.

'Indeed I did,' Mrs Arpazoglou said, collapsing into a large armchair opposite him. 'She was a very studious girl.' She gave a tight smile. 'On the surface.' She leaned towards him. 'She had a long-haired boyfriend –' she broke off, giving Mavros's hair a disapproving glance '– who had a motorbike. I saw her talking to him outside that accursed bar.'

Mavros took out the photo of Katia and Sifis that he'd taken from her room. 'Is that him?'

She nodded avidly. 'Yes. Isn't she with him now?'

Mavros ignored the question. 'Did you see her with anyone else at any time?'

The old woman shook her head. 'Only him. And her father.' A sly smile spread across her thick lips. 'I saw her father grab hold of his arm and give the young ruffian a stern talking-to.'

'And then he stopped coming to the bar?'

'Yes. But Katia was still seeing him, I'm sure of that. She used to come back from her night classes with a certain look on her face.' The old woman's tone was prurient. 'I know what she was doing.'

Mavros tried to conceal his distaste. 'Is there anything else you can tell me?'

Mrs Arpazoglou played hard to get for a time, twisting the rings on her swollen fingers. The temptation to share the knowledge was finally too much for her.

'Katia wanted to go on the stage,' said the old woman, her tone disapproving. 'Or on the television, like those shameless girls showing off their bodies every time you switch on.'

Mavros looked at her sceptically. Apart from the posters on her bedroom walls, nothing that he'd heard about Katia suggested she was stage-struck. 'How do you know that?'

'Well,' the old woman said, leaning forward conspiratorially, 'I was coming in from the local street-market one morning and Katia happened to be on her way out. She held the door open for me – I was pulling my trolley, it was full of fruit and vegetables – and a piece of paper she was holding dropped to the floor. I'd stopped to catch my breath and I happened to see it. I remember it very clearly. It said, "Girls! Interested in acting? Interested in appearing on TV?"' She leaned back, nodding at him. 'There, she's run off to some terrible stage school.'

'I don't suppose you have the piece of paper?'

'No, Katia realised she'd dropped it and came back for it. She almost snatched it from my hand.'

'But Katia was devoted to her studies. She wanted to be a doctor.'

'Ha! Girls these days only want to flaunt themselves.' She gave him a superior look. 'Besides, she told me she needed it.

These were her very words: "Please give me that back. I need it." She was very impatient with me.'

Mavros wasn't convinced, but he made a note. 'Your memory is very good,' he said, smiling to flatter her. 'Can you tell me anything else about the flyer? Was there a name on it?'

'I don't remember. It was red, bright red. I tell you, she'll be spending all the money her father gives her on stage lessons.'

Mavros didn't tell her that Katia had very little money on her when she left home; or that, according to her father, she didn't have a bank account. He wondered why the woman was so resentful of Katia. Probably, like the man in the make-up, because she was young and beautiful.

'Well, if there's nothing else,' he said, getting to his feet. 'I'd be grateful if you kept our conversation to yourself. I'll inform the family of what you've said.'

'Oh, don't worry about that,' the old woman said, heaving herself to her feet. 'I don't talk to them if I can avoid it. Russian-Greeks are the lowest of the low.'

Mavros left, swallowing the abuse that the old woman deserved. She was a racist as well as a jealous old cow. Her husband was in a better place now. He hoped he'd find more to go on than her bright red flyer.

He spent the rest of the morning talking to the neighbour-hood shopkeepers. Several knew Katia by appearance and had nothing but good words for her – how she was polite, helpful to elderly customers and the like. None of that was much help. Then he went to her school, a large concrete block that housed a middle and a senior school. He knocked on the door of the staffroom during a break between lessons. Katia's teachers were complimentary about her abilities, and hadn't noticed any dropping off in her enthusiasm or her work rate in the weeks before she vanished. He could see that most of them had liked her, but with classes of over thirty and extra coaching every day, they didn't have time to pay attention to individual pupils.

Mavros was given permission to wait outside the classroom. When the last lesson ended, he stepped in and asked the group of lively teenagers if any of them could help locate her.

'But why?' asked one musclebound youth with his hair in a ponytail. 'She's only a Russian.'

Some of his friends thought that was witty, but most of the class shouted at him angrily. It was apparent that Katia wasn't the only immigrant child. There were a couple of Albanian girls, thin-faced but smiling, and a boy from the former Soviet Union like Katia – he was impossibly shy and said in broken Greek that he didn't know her well. Mavros let the majority leave. They shouted as they ran off down the corridor, their expensive trainers squeaking on the tiled floor. He recognised three girls from the photos in Katia's room and asked them to wait.

One, a short, dark-haired girl with a spatter of acne on her forehead, was curious. 'Who are you?' she asked.

'A friend of the family.' He knew that his business card would only make them wary. 'Look, Katia's parents are desperate. Is there anything you can tell me that might help me find her?'

The trio exchanged glances and then the tallest of them, a statuesque young woman with a striking figure, twitched her head. 'Not really. Katia was fun to be with and serious at the same time. She didn't waste her time joking with the boys like the rest of us.'

'So she didn't have a boyfriend?' Mavros asked, playing dumb.

'What?' shrieked the third girl. She had highlighted hair and purple lips. 'You must be kidding. Katia learned how her body works from books, not from personal experience.' She gave a lewd smile and the short girl laughed.

'It's not funny,' the tall one said, frowning. 'Katia's disap-
peared and no one cares. Except her parents –' she looked at
Mavros ' – and you. Look, we didn't really know her that well.
No one did. She kept things private.'

Mavros nodded. Since the girls didn't know about Sifis, that
was certainly true. 'She never said anything about wanting to
act or go on the TV?'

This time all three of them burst out laughing.

'You mustn't know her very well,' said the one with the
highlights. 'She gets embarrassed just reading the lesson
out.'

Mavros asked about Katia's behaviour and state of mind
before she disappeared – normal, as the teachers had said – and
let them go.

The tall one gave him a sad smile. 'I hope you find her,' she
said, shouldering her satchel. 'She's special.'

Mavros watched her turn away. Everyone except the bitter
man and the old gossip liked Katia, but no one had done
anything to find her when she'd gone. That was the way it was
in the big city. Disappearing into its anonymous blocks and
narrow streets was as easy as falling off a fence. So was making
someone vanish.

On his way down to the avenue, he rang the boyfriend. Sifis
sounded like he'd just come back from a trip down the Heroin
Trail. He knew nothing about Katia having an interest in the
stage and was as scathing as her classmates had been. Mavros
let him go back into the void he was making for himself, struck
again by how badly the young man was affected by Katia's
absence – and by how convinced he seemed to be that she
wasn't coming back. Could he have a reason to be so sure? He
decided to pay Sifis another visit later.

In the meantime, he needed to recharge his system. Stopping
at a neighbourhood restaurant he knew on the avenue, he
ordered a plate of beef and spaghetti. The waiter was attentive

and the food was good, but all Mavros could think of was the beautiful girl who'd left no trace of her passing.

The Father was at the window of the room on the seventh floor of a mid-price hotel in the city centre, blowing smoke out into the polluted air. The Son was asleep in the adjoining room, having handed the mobile phone to the old man. They were still waiting to hear the time of the pick-up. The Father knew why. He'd picked up a copy of an afternoon paper and seen the report of the shooting at the Silver Lady Club. At least she was unhurt, the woman who gave them their orders and paid their bills. But he knew the heat was rising – and that he and the Son would soon be more involved in the gang wars.

That didn't concern him. He'd been through similar times when Stratos Chiotis was in charge, and they had never lost. The pattern was always the same: ambitious young thugs who thought they could take on the established operations declaring war and committing atrocities. There weren't many of Chiotis's rivals from the sixties still in business. They'd never managed to topple the family, and one of the reasons was the Father. What he did to the upstarts was well-known in underworld circles, though people needed to be reminded from time to time as his activities were usually kept hidden from the press and public. Bodies were weighted and dropped into the sea, or buried on distant hillsides. Now things were more public. And the Son, for all his prima donna tendencies and his smartarse smile, had brought an extra dimension to the business. The boy had talent, there was no denying it.

The Father's mind went back to a day on the lake when the Son was about eight, his skinny legs protruding from torn shorts in the bow of the boat. As now, there was snow on the mountains. The Father was at the oars, his eyes on the fish that the boy had emptied on to the bottom-boards from the net.

'The perch, the carp, the eel, Baba,' the Son said in his high voice. 'They bite, Baba.'

'Of course, they bite, boy. Fish are no different from men. They fight to survive.' He let go the oars and stretched out a veined hand to grip the fully grown eel that had been caught up in the net. Instantly, under the pressure of his fingers, the creature stopped twisting and turning. 'Do what I showed you,' he ordered.

The Son gave a smile and leaned forward to take the eel in his puny hand. It started to struggle again.

'All it takes is determination,' the Father said. 'Are you determined?'

'Oh, yes, Baba,' the boy said smoothly. Taking the knife from the scabbard on his belt, he sliced round the eel's body beneath its head, pulled at the flap of bloody skin and ripped downwards. The whole thing came off like the skin of a sausage. The Son dropped the eel on the floor of the boat and watched as it thrashed around, its miniature jaws opening and closing with decreasing speed, as if it was mouthing its last words. At last it quivered into stillness.

'Not bad,' the Father said. 'But normally we smack the eel's head against the side of the boat before we skin it.'

The Son stared up at him. 'Does it matter?'

'No,' replied the Father, impressed by the boy's dexterity. 'It doesn't matter at all.'

The old man opened his eyes, taking in the grimy windows of the building opposite rather than rock-scarred mountains under a white crown. That had been when he'd first realised that the boy had potential.

He drank some water and lit another cigarette, then started to check his tools. The knife, honed to perfection, was in its leather sheath. He kept it close to him, even back home in the house above the lake. The rest of the equipment was distributed around his clothing and luggage to escape suspicious eyes.

He unscrewed the false top of the toothpaste tube and shook out the stainless steel dental probes. The wire ligatures, impossible to slip out of, were wrapped inside a woollen sweater. The rolled socks that he used as gags needed no camouflage. Nor did the yellow rubber overalls. The most important tools of all were in a talcum-powder container, small pieces of cork over their points.

The Father shook out his hooks and ran his fingers over them, feeling the curved surfaces and the vicious barbs. Everything was in order. He packed the gear into his hold-all and went back to the window, feeling his knees creak. It wouldn't be long before the work got too arduous for him, but he wasn't planning on giving the Son the satisfaction of knowing that. He was already far too full of himself. He peered down at the streets. There were people crawling like ants, cars moving slowly and blowing their horns, brightly decorated shops.

Was this what we fought for? the old man asked himself. Was this why we exterminated the Communists? To build a paradise for empty-headed shoppers? He craned his head round, looking to the north. Only a few hundred metres away was the street where the headquarters of the security police had been during the dictatorship. That was where he'd worked, that was where he'd laboured to cut out the disease afflicting the country. And he'd succeeded. The scum he'd handled changed from wolves to lambs. They no longer shouted their contempt for government and country, they no longer boasted about how they were going to return power to the people. As if the people ever wanted power. The people needed authority and strong leadership, the people knew their place.

Suddenly the Father was back in the special cells, the sound of motorbikes revving in the courtyard below to drown the victims' screams. No matter how many cigarettes he smoked, the smell of sweat mixed with faeces filled his nostrils. He didn't care. When it was cut with the metallic tang of blood, it became

the smell of victory. Muffled blows were audible in the neighbouring cell as canes were brought down relentlessly on the feet
of prisoners till they swelled up, the pain indescribable. He
turned to the person he was to work on that night. The woman
was slumped in a chair, her hair dangling in thick strands in
front of her face and her blouse torn open. He felt aroused. He
was always eager to carry out orders.

The sound of the mobile phone brought him back to the
present. He raised it to his ear. 'This is the Father.'

There was a pause. 'Ah, it's you. You're in position?' the
woman asked, her voice as unwavering as it had been the last
time he heard it months ago. It brought him pleasure.

'Of course.'

'Eight-fifty on the corner to the left. The usual driver.' The
connection was cut.

The Father looked at his watch. There were two hours to go.
He sat back to enjoy them. In recent years, the period of calm
before jobs had become almost as enjoyable as the work itself.
He let himself sink back, back to the cells.

Recalling past successes was the best way he knew to prepare
for future ones.


Mavros stood in Kanningos Square in the city centre, his eyes
on the second-floor lights of the Great Athena School of
Foreign Languages. He had been up earlier in the evening
to ask about Katia and hadn't learned much. The night school
secretary, a wizened woman, was brusque and unhelpful. She
seemed to remember Katia only vaguely. The owner was a thin
old man in a sparsely furnished office with time only for the
papers piled on his desk. He'd referred Mavros to the secretary
with a dismissive wave. After learning that the advanced
English class finished at nine-thirty, Mavros decided to wait
outside.

There was an unexpected chill in the evening air and he

stood by a kiosk with his hands in his armpits, stamping his feet. The square – named after the British Foreign Secretary Canning, who had aided the cause of Greek Independence – was being redeveloped and the air was full of dust. He hadn't expected to get much out of the people who ran the night school. The establishments were notorious for fitting as many pupils as they could into their classrooms and cramming them with knowledge in uninspiring ways.

Mavros moved closer to the entrance. As the first gaggle of teenagers appeared, he stepped in front of them and held up Katia's photograph.

'Give me a minute, will you, my friends?' he said. 'You know who this is? I'm trying to find her.'

The shouts and taunts died away, the kids glancing at each other.

'We told her old man when he came round,' said a round-faced boy in a torn T-shirt. 'None of us has a clue where she went.'

There was a chorus of agreement.

'Did any of you spend time with Katia out of classes?'

This time the voices and gestures were negative.

'She always left straight away,' said a girl with long black hair.

'Did she seem distracted before she stopped coming?'

More glances were exchanged. The girl ran her tongue along her lower lip.

'No,' she said, looking down.

'Listen, I'm a friend of the family,' Mavros said, 'but not everything you tell me is going to get back to her father.' He could see that Dmitri had intimidated the kids when he'd spoken to them.

The boy shuffled his feet. 'Well, in the last couple of months there was this guy . . .'

Mavros held up the photo of Katia with Sifis.

'Yes, that's him,' said a girl with more sober clothes than the others. 'He was a weirdo. He tried to sell you drugs, didn't he, Marko?'

The round-faced boy glared at her. 'So? It was only grass. And I didn't buy any.'

There was raucous laughter, suggesting that wasn't true.

Mavros shrugged. 'So he and Katia used to go off together after classes?'

The students signalled their agreement.

'He had a bike, a big one,' said the long-haired girl.

Mavros ran his eyes over them. 'But the night she disappeared he says he didn't meet her.'

'No, that's right,' the same girl said. 'I saw her walking up the street towards the kiosk. Then my dad came for me.'

'Did anyone else see where Katia went?' Mavros asked.

Nobody answered.

'Anything else that might help me find her?'

They were silent again.

'So she hasn't turned up?' the boy in the T-shirt asked.

'Of course she hasn't, dummy,' the long-haired girl said impatiently. 'Why do you think he's asking these questions?' She turned to Mavros. 'Are you sure she hasn't just run off with that guy?'

'Pretty sure.'

The girl twitched her head. 'No, it doesn't seem very likely. Katia wasn't like that. She was dead set on getting into university.'

Mavros remembered the flyer that the old gossip had seen. 'She never said anything about acting or going on TV?'

There were stifled laughs in the group.

'No way,' the round-faced boy said. 'Katia was far too straight for that.'

'Like you aren't,' one of his mates said, jabbing him in the ribs.

The class broke up and dispersed across the square. Only the long-haired girl remained, her head down.

'I'm frightened,' she said, shivering.

'It's all right,' he said with an encouraging smile. 'The work probably got too much for her. She'll be back when she's over the crisis.'

The girl didn't look convinced. She stood there with her arms close to her body, mobile phone in her hand.

'Can I see you home?' Mavros asked.

'It's all right. My father should be here.'

He retreated to the kiosk and looked at the newspapers that festooned it. Only when a Japanese car pulled up and the girl got in did he turn away and head for home.

# 5

Rea Chioti was running down a narrow passageway on uneven flagstones, the sound of her heels ringing out like rifle-shots. It was pitch dark, but she kept going towards a square of light ahead, not daring to stop. Behind her came the heavy tramp of armed men and no matter how fast she ran, they seemed to be getting closer. At last, breath catching in her throat, she got closer to the light. She passed under a heavy lintel and came into a circular space.

There were torches all around and behind them she could see chiselled blocks of stone. Looking up, she realised that the walls sloped inwards to form a domed roof. And then, ahead of her, she saw the raised plinth. A man stood beside it, his face turned away from her and an inlaid knife in his right hand. He was bending over the naked and motionless form of a woman laid out on the raised stone. Rea heard herself gasp as she saw that the woman's face was obscured by a mask – her gold mask with the sewn lips. She ran forward, hands outstretched, and seized the edges of the ancient artefact. Lifted it up and saw—

She came back to the real world with a start, her eyes wide. It took her a while to work out that she was in bed in the penthouse suite that her husband kept in one of the city's best hotels. She'd decided that it was safer to spend the nights there until she found out how the would-be assassin had known that she was going to the Silver Lady. She'd doubled the guard on her husband at the villa as she didn't want him to be moved. Switching on the bedside light, she sat up and took a series of deep breaths. The dream, it had taken her unawares. She'd been overwhelmed by exhaustion after she arrived at the penthouse from a foreign trade reception and checked the daily reports from her subordinates. Most of the day had been taken up with the police and lawyers going over the shooting. But it wasn't the first time she'd been gripped by such a nightmare. Ever since she bought the mask a year ago, it had been infiltrating her very being.

Rea stood up and told herself not be so melodramatic. She had work to do, she had the family businesses to run. This was no time to be allowing the past to catch up with her. Those memories were long-buried, locked in the tomb. Why were they coming back to her now?

Checking the clock, she picked up her mobile phone. She never took decisions lightly and she'd been mulling this one over since the attack.

'The bouncer who shielded me at the Silver Lady last night,' she said to her personal assistant. 'I want him here at nine o'clock.'

It was time she made some changes to her team.

Mavros woke to the unpleasant prospect of making a preliminary report to Dmitri. At least Niki had spent the night at her place, so he hadn't had to tell her about his lack of progress. He wanted to see if Katia's boyfriend went anywhere in the evening, so he would have to interrupt his client during the day at his place of work. At least that meant he would avoid the mother's devastated face. He called the Russian-Greek on his mobile and asked if they could meet. The man sounded surprised, then told Mavros where to find him.

Walking into the sunshine, Mavros decided that the orange juice he'd drunk was enough breakfast. If he stopped off at the Fat Man's place, he'd only end up arguing and he couldn't face that. The dead-ends in the hunt for Katia were oppressing him.

He went to the station and took the urban railway up to the northern suburbs.

Someone had left a morning paper on a seat and he cast an eye over it while the orange train was still underground. The police were trying to work out what had happened outside the Silver Lady Club on the coast road. It seemed that a sniper with a high-powered rifle had attempted to kill the well-known 'businesswoman' Rea Chioti. Mavros scoffed at that description, though the reality was that the family had indeed moved into legitimate lines of moneymaking like criminal operations all over the world.

The train came out of the musty tunnel into the open air. Mavros tossed the paper aside. It was obvious what was happening. The family were co-operating with the police, but no trace of the shooter would be found. In a few days, another naked and beaten body would turn up. Stratos Chiotis had always been rumoured to exact his own form of justice. No doubt his wife was the same, for all her sophisticated veneer.

Mavros got off at Eirini Station and walked north from the Olympic stadium. He could see the cranes and columns that marked the route of the motorway extension. The noise grew louder as he approached, drills rattling and cement trucks manoeuvring into position. Having an audible conversation wasn't going to be easy. Dmitri had told him to call again when he was in the vicinity so they could meet outside the site, but Mavros walked up to the perimeter fence. He wanted to see where the Russian-Greek spent his days.

There was a crowd of workers gathered in front of a partially raised wall. They were being harangued by a man in a suit and a white hard hat, his words inaudible to Mavros because of the machines. He caught sight of his client. He too was wearing a white helmet, the rest of his stocky frame in dark blue overalls. But Dmitri wasn't paying attention to the boss's speech. He was behind a hut, talking intently to a man in a bomber jacket.

Mavros moved behind the trunk of an orange tree that had escaped the attentions of the contractors. There was something about the way the men were interacting that made him curious. He watched as they both looked around to check that they weren't being observed. Then his client handed over an envelope and the other man gave him something wrapped in a dark cloth. The material snagged as Dmitri stuffed it into his pocket and Mavros clearly saw the butt of a handgun.

The man in the bomber jacket turned quickly away and walked out of the gate. Mavros stayed where he was, putting his hands in his pockets and leaning against the tree as if he was waiting for someone. When he was a few metres away, the man's mobile rang. As he passed, Mavros heard him speaking what he was certain was Russian.

Before he rang his client, he thought about what he'd seen. What the hell was Dmitri doing with a handgun? Had his daughter's disappearance spooked him so much that he wanted it for personal protection? Or was he involved with the Russian gangs who had been setting themselves up in Greece since the fall of the Soviet Union? Either way, it wasn't a development Mavros was happy about.

Uncertain how to handle the situation, he called Dmitri and arranged to meet him at the gate. He said he was on his way from the station. A few minutes later he moved away from the tree and went towards the gate. Now there was a security man on it. Had he been told to make himself scarce by Dmitri or had he been listening to the boss like the others?

'Alex!' the Russian-Greek said, extending a mud-encrusted hand. 'Sorry, I need to wash.' He was smiling beneath his beard. 'You bring good news?' He looked at Mavros's face and started across the road. 'Come, we drink coffee.' He led Mavros into a small neighbourhood *kafeneion* with the traditional marble-topped tables.

Mavros waited till they'd been served, then put his elbows on the table. 'Listen, I need to ask you a question.' He took a sip of water and steeled himself. 'Did Katia have any reason to leave home?'

Dmitri looked puzzled. 'What you mean, Alex? Katia was happy girl, she—' Then he stood up rapidly, his chair falling back with a crash that silenced the other customers. 'What you mean, fucker?' He leaned across the table, fist drawn back. 'You think I do something to her? You think I . . . no! I love my daughter, but not that way.'

Mavros held his gaze on the Russian-Greek. Then he raised his hand, the palm forward. 'Sit down, Dmitri. Sit down.' He waited till the chair had been picked up. 'That's better. No, I don't think you did anything to her. Not now. But I had to find out. You see, your wife doesn't speak enough Greek or I would have asked her. It's standard procedure in cases like this.'

'Bastard. What you learn? What I pay you for, Alex?' He drained his glass of water in one.

Mavros was satisfied that his client had spoken the truth. If he'd taken a punch, he'd have retained doubts. 'All right,' he said, and told him about Katia's boyfriend.

Dmitri heard him out and then came closer. 'Where does this filthy drug-taker live?' he demanded.

'Oh, no. I don't want you going round there and beating the shit out of him. I know you hurt him once before.'

'I didn't want him to touch my Katia.'

'It's too late for that, my friend. I'm going to keep an eye on Sifis to see if he leads me somewhere. On my own, okay?'

The Russian-Greek nodded reluctantly. 'What about the others? They know anything?'

'No one yet.' He ran through the list of people he had spoken to. 'Is there anyone you might have forgotten?'

'I don't think so.'

Mavros caught his eye. 'Why is it that Katia didn't spend time with any Russian-Greeks? Don't you people keep in touch?'

'No. I want Katia to be Greek, not immigrant. We don't have friends from old Soviet Union.'

Mavros thought about the Russian in the bomber jacket. After Dmitri's violent objection to his first question, he decided not to reveal that he'd witnessed the exchange.

'I have to go now, Alex.' His client fumbled in a pocket inside his overalls.

Mavros took out his wallet and put a five-Euro note on the table. 'I'm buying.'

His client stared at him as if he was unused to being treated, then gave a tentative smile. 'You keep in touch?'

Mavros nodded. 'One more thing. Did Katia ever say anything about wanting to go on TV or act in the theatre?'

Dmitri blinked. 'What? No, of course not. She want to be doctor. Why you ask?'

'It's not important,' Mavros said, giving him a wave as he turned away.

On his way back to the station, he thought about the construction site where he'd seen his client take possession of what he was sure was an unlicensed weapon. The most recent victim of the war that was raging in the criminal under-world had been dumped in a similar site less than a kilometre away.

Could Dmitri have had anything to do with that?


The Father and Son had been picked up in the evening as arranged. A nondescript car driven by a silent man in a suit took them away from the back streets of the city centre without attracting attention. The two men sat in the rear, each with a hold-all. Neither spoke. They never did before a job and the driver knew better than to disturb them.

The urban landscape gradually became more rundown as they headed west. Gleaming new office buildings and show-rooms were replaced by ramshackle apartment blocks, shops with steel shutters and noise-blighted schools. They reached an area that was the location of an SS prison during the Second World War. It hadn't moved much up the desirability league since then.

They were let off in a secluded cul-de-sac in front of a derelict building. The corrugated-iron sheeting that covered the windows and doors was so caked with muck that even the graffiti-artists had given up on it. The Son watched as the car disappeared round the corner. It would be back later. A single streetlamp cast the Father's shadow across the filthy asphalt, his legs the length of a giraffe's. The Son swallowed a laugh. A cat let out a screech from beneath the shell of a wrecked pick-up truck. The road surface was pocked with pools of water from broken drains and the stench was pungent. Traffic throbbed relentlessly in the distance, but there was no sign of anyone nearby.

Perfect, thought the Son.

The Father knocked three times, then once more on the shutter beneath a sign that showed the place had once been a tannery. The metal panel, obviously oiled recently, swung open. The two men stepped inside and stood in the dark after it was closed behind them.

'Welcome to the house of pain,' said the man who had admitted them, switching on a torch and shining it in the Son's face. 'Aah!' he gasped, as the Son's hand crushed his fingers. The torchlight jerked away, illuminating the Father's craggy features.

'It isn't for you to say this is the house of pain,' the old man said, stepping closer. 'You aren't the subject of our work.'

The Son laughed softly and moved the light on to the man. He was dressed in a black polo-neck sweater and trousers, his perfectly bald head making his age unclear.

'Christ,' he said, pulling his hand away and massaging it. 'You could have broken something.'

'You're right,' the Son agreed. 'But I chose not to.'

Their guide shook his head and led them down a narrow corridor to another door. He opened it and light flooded out.

The Father and Son stepped into a large room and ran their eyes around it. There were steel vats and draining trays against walls that were strung with dust-laden cobwebs. The smell inside was even more acrid than on the street, the chemicals used by the tanners having soaked into the bricks and floor. A pair of portable lamps had been set up on either side of a metal table, the light from them directed on to a naked middle-aged man. He'd been tightly bound to the surface with chains, his mouth sealed with a strip of silver duct tape. His eyes widened as he took in the two figures and their bags.

The Father went up to the table and placed his hold-all on the captive's chest. Bending forward, he examined the man's face. It was drizzled with beads of sweat, the skin on the forehead broken in a bloody welt.

The bald man went round to the other side. 'Do you know who this is, fucker?' he asked, spittle raining over the captive's nose and cheeks. 'This is the Father.' He watched as the man started to blink frantically, then inclined his head to the second figure. 'And that is the Son.' He took a rapid step back. 'Christ, he's pissing himself.' He raised his hand, then lowered it quickly when he felt the Father's eyes on him.

'What happened?' the old man said, pointing to the captive's forehead.

The bald man licked his lips. 'When we were getting him out of the car boot, he—'

'You know our requirements,' the Father interrupted. 'No physical damage to subjects.'

'That's our job,' the Son said, grinning.

The Father turned his gaze on him. 'Be quiet,' he said. He was less scathing in public, but he never hesitated to put him in his place. 'No physical damage to subjects,' he repeated to the bald man. 'Don't let it happen again.' He looked back at the Son. 'Bring that over here.'

The Son dragged a heavy table over without breaking into a sweat and watched as the Father laid out his tools on a towel he'd taken from his bag. He started to do the same further down the uneven surface.

'Who is he?' the Father asked, unrolling his yellow fisherman's overalls.

'Right,' the bald man said, the bluster returning to his voice. 'This piece of shit works for the Russians. Fyodor's lot. You know them?'

'Of course we know them,' the Son said, drawing a warning glare from the Father.

The old man held a probe up to the light, turning it between thumb and forefinger. He paid no attention to the terrified captive. 'Fyodor started off with a single nightclub ten years ago, but now he's expanded all over the city. He handles drugs, prostitution, protection, smuggling, illegal construction work and so on.' He looked across the table. 'All the businesses that Stratos Chiotis used to regard as his own.'

'You're a walking encyclopaedia,' the bald man said respectfully. 'Now, this wanker isn't a hard man. In fact, he's a fucking accountant. But he knows plenty about the Russians' set-up.' He took a small tape-recorder from his pocket. 'And we want him to sing a song about it.'

'Have you got a list of questions?' the Son asked, pulling up the zip of his protective jacket.

The bald man took a sheaf of papers from his back pocket. 'This should get you started. It's pretty technical, about bank accounts and dummy companies, that sort of thing. He is going to tell us everything he knows once you get going, isn't he?'

The Father was pulling on purple latex gloves. 'You can be sure of that.'

'Can we be sure he's telling the truth?'

The Father looked at him as if he was a child who'd forgotten the two-times table. He emptied the hooks out of the toothpaste tube and started pulling pieces of cork from the barbs.

The bald man nodded. 'Yes, we can be sure.' His smile faded when he saw the avid look on the Son's face.

The Father beckoned to the Son. 'Remove the gag.' He glanced at the bald man. 'Step away. I've told you before, this isn't a spectator sport.'

'You think I enjoy being here?' But he didn't retreat far.

The man on the table had been emitting high-pitched sounds beneath the duct tape but, as the Son leaned over, knife in hand, he went quiet.

'Lie very still,' the Son said, 'or I might slit more than your gag.'

The Father watched as the blade cut through the tape. He reached out and tore it apart, freeing the mouth below. 'Turn on the tape-recorder,' he ordered.

The Son complied and they set to work.


Mavros had been watching Sifis's apartment block for three hours. There was a disused doorway about twenty metres down the street on the opposite side where he had been able to conceal himself. The faint line of light round the closed shutters of the flat suggested that Katia's friend was in, as did the large motorbike on the pavement beneath the steps. The street was quiet enough, a few mothers with children returning home in the early evening and a couple of men parking their cars later. The only person who'd noticed Mavros was the drunk from Sifis's block. He stared into the unlit doorway and moved quickly away, as if he'd seen a ghost.

Mavros took the opportunity to steal out from his hiding place when there was no one around. Kneeling by the motorbike he presumed to be Sifis's – there weren't any others near the building – he took a long builder's nail from his pocket.

He'd picked it up from the road outside his client's place of work. As he had no transport of his own, tailing the young man would be impossible unless he disabled his bike. He put the point of the nail against the rear tyre and hammered it down with a half-brick he'd found in the doorway. Then he pulled it out to allow the air to escape.

At last the street door opened and slammed to. Sifis, wearing a torn leather jacket and dirty jeans, came down the steps unsteadily and glanced in each direction. He went to his bike.

'Fuck!'

From the shadows Mavros had a good view of the young man kicking the rear wheel, then dropping to his knees. A string of curses came from behind the bike, tailing off into a desperate sob. Then Sifis was back on his feet. He started towards the avenue at the end of the street, his head down.

Mavros gave him a start. He'd tied his hair back to change his appearance and he was wearing a different jacket from the one he'd had on when he visited Sifis. The young man's distracted air suggested that those precautions hadn't been necessary. He watched as Sifis took up a position on the corner and started hailing cabs. Although it was almost midnight, the three lanes in each direction were packed with traffic and many of the cabs were occupied, even though their For Hire signs were illuminated. A couple of vehicles with other customers on board slowed, but the young man waved them on. Obviously he didn't want to share.

Mavros was lurking behind a palm tree. This was going to take split-second timing and a fair amount of good fortune. A yellow Mercedes pulled in and Sifis fell into the back seat. Mavros sprinted forward as the cab moved away, waving his arm. He was in luck. A Honda with a damaged front wing swung across from the middle lane and ground to a halt, the driver oblivious to the blast of horns he had provoked.

'Follow that Mercedes,' Mavros ordered.

The driver glanced in the mirror as he pulled away. 'You a cop?'

'No,' Mavros said, catching the hostility in the unshaven man's tone. 'All you need to know is that you're in line for a big tip if you don't lose him.'

'It's a deal.' The driver accelerated, cutting in front of a bus.

'Don't get too close.'

'I know what I'm doing.' There was a No Smoking sign on the dashboard, but that didn't stop the guy lighting a cigarette.

Clouds of smoke drifted past Mavros to the window that he'd opened. After initially hesitating, he inhaled. It was over a year since he'd given up, but he wasn't free from temptation. The dark blue worry-beads that he used to distract himself were in the front pocket of his jeans. He took them out and, gradually, the urge to bum a cigarette from the driver passed.

They went through the centre, the lights of the department stores and banks blazing out. Mavros could see Sifis in the Mercedes ahead. His head was slumped back on the seat and he looked dead to the world. He probably needed to replenish his stock of dope. The traffic was heavy, but once they got on to the wide avenue that led to the sea the speed of both cabs increased.

'Perverts,' the driver said, glancing to the right.

Mavros took in a pair of busty transsexuals on a corner, their legs sheathed in fishnet stockings and their painted lips in come-hither pouts. 'Everybody has to pay the rent.'

'The bender,' the driver said under his breath. 'He likes them.'

Not particularly, Mavros thought, but I bet you do.

The air took on a salty tang as they swung past the racetrack to meet the shoreline. Mavros had been wondering if they would stop there. Even though the races had finished for the day, there would be plenty of illicit action going on in the neighbourhood. But the Mercedes sped on. The lights of the coast road illuminated the rippled surface of the bay. Only a swimmer with a death wish would immerse himself here despite the improvements in sewage disposal, but the southern suburbs generally had a healthier environment than most of the city. Apart from that, Mavros couldn't see the point of living down here. Niki didn't agree. She'd inherited a flat nearby from her foster-parents. The streets were as clogged and the apartment blocks as cheerless as anywhere else.

Then again, this area was handy for nightlife. The coast road was dotted with clubs and discos flashing garish neon signs. The ones whose owners weren't able to pay protection money were dark and deserted. There were huge posters of mediocre, overpaid singers on the hoardings. They passed a sign proclaiming they were in Alimos. The area was known for its yacht marina and its clubs.

Mavros made the connection. The Silver Lady with its oversized mannequin had appeared ahead. It was where shots had been fired at the crime boss Rea Chioti. He felt a stir of disquiet. Was Katia's boyfriend involved with that family?

'He's pulling in,' the driver said, decelerating.

'Do the same, but keep your distance.' Mavros sank down in the back seat, his eyes on the Mercedes. It had stopped on the pavement outside the club's parking area, hazard lights flashing. Sifis didn't get out. He was making a call on his mobile.

'Who's the guy in the cab?' the driver asked.

'Someone I know,' Mavros answered vaguely.

The swarthy man at the wheel grunted. 'I think he might be in trouble.'

Mavros watched as two men in dark suits, one heavily built, stepped over the chain that marked the nightclub's perimeter. They both looked around, then the larger one went to the offside rear door. The other got in the back from the kerbside. Sifis looked to be the filling in a pretty unhealthy sandwich.

'We're off,' the driver said, engaging first gear.

The two cars went about five kilometres down the coast road, before the Mercedes suddenly swung to the left and ran a light that was changing to red.

'Shit!' Mavros exclaimed.

'Don't worry,' the driver said, inclining his head in the direction the other taxi had gone.

A refuse lorry was blocking the road, the Mercedes's brake lights on. By the time the traffic lights changed, Mavros's cab was only fifty metres behind. They were heading up a road that led through apartment blocks built into the mountainside, but soon the houses began to thin out. At the end of the last developed area, the Mercedes stopped.

'Kill your lights,' Mavros said, as his driver pulled in.

The three men got out of the lead taxi and stood on the roadside as the vehicle turned and went back down towards the main road.

'What now?' the driver asked in a low voice. 'I don't like the look of this.'

'Neither do I.' Mavros started to run through his options. Calling the police was a non-starter. They wouldn't come out here without a good reason. Sifis was probably just collecting a stash, but Mavros didn't like the way the heavies were crowding him. They were holding on to his arms.

'Will you wait?' he asked the driver.

'Only if you pay me what's on the meter now plus that tip you promised. After that, I'll see how it grabs me.'

Mavros didn't have much choice. He handed over the cash. 'There's more where that came from if you're still here when I come back.'

'If you come back,' the driver said with a hollow laugh. 'All right, what have I got to lose? The meter's running.'

Mavros opened the door and got out, closing it behind him soundlessly. Sifis and the other men had walked into the darkness. There were no houses beyond, only the steepening flank of the mountain. Mavros felt his heart pound in his chest. This looked like a very bad idea, but he couldn't just leave Katia's boyfriend to whatever was in store for him. He got off the road, feeling rough stones and dried mud beneath his boots. He could hear voices ahead of him. At first they were low, but they soon grew louder. Then a light shone out, the flame of a cigarette lighter.

'—fuckin' arsehole? You owe us five thousand and you want a line of credit? What do you think we are, a fuckin' bank?'

'No, no,' Mavros heard Sifis gabble. 'But I've got some good new customers. They want more than I usually shift. Please—'

'Let me sort him, Yanni,' the second man said, his voice coarse. 'I've got my dusters and I've got my knife.'

'Not to mention your Glock, Pano,' said the first man.

There was a squeal from Sifis. 'No, please, I'll get the money, I'll—'

'It's too late for that, you piece of shit. We're going to—'

Mavros swallowed hard. He had to act. 'Hey!' he shouted. 'What's going on up there?'

The light was extinguished immediately. Mavros changed position, hoping he didn't walk into them.

'Fuckin' shit,' he heard the man called Yannis say. 'We better leave the bastard. Next time, Sifi. And the interest's twenty points a day. You got that? Twenty per cent. Come on, Pano.'

'I can take this guy,' said the other man. 'He won't be tooled up like us.'

'The boss said to keep a low profile. Come on.'

Mavros listened as heavy footsteps moved past him towards the road.

'You're lucky fuckers,' Yannis said. 'Both of you.'

Mavros waited till the footsteps had faded away. He heard a car engine start up and saw headlights swing round the hillside.

'Sifi,' he said in a low voice. 'It's Alex. Are you all right?'

There was silence, then the young man's voice came from some way off. 'Alex? What the fuck are you doing here?'

Mavros went towards him. 'I'll explain that to you, my friend. And then you can explain who those arseholes were.'

'Oh, shit,' Sifis said nervously, as he lit a cigarette.

'Oh, shit is right. But at least you're still alive.'

Mavros was wondering what the musclemen would have done to Katia's trembling boyfriend if he hadn't intervened. And to him, if they'd caught him.


Damis got up from the bed in the suite that had been arranged for him in the luxury hotel. He stared down at the traffic on the avenue below. The lights formed a shimmering carpet that was never still. When he'd taken the call from Lakis the Boss in the early-morning, he hadn't imagined that things would change so much. He lowered the volume of the widescreen TV and tried to put his thoughts in order.

Lakis had been short with him, told him to get dressed and wait for a car at the bouncers' flat. 'It seems you made a good impression on Mrs Chioti,' he said with undisguised irritation. 'You and your two dumb friends.'

It turned out that Yannis the Driver and Peasant Panos had been taken off security duties and given responsibility for a list of dope dealers. Damis reckoned that was asking for trouble – the pair couldn't organise an orgy in a knocking-shop. Not that he cared. Their promotion was nothing compared with his.

'I want you to move in here immediately,' Rea Chioti said to him when he was ushered into her suite. The guys on the door hadn't deigned to speak to him as they ran their hands over him and took away his automatic. 'And I want you to take orders only from me. Do you understand?'

Damis looked into the head of the family's ash-grey eyes, feeling the force of them for the first time. She was suffering from shock the night he'd saved her from the assassin's bullets, even though she'd carried herself well afterwards, and then her eyes didn't make such an impression on him. Now, standing in front of her on the thick-pile carpet, he glimpsed the strength of will that had driven her to the top of the tree.

'As you'll find out, I have certain other operatives who deal only with me,' La Chioti said, looking up at him from where she sat in a plush armchair. She was wearing a business suit that must have cost a bagful of Euros. Her legs, in sheer black stockings, were crossed above the knee. Damis was disturbed to realise that part of the power she wielded was sexual. Jesus, he thought. Am I out of my mind?

'What kind of work is it that you want me to do?' he asked, struggling to keep his voice level.

She kept her eyes on him. 'You seem to have a fair amount of initiative. I think you're wasted as a bouncer. As you saw outside, I have plenty of enforcers. What I need is someone I can trust.' She glanced down at her perfectly manicured nails, the red varnish glowing in the artificial light. 'Young man, I was betrayed the other night.' She pointed to an antique desk. 'Over there is a list of the people who knew I was going to the Silver Lady. I'll ensure that everyone in the upper echelons of the family businesses knows you're empowered to ask questions.' She gave him a cold smile. 'However, you're not empowered to punish the guilty person. You'll report your findings to me and discuss this with no one else. Understood?'

'Understood, Mrs Chioti.'

'There's a mobile telephone number on a separate sheet on the desk. Memorise it and destroy the paper in front of me.'

He complied, thankful that he'd always had a good memory for figures.

'My assistants are preparing a dossier that will make your task easier,' the head of the family said. She stood up to end the meeting. 'They'll also provide you with certain benefits in addition to your suite here – a car, funds.' She looked into his eyes again. 'Don't disappoint me. This could be the beginning of a significant career for you.'

In his bedroom Damis turned away from the window, trying to banish his employer from his mind. She frightened him, she attracted him, she held his life in the palm of her hand. Why did she think that a simple bouncer like him could find her betrayer? He had the feeling he was being used as a pawn in a game he couldn't fathom, but there was no way he could pull out now. Not that he wanted to. He was in place, he'd got the break he'd been working for since he started at the Silver Lady.

Damis clenched his fists, feeling the nails dig into the palms of his hands. This was his big chance. He owed it to Martha, lost Martha with her empty eyes and ravaged face, not to screw it up.

# 6

Mavros and Sifis came off the slope and into the streetlights. There was no sign of the two hard men, or of Mavros's taxi. He swore under his breath. Taxi drivers were the scum of the earth. Then, as they crossed the first junction, he heard a beep. The Honda with the damaged wing flashed its lights and drew up.

The driver hung his head out of the window. 'You thought I'd left you in the shit, didn't you?' he said, with an uneven grin.

Mavros took Sifis's arm and led him to the backdoor. He was impressed by the driver's nerve. 'I'm glad you did. Those two guys from the nightclub, did you see where they went?'

'They were picked up by a big Audi. There looked to be a fair amount of shouting going on.' He glanced round. 'Back to where we came from?'

Mavros wondered if he'd been spotted. He looked at Sifis. He was shivering, his brow drenched in sweat. 'Are you all right?'

'I will be when I get home.'

'Is that a good idea? Do they know where you live?'

Sifis shrugged. 'I don't care. I've got some gear left.'

Mavros caught the driver's eye in the mirror. 'You're not listening, are you?'

'What?' the unshaven man shouted. 'Can't hear a word.'

Mavros smiled and turned back to Sifis. 'You owe me, my friend. Start talking.'

The young man wrapped his arms round his chest. 'Talk?' he said listlessly. 'What about?'

They were about to turn on to the coast road.

'Do you want us to drop you off at the Silver Lady?' Mavros asked, nudging him. 'It's on our way.'

'No,' Sifis said with a gasp. 'What do you want to know?'

'Cut inland,' Mavros instructed the driver. 'Who's your contact?'

'I don't . . .' Sifis stopped himself. 'Look, we don't usually meet. I pick up the stuff in bars or clubs. This was to be a special deal. I owe them and I was trying to make up the shortfall.'

'You've only got one customer now. Yourself.'

'No, no, I'm still supplying some . . .'

Mavros grabbed his arm. 'Stop pissing me about. Do you know where Katia is?'

There was a sob. 'Of course I fucking don't! I miss her . . . I love her.'

'All right,' Mavros said, relaxing his grip. 'Is there any chance those scumbags from the Silver Lady could have seen you with her?'

Sifis raised his shoulders. 'I suppose it could have got back to them that I had a good-looking girlfriend.' His eyes widened. 'You mean, they might have grabbed her?' He thought about it. 'They sometimes do things like that to keep people sharp. But they'd have told me.'

Mavros nodded. Sifis was probably right. On the other hand, bottom-feeding musclemen like Yannis and Panos wouldn't necessarily know if Katia had been seized on the street and forced to be a dancer or worse.

'No, they can't have,' Sifis was saying, his head in his hands. 'Katia, Katia . . .'

The taxi turned north towards the city centre.

Mavros looked out of the window as the driver shot a glance

at the corner where the men-women had been standing earlier. They weren't there now. He wondered if they were pimped by some shithead who answered to the Chiotis family. It wouldn't have surprised him. He thought about what he'd discovered. Katia's boyfriend was linked to the biggest crime organisation in the city and its enforcers had their claws into him. But he hadn't established a direct link to the missing girl.

It couldn't really be classed as a night to remember.

The Son's sleep was dreamless. He woke to the sounds of the cleaner in the corridor outside his hotel room, and the shouts of the market traders below. The Father would have been up and about for hours. The old man always wandered around the city first thing in the morning when they were down on jobs. He liked the bustle of the narrow streets in the market area. He came back with plastic bags full of olives better than those available in the north and the camomile that he'd been told to drink for his stomach. And he took the opportunity to visit the fishing gear stores to buy more hooks. He needed plenty after last night. But the Father also went back to his old haunts – the Son had followed him once. The street where the torture cells used to be, that was his favourite.

Swinging his legs off the bed, the Son started to do his exercises. He counted out the number of stomach crunches as he'd been taught to do in the army, fifty, a hundred, two hundred, feeling the burn in his muscles. He kept himself in good condition, which was more than could be said for the Father. The old man had been short of breath during the job last night, wiping the sweat from his brow all the time. Not that it mattered. The subject hadn't held back. Information had gushed from him like a waterfall. That didn't save him from the probes and the hooks. The Father never believed what people said unless they were in pain. The old bastard, he thought, as he rolled on to his back and started a set of sit-ups. Why was he so suspicious? It was obvious that the guy had been telling the truth from the beginning.

He'd hung on, though. He had a lot of stamina for an out-of-condition office worker. Three hours they'd worked on him and at the end he was still conscious. A lot of that was down to the Father's skill, of course. He knew exactly how much pain to inflict.

The body would have been discovered by now. The Father hadn't been impressed when the bald man told them that, once again, he'd been ordered to dump it in a public location. The point was to pay the Russians back for the family's man who'd been found in the construction site – to pay them back and to send a message that the family was a lot more vicious than them.

The Son got up and drank down a bottle of water. He wasn't really interested in the game their employer was playing. As long as there was work, he was happy. It sounded like there was going to be more for them to do, but there had been no calls yet. La Chioti was keeping her distance. Pulling on a tracksuit, he made sure that all his equipment was hidden and went out of the room.

'You don't need to bother,' he said to the cleaner, a blonde who probably came from the former Eastern Block. 'I'm very tidy.' The woman looked at him like he was from another planet. He was tempted to make something of it, but told himself to calm down. He'd never got on with women. It was as if they sniffed out that he was different from other men. Even the whores he'd used when he was in the army, women who'd been with the worst bastards, used to avoid his eyes. That only made it more enjoyable.

Out on the street, the Son swerved round a gypsy woman with a small child in tow. Both of them were filthy, the woman's voluminous skirt reaching to her ankles and her bare feet scabby. The child reached out a hand to him. He showed it his teeth. The Father had some lunatic ideas, but he was sound on this – there were too many sub-humans in the country. One thing they'd got right in Yugoslavia was ethnic cleansing.

He tugged his baseball cap lower over his eyes. He wasn't worried about being recognised as no one in the city knew who he was, but he liked to fade into the background, to be anonymous. It was hard to do that back home. People knew the Father. Not that they had any inkling about his past. That had been carefully erased after the dictatorship. And the Father had changed his appearance, grown a moustache to hide the prominent upper lip that the people he'd worked on in the cells might have remembered.

Brushing past shoppers with his hands in his pockets, the Son relished the contact his elbows made. No one paid much attention. It was every man for himself here, every man and every woman. The old women were the worst. They pushed through the crowd with their wire trolleys, indifferent to the damage they did to people's legs. He went into a small café and ordered. The heavily sweetened coffee appeared on the tiny table a few minutes later. He sipped it and the hubbub around him faded.

He was thinking about his future. He always was these days. The Father was getting to be a liability. He'd seen how the old man's hand trembled as he fixed the hooks last night. He needed to break away. He needed to do something to show the Chioti woman how much better things would be if the Son worked on his own. But how was he to do that? The Father and Son had a reputation. People in the business were afraid of them. The accountant had pissed himself as soon as he heard who they were. Would the Son be able to command the same respect on his own? Of course he would. All it needed was the right job. All it needed was independent action. The Son was man enough to set that up.

Suddenly he was back in Kastoria, a kid in a borrowed black

suit that didn't fit him, walking to the cemetery behind his mother's coffin. The Father was beside him, but he wasn't holding his hand. There weren't many people in the procession as the family had few friends. The Son looked up at the rooftops, to the storks' nests and the uneven television aerials. Above them, the sky was a pale blue colour that reminded him of the duck eggs he found in the reed beds – pale blue that was obliterated when he crushed the eggs and felt the sticky mess leak out between his fingers.

The old woman who cleaned for them bent down and whispered in his ear, keeping her eyes off the Father, 'Your mother has gone to a better place.'

The Son nodded. He knew she had. He'd seen the Father send her there, shoving her down the stairs so hard that her head split and her brains spattered across the flagstones below. He saw the Father do that, and the Father saw him watching. He turned and raised his finger to his lips, then gave a conspiratorial smile that made the Son feel warm inside.

There was a jolt as someone banged into his table.

'Watch out, fool!' the Son shouted, his fist clenched.

The elderly man backed away, eyes bulging in shock.

The Son lowered his hand. 'Excuse me,' he mumbled.

Then the television was turned up and everyone in the café concentrated on the corpse that had been found hanging outside a warehouse in the northern suburbs.

Mavros sat on his sofa and watched as the reporter described the crime scene.

'We're at the Black Eagle Transport Company headquarters,' Lambis Bitsos said, his expression grim. 'Workers made a horrendous discovery here this morning.' The camera panned across an asphalt area in front of a modern two-storey building. Police tape fluttered in the breeze and figures in uniform and white protective clothing were moving about. 'The body of an as-yet-unidentified man was dangling from the company sign behind me. Cause of death has not been determined but the body was severely mutilated, raising fears that this is the latest in the series of gangland murders.'

Mavros lowered the volume and sipped his orange juice. The newshound was certainly being kept busy. Bitsos liked to think he'd seen everything, but even he looked startled by this killing. The body wasn't shown. The van driving away with a police escort was all that the ghouls in the channel's newsroom were allowed this time. The victim must have been in a hell of a state. He wondered if the dead man had any connection with the attempted shooting of Rea Chioti at the Silver Lady. Things were really hotting up in the Athenian underworld.

He turned the television off and forced himself to concentrate on Katia. He needed to focus on the missing girl's circle of acquaintances.

The phone rang.

'You're awake. Amazing.'

'Good morning, Niki. Everything okay?' Her tone suggested it wasn't.

'What have you been saying to Dmitri?'

He thought back to the conversation he'd had with his client at the building site. 'Ah. Well, it's a question that had to be asked.'

'Let me get this straight. You asked him if he'd abused his daughter?'

'Normally I'd have asked his wife, but—'

'Are you completely insane? You can't go around accusing people like that.'

'Calm down. I didn't accuse him. Have you any idea how many kids run away from home because their parents or other relatives—'

'Actually, I do. I'm a social worker, remember?'

'And I'm an investigator. You have to let me run this.'

She laughed. 'You're lucky Dmitri didn't flatten you, Alex.'

Mavros took his notebook from his jacket pocket. 'Listen, there's more to your friend Dmitri than meets the eye.' He told her about the weapon he'd seen. 'Do you know anything about the fights you told me he got into in the camp?'

There was a pause. 'Shit,' Niki said, her tone less combative. 'No, I don't. No one brought charges. I assumed they were just outbursts of frustration. The conditions weren't—'

'You assumed?'

'What are you getting at?'

'Dmitri seems to be quite well off for a recent immigrant. He's got a reasonable flat, he could afford to send Katia to evening classes.'

'So?'

Mavros raised his eyes to the ceiling. Niki always gave people the benefit of the doubt. 'It's never occurred to you that he might be dirty?'

'Dirty? You mean criminal?'

'Yes, I mean criminal. He's got a handgun that I'll bet is unlicensed.'

There was another pause. 'No, I can't believe that. Maybe he's worried about his safety. I imagine it's dangerous on those big sites.'

'Give me a break, Niki. We're talking about the northern suburbs, not the Wild West.'

'Ask him, then,' she said abruptly. 'But I'm telling you, Dmitri's a good man.'

'I'll see. In the meantime, don't mention any of this to him.'

'All right. Where are you with Katia?'

He gave her a quick rundown, missing out the episode with Sifis and the hard men. 'You never heard anything about her being interested in the theatre or TV, did you?'

'No, why?'

He told her about the flyer the old gossip had picked up.

'Come on, Alex. That doesn't sound like Katia. She's the most serious kid I've ever met.'

'And she had a dope-dealer boyfriend she kept quiet about.'

'You're right.' Niki gave a sharp laugh. 'We all have secrets, don't we, Alex? 'Bye.'

Mavros put the phone down, shaking his head. That was a reference to the terrorism case last Christmas. He couldn't tell Niki about it, but she knew something serious had happened and resented being kept at arm's length. She was difficult, she often drove him crazy, but he loved her. They'd been getting closer lately, but now Katia had got between them. He should have known better than to let Niki put him on to a client. He knew from bitter experience, not least on the long and fruitless search for his brother, that he had a tendency to concentrate on people who were no longer there rather than those he could reach out and touch.

After he'd showered and dressed, Mavros headed for Katia's neighbourhood. There were a couple of names on the list of her contacts that he hadn't yet spoken to. The first was a seamstress she'd worked with occasionally on wedding dresses. The woman was tiny, her body permanently hunched. She wiped away a tear when she started to talk about Katia, saying the girl was as sweet as honey, but she didn't have any idea where she could be.

Mavros went back out into the sunlight. That left only one name on the list: Makis Nikolaou. The address was nearby, a couple of streets above Katia's. As he walked up the steep incline, he asked himself if he was wasting his time. None of the rest of her friends had a clue why she'd left home. There didn't seem much chance that he'd strike lucky with this one. Anyway, if he was Katia's age, he'd be at school.

'I'd like to speak to Makis, please,' he said into the speaker by the street door.

'Really?' said a surprised male voice. 'Come up to the third floor.'

When Mavros got there, one of the doors was open. A young man in a wheelchair was waiting for him. He was overweight, his face covered in acne, but there was a pleasant smile on his lips.

'Who are you?' he asked. 'I don't get many visitors. Well, I don't get any at all now.'

Mavros said he was a friend of Katia's family. 'Can you tell me anything about her?' he asked, as he followed Makis inside.

The boy swung his wheels round in the main room. All the furniture had been moved against the walls to allow him maximum space. 'What do you want to know?'

Mavros wondered if he was simple. The smile was still in place and there was a childish innocence about him despite the fact that he must have been about eighteen. 'You know she's left home? Disappeared.'

'Katia? Of course she hasn't.'

Mavros looked around the room. There were the usual family photos, some of which showed Makis on his feet in basketball strip.

'I broke my back playing for my club,' the boy said, seeing the direction of his glance. 'It happened a year ago. Katia used to come and see me in the hospital. We were in the same class.' He gazed up at him. 'I don't go to school any more.'

Mavros saw the pain in his eyes. 'Why do you say Katia hasn't disappeared?' he said, after a pause. 'Her parents don't know where she is and neither do any of her other friends.'

Makis laughed. 'That's because they don't know her like I do.' He pushed himself closer to Mavros. 'Sit down. My mother will be back soon and I can't talk about Katia when she's here.' He winked. 'It's a secret.'

'Really?' Mavros still wasn't sure about the state of the young man's mind, but he couldn't deny he'd been hooked. 'What's the secret?'

The smile widened. 'Katia and I tell each other everything.'

'That's nice,' Mavros said, catching his eye. 'So you knew about her boyfriend?'

'Sifis? Oh, yes.' Makis laughed. 'Naughty boy. He sells drugs.'

'When did you last see Katia?'

'Four weeks and two days ago,' the young man said without hesitation.

'And you aren't concerned that she's vanished?'

Another laugh, this one accompanied by the smack of hands on immobile thighs. 'No, I told you, she hasn't.' He leaned forward and whispered. 'She's going to be a star.'

Mavros felt the hairs on the back of his neck rise. The flyer that the old neighbour saw. 'What do you mean?'

Makis gave him another wink. 'She doesn't really want to be a doctor. She wants to be an actress. Not like the idiots you see on the TV, a real actress, one who does the classics. Sophocles, that kind of thing.'

Mavros sat back and studied the young man. 'Has she gone to a stage school?'

'That's her plan. I'm going to lend her some money.' Makis put his finger to his lips. 'Don't tell Mama. She'll go mad.'

'That's very generous of you.'

'It's nothing. Katia saved me when I came out of hospital. I couldn't face it, you see, I couldn't face the idea of life in this chair. She helped me. She made me understand that we live in our minds and souls, not in our bodies.' He laughed. 'Sounds stupid, I know. But I believe it, thanks to Katia. She's a wonderful person.'

'Yes, she is,' Mavros said, keeping up the pretence that he knew her. 'So, can you tell me where she is?'

'Maybe.' Makis gave him a sly smile.

Mavros kept his cool. 'Have you heard from her since the last time she was here?'

'Maybe.'

Mavros moved closer. 'Listen, I know what happened. Katia got hold of a flyer advertising a stage school . . .'

'Don't be silly, Katia isn't a fool. Everyone knows those places are a rip-off.'

'What was she planning to do, then?'

Makis looked round to check that his mother hadn't come back. 'You seem like a good guy. But you have to promise not to tell her father.'

Mavros thought about that. He probably wouldn't tell Dmitri until he'd checked the lead, but he'd have to come clean eventually. He felt bad about deceiving the boy in the wheelchair. 'I promise,' he said, dropping his gaze.

'Good.' Now Makis was bursting to share the news. 'She went to study with Jenny Ikonomou at her house.'

'What?' Mavros was struggling to believe what he'd heard. 'Jenny Ikonomou, our national star?'

The boy nodded happily. 'That's right. She went to stay with her.'

'What?'

'Yes,' said Makis, as if it was the most natural thing in the world. 'She was having lessons.'

Mavros ran his hands through his hair. To say that the case had just taken an unexpected turn would have been a major understatement.

Rea Chioti spread the newspapers out across the table in front of the settee in the living-room of her suite. The afternoon editions had covered 'the hanging body case', as it was being called. She wasn't interested in the details. All that mattered was that the coverage was extensive.

There was a knock. Her personal assistant Maggi appeared.

'I'm sorry to interrupt, Mrs Chioti, but Mr Frixos is here.'

Rea looked at her watch. 'He's half an hour early. Tell him to wait.' She gave a tight smile. 'Diplomatically.' Frixos was a member of parliament who was useful to the family.

Maggi nodded and withdrew. The MP was no doubt panicking about the family's recent high profile. He would calm down when she upped his monthly retainer. He'd earn it by creating a storm about the influx of foreign criminals into Greece. That would give her time, which was what she needed. Time to gain the upper hand over Fyodor. She was sure the shadowy Russian, never seen in public, was behind the shooting at the Silver Lady and the death of her middle-ranking drugs controller. The police still hadn't worked out the identity of the body that had been found in the motorway construction site in the northern suburbs. Would they discover that of the man she'd consigned to the Father and Son? Only if the Russians leaked it. They were unlikely to do that. They'd be too busy working to change their systems and safeguard their operations because of what the guy had spilled. Her people were already taking advantage of that.

Rea stood up and went to the desk. She looked at herself in the gilt-framed mirror. Her hair and make-up were as flawless as ever, the expensive clothes sheathing the ageing body effectively, but she could see the unease in her eyes. She paused, extending a hand. For a moment she'd thought she was in the study in the villa, reaching for the secret door behind the painting. The mask. Even when she was away from home, it exerted its power over her. The mask – golden, silent, an image of pain and endurance. It was her life, but it was also the life of the other woman, the one she'd betrayed. Why was the part of her life that she'd suppressed for so long coming back to haunt her?

She lowered her gaze and touched the sheet of paper on the desk. It was a copy of the list she'd given to the bouncer Damis Naskos. It was a risk, but she thought that her husband would have approved. He'd told her often enough that he always shook the family businesses up when they were under pressure by bringing in fresh blood. Stratos was an innovator, that was how he'd stayed at the top for so many years. There was definitely something about the tall young man that made him stand out from the other foot soldiers.

Rea ran her finger down the names. All that Damis had to do was scare the traitor into making a false move. Then the Father would have another body to work on.

An icy finger ran up her spine. Pain, she told herself, pain was the ruling principle. Not belief in a political cause or faith in a religion, not love or any of the other empty words that people used to deceive themselves. Pain was destiny. You couldn't escape it. The only way to survive was to make sure you dealt more pain than you received.

Maybe she'd learned that too early in her life, but the lesson had stood her in good stead ever since.

Mavros got off the trolley-bus near the Parliament building and walked past its yellow walls into Syndagma Square. The traffic was at its midday peak and the air burned in his throat. As usual, tourists and Greeks from the provinces had gathered around the kilted honour guards at the memorial to the unknown soldier. Waiting for the lights to change, he thought about the boy in the wheelchair. His first reaction had been to treat what Makis said about Katia being involved with the actress Jenny Ikonomou with profound scepticism. It was like a kid in late-fifties Los Angeles saying that his friend had been taken under Marilyn Monroe's wing. No, not Monroe, she was too young and her range as a performer wasn't so great. Maybe Bette Davis. Jenny Ikonomou displayed a similar haughty disdain to the world outside her profession. But the naive boy had held real conviction in his voice. Maybe it was true that he was Katia's sole confidant about her acting ambitions. The flyer seen by the old neighbour suggested she was interested, even if she hadn't been taken in by it. But Jenny Ikonomou? How could a self-effacing Russian-Greek girl have got anywhere near the country's most reclusive star?

Mavros went into a café on a side-street and approached a table at the rear. 'Hello, Anna.' He always spoke English to his sister. Their mother had insisted that her children use that language at home and the habit persisted when they were on their own. 'Sorry I'm late.'

She put down her magazine and presented a smooth cheek to him. 'Alex. How nice of you to dress so appropriately.'

Mavros glanced around the place. It was the kind of high-price, pseudo-high-society gossip-shop that he avoided like the plague, but he'd had little choice about meeting here as he wanted Anna's help. There were a couple of other people wearing jeans and leather, but the quality was a lot higher than what he was wearing. Next time he would insist that Anna go to the Fat Man's. That would really give her something to complain about.

He sat down, running an eye over his sister. 'What have you been doing? Appearing in a fashion show?' Her clothes were even more cutting-edge than usual, the yellow and black trouser suit set off by a pair of sharply pointed shoes that might have been designed by the Spanish Inquisition.

'Just the clothes that my job requires,' Anna said with a faint smile. She was a lifestyle journalist with columns in several of the capital's best-selling magazines. 'So, how are things?' She gave him a look that combined exasperation and concern. 'Still waiting for the perfect job to come up and kiss you on the lips?'

Mavros ordered a coffee from a waitress, who responded with a supercilious flick of her long brown hair. 'No, as a matter of fact I've got a case.'

Anna clapped her hands. 'I was beginning to wonder if you'd ever get back into the groove after—' She broke off to avoid mentioning the terrorism case. She'd been involved in it more than she'd have wished. Then her relieved expression vanished. 'Don't tell me, you want something from me.'

Mavros shrugged. 'Well . . .'

'Typical. I might have known. I thought we were having a get-together.'

'Calm down, Anna. There might be something in it for you.'

His sister gave a bitter laugh. 'How many times have I heard that?' She waited as the waitress placed Mavros's coffee on the table with an insincere smile. 'Go on, then,' Anna said, betraying interest. 'But I'm not promising anything.'

'Jenny Ikonomou,' he said in a low voice.

Anna raised her eyes. 'Our national star? What about her?'

'Have you met her?'

'Don't be silly, Alex.' She twitched her perfectly painted lips. 'Ordinary mortals aren't allowed into her company.'

'Do I detect the odour of rancid grapes? What did she do? Refuse you an interview?' He sipped his coffee and was pleased to find that it was nothing like as good as the Fat Man's.

'Worse than that. We set up an in-depth profile, the first for over a year. I organised a photographer, stylist, wardrobe people, the lot. At the last minute she changed her mind. Pressure of work, supposedly.' Anna sniffed. 'Pressure of not giving a shit, more like.' She turned the pages of her magazine and pointed to a photograph of the actress getting out of a black Mercedes. 'Look at her. She hates the press, she hates publicity. I reckon she even hates her fans.'

Mavros examined the shot. It showed a striking middle-aged woman dressed in a close-fitting evening gown, her hair so lustrous that it must have been dyed. She was staring into the lens with what would be described as antisocial loathing in a normal person, but was seen as wholly justified amour-propre in a successful actress.

'She does look fierce,' he conceded. 'But she's very popular.'

Anna nodded. 'She's supposed to represent the best of Greece. Refusal to conform, passion, self-belief, all that Mediterranean egotism.' Although she was married to a Greek, Anna shared Mavros's ambivalence about some aspects of the people. 'There's no question that she's a good actress. Her Antigone was enough to make the stones weep. She even managed to make those turgid TV adaptations of classic novels watchable.'

'She was good in that Hollywood movie about the German occupation, too. Christ knows how she managed to make that character who fell in love with a Nazi officer sympathetic.'

'Yes,' Anna said reluctantly. 'But that doesn't make her a good human being.'

Mavros ran his hand across the stubble on his chin. 'Have you ever heard of her taking in aspiring actresses?'

His sister raised an eyebrow. 'Now we're getting to it. What is this case you're working on, Alex?'

He told her about Katia, knowing that, unlike other journalists, he could rely on Anna to respect the confidence.

'And you think Jenny Ikonomou goes around inviting young women into her home?' Anna struggled to restrain laughter. 'Forget it, Alex. Haven't you heard of the Pink Palace?'

He looked at her blankly. 'You know I don't follow society gossip.'

'Well, maybe you should,' she said sharply. 'It would stop you wasting my time.'

Mavros raised a hand to placate her. 'The Pink Palace?'

'That's what she calls her house in Kolonaki. It might be pink, but it's like a prison. She never invites anyone there. She hires hotel ballrooms for her parties.'

'It's like a prison,' Mavros repeated.

Anna stared at him. 'Not like that, Alex. She's just the most private person in Athens.'

'Does she run a stage school? Some actors do.'

She laughed. 'Only the ones who don't get enough work. La Ikonomou is very much in demand.'

La Ikonomou. That made Mavros think of the gang boss Rea Chioti. Some of the papers gave her the French definite article too. Powerful women put journalists' backs up, especially those belonging to male crime reporters.

'I wish you luck if you're thinking of trying to talk to her,' Anna said, gathering her things together. 'Jenny Ikonomou doesn't like opening her mouth unless she gets well paid for it.' She put a banknote on the table. 'What kind of expenses can you get from your client?' she asked with a mocking smile.

'He's a working man,' Mavros said, giving her an irritated look and then relenting. 'Sorry. Thanks for taking the time.'

Anna leaned forward and kissed him. 'Take care, Alex. I tell you what, I'll fax you the most recent feature that I saw about her.' She smiled and headed for the door.

Mavros watched her go, only realising as she disappeared down the street that he hadn't told her he was giving up the search for Andonis. Somehow he felt that the decision wasn't official until he'd let his sister know. Too late.

The noise, insistent and regular, eventually got through to Sifis Skourtis. For once Katia wasn't in his thoughts. At first it seemed the tapping was in his dream, a branch hitting the window of the bedroom where he spent summers as a kid. His grandfather's house was in a clearing surrounded by oak trees, high in the northern mountains. He used to lie there waiting for the morning to come, waiting for the old man's shout. Then he would escape the rattle of branches on the pane that made him think of demons and unquiet spirits, going downstairs to help with the goats. The smell of their milk, sweet and rank at the same time, stayed with him for years.

Then Sifis realised that he was alone in the flat in Athens. He hadn't been back home for years, and the only smell in his nostrils was of the smoke and muck that had impregnated his clothes. He was in the flat, his stash gone and his gut heaving, but still the tapping went on.

'What the fuck?' Sifis mumbled and rolled off the bed. He managed to get to his feet and stood still, trying to locate the source of the noise. It was coming from the door.

'Who's there?' he said from the hallway, his voice low and unsteady. 'Who is it?'

No reply.

He went to the spy-hole and peered through it. He couldn't see anything. Rubbing his eye, he realised that something was covering the tiny circle of glass.

'No,' he whimpered. 'Leave me alone. I'll get . . . I'll get the money.'

Still there was no reply.

Sifis went back to the main room, banging against the walls. He scrabbled on the table, knocking aluminium wraps and syringes, spoons and lighters, to the floor.

'No,' he gasped. 'Leave me alone.' But the tapping continued, rising in volume.

'No!' Sifis screamed, running to the door and undoing the chain with twitching fingers. 'No!'

'Yes,' said the figure that barrelled into him, knocking him flying back down the hall. 'Yes, you shithead.' The arm came up and aimed the black pistol with its matching silencer at Sifis's forehead.

The last sound the young man heard was the scream that died prematurely in his throat.

# 7

It seemed to Mavros, as he stood in the square looking up at the Parliament building's neoclassical façade, that he had two choices. Either he rang the bell of the so-called Pink Palace and refused to leave without an interview, or he called in advance. Given the amount of security he was sure the star would have, he decided on the latter. His mobile phone's directory service put him through.

'The Ikonomou residence,' said a male voice.

'Ah, yes,' Mavros said, waving away an insistent lottery-ticket salesman. 'Could I speak to Mrs Ikonomou, please?'

'Your name, sir?'

'Mavros.'

'Well, sir, as your name isn't familiar, might I suggest that you contact Mrs Ikonomou's public relations—'

'No, you may not,' Mavros interrupted. He'd learned that the gatekeepers employed by rich people only responded to a heavy hand. 'This is an urgent matter. I need to speak to Mrs Ikonomou in person.'

There was a pause. 'I see. I'm afraid I'll need more information.'

'I'm afraid you'll be looking for a new job if you don't co-operate.'

'Sir, I can't help you unless you tell me what this concerns.'

Mavros saw that he'd have to be more forthcoming. 'All right. It's about a young woman called Katia Tratsou.' There was a longer pause. 'That name means something to you, does it?'

'Please hold the line.'

Mavros started walking towards the upmarket area of Kolonaki. It looked like he was making progress. He was pretty sure that the guy on the phone recognised the missing girl's name. As he crossed the road, narrowly avoiding a taxi running the light, he heard the voice again.

'Very well, sir. Mrs Ikonomou will see you now. Is that satisfactory?'

'Give me the address.' He recognised the street name. It was one of the city's most exclusive. 'All right, I should be there in ten minutes.' He cut the connection and raised his fist in triumph, provoking a languid stare from the heavily armed policeman outside a ministry. Then he wondered why the famously reclusive actress would have agreed to see him without hesitation.

As he walked up the steepening hillside, the traffic noise began to fade. The apartment blocks here were faced by high-quality marble and the parked cars were in better condition. The ones on the street were only the residents' second vehicles, those they used in the city centre; the cars they kept to show off to their friends and to drive to their seaside villas were safely stored in basement garages. Even the roadside orange trees seemed cleaner in this niche of luxury. The locals probably paid squads of immigrant workers to polish the fruit and leaves every night.

Jenny Ikonomou's house was on the highest street, backing on to the tree-covered hill. He could see how the building had got its name. It was tall and wide, its balconies festooned with plants, and the front wall had been painted in a pastel shade of pink. For all the ostentation, the Pink Palace smacked of good taste rather than tackiness. The actress had obviously thought carefully about how to project her image. The house would appeal both to her uncritical fans and to the design-obsessed intelligentsia. Mavros had to admit he was impressed. At the same time, the building had an air of impenetrability. The windows were shuttered in steel, as were the balcony rails and the door-frame that was surrounded by opaque glass bricks.

He pressed the single button on his left when he reached the top of the pale grey steps. Looking up, he saw a camera above the steel door and mugged to it.

'State your name, please, sir.' The voice was modulated by the electrics, but Mavros recognised it as belonging to the man he'd spoken to earlier.

'Mavros by name and by nature.'

There was a pause as the guy took in the witticism, 'mavros' meaning 'black'. Then there was a loud buzz and the door swung open. Mavros walked in and found himself in a large but minimalist entrance hall, the marble floor gleaming and the white walls hung with small abstract sculptures in green bronze. The effect was markedly different from the building's exterior. A door at the rear opened and a man in a grey suit came forward. Dark eyes shone beneath heavy eyebrows and a completely bald head. He placed his feet delicately on the ground, more like a ballet dancer than a butler.

'Good afternoon, sir,' he said, taking in Mavros's hair, leather jacket and jeans. 'I'll need to see some identification.'

Mavros held his eyes for a moment, then slipped his laminated ID card and a business card from his wallet.

'You're a private investigator?' the bald man asked, walking to the door at the rear. 'You don't mind if I photocopy your ID?'

'Be my guest,' Mavros called after him. 'But mind the edges, they're sharp.'

The man ignored that. When he returned to the hall after several minutes, he beckoned Mavros forward with a movement of his fingers. 'Thank you, sir,' he said, handing back the plastic card. He was carrying a cardboard folder under his arm.

'I'll take you to Mrs Ikonomou. She's on the roof garden.' He pressed a button on the wall.

Mavros followed him into the steel cubicle after the doors parted noiselessly. 'So, do you know Katia Tratsou?' he asked. 'Sorry, you haven't told me your name.'

The bald man looked at him as if he'd asked for the code of Jenny Ikonomou's safe. 'My name is Ricardo,' he said with a thin-lipped smile. 'I'm afraid I can't help you with the other one.'

Mavros watched him impassively, trying to work out if he was telling the truth or playing dumb. It was hard to believe that Katia could have been in the house without him knowing. Then again, it was hard to imagine Katia getting anywhere near the country's leading thespian.

'Over there,' the man said as the door slid open. He pointed to a profusion of greenery beyond a swimming pool.

'You aren't coming?'

'Mrs Ikonomou wishes to see you privately.' The bald man nodded punctiliously and vanished behind the door.

'Thank God for that,' Mavros said under his breath. He was hoping the actress would be more forthcoming than her servant.

He walked past the pool, the water glinting in the sunlight. Bushes in large pots and fruit trees in beds laid into the concrete roof were growing against a bamboo windbreak that would keep the paparazzi and the actress's adoring fans at bay. Further on, beneath a vine-covered pergola, a circle of plush chairs had been drawn up around a low table. A woman was sitting with her back to him.

'Sit down,' she said, neither turning round nor getting up. Smoke rose in a cloud about her. The voice, low and throaty, was instantly recognisable.

Mavros entered the circle of chairs and extended his hand. Jenny Ikonomou looked up at him and declined to take it. She nodded across the table, keeping him at a distance. She was wearing a pale yellow silk robe that completely covered her body, her dark hair swept back in a matching band.

'Thank you for seeing me, Mrs Ikonomou.'

'At such short notice. Help yourself to coffee.'

Although she must have been in her fifties, the actress was in good condition, at least above the collar. Her face was largely wrinkle-free, although Mavros couldn't tell how much make-up had been applied or whether she had been under the knife. Her famous brown eyes, the ruin of more than one rich man including her late husband, had lost none of their power and, close up, he wasn't sure if the mane of raven-coloured hair was dyed after all.

Mavros filled a cup from the flask on the table. 'I think your man Ricardo has told you why I wanted to see you.'

Jenny Ikonomou blew out smoke and laughed. 'Ricardo doesn't work for me. He's my brother. From time to time it amuses him to play the servant.'

'So acting runs in the family?'

'No, Ricardo isn't part of my world,' the actress said, looking away. 'He told me that you're a private detective. Have you been engaged to find Katia?'

'That's right. By her parents.'

'Is what you're wearing the uniform of your profession?' she asked drily.

Mavros looked into the dark eyes. 'Mrs Ikonomou, I think it would be better if you answered my questions first. Can you confirm that Katia stayed in this house?'

If the woman across the table resented the way he'd taken control of the conversation, she didn't show it. She took a deep breath. 'Yes, of course she did. She was here for a weekend – two nights – and then she left. In fact, we both left the same morning. I was going to Thessaloniki to discuss a production we're putting on in the autumn.'

'I see. When was she here?'

Jenny Ikonomou leaned forward and opened a leather-bound diary. 'She left on Sunday March the twenty-fourth.'

That squared with the last time Katia had been seen by her parents. 'Have you heard from her since?'

She looked at him and shrugged. 'No. I suppose she could have sent a note, but I know she's busy with her studies.'

'What exactly did you do with Katia when she was here?'

'We talked about acting and its relationship to life. I gave her an idea of how she should develop her talent and we ran through some scenes. She was very promising.'

'Can you tell me how Katia found her way here?'

Jenny Ikonomou lit another cigarette. 'I saw her walking down the street and I told my driver to stop the car.'

'What? You're telling me that you can spot someone with talent just like that?'

Her gaze was unwavering. 'Of course. In the same way you can tell when people are speaking the truth, I imagine. It's instinct, it's years of experience.'

Mavros wasn't sure if she was being straight with him. 'Can you remember where you picked her up?'

She blew out smoke. 'Yes, I can. It was in Kanningos Square, one evening on my way home from a reception. I never stay long.'

Mavros remembered the time Katia's evening class finished. 'About nine-thirty?'

'I should think so. I saw this girl with perfect poise and I knew she had something. What I didn't know was whether she had the dedication. That's why I invited her for the weekend.'

'And did you discover whether she had the appropriate dedication?'

'I think so. She was going to finish her final year at school – I encouraged her to do that – and then she was going to speak to me again.'

What Jenny Ikonomou said fitted with the boy in the wheelchair's story. 'Do you often pick up young women on the street?' he asked, his tone deliberately suggestive.

'No,' she said, returning his gaze coolly. 'Only when I see an outstanding individual like Katia.' She leaned forward again. 'Now, will you please tell me what's happened to her?'

'She's vanished,' he said bluntly. 'No one has seen her since she left this house.'

'What?' The actress's eyes were wide, her hands going to her cheeks. It was a histrionic display, but also convincing. 'That can't be.'

'I'm afraid it is.'

'Have the police been informed?'

'Yes. She's on their long list of missing persons. They don't do much to reduce it.'

Jenny Ikonomou jerked her hand back as her cigarette burned her finger. She raised it to her lips, blinking.

'Are you all right?' Mavros said, getting up.

She waved him away. 'My God, this is awful. Is there anything I can do?'

Mavros watched her. It was a convincing performance, but what else would you expect from the country's leading actress? 'Not unless you can tell me anything more about Katia. Did she give any hint that she might be thinking of leaving home?'

'None at all.' Jenny Ikonomou stood up, her form beneath the robe surprisingly lissom. 'In fact, I encouraged her to call her parents and tell them that she was staying with me, but she said they wouldn't worry. She pointed out to me that she was over eighteen. And she'd been going to stay with a friend.'

He wondered if Katia was capable of lying like that. Would she really have left her parents in agony over the weekend?

'I want to help,' the actress said. 'Can I pay your fee?'

The sound of a bell came from the summit of the hill behind the house, the whitewashed chapel silhouetted against the backdrop of the sky.

'No, I can't compromise my existing client.'

She stepped round the table and approached him. 'What have you discovered about Katia so far?'

He met her gaze. 'Only that she came here, Mrs Ikonomou. And that no one has seen her since.'

The actress looked away. 'Keep me advised of any developments, please.'

He realised he was being dismissed. He walked across the roof-garden and pressed the lift button. The door opened to reveal the bald Ricardo.

'So you're Mrs Ikonomou's brother,' Mavros said as they started downwards. 'There was me thinking you were a servant.'

There was no eye contact. 'It happens.'

'Since that's the case, maybe you know about the security system here. There's CCTV, isn't there? I don't suppose you've got the tapes from around March the twenty-fourth?'

'No. They're reused every second day.'

'Pity,' Mavros said, unsurprised. Most systems worked that way. 'And you didn't meet Katia Tratsou?'

'No.' The actress's brother gave him a sharp look. 'I was away then. Any more questions?'

Mavros smiled at him. 'For the time being, no.'

As he walked down the long hallway to the door, he felt Ricardo's eyes burning into his back.

Damis walked into the Silver Lady, his shoulders back and his expression grim. To his surprise, Peasant Panos was on his own in the main area, hands in his pockets.

'What are you doing here?' Damis asked. 'Where's Yannis?'

'Fucker,' Panos said, his eyes down.

Looking around the club, Damis saw they were alone. 'Me or Yannis?'

'Both of you.' Panos stepped forward, his hands out now, fists balled. 'You've gone off to play with the boss woman and now he gets all the good jobs here.'

'What do you mean?' Damis asked, lowering his voice.

The door of the office at the rear opened and Lakis the Boss walked out, Yannis behind him. They both looked coked up, their eyes bright.

'Well, well, look who's here,' Lakis said with a slack smile. 'Got tired of sucking up to Mrs Chioti already?'

Yannis gave a manic cackle. 'Yes, Dami, what'you doin' at the Lady? We're workin', you know?'

'Good to see you, too, Yanni,' Damis said, ignoring Lakis. 'Glad you're being kept busy.'

Lakis came forward, his eyes narrowing. 'What the fuck do you want? This is my territory.'

Damis shot one hand round his former boss's throat. 'Listen to this, you piece of shit.' He stared at the others to keep them back. 'I've got orders from Mrs Chioti to find out who knew she was coming here.' He pulled the choking Lakis closer. 'So, have you been a good boy?'

Lakis was gasping, his eyes bulging. 'Yes . . . ah . . . let . . . let go . . . ah . . .'

Panos swallowed a laugh. Yannis wasn't sure who to back, his suddenly influential former colleague or his boss.

'Did you know Mrs Chioti was coming?' Damis asked, squeezing harder.

Lakis's tongue was swollen. 'No . . . no . . .'

'Are you sure about that?'

'I'm . . . yes . . . sure.'

Damis raised his other hand round and drew it back. 'Prove it.'

'No!' Lakis said, wincing. 'Check . . . phone . . .'

'Good idea,' Damis said, lowering his fist. 'I'll check the numbers you called. Then we'll be sure.' He let the other man go.

'Bastard,' Lakis said, clutching his throat.

Damis smiled at him. 'I'll be watching you, you can be sure of that. Now I'm going to have a conversation with the manager of this dump.'

Yannis tapped his shoulder. 'Hey, wait till I tell you what I've been doin'.' He froze when Lakis glared at him. 'Some other time,' he mumbled.

'I'll be in touch,' Damis said, heading to the office. Lakis's name wasn't on the list he'd been given. He'd enjoyed putting the squeeze on him, even if his former boss probably didn't have the balls to betray the head of the family. But the slimeball who ran the Silver Lady was another matter.

He was beginning to enjoy his new job.


Mavros went back to his flat after he left the Pink Palace. He wanted to do some research on the actress. Although she seemed sincere, he wanted to see if there was anything suspicious in her background. She wouldn't be the first society woman with secrets. Perhaps she picked up young women on the street for less noble reasons than the pursuit of art. He was clutching at straws, but he didn't have much choice. The more he searched, the further Katia seemed to get away from him.

When he got home, he turned on the radio. What he heard made his stomach clench.

'. . . in an apartment in Schina Street to the east of the park. The police have confirmed that the dead man is Iosif, known as Sifis, Skourtis, aged twenty-five, occupation unknown. According to the forensic surgeon, the victim was killed earlier today by a single shot to the head from a pistol that was probably fitted with a silencer, as no shot was heard in the building. Sources suggest that the victim was involved in the narcotics trade and that his death may be the latest in the recent outbreak of gangland murders.'

Mavros turned on the television, his throat dry. One of the channels had interrupted its usual afternoon chat show. The reporter Lambis Bitsos was speaking to camera at a police line in the dead man's street.

'. . . and Commander Nikos Kriaras, head of the organised crime division, has just arrived to take command of the investigation.' The camera moved to the left to show a uniformed man with thick black hair getting out of a police car. 'Commander, is this death connected with the mutilated bodies found recently? Commander?'

The policeman came over to the reporter. 'You should know better than to jump to conclusions.'

Bitsos stood his ground. 'But the fact that an officer as senior as you is on the scene suggests that you see a link.'

Kriaras frowned. 'I see only what the evidence shows and you haven't given me the chance to examine anything yet. Excuse me.'

The report ended and Mavros turned down the volume. Sifis hadn't survived more than a day after his run-in with the enforcers from the Silver Lady. He felt the case slip even further away from him with the death of Katia's boyfriend. Sifis was a waster, but he didn't deserve to die like that. Then Mavros realised that things were even blacker. His fingerprints and his phone number were in Sifis's flat. There was a chance that the scene-of-crime team wouldn't spot them, but if they did he'd be in serious shit – his prints were on file in the computer in police headquarters. There was only one thing for it. He was going to have to come clean. Before he did that, he wanted to be fully informed. He rang the reporter Bitsos on his mobile.

The call was answered with a monosyllabic sound that was more like a grunt than a word.

'Is that you?'

'And you are?'

'Stop playing games, you old pervert. It's Mavros.'

There was a pause. 'Not the famous Alex Mavros, private investigator to the rich, famous and extremely secretive? Not the rat who promises his so-called friends exclusive stories, picks their brains and then shuts his mouth tighter than a cat's arse? What joy. I'm the chosen one. At last he's going to cough up the story he's owed me for months.'

'Cut the crap, Lambi, I'm in trouble. I need your help.'

'You need *my* help? You'll need a surgeon's help if you don't get off the line. I'm working. Good—'

'Don't hang up!' Mavros shouted, realising he was going to have to trade. 'I knew the dead man.'

'You knew . . .' Bitsos changed his tone. 'Why didn't you say so, Alex? How nice to hear from you. Have you got any idea why he was killed?'

'Maybe.'

'Not good enough. I'm hanging up.'

'Yes,' Mavros said quickly.

'We'd better meet then. I've got deadlines. How about Café Sonia in half an hour?'

Mavros agreed and cut the connection. He called a radio taxi, knowing that he'd never find one on the street at this time of day. As the cab wove its way through the traffic, he had another thought, one that made his heart pound. Katia's father had received a handgun up at the construction site. Could he have discovered Sifis's address and tracked him down?

Sonia was a well-known establishment on the avenue, not far from the crime scene. Mavros walked in to find Bitsos bent over a laptop, phone pressed to his ear. The reporter looked up when Mavros approached and gave him a suspicious look.

'So, Alex,' he said, when he finished his call, 'you've finally realised it's time you paid your debts.'

Mavros raised his eyes to the ceiling. 'Forget the past, Lambi. Maybe this time I'll get you the story you want.'

'*Maybe*,' Bitsos said, making space for the plate heaped with spaghetti that the waiter had brought. 'I don't like that word. You eating?'

Mavros shook his head. Sifis's death hadn't done anything for his appetite. He watched as Bitsos, skinny and permanently hungry, laid into his meal.

'There's no maybe about it, my friend,' the reporter said, his mouth half-full. 'Either you give me a good story or you start walking. You think I haven't got enough to think about right now?'

'You certainly seem to be on the TV all the time.'

'Mm. My paper's happy because it makes them look good.' Bitsos ran his hand over his thinning hair. 'I'm not sure. Do you think I should wear a hat?'

'How about a burka?' Mavros asked, unable to resist puncturing the journalist's vanity. 'Sorry,' he said, remembering he needed a favour. 'No, you look fine on screen.'

The reporter eyed him dubiously as he chewed. 'All right, you knew the dead guy. How?'

Mavros filled him in, omitting any mention of his client and concentrating on the meeting with the heavies.

'From the Silver Lady, eh? You know that's a Chiotis place?'

'Yes, I saw the reports about the wife getting shot at there.'

'So Skourtis sold drugs for the Chiotis family.' Bitsos shrugged. 'Seems a bit unlikely they'd have had him killed for a missed payment. The usual practice is to get the dealers in for as much as possible so they're even more committed to shifting the product.'

'Maybe he wasn't just a low-level dealer.'

The journalist made a note on his pad. 'Or maybe your missing girl did for him.'

'I don't think Katia's capable of killing anyone.'

Bitsos waved a finger at him. 'No, I don't mean that she pulled the trigger. Maybe she's the link to the Silver Lady.'

'Working there, you mean?' Mavros kicked himself for failing to think of that possibility. Bitsos was sharp and his years at the shit-face had made him cynical. But Mavros couldn't really see Katia slumming it as a dancer at a club when she'd just spent a weekend with Jenny Ikonomou.

'Could be a hooker by now. Doesn't take those bastards long to turn nice girls into dope fiends who'll do anything for their next hit.'

'Jesus.'

'What? She had a dope dealer for a boyfriend. Maybe he started her on that road.'

Mavros chewed his lip. 'He said not.'

Bitsos laughed. 'And you believed him?'

'The Chiotis family's in trouble these days, isn't it?' Mavros said, fishing for information. He had to follow the lead to the Silver Lady and he wanted to know what he was up against.

'You could say that. On the other hand, you could say that their rivals are further down the sewer.'

'The opposition being?'

Bitsos's eyes glinted. Despite his complaints about Mavros's failure to pay him back, the reporter liked nothing better than to show off his encyclopaedic knowledge of the Athenian underworld. 'The main opposition being the Russians. There's a guy who calls himself Fyodor. He made the trip from the former Soviet Union not long after the break-up. He keeps his head down, but he's built up a major network. That transport company where the last body was found is his. He's got all sorts of operations, some of them legitimate and others very definitely not.'

'Drugs, hookers, protection, smuggling, that kind of thing?'

'That kind of thing.' Bitsos wiped his plate with a piece of bread. 'He has some really nasty fuckers working for him. Mind you, so does the Chiotis family. That guy who was found hanging from the company's logo, I reckon he was a numbers man – he was thin and weedy, his hands had never squeezed anything harder than a lemon. You should have seen the state of him. We weren't able to print the photos. The poor bastard had fish hooks all over his body, would you believe?'

Mavros shivered. If Katia had got herself involved with people like that, he was taking a big risk going after her. Her boyfriend had already paid the price. 'Anything you can tell me about the scene at Sifis Skourtis's place?'

Bitsos glanced at his notes. 'Nothing special. Plenty of drug traces, mainly heroin and grass. They've found some finger-prints in the main room too. Probably customers.'

Mavros kept his eyes down.

'There were no witnesses, no one heard the shot. They reckon the time of death was between nine and ten this morning. Everyone else from the building was either out or still in bed. There are a couple of night-shift workers.'

'Who found the body?'

Bitsos grinned. 'Local resident, piss artist by the look of him. He came back from work at one o'clock, saw the open door and made the mistake of walking in. Blood all over the hall, then vomit all over the landing, the latter his.'

Mavros rubbed his chin. That was another reason to speak to the commander. The drinker had seen him twice, once lurking outside. Maybe he wouldn't remember, maybe he'd be too scared to talk, but Mavros couldn't be sure.

'What's the matter with you, Alex?' the reporter said with unusual concern. 'You look strung out. Drink some water.'

'Listen, I was in that flat not long ago. I have to talk to the commander.'

'Be careful what you tell Kriaras, Alex. He's about as reliable as a cardboard house in a hurricane.'

'I've noticed.'

Bitsos raised a hand for the bill. 'Make sure you only tell him the bare minimum.' He tapped his nose. 'And if he lets anything drop, I want to hear about it.'

Mavros got to his feet and put some money down. 'I'm paying. I'll be in touch.'

'Make sure you are. And be careful at the Silver Lady. The assassination attempt will have made them jumpy.'

They're already jumpy, Mavros thought as he walked on to the avenue. A sensible man would leave the low life to fight it out among themselves. Then he thought of Katia's parents. He had to find her for them, no matter where she was.

The Father was at the summit of the hill, looking down at the city all around. He hadn't told the Son where he was going and he'd be out of contact if there was a message from the woman, but he was entitled to time on his own. In the morning he'd stood on the street where the interrogation centre used to be. He was a young man when he worked there. Recalling that work made his spirit soar.

Now the Father took in the city that he'd loved so much and felt despair rise up. Over to his left was the suburb where he grew up. He'd never returned to it. When he joined the army, the place was full of Communists. Many had been hunted down during the dictatorship, but since then the jackals of the Left had prevailed there as everywhere else. It wasn't safe for him to go back, even with his moustache and the passing of the years. Straight ahead was the Acropolis, the Parthenon's ruined perfection a symbol of the country's decline. The ancients had the right idea – no votes for workers and women. It was only in modern times that society had been corrupted by progressive ideas. The bastards even hated the nation now, the nation that thousands of men had given their lives to save. The ingrates.

The Father curled his lip as a group of Albanians in cheap clothes clustered round him, their voices coarse. There was a million or more of them in Greece. They were gradually taking over the country and no one cared. They were welcomed because Greeks were too busy sitting on their arses to do a real day's work. It wouldn't be long till the foreigners were in charge. At least the Americans who supported the Colonels had been anti-Communist. Now there was the European Union, socialist bearers of corruption. And there were the Russians, who were trying to oust the family by importing their filthy drugs, their whoring women and the violence they'd learned in Afghanistan and their other failed wars. That was the worst irony. The war against Communism had been won, but its former followers were setting themselves up in the countries that had ground down their mother states. The godless scum! Stratos Chiotis was a true fighter. He'd declared war on them from the start. But now he'd been replaced by the woman. The world had gone mad. Women ordering men about? At least that one had learned the virtue of pain.

Moving to the chapel, the old man stood by the entrance and breathed in the scent of incense. It reminded him of his childhood, Sundays with his grandmother in the neighbourhood church. Boys weren't expected to go regularly but he wanted to, especially during the long period of Lent. He enjoyed the harshness of religion. The church banned chairs and allowed only the old and infirm to hang from uncomfortable frames during the ritual. He gloried in the agony of the Passion and the terrible breaking of the Saviour's body. But it was when he joined the army, following his martyred father into the ranks of the just, that he really understood how important pain and suffering were.

The Father heard the priest chanting the liturgy and the years fell away. He was young again. Similar sounds were coming from the radio in the sergeants' mess. They had it playing over the prisoners' screams. It was a Sunday and the service lasted most of the morning. There were no rest days in the cell block. Military policemen willingly worked long hours. Theirs was a sacred duty.

He was in uniform, his tie knotted tightly despite the temperature inside the building. He was smoking a cigarette, a newspaper in front of him. 'Christ and the Holy Mother,' he said to the sergeant across the table, 'those bastard students, setting bombs to murder policemen. The sooner our leaders let us put them against a wall the better.'

His colleague grinned and wiped sweat from his forehead. 'Wouldn't you prefer to carve them up first? You like breaking the fuckers down, don't you?'

The Father spat a fragment of tobacco on to the floor. He didn't like the other's tone. 'Yes, I'm dedicated to my work. Is there something wrong with that?'

The sergeant, an older man whose stomach was stretching the fabric of his tunic, dropped his gaze. 'Nothing,' he said in a cowed voice. 'Did the boy in cell seven talk?'

'Not enough,' the Father said, scowling. 'He thinks he's a hard man, but I've got a surprise for him.'

'Going to use the electrics on his balls?'

'I've already tried that.' The Father ran his hand across the smooth skin of his face. No matter how many hours he worked, he always made sure he was well-turned out. Shaving was part of a soldier's duty. 'This time I'm certain he'll give us the names of the others in his pathetic little resistance group.'

'Why are you so sure?' the sergeant asked, raising an eyebrow.

The Father smiled, noting the effect that had on his colleague. 'Because we picked up his girlfriend.' He stood up and straightened his tunic. 'And I'm going to work on her in front of him.'

'. . . the sufferings of our Saviour on the cross . . .' The priest's voice brought the Father back to the hill above Athens. The Albanians were all around him.

'Heathens,' the old man said under his breath. 'But the reckoning is coming.' Then he pushed his way through the group and headed down the steps, eager to re-enter the world of pain.

# 8

Mavros walked down the avenue to a row of phone booths. The commander had always been paranoid about being contacted, insisting that he be called from public land-lines to reduce the chance of surveillance. The run-in they'd had during the terrorism case at Christmas and his recent promotion to chief of the organised crime division would have made him even more nervous.

Leaning against the scratched plastic of the booth and pressing the receiver hard against his ear to reduce the traffic noise, Mavros slotted in a phonecard and called the restricted number.

'Yes?' Kriaras never identified himself.

'It's Mavros.'

There was a pause. 'What do you want?'

'I need to talk to you about the Sifis Skourtis killing.'

'You know something?'

'Yes.'

'Well, go to headquarters and make a statement.'

'This is urgent. And you might not want everything I know to go on the official record.'

'Are you strongarming me?'

Mavros laughed. 'No comment.'

'Don't play games. Very well.' The commander gave the name of a nearby street. 'In ten minutes.'

Mavros set off down the avenue. Kriaras sounded like he was under pressure. That meant there was a chance he could play this to his own advantage. Unless the commander's promotion had turned him into the kind of policeman who observed the rules. Mavros didn't think that was very likely.

Arriving at the street on time, Mavros crossed to the side adjoining the park. An unmarked dark blue Citroën with tinted windows flashed its lights. He checked he was unobserved and sauntered over. The back door clicked open.

'Niko,' he said, smiling at the uniformed man as he got in. 'Good to see you.'

'I'm very busy,' Kriaras said, giving him an acid look. His dark curls were neatly styled for the benefit of the TV cameras, but the face below was lined. 'This had better be good.'

Mavros looked at the heavily built driver, who was wearing a leather jacket and dark glasses. 'What about the man in black up front?'

'What about him?' Kriaras said, looking at a file on his knees. 'He hears only what I tell him to hear.'

'And have you told him to go deaf during this conversation?'

'That depends on the content. Spit it out.'

'Nice, Niko, very nice. Okay, here it is.' Mavros told him about Katia and her connection with the dead man, but didn't mention the musclemen from the Silver Lady or his client's weapon. 'So your people will probably find my prints in there,' he concluded.

The commander let out a sigh. 'You really have a talent for sticking your nose into things that any normal person would keep away from.'

Mavros shrugged. 'Got to keep you guys on your toes.'

'Who do you think put a bullet in the unfortunate young man's brain?'

'Now you want me to do your job for you?' Mavros raised a hand when he saw the look on Kriaras's face. 'All right. He was a drug dealer. Either the opposition got to him, or his own people did.'

'Any idea who he was working for?'

'You're the organised crime expert.'

Kriaras jammed an elbow into his ribs. 'You're not making this easy for yourself, Alex. Do you want to spend a night in the cells?' He pointed to the driver. 'With the big man for company?'

'No, thanks.' Mavros saw that he was going to have to give the commander more. 'I tailed him to a club in Alimos last night.'

'Really. Name?'

'The Silver Lady. I saw Sifis talk to a couple of heavies.' He still didn't want to come clean about the episode on the hillside. Kriaras would haul in the nightclub staff and that wouldn't make the search for Katia any easier. He was pretty sure those guys, or others like them, had dealt with Sifis. He didn't feel good about what had happened to the young man, but there was nothing he could do for him now. Katia had priority.

Kriaras was writing notes in a clear hand. 'You know who owns the Silver Lady?'

'The Chiotis family.'

'Bravo. Mrs Chioti was nearly killed outside the Silver Lady. The family is involved in a fight to the death with other criminal operations.' He nudged Mavros again. 'Are you sure you aren't out of your depth?' He gave a tight smile. 'It wouldn't be the first time.'

Mavros let that go. 'You think Sifis had something to do with all this mayhem that's been going on?'

'It did cross my mind,' Kriaras said ironically. 'The gangs are executing each other's personnel. Maybe that's what happened here.'

'Could be,' Mavros said, running his hand over his hair. He'd seen his client receive a gun from a Russian. He should be telling Kriaras that, but he couldn't bring himself to hand Dmitri over till he was sure he was guilty.

'This girl you're looking for, have you made any progress?'

'Not much.' He wasn't going to mention the link to the actress. 'It could be she's working at the Silver Lady.'

'Are you going to check the place out?'

'I haven't got much choice.'

Kriaras looked thoughtful. 'Watch your back down there.'

'Thanks for the warning. Anything else I should know before I enter the lion's den?'

The policeman gave that some consideration and then twitched his head. 'No. Your co-operation is noted.' His brow furrowed. 'But if I find out that you know more about this death than you've told me, I'll come down on you like a landslide.'

'Great,' Mavros said under his breath. He wanted to ask about the Russian Fyodor's operation, but that would be too obvious a pointer to Dmitri. 'I'll be in touch if I find anything.'

The commander smiled humourlessly. 'Of course you will. In the meantime, don't swim with the big fish, Alex. The last time you were almost swallowed whole.'

Mavros narrowed his eyes. 'So were you.'

He got out of the car and walked away. He'd talked his way out of Sifis's killing, but he was still no nearer finding Katia. Seeing Kriaras had brought back bad memories. The policeman had some very questionable friends.

Damis walked into the headquarters of a Japanese car dealership on the avenue that led to the sea. The afternoon sun was glinting off the glass front of the futuristic building. A four-by-four on a tilted display stand looked like it was about to take off and smash through the windows to join the herd of similar vehicles on the wide road.

'Can I help you?' asked a thin but beautifully dressed girl at the reception desk.

'Mr Gikas is expecting me,' he replied, glancing at his watch. 'At three-thirty.'

'Ah, yes,' the girl said, understanding that the visitor would not be giving a name. 'Sixth floor.' She pointed to the hall behind. 'Take the furthest lift.'

Damis did so. When the doors opened, a security man in a cap that was too small for his enormous head beckoned him in. Damis smiled and spent the trip watching him closely. It didn't seem likely that the guy would make a move, but maybe his boss was feeling nervous.

'End of the corridor,' the man said, stepping out and standing by the lift.

Damis didn't bother replying. The top floor was obviously where the dealership's owners worked, a series of wooden doors running down a wall faced with polished stone. When he got to the last one, he knocked and went in without waiting for an invitation.

'Good afternoon,' said a small man in his fifties. He was standing at the window that took up the whole of the far side of the room. 'I don't think we've met.'

Damis had seen Gikas at the Silver Lady more than once. He came with his wife, a tight-faced woman who overpainted her lips and chain-smoked small cigars. 'Apparently not. You know why I'm here?'

The car dealer gave an uneasy smile. 'Mrs Chioti said you were carrying out an investigation for her. She didn't specify the—'

'Two nights ago,' Damis interrupted, going up to him. 'What happened?'

'I . . . I was working late,' Gikas said, stepping back. 'I—'

'What happened outside the Silver Lady?' Damis asked, stepping close and placing his hands on the glass to either side of the diminutive man's shoulders.

'Oh . . . I see . . . well, there was that shooting. Terrible thing. Thank God Mrs Chioti—'

Damis moved his face closer. 'You knew she was going to be there.'

Gikas licked his lips and blinked. 'I . . . yes, I was going to meet Rea at the villa that evening to go over some figures with her. She . . . she rang me and told me to meet her at the club instead.'

'What time did you take the call?'

'I'm not sure . . . I . . . please, you're making me nervous.'

Damis looked over the car dealer's shoulder. 'Long way down, isn't it? Do these windows open? Yes, of course they do.' He flicked the catch and slid the glass panel aside, then pushed Gikas backwards on to the narrow balcony. 'I'm waiting for an answer. What time did she ring you?'

'Nine-thirty or . . . or thereabouts.' The man's voice had broken like a teenager's.

An hour before Rea Chioti arrived at the Silver Lady, Damis thought. Time to get a hit man there if preparations had been made. 'Did you tell anyone she was going to the club?' he said, one hand behind Gikas's neck and the other at his throat.

'Only the Silver Lady, to make sure they had good champagne. I'm not sure who I spoke to.'

'You're not sure who you spoke to?' Damis scoffed.

'No . . . I . . . no.'

'You definitely mentioned that Mrs Chioti was going to be there?'

The dealer hung his head. 'I . . . yes.'

'Did you tell anyone else? Your wife?'

'No . . . no.' The dealer's eyes were bulging, his lips flecked with spittle. 'I know the business, I never talk . . .'

'Is your phone system secure?'

'Yes, it's checked every day.'

Damis took the hand from behind the small man's neck so that he was holding him only by the throat and jerked him into the air. 'I want all your mobiles, as well as printouts of the office phones for that evening.'

'Yes . . . yes . . .' Gikas turned his head and gasped when he saw how far over the edge he was. 'Please, I'll give . . . I'll give Rea everything she wants.'

Damis stared into his eyes. They were damp and fearful, but he could see nothing else in them. If there had been an attempt to bribe him, he'd have known Gikas was guilty. He let him down and pulled him inside. 'All right,' he said with a smile. 'There was a security operative in your executive lift. Get him in here, please.'

The car dealer was clutching his throat, his breathing rough. 'Why?'

Damis flexed his hands. 'I'll need something to do while you're gathering up your mobiles and organising the print-outs.'

Gikas gave the command into an intercom.

'Phones,' Damis said, pointing to the desk. He watched as the quivering man took a mobile from his suit pocket and then another two from his briefcase.

There was a knock on the door.

'Come in, you fool,' Gikas said hoarsely.

'Anything wrong, boss?' the gorilla asked, giving Damis a suspicious look as he stepped towards him.

'Yes,' said Damis, smashing his elbow into the security man's abdomen. 'Your tie isn't done up properly.' He bent over the figure writhing on the floor and wrapped the strip of fabric round the thick neck. 'He can live or he can die,' he said to the car dealer. 'Your choice. Are you sure you've remembered all your phones? Are you sure you've told me everything?'

Gikas's mouth opened and closed. 'Yes,' he whispered. 'Yes, there's nothing else.'

Damis held his position for a few more moments, then lowered the security man's head and let go of the tie. 'Good,' he said, rolling the man on to his side. 'I'm glad we understand each other.'

Ten minutes later he was out of the offices, his suit pockets full of phones and a sheaf of paper under his arm. Mrs Chioti's people would check the numbers, but he was certain that the dealer wasn't the one who'd betrayed her. He'd seen all the people on the list now. Most of them had convinced him of their innocence. That meant he had to ask more questions at the Silver Lady. So much for moving up the ladder.

Mavros was climbing the stairs to Niki's second-floor flat in Palaio Faliro when his mobile rang. He stopped and fumbled for it in his pocket. Fortunately the caller didn't hang up.

'Alex? Is Dmitri.'

'Hello, Dmitri,' he said as the timer on the light ran out and he was plunged into darkness. 'Shit.'

'What's the matter? You have news?'

'No,' Mavros said, going up to the next landing and feeling for the switch. 'Sorry, Dmitri. There's nothing.'

'What you spend the day doing?'

'Listen, I can't talk now. I'm working.'

'Ah, all right, Alex. You call me tomorrow, yes?'

'Okay.' The call was terminated. Mavros felt bad about deceiving his client. The Russian-Greek didn't sound like a man who'd shot someone earlier in the day. His voice conveyed the usual mixture of concern and impatience, but nothing else. Mavros told himself not to harbour suspicions about his client. Dmitri would have been at work on the motorway in the morning when Sifis was murdered.

'What's the matter?' Niki asked after he'd let himself in. She was standing in front of the mirror in the hall, fixing her earrings.

'Oh, nothing,' he said, kissing her and taking in her black cashmere top and short red skirt. 'You look good.'

She returned his gaze with a mock-lascivious smile. 'So do you. It's amazing what putting on a clean pair of jeans can do.'

'These aren't just clean, they're new.'

'At least they were when I gave them to you last Christmas.' Niki moved into the sitting-room. The flat she'd inherited was spacious. She was gradually replacing her foster parents' furniture and there was a weird mishmash of styles – intricately carved traditional wooden trunks surmounted by blink-inducing abstract paintings done by a friend. 'There's a bottle of wine open.'

Mavros filled a glass and joined her on the sofa.

'This is cosy,' she said, leaning against him. 'Pity we have to go out.'

'You don't have to come.'

'No, I want to. Do you really think Katia will be at this nightclub?'

He raised his shoulders. 'It's not too likely, but I have to rule it out and going as a paying customer seems the safest way.'

Niki's eyebrows shot up. 'Safest? Oh, you mean because of the shooting the other night.'

'Mm.' Mavros turned to her. It struck him that taking Niki into the most dangerous nightspot in Athens was an unnecessary risk. 'Look, maybe this isn't a good idea. I'll go on my own.'

'No way,' she said forcefully. 'You invited me and I'm coming. Besides, I know Katia. I'll be able to recognise her even if she's in a costume and covered in make-up.'

That was why he wanted Niki along. He should have known better than to try to derail her at this late stage. He took a sip of wine. 'There's something else.'

Niki drew back. 'You're full of mysteries today, Alex. You invite me to a nightclub for the first time ever, then you tell me that Katia's boyfriend has been murdered. What next?'

He described his visit to the actress, watching as her jaw dropped.

'So you were right,' she said when he finished. 'Katia *was* interested in going on the stage. How come she only told the boy in the wheelchair?'

'Katia's like me. Full of mystery.'

'Ha. I always thought she was caught up in her studies, but it seems she had different dreams.'

'La Ikonomou said she has real talent.'

She turned to him, her expression serious. 'We have to find her, Alex.'

'Let's get started then.'

Niki gave him a coy look as he got up. 'What was Jenny Ikonomou like?'

Mavros laughed. 'I thought you hated people like her. Painted loudmouths, you called them, I seem to remember.'

She glared at him. 'I didn't mean her. She's far above the morons you see on the TV boasting about how many cars and houses they've got.'

'You're right,' he said, extending a hand to help her up from the sofa. 'If you think Katia and I are mysterious, you should see our national star. I looked into those huge eyes and there wasn't a hint of who she really is.' He pulled Niki close. 'It's as if she puts so much into the characters she plays that there's nothing left. It's frightening.'

'Oh, baby,' Niki said, her breath warm against his throat. 'Did she make the big, tough private investigator shiver in his boots?'

'Yes,' he said, remembering the actress's cool gaze. 'She did.'

If that was the effect she'd had on him, what had she done to Katia?

Jenny Ikonomou allowed her driver to open the car door for her in the garage beneath the Pink Palace and then sent him home. She took the lift to her bedroom and locked the door behind her.

'Fools,' she said, kicking off the shoes that had been hurting her all evening and pouring herself a brandy. 'Doltish money men who know nothing of the theatre.' She'd been at a sponsorship event in a lavish hotel ballroom. It was a waste of time. She knew the bankers and businessmen would give as little as they could get away with to the arts.

She picked up the phone and pressed the internal connection to her brother's room. There was no answer. Ricardo was out, as he usually was at night. She'd see him in the mornings, his evening suit creased and the stench of cigarettes and cheap perfume coming off him in waves. He spent his time trying to impress young women. No doubt there were plenty who were taken in by his mysterious air and his heavy wallet. At least he didn't sponge from her any more. When he was young, she'd paid more than she should have for his drugs and gambling. Ricardo had cleaned himself up, but in the process he'd become distant, his eyes allowing no access to the person within. But who was she to talk? She wore so many masks that she couldn't remember who she was any more.

Jenny went into her dressing-room and opened the door to the walk-in wardrobe. It was filled with haute couture, the creations of gaudy freaks who thought they were artists. But again, who was she to talk? At least fashion designers produced things that people could buy. What did she produce? The illusion of profundity, the fantasy that through the characters she played people could gain some understanding of who they were. What idiocy! Life had shown her that it was impossible to understand yourself, so how could anyone expect to get inside the thoughts and dreams of another person? She recalled all the masks she had worn, the layers of make-up that formed a barrier between her and the outside world. People thought that Jenny Ikonomou projected powerful emotions, but she was nothing more than an empty shell. What was once inside her had been eaten away by guilt.

The actress lifted up the sleeve of a Dior gown and pressed

the silk to her eyes. It grew damp, her tears soaking into the fabric like blood from a wound. How had she come to this? She'd grown up with more advantages than other children. Her father was a wealthy doctor with a house in an exclusive area of the city and an estate on the island of Aegina. She'd gone to theatre school in Paris. Then, in her thirties, she'd married the industrialist who gave her his name and, on his death ten years ago, his fortune. What more could she have asked for?

She let the sleeve drop and backed out of the wardrobe. Independence was the answer to her question. She felt like she was in a straitjacket even when she was young. That was why she joined the Communist youth party, that was why she spent her evenings in interminable meetings with eager-eyed comrades. And that was how she'd met them, the people she'd admired most . . . the people she'd betrayed. All of them came from the small group that she'd known for less than two years of her life, but had been weighing on her ever since. Why had she been so foolish? If she'd taken her parents' advice and concentrated on her studies, she'd never have fallen into the pit of snakes that had poisoned her life.

Jenny sat at her dressing-table and stared into the damp eyes reflected in the mirror's surface. You failed them all, she said soundlessly. You failed your comrades, you failed your brother and now you've failed that sweet child Katia. Everything you touch turns to dust. You're a demon, a murderess, a swallower of souls.

The star of stage and screen leaned forward until her forehead touched the surface of the dressing-table, and wished that the next sound she heard could be the whisper of an axe-blade falling.


Mavros got out of the taxi and looked up at the huge mannequin above the Silver Lady.

'Very tasteful,' Niki said as she joined him on the pavement.

'How did they get a permit for her?' She moved closer to him and feigned shock. 'Oh my God, Alex. She isn't wearing any clothes.'

'I didn't notice.' He took in the scene in front of them. Expensive cars were being directed into the parking area by bulky men in ill-fitting suits. There was a line of couples queuing on the red carpet that led to the club's front door. He didn't see either of the men who'd been with Sifis on the hillside.

'This is going to be expensive,' Niki said as they joined the queue. 'I'll pay my share. I don't want you charging my expenses to Dmitri.'

'I'm not going to charge him mine either,' he said, glancing back across the road. The reports said that the sniper had been in one of the buildings across the road. The distance must have been around a hundred and fifty metres. That was nothing for a professional shooter. Rea Chioti had been lucky, unlike the two men from her entourage.

'You'd hardly know there was an attempted murder here the other night,' Niki said, handing her sequined bag to a female security operative to check.

Mavros raised his arms and allowed a bouncer to run his hands down his body. 'You think they can afford to close?' he said in English. 'They'd have fixed it with the police to clear up the scene in record time.' He smiled at the security guy and received a suspicious glare. As they passed into the club, he wondered what kind of relations Kriaras had with the Chiotis family. He'd shown some interest when Mavros said he was going to check the club.

Niki ran an eye round the interior as they waited to be directed to a table. 'Not bad,' she said, pressing close to him to be heard above the din of bouzoukis. 'The management have spent some money on this place.'

He nodded. Unlike most clubs, the Silver Lady's decor was

almost tasteful. The walls were painted dark blue and the lighting was surprisingly restrained. The furniture looked less impressive. Each table bore a vase in the shape of the silver lady, a single red carnation coming out of her head. The clientèle lowered the tone further. Groups of young couples were shrieking at each other and dancing suggestively on a raised platform in front of the musicians.

'This way, madam and sir,' said a young woman in a tight top and short skirt. She led them to a table in the far corner. It was far from being the best seat in the house, but Mavros wasn't complaining. He had a good view of the passage at the edge of the stage and the doors beyond. Girls in skimpy costumes were gathering there for the next act. He ordered a bottle of wine and a platter of fruit. The prices were extortionate.

They watched the performers as they came up on to the stage. There were six of them, three blondes and three brunettes. By the end of the act, the minimal amount of clothing they'd been wearing was on the floor, only G-strings and nipple-tassels remaining.

'Delightful,' Niki said as the girls trooped off to raucous cheers from the crowd. 'Definitely not Katia. I can't believe she'd get involved in this kind of performance.' She turned to Mavros. 'I suppose you enjoyed that. Honestly, men are pigs.'

'Calm down,' he said, watching a blonde waitress at a table nearby. 'I'm working.' He inclined his head to the girl.

'No, that's not her. Similar, though. What are you saying, Alex? That you're not having a good time among all this female flesh?'

Mavros shrugged then sat up straight. Two men in dark suits were going into the toilets. One of them was almost bursting out of his jacket and the other had a pair of sunglasses pushed up on his head. He'd seen them before. 'I'll be back in a minute.'

'Oh, darling, don't leave me unchaperoned,' Niki said with a mocking smile.

As he crossed the floor, the music started up again and a young woman in an evening gown and a feather boa approached the microphone. Mavros followed the men into the toilets, wrinkling his nose. The management had spent more money on the decor than on disinfectant. Voices were coming from one of the cubicles.

'. . . cut the lines straight, Pano? This is like sniffing a slalom.'

'Get out the way, it's my turn.'

Mavros could see two pairs of feet beneath the door. He went over quietly.

'That fuckin' Damis. Who does he think he is? He was one of us till a couple of days ago. Here, shift over.'

'Yes, giving all that grief to the boss. Lakis is spitting blood. Here, Yanni, you don't think Lakis could have said something about Mrs Chioti coming down here?'

' 'Course not, Pano. Are you out of your mind? Damis is just tryin' to make a big impression. Got any more?'

'No, that's it. Look, I don't want you going off on any other jobs on your own, okay? We're in this together.'

'The terrible twosome, eh?'

The toilet flushed.

Mavros moved quickly to the door, banged it and then bent over a sink, making a loud, vomiting noise. He ran the tap, keeping his head down.

'You all right, friend?' said the muscleman called Panos.

Mavros let out a groan.

'Keep it in here,' the other man said. 'This is a respectable club.'

The men left, their laughter undisguised.

Of course it is, Mavros said to himself. These were the guys he'd seen get into the taxi with Sifis. What was the solo job that the one called Yannis had gone off on? Could it have been the shooting of the drug dealer? He dried his hands and ran them over his hair. Even if the heavies were involved in Sifis's death, he was no nearer finding Katia. At least they hadn't recognised him. He went back into the club, blinking as the smoke stung his eyes.

'What kept you?' Niki asked.

'Upset stomach.'

'You're a sensitive soul,' she said ironically. 'Were you talking to those gorillas?'

'They don't know where Katia is.'

'What? You asked them if . . . oh, very funny.' She gave him a threatening look and sipped from her wineglass. 'God, this is horrible.'

Mavros watched as two more girls came on stage, to be greeted by loud shouts of approval. They went into a clinch and started moving slowly to the sound of a saxophone. As they started undoing each other's shoulder straps, he saw a tussle break out in the passage beyond. A tall young man in black had his hand round the throat of a much smaller individual who was mouthing words at him and moving his arms up and down like a scarecrow in the wind. The two men from the toilets were standing by, remonstrating. They looked like they wanted to intervene, but didn't have the nerve.

'How civilised,' Niki said.

The tall man was smiling at his victim, his feet apart and his shoulders locked solid. It was only when another man, bald-headed and frowning, appeared from further down the passage that he relaxed his grip and let the smaller man go. The music rose to a crescendo and the girls on the stage dropped their dresses to reveal red camisoles and stockings.

'Christ!' Mavros said with a gasp.

'They're not that attractive.'

'No, it's not that,' he said, leaning forward to make sure. 'I know that guy.'

'Which one?'

'The bald one. I met him this morning. He's Jenny Ikonomou's brother.'

Niki looked indifferent.

'It looks like he has some influence here.'

'Maybe you could ask him to do something about the wine,' she said, picking up a piece of apple. 'Like not pee in it.'

They stayed another couple of hours, but saw no sign of Katia. There were no further altercations between dark-suited men. Eventually Mavros beckoned to Niki.

'Let's get out of here before our eardrums crack.'

'Aren't you going to ask if anyone knows Katia? Show her photo around?'

Mavros narrowed his eyes at her. 'Are you out of your mind? These people don't take prisoners.' But as they walked out into the smoke-free air, it struck him that taking prisoners might have been exactly what they'd done.

Rea Chioti eased her feet back into the high-heels she'd slipped off earlier in the evening and went to the mirror to touch up her lipstick. She hadn't expected to hear from the young man Damis until the morning, but he'd been so insistent that she'd invited him up to the penthouse.

What are you doing, woman, she asked herself. You're fifty-six years old, you haven't had a man since Stratos lost the ability and now you're tarting yourself up for an ex-bouncer. But she continued to apply the crimson lipstick for all the self-mockery in her eyes. It was important to impose yourself on people. Her husband had taught her that, though she'd already understood it. She stepped back and examined her image in the glass. Her auburn hair had held its shape since the morning and her body looked firm enough beneath the layers of expensive fabric. Stratos had taught her many things about the business, but she already knew how to handle people – how to make them appreciate her power. She'd been brash and naive when she was a young woman, but she'd soon become more calculating. She had the woman she'd betrayed to thank for that, the woman and the misguided, beautiful man who loved her.

No, Rea told herself, staring into the mirror. Keep them away. She composed her face, the smooth cheeks and curved eyebrows giving it the look of a mask. That was how it had to be, a mask that hid her from the world; a mask like the golden one she kept hidden in the villa. The young man called Damis was no different from the rest. He was in awe of her power. She would play with him and that way her weakness would be concealed.

There was a knock on the outer door.

Rea positioned herself in the middle of the rug. She had noticed that people tended to be more subservient when she met them standing up. 'Come in,' she said, knowing that her security staff would have checked the visitor.

Damis closed the door behind. 'Good evening, Mrs—'

'It's late,' she interrupted. 'What's so urgent?'

'I'm sorry,' he said, not looking particularly contrite. 'I think I've made some progress.'

'Indeed.' Rea sat down and crossed her legs, catching the way his eyes lingered on them. 'You know who betrayed me?'

'I think so.' If Damis expected to be invited to sit, he didn't show it. He stepped closer and gazed down at her, a loose smile on his lips. 'There isn't any doubt in my mind.'

'You're very sure of yourself,' she said, examining her nails. 'I don't remember authorising you to hang the owner of the largest car dealership in Athens over his office balcony.'

'He complained?'

'I wouldn't say that. People don't complain to me. He made an observation.'

'So did I. He isn't guilty.' Damis glanced round at the sideboard. 'Can I fix you a drink?'

'Keep to the business in hand,' Rea said, raising a finger. 'Gikas is too frightened to act against me. So are most of the people I employ.'

Damis nodded. 'But fear can make some people irrational. Do you know a man called Angelos Lazanis, Lakis for short?'

She gave him a blank look. 'Should I?'

'He's my ex-boss at the Silver Lady. A smallish man with the face of a fox.'

'Ah, the one who's in charge of security at the club?'

'Correct,' Damis said, moving nearer. 'On the evening of the attack, Gikas made a call to the Silver Lady. He wanted to speak to the manager Mr Ricardo, but he was away from his desk. Closeted with one of the girls, as a matter of fact. She saw the clock above his head as he was . . . well, you get the idea. It's impossible to prove, but I'm certain that the person who took the call was Lakis. He's often in Mr Ricardo's office and I've heard him answer the phone without identifying himself.'

Rea's face was impassive. 'Gikas told him I was coming?'

'Yes. He wanted to make sure that the best champagne was in stock.' Damis raised his shoulders. 'It seems he wanted to impress you.'

'And you think that this Lakis alerted the assassin?'

'I do. I got your people to check the numbers he called from his mobile phone. They all checked out. But I took a look in his flat without telling him. I found another mobile there. Three minutes after Gikas called the club, Lakis used it to ring a number belonging to a stolen mobile phone. I can't prove it was the sniper but if you give me the go-ahead, I can get a confession from my ex-boss. He's the only person in the frame.'

Rea stood up. 'No. I have people who are specialists in that field.' She pointed behind him. 'Now you can bring me that drink. A large cognac.' She smiled at him. 'Pour one for yourself. This could be the making of you.'

He smiled back at her. 'As long as I can be of service, Mrs Chioti.'

Rea watched him as he turned away. The young man clearly had talent, as well as an attractive face and a fine body. Why was it she could hear alarm bells ringing in her head?

# 9

Mavros leaned forward to the taxi-driver. 'Take the first right.'

'What are you doing?' Niki asked. 'There isn't much traffic on the coast road.'

'Pull up here.' Mavros turned to her and switched to English. 'I'm going back to the club. See if I can talk to the girls.'

'I thought you said that was too dangerous.'

He laughed. 'Haven't you realised? I live for danger. Don't put the chain on the door.'

Niki looked unimpressed. 'I have to compromise my personal safety so you can go and chat up a gang of hookers?' She put a hand on his arm. 'Be careful, Alex.'

He kissed her on the lips. 'I'll try not to be too late.' He waved after the cab, seeing Niki turn away with a flick of her head. He could have given her more warning, but the fact was he'd only decided to go back as they pulled away from the club. There was too much going on there to ignore – Sifis going down, the heavies who threatened him snorting coke and hinting at a solo job, the big guy putting a hold on the other one and being warned off by Jenny Ikonomou's brother. Even if he didn't find Katia, he might be able to dig up something that would impress Kriaras or Bitsos.

He spent the next hour on a bench by the chain fence around the Silver Lady. It was outside the ring of light, but close enough for him to see people as they left. So far, only customers had headed down the red carpet. The workers would be the last to leave. His plan was to follow one or more of the girls and ask about Katia. If he was lucky, they wouldn't all be accompanied by the gorillas who handled security.

The wind had dropped and the waves were running gently up the narrow pebble beach below the raised breakwater. It was a moonless night and there was a great blanket of stars across the sky. A faint blur of light and the outline of a pyramid peak were visible to the south. The island of Aegina. For a few moments Mavros wished he was there, away from the noise and filth of the city. Then he remembered the case he'd investigated on another small island. Drugs, deviancy, repressed anger and murder had been its main features. At least the criminals in the big city were open about their rapacity.

A door opened at the back of the club. Mavros stayed where he was, keeping very still. Two girls appeared in the rectangle of light. They were dressed in jeans and bomber jackets, their heads down. There were two men in dark suits behind them.

'It'll be fun,' said one. Mavros recognised the voice of Yannis. 'I'm a great driver and the Mercedes has lots of room in the back for us to get friendly.' He laughed. 'Doesn't it, Pano?'

'Yes,' said the big man beside him. 'Are you sure we can take the car?'

'Of course,' said Yannis. 'We're not the scum of the earth any more.'

Mavros watched the foursome head to the car park, the women markedly less enthusiastic than the men. There was no chance of asking them about Katia with the loudmouths in tow. He decided to wait. The Silver Lady had closed and there would soon be more sad-eyed women leaving.

Time passed, his feet and hands tingling in the cold, but he didn't have any luck. The dancers and waitresses who came out were either accompanied by men with lust in their eyes or had cars waiting for them. This was turning out to be a wasted night. Then he saw the lights in the opaque windows on either side of the door go out, and decided to see who was last to leave. He heard the door open, but wasn't able make anyone out in the darkness. There were footsteps moving alongside the building and a man came into view. It was the tall guy he'd seen with his hand round the throat of the much smaller one in the passage beyond the stage. An engine started and came nearer, a black Audi reversing to the club's rear door.

Mavros moved forward cautiously. By the light from the car's interior he saw two men standing at the door, one slumped forward and the other supporting him. The man at the wheel got out and helped the others into the back seat. As they bent down, Mavros recognised the other two. The one who seemed to be unconscious was the skinny guy who'd been in the clinch with the tall man earlier. The other, his bald head now covered by a black cap, was Jenny Ikonomou's brother Ricardo.

Realising he had very little time, Mavros backed off and headed for the road. The Audi would soon be away and he had to find a taxi. Although the coastal road was as good a place to get one as any at this time of night, he'd still need some luck. It was one of the few times in his life that he wished he had a motorbike. He glanced to his right and saw the car with the three men in it moving towards the car park exit. He swore under his breath. He didn't know which way it was going to turn – left towards the city or right towards the coastal strip.

There was a high-pitched honk from the other side of the road.

'Over here, Alex.' Dmitri Tratsou was waving to him from the wheel of a battered Lada.

Keeping his eye on the car park, Mavros ran across the lanes between cars that were breaking the speed limit. To his relief he saw that the Audi was indicating left. He pulled open the passenger door.

'I see it,' his client said, his eyes on the mirror. He had the engine running and, when the black car passed, he pulled out and slotted in about fifty metres behind in the central lane.

'What the hell are you doing here?' Mavros demanded, looking to the front. 'Don't let him get too far ahead.'

'I know what I do. You see Katia?'

Mavros jerked his head back in the negative gesture. 'Who told you she might be at the Silver Lady?'

Dmitri accelerated through a light that was changing. 'I have friends, Alex.'

'You also hired me. Didn't you think of sharing that information with me?'

'Calm down, my friend. Seems you already know.'

Mavros watched as the Audi passed a tree-ringed square. 'Get closer. He's pulling away.'

The Russian-Greek pushed the Lada hard and made up some ground. 'Who are these men?'

'They work at that club.' He glanced at his client. 'Why are you so keen to tail them?'

'I ask you the same question, Alex.'

'Careful. He's slowing down. The road splits here. Make sure we go the right way.'

Suddenly the Audi accelerated, overtaking a container lorry.

'He's going left,' Mavros said. 'The Piraeus lane.'

'You sure?'

'Yes! Pull out!'

The engine rattled in its blocks as the Lada was forced alongside the thundering lorry.

Mavros watched as the Audi moved further ahead, staying in the outer lane. 'Yes, he's heading for Piraeus,' he said, relaxing. 'No, he's cutting in! Get across!'

Dmitri tried to squeeze more from the Lada, but the lorry was keeping up with them, its driver smiling grimly. At what seemed like the last moment, the Russian-Greek managed to get past him and slip into the lane. Ahead of them the Audi, moving slower now, was approaching the junction.

'Good, eh?' Dmitri grunted.

Before Mavros could respond, the Audi veered to the left again.

'Ach, hell!' Tratsou said, glancing in his mirror. The lorry was right behind them. He made an attempt to follow the car in front, but quickly realised that he would hit the bollard separating the lanes and corrected his course.

'Bastards,' Mavros said as the Audi disappeared on the loop towards the port. They came on to the avenue that led to central Athens, the nearest junction several hundred metres ahead.

'They saw us,' Dmitri said, shaking his head. 'Sorry, Alex. This car no good for high-speed chases. I turn to Piraeus?'

Mavros sat back. 'No, forget it. We'll never catch them now.' He looked at his client. 'It's time we had a talk.'

'I take you somewhere?'

'Yes,' he said, remembering that Niki was expecting him. He gave directions. 'Who told you that Katia might be at the club?'

Dmitri kept his eyes on the road. 'I already say. A friend.'

'Listen, you've got one choice and one choice only. Either you answer every question I ask you or I walk away. I'm serious. I can't work for you if you keep things from me.'

The Russian-Greek pulled into a space and turned off the Lada's engine. 'All right, Alex. I know men, some from former Soviet Union, some I meet here at work. They . . . they are not good men.'

'You mean they're criminals.'

'Yes.' Dmitri looked down. 'I try to keep away from them, but since my Katia disappears, I talk to them. Ask them if they know where she could be.' He glanced at Mavros. 'You know, many girls from old Communist states, they find no other work. They . . . they sell their bodies.' His face above the unruly beard was pale in the lights from the street. 'I don't believe my Katia do this, but maybe . . . maybe they force her.'

Mavros decided to take a chance. 'Did you bring your gun?'

His client's head jerked back. 'My gun? I don't—'

'I saw you receive it.'

'You spy on me?'

'No. I happened to see the handover and then I heard the guy speaking Russian on his phone.' Mavros glared at him. 'Have you got it with you? What were you intending to do with it?'

'Get my Katia back,' Dmitri said, his head dropping again.

'Let me see it,' Mavros said, taking out his handkerchief.

The Russian-Greek checked that the street was empty and fumbled in his pocket. 'Good gun,' he said. 'Glock. Cost me a lot of money.'

Mavros released the ammunition clip and let it drop into his lap. The weight suggested it was full. He held the weapon to his nose. It didn't smell like it had been fired recently.

'Ah, I understand,' his client said. 'You think I kill that piece-of-shit drug-pusher. I saw report on news.' He gave a slack smile. 'I want to kill him, but I not know his address. And I work all day. You can ask at site.'

Mavros handed him back the gun and then the clip, using his handkerchief. 'All right. But you can see why I was suspicious. Did your friends give you any other places to look for Katia?'

Dmitri pulled out a piece of paper from his jacket pocket. 'Other clubs, some . . .' he broke off and bit his lip '. . . some brothels.'

Mavros took the list. 'I'll keep this. I don't want you causing trouble, especially not with that thing. Get rid of it.'

The Russian-Greek's expression was suddenly aggressive. 'You have nothing to tell me, Alex? I pay you for what?'

Mavros held his gaze. 'I've got some angles to follow up, but I'm keeping them to myself. After tonight you can hardly blame me. I'm the one who's looking for Katia, okay? You go to work, and then look after your wife in the evenings. If you don't like the way I'm running this investigation, you can fire me.'

For a few moments he thought Dmitri might do that. Then, after a series of long sighs, the Russian-Greek started up the Lada and drove on. Mavros didn't feel good about shutting him out, but the worst thing that could happen now would be for his client to burst in waving a gun. Especially since it looked like Jenny Ikonomou's brother worked for the Chiotis family.

But where did that leave the beautiful, stage-struck Katia?

The Son knocked the agreed number of times at the rear door of a crumbling building in a suburb beyond the port. It was five in the morning and the first sounds of the new day were audible: birds waking up on the rooftops, people on the early shift going by on noisy scooters, a couple of dogs fighting over a plastic bag.

'We'll be leaving in broad daylight,' he said in a low voice.

'Does that worry you?' The Father's voice was scathing. 'What are you, a woman?'

The Son's face hardened. When the door opened, he pushed past the bald man and carried his bag down a dripping corridor. There was a room lit up at the end.

'Who's this?' he demanded, taking in the scene. A bound and gagged man was slumped in a chair beside a long work bench, but he wasn't the one who'd caught the Son's attention. There was a tall, muscular young man in a dark suit to the rear.

'He's with me,' Ricardo said.

'The agreement is that no one sees us at work except you,' the Son said, glancing at the Father.

The old man stepped forward and put his bag on the bench, his eyes locked on the tall young man. 'You've seen us and we've seen you,' he said, the words heavy with menace. He turned to the bald man. 'Why the delay?'

'Sorry. We had to lose some arseholes.'

The Son bent over the man in the chair. 'You were followed?'

'Don't worry,' the bald man said. 'It was nothing. We shook
them off easily.' He gave the Father a slack smile. 'Believe me,
they've got no idea where we are. I'll deal with them later.'

'Be sure you do,' the Father said, unzipping his bag. 'You
know who we answer to.' He looked at the tall young man. 'It's
time for you to leave.'

'No, let him stay,' Ricardo said. 'He's Mrs C's blue-eyed
boy. He should see what happens at this level of the business.'
He laughed. 'Besides, he smoked this fucker out. You want to
see what happens to him, don't you, Dami?'

'No names,' the old man growled.

'Sorry.' The bald man looked chastised. 'This is an easy one
for you.' He inclined his head towards the man in the chair,
who groaned as the Son's probing fingers brought him round.
'He's one of ours who's gone bad. We need to know who he's
been talking to. And anything else you can get out of him.'

When the Son had put on his waterproof overalls, he took
hold of the captive's chin. He ripped the tape off in a single
movement. The man squealed.

'Do you have any idea how much shit you're in? Do you
know who we are?' He pointed to the old man. 'That's the
Father. Guess who I am.'

'The Father . . . the Father and the Son . . . no, no, I . . .'
The bound man jerked his head round. 'Dami, tell them I'm
clean.' He looked to the front. 'Ricardo, this is all wrong.'

'Fuck you, Laki,' the bald man said. 'We know you called in
the shooter. Now you're going to tell us who got to you.'

'No . . . no . . .' The captive started to gabble incoherently.

Damis stepped round the chair. 'Maybe he'll tell me.' He
took in the tools that the Father was lining up on the work
bench. 'Maybe there won't be any need for . . . for whatever it
is you're going to do to him.'

'Losing your nerve?' Ricardo jeered. 'That won't go down well with Mrs C.'

'That's enough,' the Father said, pulling on latex gloves. 'Get him on to the table.'

'I'll do it,' Damis said, bending over. He took out a clasp knife and sliced through the rope round the captive. 'Oh shit, I—' He broke off and slowly raised the upper half of his body. 'Laki, don't . . .' The man in the chair stood up and darted behind him.

'You see, I'm holding the knife to his throat?' Lakis said, his other arm round Damis's neck. 'Raise your hands, all of you!' He watched as the other three complied. 'Right, you piece of shit. You and I are going for a walk.' He nudged Damis. 'To the door. Slowly, very slowly.'

'What makes you think I won't go for my gun?' Ricardo asked. 'You think I care if you slit his throat?'

Lakis gave a cracked laugh. 'You said it yourself, fuckwit. Damis is the boss's new toy boy. What do you think she'll say if you bring him back without a voice box?'

The Father's eyes were on the Son.

'That's it,' Lakis said, panting. 'Nearly there.'

'Just one thing,' Ricardo said as the pair reached the passage. 'You'll need this.'

Lakis's head and upper arm appeared round Damis's shoulder. 'What?'

Before his eyes could register that the bald man was holding up a key, there was a blur of movement from the Son's hand followed by the sound of sharp metal penetrating flesh. With a shriek Lakis dropped to the floor, writhing and kicking.

'Jesus Christ,' Damis said, kneeling down and trying to steady Lakis's violently twisting head. A steel shaft about half a metre long was proturding from the man's left arm.

'Good,' the Father said to the Son. 'Now get him on to the table. Quick.'

'Isn't this enough?' Damis asked, his hands drenched in blood.

'He's going to talk before he dies,' the old man said.

The Son came over and pulled Lakis up, giving Damis a slack smile as he did so. 'Too shocking for you, pretty boy?'

Damis swallowed and put his hand under Lakis's other arm. When they got to the bench, he held the injured man's heaving shoulders down as Ricardo ran a length of rope under and over several times. Soon Lakis was secured, his head in the Son's vicelike grip.

'I'm going to get my fish spear out of your arm later,' he said, his mouth close to the captive's ear. 'First you're going to talk.' He glanced up at the Father. 'I promise you're going to talk.'

Damis watched as the old man pulled open Lakis's trousers and bared his groin. Then, his jaw dropping in undisguised horror, he saw the Father pick up a glinting fish hook with multiple barbs.


Mavros crept into Niki's bed and received a semi-conscious embrace. She quickly fell back into sleep, but he wasn't able to follow her. The case refused to let him go and he found himself reviewing images of the people he'd seen the previous day: the reporter Bitsos sniffing for anything that might make a story; Commander Kriaras warning him about the Chiotis family; the gorillas in the nightclub doing lines of coke and fighting with each other; Dmitri, the lines on his face deepening with every hour that passed; the actress Jenny Ikonomou with eyes like bottomless wells; her brother Ricardo, his face blank, giving nothing away. Behind them all was the smiling Katia, who'd disappeared into the void. Was she at the centre of this web, or had he missed some vital clue?

He came round to the sound of Niki closing the wardrobe door.

'Oh, you're awake,' she said, with a distracted smile.

'I am now.'

'I'm late. I made coffee.' She leaned over the bed to kiss him. 'Bye. You didn't see Katia?'

'No, but I ran into her father at the Silver Lady.'

'What was he doing down there?'

'Looking for her. Or so he said.'

Niki stopped at the bedroom door. 'What's that supposed to mean?'

'Nothing.' He didn't want to bring up his suspicions of his client again. Besides, he was inclined to believe him after the conversation they'd had last night.

'All right,' she said, unconvinced. 'I'll see you later.'

'Don't know. I might be working. I'll ring you.'

She waved and left.

Mavros had a shower and got dressed, his clothes stinking of smoke. He was on his way out of the flat when his mobile rang.

'You know who this is.'

Mavros recognised the policeman's voice.

'Were you at the Silver Lady last night, like you said you were going to be?' Kriaras's tone was harsh.

'Why?'

'Answer the question!'

'Yes, I was. What's happened?'

'There's something I want you to see. I'll send a car.'

Mavros told him where he was. While he waited, he ran through the events at the end of the night. Ricardo and the tall man had left the club with the guy who was unconscious. On the way towards the city, they realised they were being followed and shook Dmitri and him off. It struck him that they'd got close enough to be seen by the occupants of the Audi, so there was a chance Ricardo had recognised him. He wasn't sure whether to be worried or pleased. Maybe that would put the squeeze on the actress's brother and make him do something stupid.

When a horn sounded outside, Mavros went down and got into the back of an unmarked car driven by a plainclothes officer he didn't know.

'Where are we going?'

'You'll find out soon enough,' the driver said, accelerating away. They turned to the east and started to climb the flank of the mountain.

Was Ricardo the key to Katia's disappearance, Mavros wondered. Although he'd denied seeing her at his sister's house, he was in with the Chiotis operation. It had plenty of vacancies for attractive young women. Where had he been going with the comatose man in the Audi during the small hours? Mavros began to get a bad feeling.

The car was climbing through the highest suburb. This morning the residents had a choice view of the pollution cloud that was smothering the city centre. The driver headed up a steep road that ended in an outcrop of rock. There was a cluster of police cars and other official vehicles. Reporters and cameramen were standing behind a blue-and-white tape that had been strung between the railings outside the last houses.

'Follow me,' the policeman said, pulling out his ID.

Mavros saw Bitsos in the crowd. The reporter gave him an inquisitive look and then had the sense to conceal his interest. Mavros ducked under the tape and walked between an ambulance and a police van. A track had been trampled through the new grass and spring flowers that were growing around the rock. He could see Nikos Kriaras standing with his head bowed as he examined something on the ground. As Mavros drew closer, he saw it was a body.

'So, Alex,' the commander said sternly. 'You should be interested in this. You're the only person I know who admits to being at the Silver Lady last night.' He smiled coldly. 'That makes you a suspect.'

Mavros tried to keep cool.

Kriaras squatted down and pointed to the naked body lying on its front. 'Male, aged between thirty and forty, time of death approximately six a.m. this morning, cause of death shock and/or loss of blood. An anonymous caller directed us here at eight a.m. There was a wallet placed between the dead man's buttocks. The photo on the ID card matches. His name is Angelos Lazanis, accountant.' Kriaras laughed drily. 'How many accountants wind up like this? The wallet also contains a book of matches with the Silver Lady's logo on it.' He signalled to a technical officer in white overalls. 'Turn him over.' He watched Mavros as the front of the body came into view. 'What do you think of that?'

Mavros blinked. He'd seen more bodies than he wanted to in his professional life, and viewing them didn't get any easier. People did sickening things to their fellow men. He forced himself to run his eyes down the victim. The head was undamaged apart from lacerations and dried blood on the lips. It seemed the victim had bitten through them in his agony. There was a major wound to his upper left arm, as if a sharp object had almost passed through it. But it was the groin that made him gag. There were small metal shafts protruding from the penis, scrotum and surrounding flesh. Short lengths of line were attached to the eye at the end of each one.

'Fuck,' Mavros said under his breath.

Nikos Kriaras took his eyes off him and stood up. 'Fish hooks. There are thirteen of them. We think that the lines were longer than they are now. The damage to the tissue suggests that what the surgeon calls "significant traction" was applied. In other words, the hooks were inserted and then pulled.'

'Maybe he was strung up like the guy at the transport company,' Mavros said, shaking his head.

'You could be right.' Kriaras glanced at the technician. 'All right, get him to the morgue.' He led Mavros away. 'Did you recognise him?'

'Yes,' he said, without hesitation. 'He was in the club last night. He was wearing a dark suit when I saw him.'

'Do you think he worked there?'

'Not sure. He was in a scuffle with another guy in a suit. It got broken up.'

Kriaras's eyes were on him again. 'Anything else you noticed about him?'

Mavros returned his gaze as frankly as he could. 'No. I was looking for a missing girl, remember?' What the victim had gone through turned his stomach, but if he told the commander about Ricardo and the other guy taking the dead man away, he would lose the only lead he had to Katia.

'Very well.' Kriaras turned away. 'Give a statement of your movements last night to my men.' He looked over his shoulder. 'And don't talk to any reporters until I've had my say to them.'

'Are you treating it as another gangland killing?'

'What else? The war's hotting up and they're using us now, the scum.' The commander spat on the ground. 'The anonymous calls, the wallet up his arse. One side's telling us who the victim is so that we publicise it and put more pressure on the opposition.' He walked away down the slope.

Mavros watched him go. He had the feeling that he'd become a pawn in some game that Kriaras was playing. But it wasn't the commander who worried him most. Ricardo and the tall man with him were responsible for the torture and murder of Angelos Lazanis, he was sure of that. If Ricardo had seen him and Dmitri, they could be next in line for the hooks.

The Son was standing on the external wall of the port of Piraeus, watching a cruise liner negotiate the narrow passage that led to the Saronic Gulf. The ship was like a great yellow brick. It had none of the sculpted lines that enabled most vessels to slip through the water like fish. The square-ended boat that he and the Father used on the lake back home was better attuned to its environment. This monstrosity was an expanded version of the high-sided trucks that took sheep and pigs to the slaughterhouse, the animals crammed into restricted spaces. The Son looked up at the passengers who were waving at him from the upper decks. He kept his hands in his pockets. People were cretins. Who would pay to be cooped up with hundreds of others in a floating prison?

He turned his eyes to the open sea. There was a smudge on the horizon beyond the ships that were waiting at anchor. It was the first of the islands. He'd have liked to take a ferry to see how the fishing was over there, but he couldn't leave the city now. Men were casting lines from the wall. The windows on the breakwater's superstructure had been broken years ago and never replaced. Despite the bright sunlight and the breeze that was cutting up the surface of the water, it was a depressing scene. What kind of fish would they catch here? Dull-eyed scavengers that fed on the filth pumped from the city, grey-skinned predators stunted by chemicals from the nearby factories.

The Son watched a baited hook as it flew through the air. The Father had surprised him last night. There was a good chance that the squealing traitor wouldn't answer their questions after he'd been hit by the fish-spear. But no, even though his hands weren't steady, the Father used his hooks with consummate skill, looping the lines round the pipes on the ceiling and fixing the tension on them so that the victim floated in midair. The vermin spilled everything about the opposition people he was dealing with. It was no surprise to learn that the Russians were behind the assassination attempt. Ricardo looked pleased, probably because the bastard's confession had taken suspicion away from him – apparently the subject was a minion of his at one of the family's nightclubs. The other guy, the tall one, he wasn't so keen. He was already in the shit for allowing the victim to hold his own knife on him. His eyes went glassy when the hooks were applied and he struggled to hold on to the contents of his stomach. A wimp like that didn't have any future in the business.

The barking cry of a seagull made the Son look up. He'd never gone queasy like that. The Father had trained him well. By the time they went on a job together for the first time five years back, the Son was ready. He'd watched the man they were working on wriggle and gasp, his eyes bulging, the Adam's apple almost bursting from his throat, and felt nothing but satisfaction that the work was successful. Not that the old man had shown much approval, let alone pride. The Father lived in a world where pain was the only currency. He exchanged the pain of others for money. He hadn't always been like that. During the dictatorship he'd been driven by hatred of the Communists, of anyone who resisted the Colonels' rule. The fool had actually believed that the old traditions – nation, Church, army – were worth something. What happened to family?

He watched as one of the anglers reeled in a small brown fish that flapped feebly. The Father was a hypocrite like everyone else. At the same time that he was breaking the opponents of the regime, he was working for Stratos Chiotis, who was in with the Colonels. They were all criminals. The Son swallowed a laugh. That was why he was superior to the Father and everyone else. He didn't allow himself to be distracted by notions of right and wrong, he wasn't affected by ideas or emotions. That was why he'd be the best. He looked down at the fish as it gasped its life out on the concrete, feeling no pity. He was fascinated by fish, their empty eyes, their permanent hunger, and the speed with which they caught their prey. But they were nothing compared with him. He was the new order, bred to show no mercy to the weak. Even when those included the Father.

It would soon be time to make his move.

Mavros pushed open the door that the Fat Man left dirty to discourage all but the locals. The café was half-full, the market traders taking a break from fleecing the tourists. He acknowledged the ones he was on speaking terms with. Some of them were too grasping to merit even a nod.

'Smile, Yiorgo,' he said to the figure behind the chill cabinet. 'Your loyal customers deserve friendly service.'

'Bend over and I'll give you friendly service,' the Fat Man said, with a scowl. 'Where the hell have you been?'

'Busy.' Mavros went out to the enclosed yard at the rear. It was a pleasant morning, but that wasn't why he was sitting down there. He wanted privacy. He smoothed out the pages his sister had faxed him and found the passage that had caught his eye on the way down from his flat.

'You're too late for anything to eat,' the Fat Man said, coffee and a glass of water on his tray.

'You mean there are no pastries? I'm starving. Why didn't you keep me any?'

'Because you haven't been in the last few mornings.'

Mavros glared at him. 'You ate the last piece yourself, didn't you?'

The café owner looked sheepish. 'Well . . .'

'Marvellous,' Mavros said in disgust. 'I'll let you off if you answer a question.'

The Fat Man was immediately suspicious. 'What kind of question?'

'Jesus, Yiorgo, it's not the dictatorship. When will you Communists loosen up?'

'We Communists? Have you forgotten that your father and your brother both came under that heading?'

Mavros raised a hand. 'All right, all right. Look at this.' He spread the pages across the table. 'Jenny Ikonomou.'

The Fat Man's lip curled. 'Rich, fancies herself, appears in deadly boring TV programmes. What about her?'

'It says here that she was a member of the youth party in the late-sixties.'

'So?'

Mavros looked up at the pergola and the vine hanging from it. 'Jesus, try to open up. Communication is god these days.'

'Communists are atheists, remember?' Yiorgos shuffled his feet in the gravel. 'What do you want me to say?'

'Did you know her?' Mavros said, emphasising each word. 'No.'

'Come on, you were the link man between the youth party and the comrades often enough. You must have come across her.'

'Jenny Ikonomou? No, I swear on Lenin's tomb.' There was a hint of a smile on his lips.

Mavros stared at him and then laughed. 'Oh, I get it. She had a different name then.'

'Bravo,' Yiorgos said, clapping. 'Who's a clever investigator? Her family name was Zanni.' He leaned closer. 'What's this about, Alex?'

Mavros shrugged. 'She's come up in a case I'm working on.'

The Fat Man grunted. 'What was that about communication being god?'

'Client confidentiality. What do you expect?'

After a pause, Yiorgos sat down heavily. 'All right, where's the harm? I don't think she'll have paid her dues for a long time. For what it's worth, here's what I remember about Jenny Zanni. She was one of those rich kids who want to see the other side of life. She was enthusiastic, the others liked her, especially the boys, but there was always something fake about her. Makes sense that she became an actress.'

'Was she involved in any resistance activities?'

'Don't know,' the Fat Man said, his eyes shifting away. 'You know how we worked. Cell structure, need-to-know basis. She was in with Manos Floros's group.'

'Floros? The one who was found in the sea off Rhodes?'

'That's right.' The café owner's expression darkened. 'The fucking bastards. They beat the shit out of him and then chucked him overboard when he was unconscious.'

Mavros made a note on one of the pages and then looked at the Fat Man. Even though he'd decided to give up the hunt, he couldn't resist. 'Did she know Andonis?' He spoke his brother's name softly, wary about raising his smiling face, but he stayed away.

Yiorgos heaved himself up. 'I don't know. She might have. You know how inspirational Andonis was, especially in the youth party.' His eyes moved towards the interior. 'Oh, shit. Here's one of my favourite human beings.'

Mavros looked up and saw the cadaverous form of Lambis Bitsos coming towards them.

'I thought you might be here, Alex,' the reporter said, giving the Fat Man a cursory glance. He'd got into loud disagreements with him more than once. The café owner had the Communist's disgust for the popular press – for him, journalists were the fleas that spread the plague of capitalism.

Bitsos took in the papers on the table.

Mavros gathered them up quickly. 'Yiorgo, we're going to need more coffee. I've forgotten how you take it.'

'Sweet,' Bitsos said with a tight smile. 'Like my character.'

'That'll be right,' said the Fat Man, lumbering away.

The reporter sat down and raised his eyebrows. 'I noticed you beat a hasty retreat from the crime scene, Alex. And didn't bother to return my calls.'

Mavros stuffed the fax pages in his pocket. 'I was busy,' he mumbled.

'Sorry?' Bitsos said, cupping his ear. 'You look like you're carrying a weight, my friend. Why did the commander bring you to the scene?'

Mavros thought about how to respond. He wanted to keep the reporter on his side. It was possible he knew something about Jenny Ikonomou's brother. 'I saw the dead man in the Silver Lady last night.'

'Did you now?' Bitsos thanked the Fat Man insincerely and sipped from the miniature cup that had arrived on the table. 'I'd forgotten how good the slob's coffee is.'

'Careful. Yiorgos and I are friends.'

The journalist shrugged. 'So are we, Alex. Supposedly. I saw what you were reading. What's Jenny Ikonomou got to do with your case?'

'You know she has a brother?'

'Oh, yes. Ricardo Zannis. He's with the Chiotis family.'

Mavros nodded. 'I saw him in the Silver Lady.'

'That figures. There's a rumour he runs it. The police have established that the dead man worked there. He was in charge of security.' Bitsos gave a sardonic laugh. 'Should have spent more time looking out for himself.'

'I think Ricardo was involved,' Mavros said. 'I saw him leave the club with the victim and another guy late last night.' He shot Bitsos a warning glance. 'That's between you and me.'

'You aren't two-timing Kriaras, are you? Don't worry, I won't be using it anyway. Ricardo Zannis has some very nasty friends.'

Mavros pulled his chair closer. 'Tell me more.'

Bitsos drank his coffee to the grounds. 'He was in the States for years, working for a Greek gang in New York. He had a bad reputation. One night he beat a pimp to death. What he didn't know – or maybe didn't care about – was that the guy worked for one of the Italian families. Result: the delightful Ricardo turned up here with his tail between his legs about ten years ago. He's kept his head down, but he's been linked to the Chiotis family for a long time.' He picked at the elongated nail of his little finger. 'That's not all I've heard.'

Mavros saw the lascivious look on the reporter's face and his heart sank. 'What?'

'Apparently he has a liking for young female flesh. He has people looking out for suitable girls.'

'Then what?'

Bitsos peered at him. 'What do you think? They vanish and he has his way with them.' His eyes widened. 'Oh, Christ, your missing girl.'

Mavros was trying to dispel the red mist that had risen up before him. Katia had been in the same house as Ricardo before she disappeared. He wondered how much the exalted actress who owned the Pink Palace knew about her brother's activities.

# 10

Damis was lying on the bed in the hotel, his breathing shallow and his stomach empty. He'd returned before the rush hour started, having got rid of Lakis's body with Ricardo. Since then he'd spent much of the time in the bathroom with his arms wrapped round the toilet. The place was equipped with gold-plated taps and pure white marble units, but he might as well have been in the filthiest squatter for all the good they did. What he'd seen, what he'd participated in, made him feel worse than a concentration camp guard.

At least Rea Chioti had cut him some slack. She'd called him not long after he got back and his heart skipped more than one beat when he saw who was with her. Ricardo was full of himself, his chest out and his face ruddy, as if he'd spent the morning exercising a horse rather than dumping a mutilated corpse.

'What's the matter, young Dami?' he said with a laugh. 'Bitten off more than you can chew?'

Damis looked at the head of the family. She was sitting in an armchair, her legs crossed above the knee and her face impassive. 'What can I do for you, Mrs Chioti?'

She ran an eye over him. 'Tell my assistant to order you a new suit.' She glanced at the bald man. 'I understand from Ricardo that you were correct. The traitor was the man you picked out.'

'I was sure it was him.'

'Yes, you were,' she said thoughtfully.

Ricardo stepped forward. 'And you were lucky, Dami. How did you manage to lose control of your knife? Just as well Lakis was in a state of panic. If he'd remembered you were carrying a gun, God knows what would have happened.'

Damis felt his cheeks redden, but Mrs Chioti didn't look concerned.

The bald man came up to him. 'You're nothing if you can't stomach a squealer getting what he deserves.'

'That'll do, Ricardo,' Rea Chioti said firmly. 'Not everyone has your aptitude for such work. I'll be in touch.'

Ricardo pursed his lips and accepted his dismissal. He winked at Damis as he headed for the door.

Damis kept his head bowed. 'I'm sorry, Mrs—'

'Don't apologise. Some parts of the business are demanding. You're young and you're learning quickly. You can take the rest of the day off.'

Back in his suite Damis closed his eyes, then quickly opened them again. The horror of seeing Lakis suspended in the air with taut pyramids of skin raised from his groin wouldn't leave him. It had been a relief to put the body face down on the rock, obscuring the wounds and the hooks with lines dangling from them like rat's tails. But there had been no relief for him since.

He rolled off the bed and started to do consecutive sets of press-ups, first with both hands on the ground, then only one. When he'd finished sets of a hundred left and right, he got up and looked out of the window. There was a crush of people in the street below, many walking straight at each other and then veering apart at the last moment. Some were young, others decrepit; some well-dressed, others in little more than rags; most aware of what was going on around them, some in their own drug-induced worlds. He clenched his fist and pounded it against the open palm of his other hand. That was what this was all about. Drugs. The way they cut people off from their friends and families, from those who loved them. From life.

Damis couldn't forget seeing Martha in the hospital's secure unit. Her clothes flapped about wasted limbs that jerked uncontrollably. Her eyes, once beautiful deep pools, were red-veined, the pupils wide and vacant. He spoke to her but she didn't hear, her lips moving constantly as she mumbled words he couldn't understand. It was her smell that was hardest to bear. He'd taken in every scent of her body. The sweet warmth of her armpits. The tang of her sex cut with the wild flowers they'd lain on. The aromatic smell of her hair when he crushed his face into it, and the perfume she used to dab beneath her ears. But now she stank. Blasts from her unwashed skin and knotted hair forced him back, his hand over his face. Martha was a living corpse. The body he'd possessed was rotting away.

Martha, he said to himself. He was doing this for Martha. If she'd been able to understand, she'd have approved. She'd always been so protective of animals and children, of creatures who couldn't help themselves. Yes, she'd appreciate what he was trying to do.

Then Damis saw Lakis again – the tortured flesh, the throat ruptured from screaming. How could he ever justify that to Martha? He'd tried to help, had deliberately dropped his knife when he was cutting the ropes, but it was useless. They might have escaped Ricardo, but the other two, the Father and the Son, they were monsters, inhuman and implacable. He hoped he'd never see either of them again.

Damis gave a hollow laugh. Who was he fooling? Ricardo didn't frighten him but, if he were to honour the oath he'd sworn after Martha had been lost to him, there would have to be a reckoning with the Father and the Son. One thing puzzled him. Rea Chioti obviously knew exactly what those men did. She employed them, but she showed no emotion. How had the woman become so immune to the pain of her fellow human beings?

Mavros went back to his flat and came up with a plan. As far as he'd been able to establish, Jenny Ikonomou was the last person to see Katia. From what the actress had said, it seemed that her brother stayed at the Pink Palace at least part of the time. The last thing Mavros wanted was to run into the scumbag before he could see her, so he decided to wait until early evening before phoning. Ricardo had been busy during the night and he'd probably be sleeping during the day. By evening he'd be back at the Silver Lady, making preparations to relieve more suckers of their cash.

He watched Bitsos report the Lazanis killing on the afternoon news. He was dozing off on the sofa when it occurred to him that his mother might have met Jenny Ikonomou. The Pink Palace wasn't far from Dorothy's apartment building and she had friends who worked in the theatre. He rang her.

'Jenny? Yes, I know her, dear. Though she hasn't come to many parties since she disposed of her husband.'

'What do you mean "disposed of", Mother?'

She laughed. 'Well, she was a lot younger than him and she's a passionate woman.'

'Is she?'

'We knew her parents,' Dorothy continued. 'Spyros used to be scathing about them. I don't remember their names. He was a doctor. He used to treat the society fools, the ones with more money than brains, and she was a terrible snob. They had a huge place over on Aegina and—'

'She was in the youth party,' Mavros put in.

There was a brief silence. 'Really? I didn't know that.'

'Andonis never brought her to the house?'

His mother gave a soft laugh. 'Your brother used to sneak girls in the back way. He said it was for reasons of security, but I knew better. I don't remember her, though.'

Mavros found himself smiling at a recollection that came up out of the void – Andonis with a finger raised to his lips when the nine-year-old Alex had caught him in the corridor outside his bedroom with a flustered girl. His brother's bright blue eyes and winning smile meant he was never short of female admirers.

'Are you there, dear?'

'Yes, Mother. Did you ever meet her brother?'

'Her brother? No, I don't . . . oh, wait a minute, a completely bald man?'

'That's right.'

'I did. Horrible type. There was a scandal about him. All hushed up, of course.'

Mavros realised he was pressing the receiver hard against his ear. 'What was that?' he asked innocently. His mother claimed she never gossiped, so he had to be careful.

'It was very unsavoury. He was supposed to have raped a girl on the set of one of his sister's films.' Dorothy lowered her voice. 'And the thing was, she really *was* a girl. Only fourteen, the daughter of a cameraman who'd taken her there for a treat. It cost them a lot to brush that under the carpet.' She stopped abruptly, as if she'd suddenly realised that her tongue was running away with her. 'Why do you want to know, Alex?'

'Oh, nothing. I was talking to Anna and Jenny Ikonomou's name came up.' Diverting attention to his sister always got him out of jail.

'Indeed,' Dorothy said sharply. 'I've learned to be careful what I say in front of Anna in case it appears in some magazine.'

Mavros ended the call. What his mother had told him was useful background material, but it didn't help him with his approach to the actress. He had to find a way to gain her confidence. The more he thought about it, the more convinced he was that she hadn't told him everything she knew about Katia. But how could he get her to lower her guard, at least until he was inside the house? He spent the rest of the afternoon thinking.

At seven-thirty he called the Pink Palace. If Ricardo answered, he would put the phone down – he'd activated the option to withhold his number.

'Ikonomou.' It was her.

'This is Alex Mavros. You were good enough to see me yesterday.'

'Yes?' the actress said, her voice almost inaudible.

'I'm calling again about Katia, the young woman who stayed with you. I'm happy to say that she's contacted her parents. She's safe and well. The only thing is, she's mislaid an earring and she thinks it may be in your house.'

'Katia is well?' Jenny Ikonomou said, her voice louder. 'She wants to come to my house?'

'Ah, no,' Mavros said, elaborating the story he'd formulated. 'She's actually in Italy. She met a boy and had a rush of blood to the head. You know how young people are. Her parents have asked me to retrieve the earring. Apparently it was her great-grandmother's and it has sentimental value.' He waited nervously to hear if the ruse had worked.

'You're sure that Katia is all right?' the actress repeated. 'She's in Italy, you say?'

'Yes, I spoke to her myself. Would it be possible for me to come round now, Mrs Ikonomou?'

'Well . . . yes, I suppose so. Very well.'

Mavros grabbed his jacket and headed for the door. It looked like his gamble was working. Unless Jenny Ikonomou knew Katia's real whereabouts. If that was the case, he was walking into a bear trap he'd made for himself.

Rea Chioti was hunched over the telephone. 'Can you pick him up? That's all I want to know.'

'He's one of Fyodor's top men,' Ricardo replied. 'It won't be easy.'

'I didn't ask if it would be easy.'

There was a pause. 'Yes, we can pick him up when he goes to collect the take. But it'll be messy. He always has at least two bodyguards with him.'

'Make sure you have superior fire power. I'll give you the ex-bouncer.'

There was another brief silence. 'He's green. I'm not sure if he has the balls.'

'He put himself between me and a sniper. I wonder if you'd have done that.'

Ricardo laughed drily. 'Of course I would.'

'Do it tonight. We're at war. I want it as loud and as brutal as possible.'

'All right. You'll advise the—'

'Yes, I'll advise them.' She put the phone down on the coffee-table and thought about Ricardo. He'd become one of Stratos's most trusted lieutenants in the years before her husband's condition worsened. He was capable of the worst jobs, but she didn't fully trust him. She'd taken him away from front-line enforcement and installed him in the Silver Lady, where he'd raised the profits substantially. But the nightclub had brought him closer to vulnerable women and that was Ricardo's weakness. She'd heard stories about his viciousness to dancers and waitresses, and she wasn't impressed. Still, he was a good man to have on her side in a war and, when the Russians made their move, she'd been forced to bring him back. He was one of the few people who would work with the Father and Son.

She picked up her mobile and pressed the buttons – she never stored any numbers in its memory in case it fell into the wrong hands.

'Hello.' The Son's voice was neutral.

'Grouper,' she said, choosing a code word.

'Scorpion fish,' came the reply, without hesitation.

'Very well,' she said. The Son had sent her an encrypted list of fish names to be used. She was to select one and he would respond with one that began with the next letter in the Greek alphabet. She accepted the need for the precaution, but she wasn't impressed that fish names were used. She knew what the Father and Son did with hooks. 'I need you tonight.' She gave him the time and location of the pick-up.

'I'll be ready.'

'You mean you'll both be ready.'

'Of course,' the Son said after a pause.

Rea walked over to the window. In the distance, the wind was streaming over Mount Lykavittos, a large blue-and-white flag waving in front of the domed chapel. She wondered what was going on. The Son's tone had been different from usual, almost jaunty. He was a strange one. The Father was hard and merciless but, unlike the Son, there was a passion about him. She recalled the first time she had seen him, his cheeks red and his mouth wide as he screamed at her, told her she was a filthy whore who'd betrayed her country and the martyrs who fought to save it from the stinking Communists. The Father was committed to the patriotic cause. Or so she'd thought at the time. Later she discovered from her husband that the Father had worked for the family since before the dictatorship.

She turned from the window and went to the desk. The Father was compromised, but at least he'd once had ideals, no matter how poisonous they were. The Son was different. From what she'd heard from Ricardo and the others, he believed in nothing except inflicting pain. That was useful to her, but it also made her uneasy. Like the Father, she'd once had ideals, though they were the opposite of his. Growing up in the slums, her mother dead from consumption when she was nine and her father a trade unionist who died in the first month of the dictatorship, she'd thrown herself into the struggle for the people's rights.

She stared into the mirror. If only she was back at the villa in front of the painting in the study. She could have opened the safe and looked into the bulging eyes of the mask, the golden mask of silence. There was so much she had buried, so much of her life that she'd consigned to the abyss. The Father had taught her how to do that, but now it seemed she was forgetting the lesson. She'd sacrificed the Party and her comrades because of her lust for a man who was unattainable. She'd given in to the pain and the temptation, she'd destroyed Manos and the woman he loved on a whim. She'd turned that weakness in to strength in the years she'd been with Stratos, she'd used what she discovered about herself in the cells to benefit the family business – but she needed the mask to sustain herself. The mask reminded her of that weakness and the reminding made her strong again. She needed to see it.

Rea summoned her assistant and told her to make the arrangements. She would go back to the villa to be with her husband. If Ricardo and the Son did their jobs, the Russians would soon be reeling, no longer able to mount attempts on her life. The mask, the golden mask. She needed to see the woman's twisted face, the sewn lips that had been preserved for eternity. She needed to see it like a junkie needed a fix.

Then she thought of the woman she'd ruined. Would she ever summon up the strength to speak, to break the golden silence? If she did, everything that Rea had worked for would turn to dust.


Mavros stood under the camera at the door of the Pink Palace, his heart pounding. If Ricardo opened it he was in deep shit, but he didn't have a choice. He had to speak to Jenny Ikonomou.

There was a loud buzz. He pushed the metal door and walked in. To his relief there was no one in the long entrance hall.

'Take the lift to the third floor,' came the actress's voice from a speaker.

Mavros complied and walked out on to thick-pile carpet. Jenny Ikonomou was framed in a doorway at the end of the corridor. She was wearing a pair of tight-fitting jeans and a white blouse, her dark hair loose on her shoulders. The change in her appearance from the last time he'd seen her was striking. She looked twenty years younger.

'Alex Mavros,' she said, blowing out smoke. 'I didn't expect to see you again.'

He raised his shoulders. 'I must apologise, Mrs Ikonomou. My clients' daughter is proving to be a source of irritation to a lot of people.'

She stepped back into a large drawing-room. There were paintings by modern Greek masters on the white walls. 'Katia caused no irritation when she was here,' she said, sitting down and waving him to the sofa opposite. 'So, she is well?'

'Yes,' Mavros said, looking around. The ambience was one of understated elegance. A row of terracotta masks stood on a sideboard. 'Are those ancient?' he asked, taking in the varied expressions.

Jenny Ikonomou laughed. 'Of course not. Not even I can buy such things. They're copies of fifth-century originals. Do you like them?'

Mavros wasn't sure. Some of the faces were grotesque, others displaying naked emotion. 'Your brother isn't here this evening?' he asked, turning back to her.

'My brother comes and goes,' she said, giving him a blank look. 'But you didn't come to talk about Ricardo. Is Katia on her way home?'

'I'm not sure,' he said, looking down. 'Her parents certainly hope so.'

'Ah, to be young,' the actress said with a sigh.

Mavros took the cue. 'You were in the Communist youth party, weren't you? You must have known my brother Andonis.'

Despite his decision to end the hunt, he couldn't pass up the opportunity.

Jenny Ikonomou busied herself extinguishing her cigarette, but Mavros could see that she was agitated. Taking another from the pack, she looked up at him. 'You're Andonis Mavros's brother? Spyros's son? My God, I didn't realise.'

'Did you ever meet Andonis?' Mavros was expecting his brother's face to rise up before him, but again there was nothing.

'I . . . no, no, I didn't.' The actress glanced towards the line of masks. 'I knew of him, of course. It was a terrible tragedy that he disappeared.' She glanced back at him. 'There's never been any trace, has there?'

'No.'

'Those bastards,' she said bitterly. 'They were cowards. They ruined people's lives and they didn't have the nerve to own up to it.'

'Did they take you in?'

She inhaled deeply. 'I was arrested, yes.'

'Tortured?'

She stared at him through the smoke she'd blown out. 'Why are we having this conversation?' She twitched her head. 'They hurt me. But it was nothing compared with what my friends went through.' She stood up. 'Now, you wanted to see the room that Katia stayed in. It's been thoroughly cleaned. I don't think you'll find anything. What was it again? Earrings?'

'A single earring.'

'Follow me,' she said brusquely, her appetite for conversation clearly exhausted. She led him to the lift and they went up one floor. There were two doors on each side of a dimly lit hallway. She went to the first on the right and opened it.

'Are there only guest rooms on this floor?'

Her expression suggested that the question was inappropriate. 'Yes,' she replied, as she turned on the lights and went inside.

Mavros followed her. The room was substantially larger

than Katia's bedroom in her parents' flat. There was a double bed covered with an African blanket. The walls were pale peach, framed Toulouse-Lautrec prints facing each other. Instead of a dressing-table, there was a long mahogany table under the window. The surface was bare apart from a glass ashtray and some art books. There was a partially open door in the corner, expensive bathroom fittings visible through it.

'Very nice,' he said, standing in the middle of the room.

'Katia was the last person to stay here.' The actress went over to the double doors of a built-in wardrobe and opened them. 'Nothing in here apart from fresh bed linen and towels. I really think you're wasting your time.'

Mavros shrugged. 'Don't worry, I'm being paid for it. Shall I come down when I've finished?'

She turned away. 'All right.'

Mavros watched her go, relieved that she'd taken the hint. He couldn't have searched with her standing over him. He closed the door and ran his eye round the room. It had certainly been cleaned fastidiously since Katia was there. He wondered if there was anything to be read into that. Probably not, since Jenny Ikonomou hadn't denied the missing girl's presence. Her brother had been less forthcoming, though.

He decided to prioritise locations, given that he couldn't expect to spend long in the room – locations where Katia might have left some trace that had escaped the cleaner's eye. The bathroom was completely clear, shelves and surfaces bare, and the pockets of a white towelling dressing-gown behind the door empty. He went to the wardrobe and pulled out the fitted drawers. Nothing. There were only empty hangers in the main section. He took a step back and peered up at the top shelf. Again, nothing. Then he checked the width of the shelf and realised that the rear part wouldn't have been visible, even to a tall woman like Jenny Ikonomou. He brought a chair over and stood on it.

'Eureka,' he said under his breath. He stretched forward and brought out the pair of worn trainers that were lodged deep in the corner. They were size 38 and looked similar to those in Katia's own room. Then he remembered that he'd found things in a shoe there. Did she make a habit of hiding things in her footwear?

Mavros sat down and stuck his hand into the first shoe. It was empty. Taking a deep breath, he did the same with the other. There was something in the toe. He wriggled his finger and dug out a tightly folded piece of paper. The handwriting on it was in green ink and he recognised it immediately – he'd seen it in Katia's schoolbooks. She had written this. He unfolded the sheet, which had been torn from an exercise book, and started to read, thankful that she'd used Greek rather than Russian.

*Saturday 23 March. Wonderful day! Worked with Jenny – she asked me to call her that – on diction and movement in the morning. Then we had lunch on the roof garden. After that Jenny went off to sleep and I worked on the texts she gave me. In the afternoon we ran through some speeches. I did the best I could with Elektra. Then she asked me to do Lady Macbeth. At first I thought it was disgusting, she was encouraging her husband to kill the king, calling him a coward and saying she'd do the killing herself. But something strange happened, as if a switch clicked in my head. Suddenly I was Lady Macbeth, forgetting the book in my hand and moving around the room like a big cat circling its prey. It was amazing! And at the end Jenny actually clapped. She'd been so stern, but now she clapped and smiled, saying bravo and kissing me. I wish I could do this every day of my life! But on Monday I have to go back to school. Jenny won't hear of me stopping before exams. But I'll come to her as soon as they're finished. She'll find me a job helping her and I'll be able to study what she does in every part. It'll be wonderful. I don't care what the others say. Sifis, Papa, Mama, they'll all try to discourage me, but I know I'm right. Only Makis supports me. He was so happy when I called. He'll keep it secret, I know he will. I was born to act, I told him. The great Jenny Ikonomou said so herself!*

*This evening wasn't so nice. Jenny was tired and she didn't talk much. Her brother Ricardo ate with us. His eyes were on me all the time. I wish he'd left earlier than he did. At least I didn't see him again, at least he didn't talk to me like he did last night. Horrible man.*

*Now I'm sleepy, I can feel my eyes closing. But I have to finish this. Because the last, the best thing Jenny said was that she wanted me to come to her house in Aegina at Easter. Mama and Papa won't like it, Papa especially. He likes to make a family occasion of the holidays, even though I'm not his little girl any more. I wish he hadn't been so horrible to Sifis. I'll tell them I was with a girlfriend. Papa will be furious that I didn't let them know before, but he has to realise. This is my new life. I'm eighteen, I'm a grown woman. No one can tell me what to do anymore, not my parents, not the man in my life. I want Sifis, but I want my future even more. Thank God there are people as kind as Jenny Ikonomou in the world! What a weekend this has been!*

Mavros folded the page and put it in his pocket. He replaced the shoes so there would be some proof that Katia had stayed, should the actress go back on what she had said. The person who concerned him now wasn't Jenny Ikonomou, but her brother. Katia had felt his eyes on her. The scumbag had a reputation for mistreating young women, and he worked for the city's biggest crime family. He had clearly lied about not seeing Katia in the house. It didn't take much imagination to see a solid link to Katia's disappearance there now.

He closed the wardrobe doors and put the chair back. As he was turning away, the bedroom door opened without warning.

Ricardo stepped in. 'Alex fucking Mavros. What the fuck are you doing here?'

Mavros raised his shoulders. 'Didn't your sister tell you? I'm looking for—'

'An earring that the girl supposedly lost.' The bald man moved closer. 'Found it, did you?'

Mavros put his hand in his jacket pocket and took out the piece of jewellery that he'd bought in the Flea Market. 'Yes, I did. Thank you for asking.'

Ricardo stared at the earring. 'Out,' he said, pointing to the door with a rapid movement.

Mavros left the room. 'I was going to say a word to Mrs Ikonomou.'

'Say it to me.'

'I don't think so.'

Ricardo ushered him into the lift. As soon as it started, he stood in front of the doors. 'You and I need to have a conversation, wanker. I saw you in that clapped out car last night. What the fuck were you doing tailing me from the Silver Lady?'

'Who said I was tailing you?'

The bald man's teeth were visible between his thin lips. 'Don't play games, you piece of shit. If I see you here again, you'll regret it. If you contact my sister again, you'll regret it. If you show up within a kilometre of me again, you'll be picking your teeth off the pavement. Clear?'

Mavros sighed. 'So hostile, Ricardo. Anyone would think that you had something to hide.' He decided to see if his story provoked a different reaction. 'Didn't your sister tell you? The young woman Katia has turned up in Italy.'

Ricardo's eyes widened. He still blocked the doors after they'd opened on the ground floor. It looked like he was about to say something, but finally he let Mavros pass without a word.

Out on the street, Mavros walked swiftly away. He was sure the actress's brother knew something about Katia. A look of confused relief had flashed across his face when Italy was mentioned. But this had turned into a dangerous strategy. If Ricardo was involved in Katia's disappearance, he would know that Mavros had been lying. He'd have to watch his back even more carefully from now on.

From the third-floor window, Jenny Ikonomou watched the investigator's shadowy form move down the street until it disappeared. When she'd told Ricardo that he was in the bedroom Katia had used, her brother's face took on the blank expression that she'd dreaded from childhood. She knew it was wrong to admit Alex Mavros, but she couldn't help it. She liked the girl, was disturbed that she'd disappeared. And Katia was safe now. So why had Ricardo been so keen to eject Mavros?

The actress sat down and reached for a cigarette. There was no point in tormenting herself over her brother's moods. She'd learned long ago never to ask questions and never to criticise him. Ricardo had been a closed book to her since they were children. Her father had been overjoyed when a son came seven years after her. He made no attempt to disguise his preference for Ricardo, even insisting on the unusual name to emphasise his importance. He grew up in the bright light of their father's adoration. Their mother had almost died giving birth to the oversize baby and had never forgiven him for the pain, but that made no difference. She paid little attention to either of the children, being obsessed by the family's standing in society. When Ricardo proved himself to be a waster and a bully, it was too late. Their parents did what they could, spending more than they should have to rescue him from the law and then to set him up in the US. They even sold the estate in Aegina, though she'd been able to buy it back when she married one of the country's richest industrialists.

Jenny sat in a cloud of smoke and wished that she'd cut ties with Ricardo long ago. She knew he was involved with un-savoury people. He might even be behaving like he had done in New York. Though she tried not to show it, he frightened her and she knew he frightened other people. That poor girl Katia had quivered like a mouse when he eyed her up. Thank God she was safe. If only Jenny had the strength to throw him out of her house, but it was no good. She'd promised to protect him from himself when she was young and idealistic, and she could never break that promise. Not just because of him, but because of the people she'd wronged. She owed it to them, her former comrades, the ones she'd worked with to change society. They were lost now, one of them long dead and the other suffering in silence, but she'd be true to them. If she saved one soul, her brother's, that would be some recompense for what she did to them.

They came back to her in a flurry of images. Alex Mavros's questions had brought them to the surface. He was Andonis's brother, Andonis Mavros who had inspired them in the youth party. Why did she lie to Alex? Why did she tell him she'd never met Andonis? How had she failed to recognise the features they shared? The investigator's hair was longer and his eyes were different. Perhaps subconsciously she'd refused to allow herself to make the connection. She remembered the end-of-term party. Andonis Mavros had been there, in the flat near the Polytechnic. That party had marked the beginning of the end for Manos Floros and his comrades. She'd danced with Andonis, his eyes a brilliant blue that enslaved women and men alike. Then she'd watched Manos. He was strong and brave like Andonis, but he chose his friends less carefully. That night he was surrounded by the women who dragged him down. She included herself in that number.

'Are you all right, big sister?' Ricardo's voice cut into her thoughts. 'You don't need to worry about that asshole Mavros any more.'

She kept her eyes down. Ricardo faced the world with vicious disdain. He'd never got over the spoiled life of his early years. But she didn't want to think about him. She wanted to go back to her own youth, when she'd thought for a short, sweet time that she could do something about the injustice all around her. Manos had convinced her of that and she'd loved him for it. But so had the other women, and one of them had wanted him for herself alone. Why was there so much self-ishness in the world?

'I'll be back late,' her brother was saying, smoothing the creases of his suit and smiling ironically. 'Don't wait up.'

As if she would. Jenny had better people to devote her attention to. Alex Mavros had taken her back to them with his questions. Did he have any idea of the memories he'd stirred up? But at least the missing girl was found. The long-haired investigator with the flaw in his left eye had finished his work. He was different from Andonis, he was darker and taller, but there was a similar doggedness about him, a similar subtle intelligence. She found herself regretting that she wouldn't be seeing the youngest of the Mavros men again.

# I I

Even though it was well into the evening, drills were blasting away at the palatial hotel in Syndagma Square – no expense was being spared to refurbish it in time for the Olympic Games. Mavros took out his mobile as he crossed the open space and called his client's home number.

Mrs Tratsou answered, her voice almost inaudible.

'Is Dmitri there?' Mavros asked, remembering her lack of Greek. 'Dmitri?'

'Mowbeel, mowbeel.'

Mavros cut the connection and found the number in the phone's memory. He was still suspicious of what his client was up to.

The call was answered with a gruff monosyllable.

'Dmitri? It's Alex.'

'Can't speak now.'

'Where are you?' Mavros demanded. 'You should be at home with your wife.'

'I . . . I have work. I call you later.'

Mavros swore under his breath as the call was terminated. He could tell his client was hiding something. He'd heard no background noise from the motorway site during the brief conversation, so he didn't think Dmitri was working overtime. He stopped by a cypress tree, sure that his client was looking for Katia. It didn't take him long to conclude where he'd be. Dmitri had been outside the Silver Lady last night and he'd been involved in the abortive tailing of the Audi. He had unfinished business.

Kicking the paving-stones in frustration, Mavros looked at his mobile. He could call Dmitri back and tell him to get the hell out of there, but that might blow his cover. There was only one solution. He'd have to go down there and get his client to safety. But what if Ricardo saw him? He'd been warned off and he knew the bald man wasn't joking. He remembered the state of the body he'd seen in the morning, the hooks with fishing lines tied to them, the mutilated genitals. He'd be out of his mind to risk another confrontation with the man who was probably responsible for that. He considered calling Kriaras, but dismissed the thought. What would the policeman have been able to do to help Dmitri without destroying the trail to Katia?

He got the taxi to drop him about a hundred metres before the nightclub. The huge mannequin above the entrance was gleaming in the bright lights, but the doors were dark. The club wouldn't be open for at least another hour. Looking around, he tried to work out where Dmitri might be. As he approached the chain fence at the edge of the car park, he saw that the rear door was open. Light was spilling over the bench he'd used last night. There was no sign of his client there. He looked back across the road. There was a kiosk opposite the Silver Lady, the area beyond it in shadows. Waiting till the traffic-lights changed, he ran across the wide avenue. The smells of tobacco and chewing-gum filled his nostrils as he went slowly past the yellow structure that was almost blocking the pavement. The branches of an untended oleander were protruding from the unlit space in the retaining wall. He stopped and peered inside.

A hand shot out and pulled him into the narrow alcove. The bitter leaves of the bush were crushed against his mouth.

'Dmitri?'

'Yes.' The Russian-Greek's bulky form was close to him. 'What you do here, Alex?'

'I've come to get you out. The people who run that place are dangerous.'

'No. I wait to see the girls. Last night they arrive about this time.'

'Then you'll leave?'

'Okay,' Dmitri said reluctantly.

Mavros stood there, his arms jammed against his body and the Russian-Greek's beard tickling his cheek. About half-an-hour later he saw a blue minibus drive across the nightclub's parking area and pull up by the rear door. He felt Dmitri's arms move upwards. He was looking through a pair of binoculars.

'Soviet Army,' his client said. 'I take with me when I finish service.'

Mavros tried to make out the faces of the girls who were climbing down from the vehicle. Some of them were blonde, their heads down and their shoulders slumped. They looked like Christians about to be thrown to the lions.

'No,' the Russian-Greek said with a sigh as he lowered the binoculars. 'Not my Katia.' He leaned forward so that his head and shoulders were in the glow of the nearest street-lamp and looked left and right. 'Girls come in cars also. We wait.'

Mavros groaned and pulled him back under cover. 'She isn't there, Dmitri. I sat through the show last night.'

'You not find my Katia, so I have to do it myself, Alex,' his client said in a hoarse whisper. 'If you are scared, leave me.'

Mavros bit his lip. He shared Dmitri's pain. He wanted to find Katia too, but hiding in a bush wasn't the way to do it. 'Look, let's—'

He wasn't able to finish the sentence. There was a screech of tyres and a large black car appeared on the road in front of them. Before they could move, two musclebound men in suits leaped out of the nearside doors and crowded up to the space in the wall. Even in the restricted light, Mavros could make out the muzzle of a matt-black automatic pistol. It was jabbed into his abdomen.

'Out,' said a harsh voice. 'Into the car, both of you. Any noise and you're dead.'

They were bustled into the back seat, hands running over them to check for weapons. To Mavros's relief, it seemed that Dmitri didn't have his gun with him. They were squashed between two men, the driver on his own in the front. As the car accelerated away, Mavros realised that he'd seen all three of them before. The man at the wheel, sunglasses pushed up on his head, was Yannis, one of the coke-sniffers. The gorilla beyond Dmitri was Panos, the other guy from the Silver Lady's toilets. He took a deep breath. They were also the men he'd seen with the doomed Sifis that night on the mountainside when he intervened. Would they recognise him now he wasn't leaning over a basin? That wasn't his only problem. The tall heavy on his left was the one who'd had his hand round the throat of the man who was hustled into the Audi and had subsequently turned up dead. Would he recognise the pair of them from the chase in the Lada? He glanced at his client. Even though Ricardo wasn't there, they were in very deep shit.

'Head for the old airport perimeter fence,' the tall man said. 'You know the spot.'

'Oh, yes, Dami,' the driver said with a coarse laugh. 'Where we take the bad boys.'

Mavros watched as they turned off the coast road and headed inland. It wasn't long before they cut down a back-street and reached a quiet dead-end. The high wire surrounding the former airport was in front of them. The nearest buildings were commercial properties with few lights on in them. There was no one around. Mavros was trying to work out if the fact that they hadn't been blindfolded was good or bad. Either their captors didn't regard them as important enough to take the trouble, or they didn't care that they could be identified – meaning they were going to dispose of their captives.

His mouth went dry. 'Look,' he said. 'You're making a mistake. We—'

'Pano, get the other guy's ID,' the man called Damis said, extending his hand to Mavros. 'I want yours.' He gave a hard man's stare and brandished his automatic. 'Carefully.'

Mavros moved forward in the cramped space, eased his wallet out of his back pocket and handed it over.

'Well, well,' Damis said, holding up one of his business cards. 'Look what we've got here. A private investigator by the name of Alex Mavros.'

There were groans.

'This one's called Dmitri Tratsou,' Panos said. 'What kind of name's that, shithead? Are you foreign?'

'I am Greek,' Dmitri said, glowering at him. 'From former Soviet Union.'

'Jesus,' the driver said, turning round. 'He's a fuckin' Ivan. We'd better tell Ricardo.'

Damis raised his hand. 'Wait a minute. Let's find out what they were doing outside the Silver Lady.' He turned to Mavros. 'And don't tell me you were feeling each other up.'

Mavros was choking inside the Mercedes. The air was heavy and rank now that the air-conditioning wasn't running. He decided to tell the truth. It might even be that the musclemen would let something slip. 'We're looking for his daughter Katia. I don't suppose you know her?'

Yannis burst out laughing. 'And if we did, we'd tell you, tosser?'

Damis gave him a stern look. 'Be quiet.' He nudged Mavros. 'This Katia, she's gone missing?'

For a moment Mavros thought he saw sympathy in the man's dark eyes. 'Yes. There's a photo of her in my wallet.'

Damis looked at it, then showed it to the other two. 'I haven't seen her. You?'

The other two men looked blank.

'Nice face, though,' the driver said. 'I could—' He broke off when he saw Dmitri's expression. 'What are we going to do with these assholes?'

Mavros waited as the tall man kept his eyes on the photo of Katia. His heart was thundering in his chest. Would he buy their story? If he recognised them from last night, would he take that as an explanation for the tailing of the Audi? Why should he, since there was no girl in the car?

'All right,' Damis said, handing back the photo and wallet. 'I hope we understand each other. There's no Katia at the Silver Lady. I don't want to see either of you near the club again.' He opened the door. 'Get out.'

Mavros followed him, while Dmitri was hauled out by the gorilla called Panos.

'Give him a little souvenir,' Damis called over the roof of the car.

Mavros heard a dull thud followed by an expulsion of air as Dmitri went down. There was a cackle of laughter from the driver.

'Okay,' the tall man said in a low voice. 'You heard what I said. Keep your distance. This isn't a game.' He drove his fist into Mavros's midriff.

From the ground Mavros heard the doors of the Mercedes close and the engine start.

'Christ, it stinks in here,' Yannis was saying, his window sliding down. 'We should have handed them over to the Father and Son. They'd have given them some real pain.' Then he accelerated away, sending gravel flying.

Mavros had one hand over his eyes and the other on his belly.

'You okay?' His client was on his knees, gasping for breath.

'Yes.' Mavros felt his abdomen with his fingertips. The blow had scarcely winded him. 'You?'

'I've had worse,' Dmitri said with a grin. 'Much worse. These men fools, not serious gangsters.'

Mavros got to his feet. Yannis and Panos certainly struck him as fools, but not Damis. He was on a different level, more authoritative and thoughtful. But there was something strange about him. Had he mistimed his punch, or did he have some reason for pulling it? The guy who hit Dmitri had done a much better job, whatever the Russian-Greek said.

'Come, we go for drink, Alex.'

Mavros was examining his clothes. The area seemed to be the dog toilet of south-east Athens. 'Do you know how we look? Not to mention smell. I've got a better idea.' He took out his phone.

'Is that the Glezou Laundry? I need your services. About fifteen minutes.'

Dmitri was peering at him in the gloom. 'We go to clean clothes?'

'If you're lucky, you might get a drink too.'

They found a taxi two streets away. The driver was a smoker and didn't notice the state of his passengers until it was too late. During the drive to Niki's flat, Mavros ran over what had happened. He couldn't understand why the tall man called Damis had let them off so lightly. He was also wondering about the driver's last words. Who were the Father and Son? Could they have been involved in the killing of the man Damis and Ricardo had bundled into the Audi?

He knew who would be able to help him.


Damis was beginning to feel the strain. He went into the toilets at the nightclub and locked himself in a cubicle. It wasn't just the operation to snatch the Russian that Mrs Chioti had ordered him to play a part in, though that was worrying enough. Yannis and Panos were full of themselves for spotting the guys hiding in the hole in the wall opposite. He'd said he'd tell Ricardo about the private investigator and the bearded man who were looking for the girl, but he didn't intend to do that.

Not tonight, anyway. There was too much going on and he didn't want any more distractions. He was taking a risk. Ricardo would find out sooner or later, even if Damis didn't volunteer the information. How could he justify keeping quiet about it? The investigator Mavros, Damis had heard of him. He was a hot shot. He'd solved a high-profile murder case on one of the islands last year. It had been in the papers and on the TV. Was he really after a missing girl or was there more to his surveillance of the Silver Lady? And what the hell had he been doing tailing them in the ancient Lada?

The outer door banged.

'Dami?' It was Panos. 'You in there?'

'Yes.' He flushed the toilet and went out to the row of wash basins.

Panos was closely followed by Yannis.

'Not shittin' yourself, are you?' Yannis asked.

Damis stood upright and grabbed the lapels of the driver's suit jacket with his wet hands. 'No.' He lifted him off the ground and sniffed. 'I think you might be, though.'

Panos started to laugh raucously.

'Christ, loosen up,' Yannis said, wiping his jacket.

'Oh, I'm loose,' he replied. 'What do you want?'

'We're going in five minutes,' Panos said. 'You're in the front car with Mr Ricardo, Yannis and me are covering you.'

Damis strode out, his head held high. He needed to show the other two that he was worthy of the promotion Mrs Chioti had given him. They'd benefited too, though the idea of that pair of idiots riding shotgun didn't fill him with confidence. Neither did the fact that Ricardo was in charge of the operation. He was a sick bastard, but he was experienced and he had a sharp eye. Damis knew that the bald man had doubts about him because of what had happened with Lakis, not that it had done Lakis any good. The Father was bad enough but the Son . . . With his cold eyes and the ruthless way he'd launched the fish spear, the Son would have given Pol Pot nightmares.

'You're driving,' Ricardo said as they approached the Audi. 'I've told Yannis to keep about a hundred metres behind us.'

'Where are we going?'

The bald man glanced at him as he was fastening his seat belt. 'I'll tell you when I'm sure we're not being tailed.'

Damis didn't react to that. He was half-expecting Ricardo to mention the Lada and its occupants, but he didn't.

'Testing,' the bald man said into a walkie-talkie. 'You receiving, Pano?'

'Yes, boss.'

'Okay. Let me know if you see anyone on us.'

'Yes, boss.'

Ricardo dropped the receiver between his legs. 'Head for the city centre.'

Damis turned left on to the coast road and accelerated away.

'So, how do you feel about the job tonight?' Ricardo's eyes were on him again. 'Looking forward to picking up one of the opposition's top men?'

'Sure,' Damis replied evenly.

'Of course, you didn't have much choice. Mrs C threw you in without a second thought.' Ricardo gave a hollow laugh. 'She didn't seem to care that you almost let Lakis escape.'

'It was an accident.'

'Oh, I know that. Why would you have dropped your knife deliberately?' He leaned closer. 'It wasn't as if you liked Lakis.'

Damis glanced in the mirror and pulled out in front of a van. 'No, I couldn't stand the wanker.' He looked at the bald man. 'The Father and Son, they're really something.'

Ricardo lit a cigarette. 'They certainly are. Did you see the way they hooked the bastard up? No wonder his heart gave out.' He adjusted the rear-view mirror on his door.

'Have they always worked for the family?'

'As long as I've been around.' The bald man blew smoke over him. 'You don't want to be asking questions about them. And you don't want to tell anyone else about them. They're the family's secret weapon.'

Tell that to Yannis, Damis thought. He wondered if the investigator Mavros had heard the Father and Son being mentioned. He realised that he was being warned off and kept silent. When they approached the junction that led to the western suburbs, Ricardo told him to bear left. He did so, aware that the other man was beginning to breathe more heavily. They must be getting close to the scene.

'Pano?' Ricardo said into the walkie-talkie. 'Anybody on our tail?'

'No, boss.'

'Tell Yannis to close up now.' The bald man turned to Damis. 'Turn left at the next junction. After about half a kilometre you'll see some warehouses on the left. I've got a couple of guys in a car there. Pull up behind the parked lorries.'

Damis did as he was told. The buildings were lit up for security, but the truck park was in the shadows.

'Turn off your lights,' Ricardo said as they coasted to a stop, repeating the instruction to the car behind.

'Now what?'

'We wait.'

Half-an-hour passed, cars speeding past on the wide avenue and train wheels rattling on the rails nearby. The car was full of Ricardo's smoke and Damis was sweating in the enclosed space. Finally the walkie-talkie crackled.

'They're on their way. Two cars. Target's in the front one, sitting behind the driver.'

'You hear that, Pano?' Ricardo said in a low voice.

'Yes, boss.'

'Take the rear car out when I give the word.'

'Yes, boss.'

Ricardo put the handset down. 'Jesus, where do we find these morons? Yes, boss. No, boss. Can I kiss your arse, boss?' He leaned forward and opened the glove compartment. 'You know how to operate these?'

Damis looked down and saw a pair of Uzi machine-pistols. 'Yes, boss.'

Ricardo glanced at him and then laughed. 'Maybe you've got some balls after all. We're taking the lead car. Make sure you don't hit the guy in the back seat.' He looked ahead. 'Start the engine. You see them?'

'Yes.' Damis turned the key in the ignition. A couple of top-of-the-range BMWs were moving slowly across the parking area.

'Any moment now a friendly truck driver is going to put the shits up them.'

Damis watched as exhaust fumes appeared from a lorry to their left, its lights staying off. Then it moved forward, accelerating surprisingly quickly.

'Go, go!' Ricardo shouted.

Damis drove forward, aware of Yannis's Mercedes alongside before it veered off to the right. He aimed the Audi at the front BMW. It had been forced to stop by the lorry. He hit the brake and stopped the car about ten metres from them. Ricardo was out in a flash, his machine-pistol stuttering. The front window shattered and the driver and the man next to him fell forward, their heads exploding in crimson.

Damis opened his door, Uzi in his right hand, and loosed off a long burst over the roof of the front car. He heard a fusillade of shots as Panos and Yannis emptied their weapons into the second BMW.

'All right!' Ricardo shouted. 'We have him.' He leaned into the back seat and hauled a fair-haired man out. 'Don't try it.' He smashed his weapon down on the man's arm and a silver-plated automatic fell to the floor. 'Help me, Dami.'

Together they dragged the man to the back of the Audi. Ricardo looped plastic straps round his wrists.

'Open the boot.'

When it flipped up, they heaved the captive in, forcing him to bend his knees.

'Okay, get moving,' Ricardo said, moving to the passenger door.

'Where to?'

'The motorway heading north.' Ricardo gave a dry laugh. 'The Father and Son are entertaining out of town tonight.'

Damis reversed and carved an arc round the other vehicles. The truck's door was open, the driver running towards a car. Panos gave Damis a broad grin as the Audi passed him. Three bodies were half-in, half-out of the second BMW, their limbs flung wide and their chests covered in slicks of blood. Damis swallowed the bitter liquid that had risen up his throat.

It looked like the latest victory in the gang war belonged to the Chiotis family, even before the Father and Son got to work.

The apartment block's door was buzzed open a couple of seconds after Mavros rang the bell.

Niki was waiting for them on the landing outside her flat. 'What's going on, Alex?' she asked, her voice tense. 'Dmitri? What have you two been doing? God, I see what you mean about cleaners,' she said, sniffing the air. 'Get those clothes and shoes off out here. I don't care what the neighbours think. You're not coming into my flat stinking like that.'

Mavros shrugged and started to undress, signalling to his client to follow suit.

'You can keep your underwear on,' Niki said, handing them each a towelling robe. 'Assuming you didn't make a mess of that too.' When they were ready, she went inside with a brimming laundry basket.

'What she say?' Tratsou asked.

'Nothing. She thinks that men are cowards.'

'Pah! You tell her what happened to us.'

They followed Niki into the flat. Mavros wasn't sure if telling her was a good idea. He took his phone from his jacket, relieved that the leather didn't have the dog muck on it that his trousers did, and found the number he wanted. He waved Dmitri into the main room and went to the bedroom.

'Lambi, it's Alex.'

The crime reporter gave a sardonic laugh. 'Alex Mavros the groupie? Have you paid your respects to Jenny Ikonomou yet?'

Mavros ignored that. 'Look, I need to ask you something.'

'Not again,' Bitsos groaned.

'Have you ever heard of a couple of underworld operators called the Father and Son?'

There was silence down the line.

'Are you still there?'

'I'm here.' The reporter's voice was low. 'Where did you hear about them?'

Mavros knew he'd have to barter information. 'I heard a gorilla from the Silver Lady Club mention them. Are they hit-men?'

Bitsos grunted. 'After a fashion. Look, this is not a good conversation to be having right now. I'm in a public place.'

'Put your hand round your mouth, you old lecher. Like you do when you ring up your porn dealer.' Then Mavros realised that Bitsos wasn't just being security-conscious. He sounded shit-scared. 'Who are the Father and Son?'

'Shut up, Alex. I'm not joking, I can't talk about this on the phone.'

Mavros raised his eyes in frustration. 'Get in a cab then.' He gave Niki's address. 'I'll even pay your fare.'

'You'll pay a lot more than that.'

Mavros dropped the phone into the pocket of his robe and went into the sitting-room. Niki was standing over Dmitri, who was leaning back on the sofa with a glass in his hand.

'Is this true, Alex?' she demanded, her eyes wide. 'You got beaten up by bouncers from that nightclub?'

He glared at his client. 'Well, not exactly beaten up. Look, my delicate features are still—'

'Stop it, Alex,' Niki said, coming over to him. 'It isn't funny. I don't . . . I don't want you getting hurt.'

He put an arm round her, touched by her concern. There had been a time when she would have berated him all night, but she'd become much less spiky. 'Don't worry, Dmitri took more of a hit than I did.'

Niki pulled away and poured him a glass of brandy. 'Drink that and be more careful.'

Mavros was wondering what she'd say if she heard about the body he'd seen that morning; or if she was party to the conversation he was about to have with Lambis Bitsos.

'Alex, what we do now?' Dmitri asked, scratching his legs. They were so hairy that it looked like he was wearing woollen trousers.

Mavros looked at the floor. 'I'm not sure. I've got a couple of angles I'm still investigating.'

The Russian-Greek sat up straight. 'Is not good. You think you can find my Katia? I prefer to stop pay now if you don't.'

Niki put her hand on Mavros's shoulder. 'You'll find her, won't you, Alex?'

He glanced at her and saw the trust in her eyes. She really believed he could do it. That made him feel better. 'I'll find her. I promise you that, Dmitri. Excuse me, I need a shower.'

He went to the bathroom. He couldn't pass on his suspicions about Ricardo to either of them. Dmitri would march up to the bald man and provoke him, while Niki was capable of anything. She might even organise a police raid to get any under-age immigrant girls at the club taken into care. None of that would be any help to them in finding Katia. What he needed was some leverage. He hoped Bitsos would provide that.

The door bell rang soon after Mavros had finished his shower. The brandy had sent Dmitri into a seemingly deep sleep.

'Do you think you could let me talk to Lambis alone?' Mavros asked Niki.

She kissed him. 'With pleasure. I can live without seeing that lecherous ghoul again.' She went into the bedroom and closed the door. She'd only met the journalist once, in a disreputable bar. He'd described a particularly brutal murder in lingering detail, his eyes never moving from her cleavage.

'Good evening,' Mavros said as he opened the door.

'Is that all I get for taking valuable time away from covering the gang war that has the nation transfixed?' Bitsos stopped when he reached the main room. He pointed at the figure on the sofa. 'Who's the house guest? And why are you both wearing dressing-gowns?'

'He's my client. Our clothes are in the washing-machine.'

The reporter raised an eyebrow. 'Is he the one with the missing daughter?'

'That's right.' Mavros handed him a glass of brandy. 'Niki's gone to bed.'

Bitsos took it over to the dining-table and sat down. 'What a pity. Still no sign of the girl?'

'No.' Mavros sat down opposite him. 'Listen, I'm pretty sure Jenny Ikonomou's brother Ricardo snatched her but I can't prove it. Short of strongarming him.'

'I wouldn't recommend that, my friend.'

'No. He's already warned me off. Of course, that only made me more suspicious.'

Bitsos looked around the room. 'Is there anything to eat?'

'Jesus, have you got a tapeworm? How many times have you

eaten today?' He went to the kitchen and found a plate of stuffed vine leaves that Niki had made.

'Ah,' said Bitsos, his face lighting up. 'My favourite.'

Mavros watched him eat. 'All right, here's what happened.' He glanced over his shoulder. 'My comatose friend and I had a run-in with some heavies from the Silver Lady tonight. As they were driving away, I heard one of them mention the Father and Son. How they could have really hurt us. So who exactly are the Father and Son?'

The reporter finished chewing and pushed the plate away. 'Look, you don't want to get involved with them.' He took in Mavros's expression. 'Oh, for fuck's sake. There have been rumours about these guys for years. Never anything more than that, mind. They work for the Chiotis family. It seems that even the enforcers in the other gangs are terrified of them.'

'They're executioners?'

Bitsos picked a piece of food from his teeth. 'Not exactly,' he said, bending forward and lowering his voice even further. 'The word is they torture people.'

'Like the guy we saw this morning?'

'Could be. The problem is no one will ever go on record about them, so the police don't know any more than we do.'

'How come you never mention them in your articles?'

The reporter sat back. 'Are you crazy? I want to keep my skin in one piece, thank you very much.'

Mavros looked at the Russian-Greek. He was still slumped in the sofa, his breathing regular. 'Do you think they torture women?'

Bitsos frowned. 'Who knows? I've never heard . . . oh, I see, you mean your missing girl.'

'I'm wondering if Ricardo might supply them with young women,' Mavros said, feeling his disgust at the idea rise as he put it into words. 'It's not exactly unusual for gangsters to provide their hired men with women, is it? If these guys are as fearsome as you say . . .' He let the words tail off. 'What else do you know about them? Are they really a father and son partnership?'

'Who knows?' Bitsos raised his shoulders. 'There isn't much else. A couple of years ago, during the last gang war, I talked to one of the Chiotis family's men, a former tough guy who'd been pensioned off. He was bitter that he'd been sidelined, so he tried to sell me his story. He mentioned the Father. At first I thought he was talking about Stratos Chiotis, but I soon realised he meant someone very different.' He emptied his glass. 'Someone even worse. In the old days the gangs didn't carve each other up and leave the bodies in public places. Not the important victims, at least. They tied them to anchors and dumped them in the sea. So no mutilated bodies, no poor bastards with hooks in them, ever turned up. But that didn't mean it wasn't happening. According to my informer, the Father could get anyone to speak. It seemed to work. The Chiotis family was always one step ahead of the opposition.' He dropped his gaze. 'Look, Alex, you aren't going to like this. The story was that the Father was . . .' He broke off.

'Come on.'

'Shit, all right. The Father was said to be a torturer during the dictatorship.'

Mavros sat back, reeling. He'd started the search for Katia with a vow to give up on Andonis and here was Bitsos taking him back to the time that his brother disappeared. 'Why didn't you tell me this before?'

'Tell you what, for Christ's sake?' Bitsos said angrily. 'It's only hearsay. The guy who talked to me was found dead a week later. Heart attack, supposedly. I got the message and kept my head down. Anyway, you know what happened with the regime's torturers. A few of the bastards were put through show trials after the Colonels fell and the rest vanished. If the one who calls himself the Father knew Stratos Chiotis back then, he'd have had no problem setting himself up with a new identity.'

Mavros got his breathing back to normal. 'You're right. It's all hearsay. There's probably no connection with Andonis.'

'Or with your girl,' the reporter said, picking up another stuffed vine leaf. 'Forget the Father and Son. They're so well protected that you'll never get near them. Forget Ricardo too. If he's got your girl, she's had it.'

'Nice, Lambi,' Mavros said acidly. 'Very—'

The reporter's phone rang. He answered it and listened, his expression hardening.

'Right, I'll be there as soon as I can.' He stood up and backed away from the table.

'What is it?'

'There's been a shoot-out in a parking lot in Tavros. At least three dead.'

'Next round in the gang war?'

'I reckon.' Bitsos headed for the door.

'Hey,' Dmitri said, staggering to his feet. 'I know you from television.'

The reporter frowned at him and kept walking.

'Let me know if you find anything that might help me,' Mavros called.

'Ditto,' said Bitsos over his shoulder.

'This man from television is your friend, Alex?' his client said, rubbing his eyes. 'He tell you something about Katia?'

Mavros went towards the kitchen. 'No, Dmitri, he didn't.' He wasn't going to share what Bitsos had said. The reporter hadn't provided any more options and Katia was as lost to them as she'd been from the beginning. What was worse, the shadows from his own family's past were gathering again.

The Son walked into the deserted shack in the mountains north of Athens with a spring in his step. It was a beautiful night in the countryside, the stars brighter than they were in the city. And he was on his own. As far as the Father knew, they weren't required tonight and the Son had gone whoring.

Ricardo's face was a picture when he looked up. 'Where's the Father?'

'Ill.' The Son smiled. 'Don't worry. I know what I'm doing.'

The bald man studied him and then nodded. 'This piece of shit's an Ivan who hasn't bothered to learn Greek, so we don't have to ask him any questions. Just carve him up.'

The Son looked past the gagged captive who was writhing in his chair. The tall man who'd almost let the last subject escape was standing there. 'You can wait outside,' he said. 'We don't need you.'

Ricardo laughed. 'Go and sit in the car, Dami. This is man's work.'

The guy trudged away, trying to look like he didn't care.

The Son started to lay out his tools on an uneven table.

'What's really happened with the Father?' the bald man asked. 'He can't be ill. He's harder than stone.'

The Son stepped into his waterproof trousers. 'He's . . . how can I put it? He needs a rest.'

'Bullshit,' Ricardo said, stepping closer. 'The truth.'

The Son looked at him, the smile still playing on his lips. 'Do you know how old the Father is?'

Ricardo shrugged. 'Sixty-five?'

'Wrong. He's seventy. Do you really think he's up to this kind of work any more?' The Son picked up a gutting knife. 'We're wasting time. Either you trust me or you don't. Which is it?'

Ricardo eyed the serrated blade. 'All right. Get started.'

'You'd better stand back,' the Son said, the smile still hanging on his lips. 'I think you'll like what I've got in mind.'

The Son's prediction was accurate. By the time he'd finished, the bald man looked as pleased as a kid with his first fishing-rod.

'Dami!' Ricardo shouted. 'Get in here!'

The Son watched as the tall man came inside, hoping for an extreme reaction. But Damis took in the severed head that had been placed on a plastic sheet without a twitch and turned his gaze on them.

'Congratulations,' he said coldly. 'Mrs Chioti will be delighted. I hope.'

Only then did it strike the Son that maybe, in his haste to impress, he'd gone too far.

# 12

Mavros woke up alone in Niki's bed. Sunlight was forcing its way through the curtains. He stumbled towards the kitchen.

'Too much brandy?' Niki was sitting at the table, drinking coffee. 'Or too many vine leaves? I was going to take them for my lunch.'

'Sorry,' he mumbled, sitting down next to her. 'Bitsos ate them.'

She stared at him and then relaxed. 'Dmitri got his clothes from the dryer?'

'Yes. I didn't want to wake you.'

Niki bent down and put her arms round his neck. 'How decent of you.' She kissed his ear. 'You are quite decent, really. Apart from arriving covered in dog-shit.'

'Sorry about that. Thanks for cleaning us up.'

She laughed. 'At least you didn't ask me to clean up the journalist.' She moved her head and looked into his eyes. 'Did you find anything out about Katia?'

'Not much. I've still got some things to check.'

'Well, watch yourself. I don't want you getting beaten up again.' She glanced at her watch. 'Got to go. Can I stay at your place tonight? I've got a meeting in the centre first thing tomorrow morning.'

'Call me later. I don't know where I'll be.'

After she'd left the flat, Mavros made himself coffee and had a shower. He dressed and made the call he'd been thinking about. Then he remembered the reporter's hurried departure and turned on the television. As Bitsos said, there had been a gunfight in the parking lot of a small business centre. The death toll was now four. The camera panned down a police line. Behind it were two black BMWs with shattered windows and pockmarked bodywork. No details about the dead men's identities were forthcoming, and the usual complaints about the increase in gun crime were voiced.

Mavros went out and took a bus. On the journey to the city centre he ran though his options. One, confront Ricardo about Katia – that might earn him a one-way trip to the bottom of the sea. Two, tell the police about his suspicions of Ricardo's involvement in the murder of the man with the hooks in him. He could also ask the commander if he knew about the mysterious Father and Son, but he ran the risk of being hauled over the coals for keeping quiet until now. Worse than that, if Ricardo was arrested, he'd lose that potential link to Katia. No, he had to keep all his leads alive, no matter how unpromising they were. Three, confront Jenny Ikonomou again. He had the feeling that the actress knew more about her brother's activities than she was admitting. But how likely was it that she would condone Ricardo seizing Katia? Before doing anything, he needed more information. He hoped the man he'd called would provide that.

As the bus went up the avenue, motorbikes zigzagging around it like pilot fish shadowing a whale, Mavros thought back to the episode with the heavies last night. The one who seemed to be in charge, the one called Damis – there was something about him. The tall man hadn't reacted to the discovery that Mavros was an investigator with the suspicion usually shown by criminals. And he'd pulled his punch. Could he be the weak link in Ricardo's armoured guard?

Getting off in the centre, he headed for his flat. The streets were filled with shoppers and tourists. He turned off towards the Roman market and caught sight of the man he'd arranged to meet. Diminutive and thin, Pandelis Pikros was wearing jeans and a matching jacket that would have made most men over seventy-five look ridiculous. But even from behind the former Communist fighter had the bearing of a man who commanded respect. His hair was pure white and bristly.

'Good morning, Pandeli,' Mavros said, catching him up.

'Aleko, my boy!' Pikros stopped and seized his hand. He'd always refused to address Alex by what he saw as a foreign diminutive of Alexandhros. 'Thank God you rang and gave me a reason to get out of the house. The wife's driving me crazy. She wants me to fit new shelves in the kitchen, would you believe? I don't have time for that sort of idiocy. Why do we have joiners?'

Mavros smiled. Before he called, he'd been worried that the old man would refuse to help. He was congenitally awkward and had fallen out with the Party years ago. Since then he'd spent his time compiling a vast archive that documented the struggle of the Left. Pikros had worked with Mavros's father for years and he'd known his brother too.

'Why indeed?' he agreed. 'The workers have a right to jobs.'

The old man grimaced. 'Not that you can find a joiner these days. They're all money-grabbing capitalists who need a month's notice just to show up and give you an estimate.'

They came on to Mavros's street.

'We can either go to my place or to a neighbourhood café,' Mavros said. He was unsure about introducing Pikros to the Fat Man. They might find more to argue about than to agree on.

'Your place.' An ironic smile appeared beneath the moustache that was stained dark yellow by tobacco. 'I want to see how a successful private investigator lives.'

Mavros led him in. He opened the windows and looked around for an ashtray.

'Don't bother.' Pikros put his hand on his chest. 'I've been warned off. Apparently I've got a time bomb in here.' He gave a gruff laugh. 'I told the doctor – you'd better report me to the police then, the government's got a real downer on terrorists.'

Mavros looked at him. 'I'm sorry to hear that. Can they do anything?'

'I'm not in pain,' the old man said, sitting down. 'They've given me drugs. Which reminds me. I'd better have a glass of water to wash the next one down. I'm not allowed coffee any more either, you know. If it wasn't for the archive, I'd have slit my wrists.'

Mavros went into the kitchen and got the water. He felt bad. Pikros wasn't well. He shouldn't burden him with more work, but he really needed his help. This wasn't just about Katia. It might be about his brother too.

The old man popped his pill and washed it down. 'So, my boy, what do you need to know?' He had the archivist's trademark curiosity.

Mavros wanted to sustain that interest, so he started on the past rather than the present. 'I'm working on a case that's leading me back to the dictatorship.'

Pikros's eyebrows shot up. 'Are you now?'

'You know the actress Jenny Ikonomou?'

'I can't say I care much for the theatre or the TV, but I know of her.'

'She was in the Communist youth during the dictatorship.'

'Which organisation?'

'The main party's.'

The old man stroked his moustache. 'First I've heard of it.'

Mavros remembered what the Fat Man had told him. 'Her surname then was Zanni. She was involved with Manos Floros's group.'

'Ah!' Pikros moved forward to the edge of the sofa and rubbed his hands together. 'Manos Floros! He was one of the best.' He glanced at Mavros. 'Along with your brother

Andonis.' His expression darkened. 'The filthy murderers did for him. Tossed him into the sea like a sack of garbage. Jenny Ikonomou was in his circle?' He took out a small black notebook. 'Zanni was her family name, you say?'

'Yes. Manos Floros was tortured before he was dumped overboard, wasn't he?'

'That's right. The brave doctor who saw his body on the beach made a list of his wounds and smuggled it out to one of the Italian papers. There was international outrage.' The old man shook his head. 'The fuckers. They were worse than jackals.'

Mavros blinked, expecting his brother's face to flash up. But, again, Andonis stayed away. 'What do you know about the torturers?'

'Those cowards? Not much. Who would want to waste time on them? Anyway, I was out of the Party by then. I hadn't set up my network of contacts.'

'Did you ever hear of one called the Father?'

'The Father? As in "Our Father which art in heaven"?' The old man looked blank. 'No. I only ever heard of the scum who were put on trial. And that one who was shot by the terrorists in '74. I've never come across anyone called the Father.'

'Do you think you could take a look at Manos Floros's circle? I'm interested in Jenny Ikonomou – Zanni as was – and any other people he was close to. She was arrested. There must have been others. I'd like to know what happened to them.' Mavros caught his eye. 'And who interrogated them.'

'Who tortured them, you mean. All right, my boy. I'll see if I can find any hint of this Father.'

'And, Pandeli? If there's any connection with Andonis . . .'

The old man got up and put his notebook in his pocket. 'That goes without saying. Your mother is well? Your sister?'

'Both blooming.'

'Women,' Pikros said, with a sigh. 'They bloom, but we men are condemned to fade away.'

Mavros smiled. 'I'll see if I can help you pay for those shelves,' he said, as they went to the door.

'No, no. I don't want money for working on a hero like Manos Floros. Ring me tomorrow, my boy.'

Mavros watched the old man go down the stairs. Pikros had fought the Germans when he was a teenager and the enemies of the Left ever since, but what could he do against the power of the criminal underworld?

He walked back into the sitting-room and turned on the TV, to be confronted by a white-faced young woman who was struggling to hold her microphone steady.

'. . . something unimaginable this morning. A neighbour across the street saw a human head on the balcony of the apartment above me. According to the forensic surgeon, it belongs to a middle-aged man with fair hair and blue eyes. Police are as yet unable to make an identification.'

Mavros found himself thinking of the horrors his father and Pandelis Pikros had lived through. Their generation had fought for a better world, as had his brother's, but they'd wasted their time. People were still cutting off each other's heads, shooting each other's sons, stealing each other's daughters, and there was nothing anybody could do to stop them.

Damis was woken by the phone at midday. Ricardo had dropped him at the hotel and gone off on his own with the severed head in the boot of the Audi, giving him a hostile look. Damis knew that his comment about Mrs Chioti hadn't gone down well with him or the Son. At least the Father hadn't been there.

He'd fallen into a disturbed sleep, seeing the Russian gangster writhing in the chair he'd been tied to in the remote cottage, then his inert, headless body and the Son's sick smile. But the dream had got worse, the slumped and blood-drenched corpse suddenly topped with Martha's ravaged face. He felt himself trying to fight his way back to the real world, but he hadn't been able to surface. He was powerless to resist the compulsion that drove him to his lost lover, lowering his head to kiss her cracked and bleeding lips. Martha, he screamed. But she remained silent, imprisoned in the vacant world that the Chiotis family's pushers had sent her to.

The personal assistant's voice on the phone was business-like. 'Mrs Chioti is expecting you at the villa in an hour. Take your belongings. You'll be staying there.' She gave him directions.

Damis got ready, trying to damp down the unease that had gripped him. He should have been pleased. Only the family's most trusted people were invited to the villa. Old man Chiotis was confined there, and the best security men were assigned to it. This was what he'd been waiting for, the chance to get into the family's inner sanctum. But it had all happened too quickly. He was making enemies, not least the man who ran the Silver Lady. Antagonising Ricardo Zannis was as dangerous as it got.

He cleared his few possessions from the room and went down to the underground car park. It was deserted, the dark blue Japanese four-by-four that he'd been given in the corner where he'd left it. He drove into the sunshine and headed for the coast road, stopping halfway down the avenue to buy a newspaper. The gunfight in the parking lot was on the front page. He read the article and then made a call from the phone at the kiosk.

The traffic thinned as he got beyond the last of the suburbs. To his right the sea stretched away, its surface pale blue in the sunlight. Ships were ploughing through the water, the ridges of the southern mountains visible in the distance. For a moment he wished he was away from the trouble he was in, up on the heights with the wind in his hair. But that only reminded him of the times he had spent on the hills back home with Martha. He had to finish the job. He was doing it for her.

The road narrowed after he turned off at Lagonisi. He passed another four-by-four that had pulled into the side, two men in sunglasses watching him. They were the first of the Chiotis guards. Further on he was checked by two more men in dark suits, a chain stretched across the road behind them. There were others at the gate to the walled compound. If he hadn't been expected, there was no way he could have got close to the villa.

A servant in a white jacket was standing at the top of the steps that led to the main door. The house was a series of rectangular blocks, some connected and some separate, that had been built into the hillside. Trees and bushes had grown up against the white walls and the windows were shaded by pergolas and shutters. It was tasteful, but it was also very secure. There were no vantage points in the vicinity and no cover for snipers.

The servant showed him into a book-lined room.

'Good day,' Rea Chioti said, looking up from an antique desk. Her expression was neutral. 'I presume you don't mind staying here.'

'Of course not, Mrs Chioti.' He felt her eyes on him.

She stood up and walked towards him, her heels clicking on the tiled floor. She was wearing a knee-length skirt and a low-cut top. 'Tell me about last night,' she said, going over to the fireplace and standing in front of it with her back to him.

Damis took a deep breath. He'd decided what he was going to do. 'I didn't like it,' he said, watching as she turned to him, her face still impassive. 'Ricardo's planning was faulty. The Russian was picked up in a very public place and a lot of shots were fired. The police might easily have arrived earlier. As for the victim, well . . . I understand we're at war, but decapitating him was too much. The Son's out of control.'

'Out of control?' Rea Chioti said, her voice betraying a trace of concern. 'The Father tells him what to do.'

Damis realised he had the advantage of her. 'The Father wasn't there.'

Rea stepped back to the desk and picked up one of the phones. 'Send Ricardo in.'

Damis stood still and fought to keep his breathing regular. He hadn't expected Ricardo to be in close proximity. He saw that Mrs Chioti was playing them off against each other.

The bald man walked in with his customary arrogance. He gave Damis a disparaging look and then nodded to the head of the family. 'Good—'

'Never mind that,' Rea interrupted. 'I've just been told that the Father wasn't present last night. It didn't occur to you to inform me of that?'

Ricardo blanched. 'Ah, I . . . I didn't want to bother you during the night. It wasn't a problem. The Son did a good job.'

Rea glanced at Damis. 'I wonder about your planning, Ricardo. The shoot-out, the risk you took planting the head on the Russians' own balcony.'

The bald man clenched his fists. 'There's nothing wrong with my planning. You wanted all-out war and that's what you've got.' He turned his eyes on Damis. 'No matter what some jumped-up bouncer has been saying.'

'Be careful,' Rea said, looking at his hands. 'Damis put his life on the line. Maybe he's due for another promotion. Now, get back to work. We can expect the Russians to respond. Make sure all your people are alert to the threat.' She glanced at Damis. 'Wait outside. I'll be needing you shortly.'

Ricardo's mouth was opening and closing, as if he wanted to speak but couldn't get any words out. Damis walked past him to the door. When he was in the wide hall, he heard rapid footsteps behind him.

'Outside, asshole,' Ricardo said in a low voice. 'Now.'

Damis smiled at the white-coated servant and followed the bald man into the walled compound.

'What the fuck have you been saying to her?'

Damis raised his shoulders. 'She asked for my opinion about last night and I gave it.' He caught the smaller man's eye. 'You screwed up, Ricardo. Too much noise, too many risks. As for the Son, the guy's a psycho.' He stepped closer. 'And you're not much better.'

Ricardo drew his fist back, his face red. Then he glanced around and took in the guards, machine-pistols in their hands. 'I'll rip your guts out. And another thing. What the fuck were you doing letting that cocksucker Mavros go?'

Damis looked back at him. So Yannis and Panos had talked. He'd been expecting that. 'Do you want to cut his head off as well? He's looking for a girl, that's all. None of us has seen her.' He narrowed his eyes. 'Have you? Is that the problem?'

Ricardo was quivering with rage. 'Screw you. Mavros is finished.' He dropped his arm. 'Stay away from me. I'll be waiting, you fucking brown nose. When Mrs C gets bored with you, I'll be waiting for you.'

Damis nodded. 'It's a date.' As he walked back to the impregnable villa, he wondered what was in store for the private investigator.

Mavros tried to contact Bitsos to find out more about the gunfight and the severed head, but he couldn't reach him and had to leave messages. He paced up and down his living-room, a sense of foreboding settling over him. Where was Katia? He'd done everything he could to find her. Ricardo was involved, he was convinced of that, but the bald man wasn't going to admit it. He couldn't confront Jenny Ikonomou again until the archivist checked out what had happened to her during the dictatorship. If he pushed her too early he might scare her into clamming up. Eventually the frustration was too much for him. He took a chance and rang Kriaras.

'I've got something for you,' Mavros said when the commander answered monosyllabically.

'It had better be good.'

'It is.'

'Let's hear it then.'

'Not on the phone.'

Kriaras groaned. 'Have you any idea how busy I am? All right, where are you?'

'At my place.'

'I'm not risking being seen there. You know the road under the flagpole on the Acropolis?'

'When?'

'Half-an-hour.'

Mavros worked out how much he was going to tell Kriaras without compromising the search for Katia, then set off up the hill. As he got higher, the large neoclassical townhouses that had become hyper-trendy and ludicrously expensive in recent years were replaced by single-storey whitewashed buildings. The narrow lanes kept the number of cars down and made the area one of the most peaceful in the city centre. The flank of the citadel reared above the small houses, the blue-and-white flag flapping from a high pole.

Mavros saw the Citroën he'd been in before and went over.

'I like this place,' Kriaras said, looking out of the darkened glass. 'It's stamped with heroism. Those guys who climbed up there during the war and replaced the swastika with our flag were crazy, but at least they believed in something worthwhile.' He grunted. 'Now all that people believe in is shopping and getting high.'

'Live and let live,' Mavros said.

The commander gave him a disapproving look. 'Let's have it, then.'

Mavros took a deep breath and told him about Ricardo, the tall man and their soon-to-be-dead captive in the Audi.

Kriaras's expression was stony. 'Anything else?'

Mavros was surprised that he wasn't being savaged for the delay in passing on that information. He shrugged and started to describe what had happened to him and his client outside the Silver Lady. 'Three of them grabbed us. There were a couple of gorillas called Yannis and Panos. I saw them in the nightclub before. And there was the guy who was with Ricardo. He was called Damis.'

The commander stiffened. He leaned forward to the bull-necked driver. 'Take a walk,' he ordered, then turned to Mavros. 'Damis, you say? What happened then?'

'They warned us off and chucked us out of the car. The one called Damis gave me a pretty minor thump in the belly. Then, when they were driving off, I heard Yannis mention the Father and Son.' He was studying the commander's face, which remained unreadable. 'He said they would have given us some real pain.'

'The Father and Son,' Kriaras repeated. 'First time you've heard of them?'

'Yes. How about you?'

The policeman picked a piece of fluff from his uniform jacket. 'Why do I get the impression you're playing games with me?'

'I was asking myself the same question about you, Niko. Come on, give me a break. Who are they?'

Kriaras looked him in the eye. 'As if you haven't done your research.'

Mavros decided to give him a bit more. 'All right. They're enforcers, torturers working for the Chiotis family.'

'Anything else you want to tell me?'

Mavros went for the jugular. 'The Father was one of your lot during the Colonels' regime.'

Kriaras drew himself up. 'The torturers were in the Military Police, not under civil command.'

'All of them?' Mavros said sarcastically. 'You don't know who the Father and Son are?'

'No. There are only underworld rumours. The Chiotis family has taken great care to protect them. Not just from us, but from their rivals.'

'That's it? You're just going to let these lunatics continue shooting each other?'

Kriaras looked at his fingernails. 'There's a feeling in the government that a bloodletting is no bad thing.'

Mavros saw red. 'And what happens when an innocent bystander gets killed? What happens when young women like the one I'm looking for fall into the animals' hands?'

'The latter happens every day of the week.' The commander gave him a tight smile. 'That's why you exist, isn't it? To do the jobs we can't.'

'You aren't going to help me, are you? You're just going to stand by while the fools slaughter each other. Jesus Christ, that's cynical.'

Kriaras put a hand on his arm. 'It's realistic. Maybe you can afford a conscience, but I can't. Stay away from Ricardo and the rest of them. They're too strong for you.'

Mavros got out and slammed the door, provoking a glare from the driver, who was smoking a cigarette in the shade of a tree. The bastard police and the bastard government. They might not be as corrupt as they once were, but the result was the same. Ordinary people were left as sitting targets.

It was only as he was nearly home that the strangeness of Kriaras's behaviour struck him. The commander hadn't attacked him for keeping quiet about tailing the Audi. He hadn't even been particularly interested in the Father and Son. The thing that had attracted his attention was the name Damis. Or had he imagined that?

When he got back to the flat, he found Niki parking her car on the pavement outside.

'That's illegal, you know.'

She looked at him as if he was insane. 'Have you told the other drivers?' she said, inclining her head towards the vehicles lining the street.

'Every day,' he said, opening the street door. 'But no one listens.'

Niki came in and kissed him. 'Hello. Pleased to see me?' She kissed him again, this time pressing hard against him.

'Yes,' he said, slipping an arm round her. 'I think I might be.' He followed her up the stairs. Her backside was moving in an exaggerated way. 'Did you have a good day at the office, by any chance?'

Niki laughed as she slid her key into the door of his flat. 'As a matter of fact, I did. How could you tell?'

They fell into a tight embrace when the door closed behind them. Inching down the hallway, trying to shed their shoes, they toppled over on to the bed. Their clothes came off in flurries and landed on the floor.

'Ah!' Niki gasped, nestling his head to her breast. 'Sex in the afternoon. What can beat it?'

'Certainly not talking to stone-faced policemen,' Mavros mumbled as her legs opened beneath him.

Afterwards, he felt himself sinking away. He tried to stay in the world where girls went missing and no one cared, but surrendering to oblivion was easier. When he came round it was almost dark.

'Shit,' he said, rolling away from Niki. 'Where's the day gone?'

'Forget it,' she said, stifling a yawn. 'You've been working long hours. Give it a rest.'

'Remember Katia? The girl you wanted me to find?'

Niki touched his back. 'Calm down. I know you're taking her seriously. Maybe too seriously.'

'Dmitri,' he said, reaching for the phone. 'Christ knows what he's up to.' He rang his client's home number.

'Yes?' came the gruff voice.

'You're there.'

'Where else, Alex? You tell me to stay in with my wife and I do this.'

'You aren't planning on going out later?'

'No. Maria is cooking special dinner. I must stay. You have news?'

'No, nothing yet. I'll talk to you tomorrow.'

'See, he's behaving himself, isn't he?' Niki gave him a playful shove. 'Now smarten yourself up. I'm taking you out to eat.'

While she was in the shower, he watched the TV news. There was plenty of debate about the shooting and the discovery of the head, but nothing he hadn't already heard. Niki was right. He needed to let it go for a bit.

'Da-da!' she said as she came into the sitting-room in a short leather skirt and tight top.

'Wow,' he said, getting to his feet. 'Maybe tonight isn't going to be as much of a chore as I thought.'

Niki stuck her tongue out at him and pulled on her coat. 'Coming, lover boy?' she said with a seductive smile.

'Again?'

They went downstairs arm-in-arm. He opened the street-door and ushered her through. Following her into the cool night air, he looked across the ancient marketplace to the tall houses beyond. There was loud music coming from an open window. That was what distracted him. He didn't hear the motorbike until it was too late, the engine noise lowering as it stopped in front of them. There were two helmeted figures, the rear one holding a snub-nosed black object in one hand. As the shooting started, Mavros grabbed Niki and pushed her to the ground, his body on top of hers. He heard the motorbike rev up and then the rattling and cracking were over. The bike and its riders disappeared round the corner.

'Niki?' he said, looking down. 'Niki?'

There was blood on her mouth and hair, and her eyes were half-open. Mavros was aware of a dull pain on the top of his head, but he ignored that. He put his face close to hers. He couldn't see any sign of movement or feel a breath issue from her damaged lips.

The Father put down the mobile phone and called the Son in from the bathroom where he'd sent him during the conversation. They were in the medium-price hotel that they'd moved to after the job with the traitor. Traffic noise was coming through the loose windows, the lights of the office block across the street blazing even though few people were at their desks.

'What have you been doing?' the old man said, lighting a cigarette.

The Son stood his ground. 'What I was told to do,' he said, folding his arms across his chest.

'Don't give me that shit. You've been fucking things up.' The Father blew out a plume of smoke. 'You cut me out of a job. What other idiocy have you pulled?'

'I took a decision,' the Son said, the customary slack smile on his lips. 'This extra work is too much for you. You need to look after yourself.'

The old man staggered and dropped his cigarette on to the worn carpet.

'Look out!' the Son said, dropping to his knees. 'You'll set the fire alarm off.' He patted his hands on the floor to locate the butt. Then he froze. There was a razor-sharp blade at his throat.

The Father grabbed his hair and pulled his head back. 'No, boy,' he said, with a humourless laugh. 'You need to look after yourself. Give me a reason why I shouldn't open your jugular.'

'Because . . . because you need me,' the Son said, stretching his body upwards to put some space between his throat and the blade.

The Father drew the knife closer, making a small gash. 'I need you like I need a second asshole. Do you know how many men I've killed since I started in this business? Do you know?'

The Son let out a stifled squeal. 'Let me go, Baba.'

'It's Baba now, is it?' the old man said sardonically. 'We're all lovey-dovey father and son, are we? After you decided you were better off without me?' He pressed the blade harder and watched the flow of blood increase. 'I don't think so.'

'Please,' the Son said, his arms outstretched. 'Please, Baba. I won't . . . I won't do it again . . . please . . .'

The old man held his position. The Son's body was trembling like a tree in a hurricane. Then he stepped back, raising the bloody knife to his face. 'You're no different to me than the ones we cut up, you hear?'

The Son was on the floor, one hand at his neck and the other over his face.

'You hear that, worm?' the Father repeated, moving closer.

'Yes . . . yes, I hear that.'

'Good. From now on I'll talk to our employer and I'll decide whether you participate.' He kicked the Son in the chest. 'I made you what you are and I can unmake you whenever I want. Remember that.'

The Son lay panting on the floor until the Father left the room. When he got up, he saw that the dropped cigarette had burned into his upper thigh. The pain was nothing compared to the humiliation that had scorched his soul.

Rea Chioti stood in front of the fireplace, mobile phone in her hand. She'd been on edge all day because she'd been unable to contact the Father. She'd tried frequently, only getting the messaging service. Fear that the opposition had got to him began to mount and she'd gone to spend time with her husband. Stratos was as unresponsive as ever. She persisted in talking to him despite her certainty that he couldn't hear, whispering her fears about the Father, about the Russians, about Ricardo.

Finally, in the evening, she got through to the Son. He was full of himself, but she deflated him by telling him he had no authority to act without the Father. The Son said that the Father was ill. She knew that was a lie and when the old man came on the line, she was reassured. He was in command of the situation immediately, telling her he would discipline the upstart.

Rea opened the safe and looked at the gold mask. She'd resisted the temptation to do so earlier, even though she wanted to all day. Now was the time. If she'd seen the twisted face and sewn lips before she'd been able to speak to the Father, she'd have been crushed. She gazed at the ancient artefact and felt the strength flow back into her. The Father and the mask. Where would she be without them?

Suddenly the years were falling away. She was young again, her body firm and her mind as sharp as an executioner's sword. Her name was Roza Arseni. She was the daughter of a poor family, her father a trade union activist known to the police and often in prison. She was brought up by a grandmother who pushed her to study for the university. There she joined the Communist youth party and met him, the man she loved but who saw her only as a fellow fighter against the oppressors. Manos Floros. It was strange, she couldn't see his face. She could see the features of the woman he loved, the soft and shy Era. And she could see Jenny Zanni, who became Jenny Ikonomou, the country's favourite actress. But not Manos. He was a blank to her, his face obliterated by time and guilt. She could also see another hero, the blue-eyed and smiling Andonis Mavros. He was clear enough. The glance he'd given her at the end-of-term party had burned her. It said he knew what she was thinking, he knew that she wasn't reliable. Andonis Mavros. He'd gone from the world later.

Rea kept her eyes on the mask – the golden face with its subtle curves and terrible stillness. It was silent, the identity of the woman beneath concealed, just as hers was. No one except the Father knew what she had done. She was a traitor, a female Judas, but she was free. As soon as she understood the Father back then, saw the cold light in his eyes, she knew she was safe. Because he'd reached inside her, he knew who she really was. None of the others, not even Manos, had fathomed her. She wanted power over other people and the Father realised that instantly. He saw he could use her, but she'd used him in turn. Stratos had come to understand that. He'd given her a new life, enabled her to change identities just as he'd done for the Father. Her husband knew she had a bond with the torturer, a bond forged in the furnace of pain, but he didn't know exactly what had happened between them. It was their secret.

Rea closed the safe and stepped back, the blood coursing through her veins as if she'd had a transfusion. She was renewed, untouchable. What could Fyodor or any of the others do to her now?

She picked up the internal phone and dialled the room that Damis had been assigned.

# 13

The hospital was a picture of chaos. Family members were hunched over motionless bodies on trolleys, letting out distraught cries. Other people, some of them bloodstained, were blocking the corridors. Mavros followed the paramedics through the crowd, one hand on Niki's arm as she was wheeled into a room with a curtain down the middle. From the other side came the groans of a woman in pain.

'Niki,' he said, bending over her. 'Can you hear me, Niki?'

She remained as she had been, white-faced apart from the blood on her mouth. The paramedics had found a weak pulse before she was lifted into the ambulance and she'd been given oxygen.

'Step outside, please,' said a young doctor with his hair in a ponytail. He frowned at Mavros. 'Let me see your head.' He felt around an area on the top of his cranium, the dull ache now a sharper pain. 'You'll need stitches. I'll see to you when I've finished here.' He turned back to Niki.

Mavros went out into the tumult of the corridor and found a seat next to a disconsolate woman dressed in black.

'Ach, my boy,' she said, looking at him sadly. 'What torture they put us through.'

He nodded, putting his hand to his hair. There was sticky blood in it. He saw one of the men from the ambulance approaching, a uniformed police officer behind him.

'That's him,' the paramedic said, pointing at Mavros. 'Sorry,' he said in a low voice, as he moved away.

'What happened?' the policeman demanded. 'There was a report of gunfire.'

Mavros stood up unsteadily. 'Look, my girlfriend's in there. She's still unconscious. I'm not too good myself. Can't this wait?'

The man in blue was overweight, his face covered in heavy stubble. 'No, it can't. This is a serious matter. You must—'

'You know Commander Kriaras?' Mavros interrupted.

The policeman's eyes widened. 'Of course.'

'My name's Alex Mavros.' He took out his business card and held it up. 'Contact him and tell him I need to talk to him.' He glared at the man. 'Jesus Christ, they emptied the magazine of an Uzi at me and my girlfriend. Tell him I know who it was!'

The policeman took a step back. 'All right. Stay here.'

Mavros felt the anger drain away. 'Where else am I going to go?' He sat down heavily. That bastard Ricardo, he thought. He set this up. Or that streak of piss Damis. They didn't give a shit that Niki was with me. Christ – Niki. What did they do to her?

He went over to the door of the consulting room.

The doctor looked up, his expression severe, then pointed to a chair. 'I can't find any wound apart from this one on the side of her head and the damage to her lips. She obviously landed on her face. Lucky she didn't lose any teeth. She's still uncon-scious. I'm sending her to the radiography department. You stay here. I'll fix your head.'

Mavros watched as Niki was wheeled out. 'But we were sprayed with bullets from close range.'

The doctor swabbed his head. 'You were lucky. This gash is on your hairline so I won't have to cut your flowing locks.'

Mavros sat still as an anaesthetic was sprayed on his head. He could feel the needle, but the pain was insignificant. He thought about what had happened. The bastards aimed to miss. It was a warning, not an attempt to kill. At that range, a three year old could have wiped out a dozen people with a machine-pistol. He was relieved, but anger was coursing through him. What if Niki didn't come round? It was his fault. Not only had he drawn Ricardo's minions to them, he'd pushed her down so her head smashed into the steps. He closed his eyes and clenched his fists.

'It'll hurt less if you loosen up,' the doctor said.

Loosen up, Mavros said to himself. There would be no more loosening up. Ricardo, Damis, those morons Yannis and Panos, he'd get them all.

'There, that wasn't so bad, was it?' The doctor stepped back to admire his handiwork. 'You might need to take painkillers for the next day or two.'

Mavros got up. He didn't intend to take anything to dull the pain. It would drive him to close the case.

His mobile rang as he was on the way to radiography.

'Tell me what happened,' Kriaras said, his tone less harsh than usual.

Mavros described the attack.

'I was told that you know who did it,' the commander said when he finished.

'It's obvious. Ricardo Zannis was warning me off. He's got something to hide. He doesn't like me on his tail so he sent two of his people. But he made a big mistake. Niki's still unconscious. Who knows when she'll come round? I'm going to nail him.'

'Don't,' Kriaras ordered. 'It's too dangerous. Of course Ricardo has got things to hide. He works for the biggest criminal family in the city. You can't touch him. Leave him to us.'

'Forget it. You're just watching them kill each other, you said so yourself. If you won't do your job, then I'll have to.' Mavros cut the connection and went into the radiography department. Niki was still on her trolley, a hospital porter wheeling her out.

'Where are you taking her?'

'Neurology,' the man in white said. 'They need to do more tests. You with her?'

Mavros touched her hand. 'Yes, I'm with her,' he said, looking at her face. It was still deathly pale, the blood around her lips a blackening crust. 'Come on, Niki. It's Alex. I need you to open your eyes.'

They remained firmly closed.

The stars across the dome of the sky were bright as Damis crossed the terrace to the block beyond the villa's main building. The shutters, heavy steel painted blue, were closed and the only artificial lights were in the small courtyard outside. There was a guard with a machine-pistol slung over his shoulder about ten metres further on. He directed an inscrutable look at Damis, then resumed his patrol of the compound.

The door opened when Damis knocked. The personal assistant Maggi gave him a tight smile and led him down a narrow passage. She pressed a button outside the heavy wooden door at the end. The door swung open with a buzz.

Damis found himself in a large room with several doors leading off. It was furnished in a very different style from the other parts of the house that he'd seen. Instead of rich people's chic, this room was done in rustic style. Flokati blankets in vivid colours had been thrown over a bulky sofa and there were carved wooden chests, a heavy table and chairs. Paintings of men in helmets and oriental tunics lined the walls.

'I'm a daughter of the people,' Rea Chioti said, coming in from an adjoining room. She was wearing a green silk dressing-gown. 'I like to keep in touch with my roots.' She beckoned him to the sofa. 'Sit down and relax.' She smiled at him. 'I'm not going to eat you.'

Damis sat at the far end of the sofa from her. Relaxing was out of the question. He smelled her perfume, a stronger one than she usually wore, and saw that her feet were bare. He wondered exactly what Mrs Chioti was going to require of him.

She filled glasses from an earthenware jug and handed him one. 'This wine is from our own vineyard on the other side of the mountain. My husband never liked it – he said it was only fit for peasants – but I don't agree. What do you think?'

Damis took a sip. 'It's good. Better than my grandfather's.'

Rea was studying him. 'Where do you come from?'

'Evia. A little village in the far south.'

'I've never been to the island.' She put down her glass and looked around the room. 'Since Stratos became housebound, I haven't been anywhere.'

'Probably just as well. It isn't safe.'

She laughed. 'No, I can't even go to one of our clubs without an attempt being made on my life.' She moved closer to him, the silk of her dressing-gown making a swishing sound on the cushions. 'It's just as well you were there that night.'

He felt her eyes on him and thought about how to play this. Was she about to jump him? 'I was only doing my job.'

'You were a bouncer,' Rea said, crossing her legs and revealing well-conditioned white flesh. 'I don't know what we were paying you, but it wouldn't have been enough for you to put your life on the line for a stranger. Tell me, why did you do it?'

He tried to move further away, but the arm of the sofa dug into his back. 'Natural reaction, I suppose.'

'The natural reaction would have been to hit the ground, like all the rest of them did. Why were you different?'

Damis kept silent. He had the feeling the interrogation was only just beginning.

Rea took another sip of wine. 'All right, if you won't answer that, tell me why you wanted to be a bouncer.'

He shrugged. 'I didn't. I wanted to be what I am now. An enforcer.'

'Really?' Her eyes were on him again. 'You've got the build for it, there's no doubt about that. But there's a sadness in your eyes. A sign of weakness, maybe.'

Damis returned her gaze, his heart thumping in his chest. 'Not weakness, Mrs Chioti,' he said, trying to sound convincing. 'I'm ambitious. But maybe I've been moving too fast recently.'

She sat back, one hand on the bare skin of her chest that was revealed by the gown. 'I'll be the judge of that,' she said, her voice hardening. 'Now, as to Ricardo. What do you propose we do about him?'

Damis concealed the relief that had flooded through him. It seemed he'd passed some kind of test. 'Like I told you, he's taking too many risks. The authorities will crack down if the violence in the streets goes on much longer. That won't be good for the family's businesses, especially the drugs trade.'

'You may be right. But Ricardo's been with us for years. He's always been reliable.'

'I've seen him using cocaine.' Damis paused to see if the lie had an effect. Rea's face was impassive. 'Eventually it screws you up. And he's attracted the attention of a private investigator who's looking for a missing girl.'

'That's interesting. Tell me more.'

'I've seen a photo of the girl. She's doesn't work at the Silver Lady, so maybe it's a false alarm. But the investigator could be a problem. Alex Mavros is his name.' He watched as a flicker of what looked like recognition passed over her face. 'Have you heard of him?'

'I don't think so.'

'He's quite well-known. There were some murders on an island last year. He was on the TV and in the papers.'

'I remember that.' She looked at him. 'What sort of problem do you think this Mavros might be?'

Damis shifted his gaze from her. 'If he keeps tailing Ricardo, a big one.'

Rea's eyes narrowed. 'He's been doing that?'

'He was behind us the other night. We shook him off.'

'Well, Dami,' she said, settling back on the sofa, 'I'm glad someone finally told me. What are you going to do about him?'

'I could talk to him. Try to make him see sense.'

'Sounds like a good idea. Do it. And keep an eye on Ricardo. Without him noticing.'

He stood up. 'Yes, Mrs Chioti.'

'Where do you think you're going?' she asked, raising an eyebrow.

Damis smiled. 'You gave me my orders. I'm going to carry them out.' As he went to the door, he could feel her eyes boring into his back.

Mavros spent the night in a chair next to Niki's bed in a single room that had been found for her in the neurological wing. She'd been hooked up to a monitor, a saline drip running into her arm and another tube into her nose. He slept for no more than a few minutes at a time. Whenever he checked her, he spoke to her. She made no reaction to his voice and her breathing remained shallow.

'You should go home,' a fresh-faced nurse said when she pulled back the curtain in the early morning.

'Not till she wakes up,' he said, wincing as he touched his head.

'That looks nasty. Did you get any sleep?'

'A little.' Mavros turned on his mobile. He saw that he had several messages. 'When will the doctor be in?'

'Soon. Don't worry, we see it all the time. People tune out from the world for a while and then they come back better than ever.'

Mavros didn't find that very comforting. He went to the window and looked down over a building site wreathed in clouds of dust. Checking the phone, he saw that three of the messages were from the reporter Bitsos. Two of the others were from his mother and sister. He called them to reassure them – both had seen the TV news and recognised the outside of his flat. Then he called Bitsos.

'Jesus, are you all right?'

'I am, but Niki took a blow to the head. She hasn't come round yet.'

'I'm really sorry.' There was unexpected compassion in the reporter's voice. 'Look, can you give me a rundown of what happened?'

Mavros raised his eyes to the damp-stained ceiling and told him what he wanted to know.

'You reckon it was the guys from the Silver Lady, Alex?'

'Who else?'

'I told you to be careful. You're lucky they weren't aiming to kill.'

Mavros glanced across at Niki. 'It might well come to the same thing. I'll tell you what you can do. Print a story pinning this on Ricardo Zannis. That'll make the bastard think.'

'I can't just write what you want. Have you got any proof?'

'No, I haven't. Christ, you're as spineless as the cops. No one wants to do anything about these lunatics.'

'Get me proof and I'll print it.'

'Since when were you scumbags so fastidious? Piss off if you can't do anything to help.' He terminated the call.

'Alex?' The voice from the bed was weak and cracked.

He ran across the room, dropping his mobile. 'Niki.' He bent over her and examined her face. She was blinking, her eyes gummed up. He went to the sink and ran water on a cloth, then dabbed them gently. 'Niki, how are you feeling?'

Tears blossomed from her bloodshot eyes. 'Oh, Alex,' she said, looking around. 'Where am I? My head hurts. And my mouth.'

'Keep still, my love.' He pressed the call button. 'You're in hospital. You took a blow to your head and – what is it?'

There was a smile on her broken lips. 'You called me "my love". You've never . . . you've never said that before.'

Mavros leaned over and kissed her on her damp cheek.

The door banged.

'That's enough of that,' the nurse said with mock severity. 'You see? I told you she'd come round.' She came closer and checked the monitor. 'Good. I'll fetch the doctor.'

Mavros squeezed Niki's hand. 'Do you remember what happened?'

'No.'

'But you remember me.'

She laughed weakly. 'You're the brave knight who's come to rescue me.'

'You really have got problems.' He realised that he was trembling with relief. 'I'm sorry. This is all my fault.'

'I know,' she said, blinking. 'And you're going to pay.'

Mavros stayed in the hospital till midday. Doctors and nurses bustled around Niki. They seemed happy with her progress, but wanted to keep her in for a couple of days to make sure there was no residual damage. She was exhausted and soon fell into a deep sleep. At first Mavros thought she'd regressed to the comatose state, but he was told not to worry. He decided to leave the hospital. He had things to do that wouldn't wait.

Standing on the avenue waiting for a taxi, he saw the after-noon papers being pinned up at a kiosk. There had been a gunfight outside a bar in the northern suburbs that left one man dead and four wounded. They were Albanians. It wasn't clear if the Chiotis family was involved.

When he got back to his street, he saw a police car outside his building.

'Alex Mavros?' a uniformed officer asked, getting out.

'The same.'

'Commander Kriaras sent me. You're to have a guard.'

Mavros looked at the holes in the wall and door. His neighbours wouldn't be impressed. He called Kriaras.

'I don't want a guard, for Christ's sake. My girlfriend's in hospital and she can't look out for herself.'

'You don't get it, do you?' the commander said testily. 'That guard is to stop you doing anything stupid. Not to mention illegal.'

'I promise I'll behave, Niko. What do you think I'm going to do? Put a bomb in the Silver Lady?'

'It sounded like you were ready to do that last night.'

'Look, I was uptight. Niki's come round so things are looking brighter.'

'But you still want her protected?'

'Just in case.'

'Do you promise you won't disturb the peace?'

'Yes, I promise. Now can I get on with my life?'

There was a long pause. 'All right. But I'm warning you, don't step out of line. I won't give you any more help.'

'Yes, sir.' Mavros heard a buzzing in his ear. He passed the order to the policeman and told him where Niki was. He also gave him his mobile number. 'Ring me if anything happens. I'll be round later.'

The officer nodded and drove away.

Mavros went inside. As he was halfway up the stairs, he heard a phone ringing and realised it was in his flat. He got there in time.

'Ah, Aleko, I was about to give up,' came the archivist Pikros's cigarette-ravaged voice. 'Are you all right? I saw in the paper that you were attacked.'

'I survived. It was a warning, not a serious attempt.'

'You work with very civilised people, my boy.'

Mavros laughed. 'True. Have you got something for me?'

'I have.' The old man lowered his voice. 'But not on the phone.'

'Can you come here? I really haven't got time to come out to you.'

'Of course. Any excuse to leave this madhouse.'

'No,' Mavros said, looking out of the window. 'On second thoughts, there might be press here. Go to a café called the Fat Man's.' He told him the street name.

'Give me an hour.'

Mavros had a shower and changed his clothes, then went down to the Flea Market. He assumed the Fat Man would be taking his normal afternoon nap. He still wasn't sure about putting him and Pandelis Pikros in the same room, but at least it would be private at this time of day. When he got to the café, he hammered on the grimy door. After a while, he heard heavy footsteps.

'Go away!' came an aggressive voice.

'It's Alex. Open up.'

There was the sound of bolts being drawn.

'You bastard,' the Fat Man said, glaring at him. 'Why didn't you return my call?'

'I thought you'd prefer to see me in person.'

The café-owner turned away in disgust. 'I thought you'd been shot to pieces.'

Mavros followed him in, leaving the door ajar. 'How did you find out?'

'I heard it, for Christ's sake. One of the locals came round and told me your doorway had been used for target practice and that an ambulance had taken two people away. Bastard.'

'Sorry, Yiorgo,' Mavros said, putting his hand on his friend's shoulder. 'I had other things on my mind.' He told him about Niki.

'Shit, I'm sorry,' the Fat Man said, bowing his head. 'But she's going to be okay?'

'Looks like it.'

'Thank God for that.' Like many atheists, Yiorgos had a habit of invoking the deity in times of need.

'Hello? Aleko?' Pandelis Pikros appeared in the doorway. 'Ah, there you are.' He looked around. 'Nice place for a meeting.'

Mavros swallowed a smile and introduced the old man. 'Pandelis was in the Party,' he added.

The archivist snorted. 'Until the fools got a thirst for each other's blood and broke into warring factions.'

The Fat Man, loyal to the comrades for all his irritation with them, was unimpressed. 'It may have escaped your notice, Aleko –' he used the unfamiliar name with heavy irony '– but I'm closed.'

'Do me this favour,' Mavros pleaded. 'I'm trying to avoid cops and journos. Not to mention trigger-happy gangsters.'

Yiorgos stared at him, then went to the door and locked them in. 'All right, but I'm going back to bed. You can make your own coffee.' He lumbered off to the mattress he'd installed behind the kitchen.

Pikros sat down at a table. 'Bring me some water, Aleko,' he said, his expression serious.

'Are you all right?'

'Fine.' The old man shook his head. 'No matter how many times I go back to those years, they still get to me.'

Mavros put the glass he'd filled on the uneven tabletop. 'That bad?'

Pikros drank and then wiped his lips with the back of his liver-spotted hand. 'It's the hopelessness, my boy. Young lives destroyed, so much pain.'

Mavros sat down opposite him. 'I'm sorry. I shouldn't have—'

'You did right,' the archivist interrupted. 'These things shouldn't be forgotten. That's the problem with the national reconciliation that the politicians trumpet. The ones who died are forgotten, and the ones who survived feel betrayed.'

Mavros took out his notebook as the old man started to talk in a low voice.

Rea Chioti put down the phone and got to her feet. She walked across the study and opened the door that led to her assistant's office.

'Is Damis in the villa? He isn't answering.'

'No, Mrs Chioti. He drove out of the compound when you were with your husband. Do you want me to try his mobile?'

'No, leave him be.' Rea went back into the study. The young man would probably be watching Ricardo and she didn't want to disturb him.

Stepping across the tiles, she stood facing the fireplace, her eyes on the portrait above. The golden mask was drawing her to it, but she didn't intend to open the safe. The ancient artefact was less powerful in daytime, although recently its influence over her had been increasing. The unease that she'd begun to feel was growing. That was why she had gone to Stratos's room. Normally she only sat with him in the evenings, but she was under pressure now and talking to the motionless, twisted figure brought her some comfort. The war with the Russians, the Father and Son, Ricardo – they were all squeezing the air from her lungs.

Rea broke away from the mask's unseen power and went back to her desk. She'd brought her hand down hard on the wooden surface when she heard about the attack on Alex Mavros. She knew instantly that Ricardo was behind it. Her first reaction was to tear him to shreds. Then she thought again. She'd already taken steps to control him. Damis would handle Ricardo. There was something about the young man, a subtle intelligence inside the muscular frame. He'd already proved himself to be quick-witted and resourceful. Stratos had taught her that personal ties with trusted lieutenants were essential. That was why he had cultivated a working relationship with the Father. She'd tried to create a bond with Damis. She'd have liked to feel his hard body close to hers, but she couldn't blame him for making a hasty exit. No matter what she did to improve it, her own body was ageing and unappealing. No doubt he was also frightened of intimacy with the wife of Stratos Chiotis. But Damis didn't seem to be the type that scared easily. There was a darkness in him, a concealed centre. She could see that in his eyes. It might be a good idea to run a check on his background.

She felt her head rise towards the concealed safe. As if she didn't have enough to contend with, there was the question of Mavros. Not Alex. She wasn't concerned by a lone private investigator, no matter how much of a splash he'd made in the media with one of his cases. The family had plenty of contacts in the government and the police who could shut him up without difficulty if he became insistent. That was another reason she was livid about the attack on him. No, Alex Mavros was nothing. Damis would deal with him. The problem was his brother Andonis. How was it possible, after all these years, that a name from her youth could disturb her so much? She'd lain awake overnight, blinking to shut out the images of faces she'd consigned to oblivion years ago. Manos Floros, his Era, Jenny Zanni, and now Andonis Mavros – the look he'd given her was still raw. He'd known what she would become before she'd understood it herself. He'd known she was a traitor.

She stood up and went to the safe, then fumbled with the combination. Was it any wonder she needed the mask to protect her? She'd suffered too. Could none of them understand that? She'd endured the same pain as them, her face contorted, her eyes bulging like the woman's beneath the golden surface. At least her pain had stopped. But now it was back again.

Rea looked into the uneven eyes of the mask and swallowed a scream.

Mavros put his mobile on the table. 'Sorry about that, Pandeli. It was the hospital. Niki's latest scan is clear. They don't think there's any damage to the brain.'

'That's good, my boy.' The archivist peered at Mavros's head. 'Did they give you a scan too?'

'No. It's only a surface wound.'

'Maybe they should have. You need your head examined, getting involved with these madmen.'

Mavros raised his shoulders. 'It's what I do. There's a young woman missing and I'm not going to let those bastards have her.'

The old man gave him a sceptical look. 'What's she got to do with Manos Floros and his circle?'

'That's what I'm trying to find out. We've established that Jenny Ikonomou, or Zanni as she was back then, was in that group. And that she was arrested on the same day as Manos Floros.'

'March the seventeenth 1968,' Pikros said, nodding. 'Manos, Jenny Zanni, and another woman by the name of Era Bala were taken to security headquarters. Now, according to statements made by other inmates during the trials of the torturers after the dictatorship, Manos and the woman Era were beaten and tortured. One of them caught a glimpse of Manos in a corridor. He couldn't walk, he was being dragged along.'

'The *falangas*,' Mavros said. He'd always been horrified by the torture in which the prisoner's feet were beaten. He feared his brother might have been subjected to it.

'Yes, but that was only the beginning.' Pikros shook his head in frustration. 'Of course, none of this is confirmed in the official records. They were either incomplete or destroyed before the investigation. All we have to go on are the statements of witnesses or the prisoners themselves, which don't exist in Manos's case.'

'What about Jenny Zanni and the other woman, the one called Era?'

'Well, Jenny doesn't seem to have stayed inside for long. Her father was a—'

'High society doctor,' Mavros completed, remembering what his mother had told him.

'Well done, Aleko,' the archivist said with a wry smile. 'It seems that he got her out. He was in with the regime.'

Mavros thought about the actress's distracted look when he'd asked about Andonis. She'd suffered back then, but how much? 'What about the other woman?'

Pikros was chewing the end of his moustache. 'Gone.'

Mavros felt a stab of foreboding. 'You mean like Andonis?'

'No, no,' the old man said rapidly. 'She was sent to hospital on April the fourth. Those fuckers were good at keeping records when they wanted to. From what I can find, she was in a terrible state. She was discharged after four months. One of the comrades saw her the following September, but there's been no sighting since then. She was an only child and her parents died when she was at high school.'

'Dead end,' Mavros murmured.

'That's not all,' Pikros said, raising a hand. 'She and Manos were very close. There were rumours they were a couple even though, as you know, the youth party disapproved of such liaisons. She'd been told in the hospital about Manos's body being washed up in Rhodes. The comrade who saw her said she was a broken woman.'

'Christ.'

'Christ indeed. Not that he did her any good.'

Mavros glanced at his notes. 'Any other names?'

The old man removed a folded page from his jacket pocket.

'I made a list. Next to each name is a line about what happened to them, as far as I could trace.' His voice was sombre. 'You'll see Andonis is on there. Sorry, my boy. Your brother knew Manos Floros quite well, although they disagreed about strategy. I've left . . . I've left a blank space after his name.'

Mavros took the page, his heart pounding. He'd checked some of the names in the past when he'd been looking for traces of his brother, though he hadn't concentrated on the Floros group as there were many other activists closer to Andonis. Several of the names were followed by the dates of their deaths in Pikros's neat hand. Some had died during the dictatorship and others in the twenty-eight years since – often from natural causes, but several by suicide. The regime's poison was still working its way through the body politic.

'Who's this one you've put an asterisk by?' Mavros asked. 'Roza Arseni. There's nothing after her name.'

The archivist sat up straight. 'Yes, she interests me. From the little I've been able to find, she was very close to Manos. According to one of my contacts, there was a foursome that stuck together: Manos, Era, Jenny and this Roza. I'd forgotten, but reading through the files, I realised I knew her father. He was a good man, a union leader in one of the cigarette factories.' He looked down. 'He died in the first year of the dictatorship.'

Mavros gave the old man some time. 'I suppose it was to be expected that his daughter would join the Communist youth.'

'Yes, and she was quite a firebrand. I heard that Manos had to calm her down more than once. She wanted to go out on the streets and firebomb the tanks.'

Mavros looked at the name again. It wasn't one he'd ever heard. 'So what happened to Roza Arseni?'

Pikros had his moustache between his lips. 'She's another one I can't find,' he said, avoiding Mavros's eyes. 'She was picked up by the security police on March the twelfth.'

'Five days before the other three.'

'The boy can count,' the old man said, with a throaty laugh. 'And she was released on April the second. That was a week after Jenny Zanni and a few days before Manos was found on that beach.'

'And then?'

'And then, nothing. No one from the youth party ever heard from her again. She had a grandmother, but not even she saw Roza after that. The comrades went round several times. Of course, the old woman might have been covering for her. She wouldn't have been the first to come out of the cells having been scared off political activity for life. But they said that the grandmother seemed genuinely heartbroken. She'd brought Roza up, you see. The mother had died young and the father only had time for his work.'

'Did you check the phone book?'

'There are a couple of women with that name, but one's too old and the other's too young. No, she vanished years ago. My guess is she married and became a model mother and house-wife.'

'I'd be surprised.'

Mavros looked round. The Fat Man was lurking behind the chill cabinet. 'Why's that, Yiorgo?'

'Because she was a vicious cow.' The café owner came out into the open. 'I met her a couple of times. I saw her at a student party once. She only had eyes for poor Manos. Not that he was paying her any attention. He was in deep with another girl. I can't remember her name.'

'Era Bala,' Pikros said.

'That's her.' Yiorgos sat down beside them, his elbows making the unsteady table cant over. 'She was sweet. Very quiet, though.'

Mavros glanced at the archivist. 'Do you know what happened to her, Yiorgo? How much of this conversation have you heard?'

'You woke me up a couple of minutes ago,' the Fat Man said indignantly. 'I only heard Roza Arseni's name, you suspicious tosser. You come in here and take the place over, you—'

'Sorry, sorry,' Mavros said, raising his hands. 'Is there anything else you remember?'

'Yes, as a matter of fact, there is. Andonis was at that party as well.'

Mavros felt his stomach contract. 'And?'

'And he told me that Manos was making a mistake trusting that Roza. He reckoned she wasn't reliable, that she'd do anything to get her claws into Manos.' Yiorgos raised his sloping shoulders. 'I don't know where he got that idea from, but you know what Andonis was like. He could see right through people.'

Pikros was examining Mavros's face. 'Is this about your missing girl, Aleko?' he asked, 'Or is it about your brother?'

Mavros looked at Pikros and then at the Fat Man. 'It looks like it may be about them both.'


She was sitting at the window, watching the water that separated the island from the mountains across the strait. The surface was being cut apart by the north wind, flurries of white suddenly appearing. The walls of grey stone that led down from the ridge opposite, they reminded her of something but she couldn't place it. The uneven line that ran from summit to summit, it meant something to her. What was it? Looking down, she saw white birds, seagulls, rising from the undulating surface. There was a fishing boat with its bow to the wind, nets stretching into the depths where the fish lived, innocent of the fate that was about to gather around them. The fish, doomed and helpless.

With a jerk, she was back there, in the terrible room with the damp, stained walls, the stink of her own waste in her nostrils. A shrieking voice . . . was it hers? It was so long since she'd heard it and it sounded different – higher, more desperate. She'd always spoken in a low voice, she'd been brought up to be retiring and obedient. But now she was screaming, begging for the pain to stop.

The man with the dark eyes was bending over her, blood on his hands. 'Tell me about your Manos,' he said insistently. 'What was he planning?'

Then Manos's voice came from nearby. 'Tell him,' he said softly. 'None of it matters any more. Save yourself.'

She wrenched her head round at the sound of the blow that followed his words. There was fresh blood on Manos's face, but he smiled at her through it.

'Tell him,' he repeated. 'It's finished.'

But she wouldn't. She'd seen the marks on Manos's chest, the lines that dangled like rats' tails from the hooks that had been inserted. They'd made her watch them do it, the interrogator attaching them and then pulling on the lines while the other men held Manos down. How brave he'd been. He cursed them, he sent their corrupt lords and masters to the devil, but he told them nothing. She screamed until they stuffed a dirty rag in her mouth, one of them keeping her eyelids apart with his fingers. She saw it all. But still he wouldn't talk. Nor would she.

'You're a fool,' the torturer said to Manos. Then he turned to her and gave a slaughterman's smile. 'Hold him up,' he ordered. 'It's his turn to watch now.'

She felt Manos's eyes on her and she tried to avoid them. She needed all her courage now and the sight of his sweet face would dispel it. But she couldn't resist his power. She looked at him and felt her heart break into a thousand pieces.

'I love you,' he said. 'Forever. But you have to tell them.'

She looked down, feeling hands on her body, hands that were pulling at her clothes. The sergeant was staring at her, one hand on his groin. Then she heard him laugh. The sound stung her soul.

'You have a good body, my girl,' the animal said, unfastening his trousers. 'But your mind has been infected by the syphilis of Communism. It's time you were filled with the seed of a patriot.'

She heard Manos howl. Again he told her to talk, but she knew it was useless. They would defile her, whatever she said. Better to keep silent, never speak. For the Party. For Manos.

She turned her head away from her lover as she was penetrated. The hands on her breasts were rough, the nails splintered, and the pain between her legs was sharp. But it was nothing to what she saw to her left, her eyes bulging in horror.

In the doorway stood Roza Arseni. There was a broad smile on her lips.

# 14

After he left the Fat Man's, Mavros went to the hospital. He spent the afternoon at Niki's bedside. She came round a couple of times, smiled at him and then dropped back into the sleep that, according to the doctors, would do more than anything to get her back to normal. That meant Mavros had time to think. What he'd learned from the archivist and the Fat Man was distracting him, especially the mention of Andonis. But all it had done was provide him with another two missing women, both of whom may have been tortured. Was there a link to the Chiotis family's torturers who were known as the Father and Son? Much though he'd have liked to talk to Roza Arseni and Era Bala about the Father and about Andonis, he had to concentrate on Katia. The suspicion that the Father might have tortured his brother was nagging at him. He had to let it go. He'd established years ago that there was no reference to Andonis in any arrest records or in any of the surviving files from the security headquarters. There was no record of him anywhere after he'd disappeared. The women who'd been in the Communist youth party might have been able to help him with his brother, but they had vanished. The Father was alive and hard at work. But what could he have had to do with Katia's disappearance?

He managed to fight his way back to reality. The key to everything was Ricardo. Mavros reckoned the actress's brother could lead him to Katia and to the Father. He had to concentrate on the bald man. There was only one thing to do. He didn't care that he'd been warned off. The shooting had changed the rules. He was going to tail Ricardo, but this time it wouldn't be in his client's clapped out Lada. He called a school-friend who ran a car-hire company and got a discounted rate on a mid-range Renault.

'Are you going again?' Niki said in a weak voice, as he stood up.

'I didn't know you were awake, Sleeping Beauty.' He leaned over and looked into her eyes. 'You'll be fine here. The policeman is still outside.'

'I want to go home.'

He kissed her, avoiding her damaged lips. 'Not yet, my love.'

She smiled. 'My love. I like that.'

'I know you do. I'm going to have to ration it.'

She pushed him feebly. 'Scottish skinflint. Go and see the other women in your life.' Her eyes flickered and she sank away again.

Mavros headed for the door, wishing he could meet up with the women he was looking for – Katia, Roza, Era. He nodded to the policeman, a serious young man with a slung machine-pistol, and went out into the late-afternoon sun.

The car-hire depot was only ten minutes' walk from the hospital. He chatted with his friend for a few minutes and promised that he'd look after the car. It was a silver hatchback with only a few thousand kilometres on the clock. He'd have preferred a darker colour, but nothing else was available. He'd have to keep his distance from Ricardo.

Mavros drove to the actress's street. He found a parking space about fifty metres from the Pink Palace. Sitting there with a newspaper to conceal himself, he felt temptation rise. Couldn't he just ring the bell and ask to see Jenny Ikonomou? She said she hadn't met Andonis, but he was pretty sure she was lying. The way she'd gone into herself when the past came up suggested she had something to hide. The Fat Man and

Andonis had been at a party where Manos Floros and the other women were seen. It seemed likely that Jenny had also been there. Why was she being secretive? He tightened his hands on the wheel and told himself to forget it. Ricardo was the link to Katia, not his sister. The fusillade of bullets last night proved that.

It was almost dark when he saw lights flash from the garage beneath the Pink Palace. He started the engine. The long shape of a black Mercedes reared up on to the pavement and then turned right. Glancing in his mirror, Mavros pulled out and set off after it. He could see two heads inside, the driver with the unmistakable silhouette of Ricardo and the person in the rear seat with long hair beneath a wide hat. The star of stage and screen, he reckoned. Two birds with one stone.

The Mercedes passed through the narrow streets and joined one of the central thoroughfares. Soon it turned on to the avenue that led to the coast. Mavros wondered if Ricardo was taking his sister for a night out at the Silver Lady. He didn't think the club was exactly Jenny Ikonomou's style, but you could never tell with actors – they liked to pretend that they shared the pleasures of their fans. When the Mercedes took the Piraeus turn, he had to revise his ideas. Ricardo put his foot down and Mavros struggled to keep up. He only just succeeded, the black car being caught behind a pair of trucks as the lanes narrowed beside the railway. He followed it through the dingy streets to the port area. It swung in without warning and he realised it was heading for a ferry.

The boats on the front were for the nearby Argo-Saronic islands. The asphalt apron where they lowered their ramps allowed little space for vehicles to queue. There were enough vehicles to give Mavros some cover but not enough to suggest he wouldn't get on, despite the increased traffic in the period leading up to Easter. He remembered that Jenny Ikonomou had a house on Aegina and bought a ticket for that island after

Ricardo had driven on to the ferry. Once Mavros was onboard, he stayed in the car until Ricardo and the actress had got out of the Mercedes. They were standing on the catwalk near the ramp, so he went to the raised walkway on the other side of the hold and passed through the cabin to the steps leading to the top deck. He watched the couple as they remained close together, deep in conversation. The ferry's engines were started and diesel fumes mingled with the rank smell of the brown water. In the lights, orange peel and drink cartons were bobbing on the viscous surface.

Mavros stepped back as the actress turned towards the ferry's superstructure. When he moved forward again, he saw the ramp begin to rise slowly. As the angle steepened, Ricardo hurried down the stairs and across the ridged metal surface, then jumped down on to the asphalt beyond. The sailor by the winch shouted at him and received a dead-eyed stare in return.

Mavros swore, provoking a snigger from the teenage boy who was lighting up behind him. He watched as Ricardo passed through the gate, his arm raised towards a passing taxi. So much for tailing the bald man. He didn't think he'd been spotted, but that didn't change anything. He was stuck on the ferry, an hour and a half to Aegina and the same back. He stayed outside as the ship backed away from the quay. It ploughed through the harbour at low revs, heading for the narrow exit. The gamey smell that he'd always associated with Piraeus was still in his nostrils, but now it was cut with the tang of the open water beyond the harbour walls.

Mavros decided to approach Jenny Ikonomou. She'd gone into the saloon after her brother had jumped ship. This was his opportunity to ask about her involvement with Manos Floros and her arrest. Maybe she'd come clean about Andonis. He headed down the stairs and looked through the porthole in the wooden door. He saw the actress immediately, even though she'd pulled her hat lower. But, as he was on the point of pushing the door open, he realised that she wasn't alone. There was an elderly man in a bright red anorak sitting next to her and they were exchanging words.

Mavros stepped back. He was sure that she wouldn't open up to him in company. He'd have to wait till they arrived at Aegina. He spent the rest of the voyage in the upper saloon, watching the lights from the ships that were lying at anchor. At least Andonis's face didn't come out of the darkness like it used to. Despite the fact that the search for Katia had provided an unexpected link to him, Andonis wasn't as close as he had been. Mavros wasn't sure if that was a healthy development.

The ferry came round the point north of the town of Aegina. There was a floodlight shining on a column that had survived from an ancient temple. Mavros went outside and watched as Jenny Ikonomou and the white-haired man got into the Mercedes. He was driving. Mavros waited till the ramp came down before he went to the lower deck and got into the hire car. He was hoping the actress hadn't noticed him in the clamour of people and vehicles preparing to disembark. He'd decided what he was going to do. Since he couldn't talk to her now, he would follow her. He'd lost Ricardo for the evening and he might as well make the most of the trip to the island.

The port was brightly lit, the buildings on a curve around the yacht harbour. There wasn't much to the town and soon Mavros found himself on a road that led south. He'd been to the island often enough and he knew the general layout. It was under fifteen kilometres in length and triangular in shape. The main town was at the north-western corner. Much of the south was taken up by a mountain about five hundred metres high. The Mercedes turned left and headed for the uplands, the road gradually ascending. There was a pick-up truck between Mavros and the other car, but it pulled off in a village and Mavros was forced to drop back. He saw the Mercedes indicate right. He gave it a start and then followed up what turned out to be an unsurfaced track. The darkness was all-embracing on the mountain's flank and he could see the glow from the actress's car easily. He slowed down, aware that he was visible as well. Then the Mercedes turned right again, this time without signalling.

Mavros killed his lights and drove forward slowly. By the time he reached the place, a heavy metal gate had been closed across what looked like the entrance to an estate. He turned the car round, the springs complaining on the rough ground, and went back to a flat area he'd seen on the way. He parked and left the car, wishing he'd had the foresight to bring a torch. Fortunately there were lights on the track leading to the house. It was a large two-storey block with a red-tiled roof.

The actress took her privacy seriously. There were No Entry signs every few metres on the high wall. Mavros thought about his options. He could press the button by the gate and ask to see Jenny Ikonomou, but there was no guarantee she would grant his request. There was a good chance that Ricardo had told her not to speak to him again. The other option was to scale the walls and snoop around. Mavros shivered. It wasn't just the wind and the evening chill that were getting to him. This fortified establishment would be a perfect place to shut someone away from the outside world. Could it be that Katia was here?

He went to the far edge of the compound and followed the wall towards the west. In the distance he could see points of light on the shoreline and on the mountains across the strait. He came to a section where a tree was growing against the wall. He managed to clamber through the branches, feeling them catch his hair. When he was on the top, it was hard to see the ground on the other side. Taking a chance, he jumped. The impact jarred his knees, but did nothing worse. He was in.

Keeping to the dark spaces between the lights that had been

installed across the cultivated ground, Mavros headed for the house. The shutters on the land side were all closed. He noticed a single-storey block beyond the main building and decided to check that out first. There was a light in one of the windows, the shutters open. As he got closer, he made out a figure inside. Then he realised that there were bars across the window. Heart racing, he ran to the building. He crouched down beside the illuminated window and got his breathing under control. The silhouetted figure had hair hanging down to the shoulders. He edged forward slowly and raised his head to the bottom of the window.

The person inside was female – by the time Mavros looked, she'd turned side on. But the hair wasn't Katia's strawberry blonde and the face wasn't that of an eighteen year old. This was a person who had been ravaged by life. Her hair was grey and lank, her face deeply wrinkled. But that wasn't the worst of it. Her eyes were blinking continuously and her mouth seemed to have collapsed in on itself, the lips tightly closed.

Mavros raised a hand to the glass, but before he could touch it he felt a hard object jab into his back.

'Stand up, arsehole,' came a rough voice. 'And slowly. This is a double-barrelled shotgun with triggers so sensitive that a baby could pull them.'

Mavros did as he was told. When he was fully upright, he came face to face with the woman behind the bars.

Her eyes widened and her mouth fell open to reveal yellow teeth. She looked like she'd seen something worse than a ghost. She made the movements of someone who was screaming, her head back and her jaws opening and closing. But no sound followed Mavros as he was marched towards the house.

Damis watched Ricardo hail a taxi in the port. He followed it, allowing a couple of cars to cut in between them. He was puzzled. He'd been on Mavros's tail from the hospital. He could have approached the investigator when he was sitting outside the Pink Palace in the car he'd hired, but he'd decided to wait. Earlier in the day he'd heard Yannis and Panos crowing about the shooting outside the investigator's house – how Ricardo had given them the job. Now the tables had turned. It looked like Mavros was tailing Ricardo. That made Damis's job easier, but he couldn't leave the city so he'd resigned himself to losing them on the ferry. Then Ricardo jumped off and left his sister and Mavros on board. Had the bald man spotted the investigator?

The taxi followed the coast road to the east. Ricardo got out at the Silver Lady. It wasn't open yet and Damis was about to park, assuming that Ricardo would stay there, when he saw Yannis and Panos come out in a hurry. They got into the Audi. It was reversed round to the rear door. Ricardo appeared in the rectangle of light, a hold-all in each hand.

Damis called the number he'd been given. 'I'm sorry to bother you, Mrs Chioti,' he said, slipping in behind the Audi as it turned towards the city. 'Have you given Ricardo instructions for a job tonight?'

'No,' she said, her voice brusque. 'I'm waiting to see if the opposition have learned their lesson. You're supposed to be handling Ricardo. I hope you aren't going to disappoint me.'

'I won't,' he said, accelerating past a lorry. 'Do you want me to stop him if he takes action against the Russians?'

'I'm paying you to use your initiative.'

Damis tossed the phone on to the seat, glad that she hadn't asked him about Mavros. He wanted to keep the investigator's current location to himself. He was thinking about how to play this. Getting Ricardo out of the way was risky, but it would advance his career with the family. Did he have the nerve for it? He decided to hold off until he saw what Ricardo did.

The Audi passed to the east of the city centre and drove into the back streets above Alexandhras Avenue. It wasn't an area that Damis knew well and he found it difficult to keep the car in view. Eventually it stopped outside a bar called Bonzo's. Loud music came down the street. A pair of elderly locals passed with long-suffering looks on their faces. Damis parked down the street, angling the wing mirror so he could see to the rear.

He saw Yannis talking to a group of denim-clad youths from the front seat of the Audi. One of them pointed to a building across the street. Damis watched as Ricardo and Panos got out and went over to the street door, the bald man bending to speak into the entry-phone. Instead of going in, the pair waited outside the door. Panos lurked in a shadowy corner at the bottom of the steps.

The door opened and a bulky figure came out. Damis recognised him immediately. It was the Russian-Greek who'd been watching the Silver Lady with the investigator Mavros. Ricardo started speaking to him.

Damis got out of his car, ducking down and crossing the street. He got as near as he could.

'. . . and I can find your daughter,' Ricardo was saying.

'How do you know where she is?' the Russian-Greek demanded. 'Did you take her?'

Ricardo laughed. 'No, of course I didn't. I want to help.'

The bearded man gave him a suspicious look, then nodded. 'Very well. I come with you.' As he went down to the pavement, he caught sight of Panos. 'Wait, I know—' He fell to his knees as Panos punched him and put an armlock on him.

'Get him into the car,' the bald man hissed.

Damis knew he had to act. He stood up and went over to them. 'Who's your friend, Ricardo?'

'Don't you remember, Dami?' Panos said. 'He's the—'

'Shut up, you idiot,' Ricardo said, looking down the street and then back at Damis. 'What the hell are you doing here? This is none of your business.'

'Maybe you'd like to talk to Mrs Chioti about that. She told me no action was to be taken against the Russians tonight.' The lie came easily.

'This guy isn't one of them,' the bald man scoffed. 'You don't know what you're talking about, arselicker.'

Damis looked at Panos. 'Isn't he a Russian-Greek?' he asked. 'You saw his ID card.'

The muscleman looked confused. 'Yes . . . yes, he is.'

Damis caught Ricardo's eye. 'There you are then. He's a Russian. Mrs C said nothing happens to Russians tonight. So let him go.' He took the automatic from his jacket pocket. 'Now.'

Ricardo glared at him. 'You're a dead man. You're a fucking corpse.' He beckoned to Panos. 'Come on, jackass. Let him go.'

Damis watched as they walked to the Audi. Yannis had got out and was staring at them. The three of them slammed their doors, then the Audi pulled away and disappeared round the corner.

'Are you all right?' Damis said to the Russian-Greek. 'What's your name again?'

'Tratsou, Dmitri.' The bearded man straightened up. 'I'm fine. I can take them. They not hold me.'

Damis shrugged. 'Sorry I spoiled your fun.'

'Why do you help me?' Dmitri said, his forehead furrowed. 'You were with them the other night.'

Damis looked around. 'I think it would be a good idea of we got off the street. My car's down there. Come on. You and I need to talk.'

The Russian-Greek hesitated, his eyes on the young men who were standing outside the bar. 'Go back to your mothers!' he shouted.

Damis waited for him at the side of the four-by-four. 'Friends of yours?'

'They knew the fool who was with my Katia, the one who

was murdered.' Dmitri looked at him over the roof. 'We must follow that bald pig. He said he knows where she is.'

'That's what I want to talk to you about,' Damis said, getting into the car and opening the passenger door. 'That and Alex Mavros.'

The Russian-Greek gave him a dubious look and then climbed in. They drove off into the night.

Mavros walked into the house gingerly, the muzzle of the shotgun pressing into his back. The interior of the building was that of a typical rich man's country house from the sixties. The style was plain, the marble floors and white walls as sterile as a laboratory.

'Keep going.' The elderly man in the red anorak who'd been on the ferry with Jenny Ikonomou was clearly used to handling weapons. 'The far door.'

When they got there, he pushed Mavros to one side and knocked on the door. 'Mrs Jenny? There's an intruder. He says he knows you.' He jabbed his elbow into Mavros's ribs. 'What's your name?'

The door opened.

The actress looked surprised. 'His name is Alex Mavros, Thanasi.' She dismissed the man with a movement of her hand. 'It's all right. Mr Mavros isn't an associate of my brother's. You can lower the gun.'

Thanasis looked at his captive and gave a derisive laugh. 'You're right, Mrs Jenny. This long-haired ponce couldn't hurt a worm.'

Mavros followed the actress into a wide room with three French windows. Outside, he could see lights around a swimming-pool and rows of fruit trees stretching away. The atmosphere in this room was less frigid than in the hall. The walls were hung with brightly coloured abstract paintings, the sofas and armchairs in pink covers.

'I'm sorry about that,' Jenny Ikonomou said. 'We've had trouble with insistent male fans in the past.'

Mavros gave her a severe look. 'The woman you've imprisoned in your outhouse needs help. She's very upset.'

'She isn't imprisoned, as you put it.' The actress looked away. 'There's a nurse with her. Please sit down.'

'No, thanks,' Mavros said, stepping closer. 'Have you got anyone else locked up here? On behalf of your brother, perhaps?'

She gave him an agonised look. 'Please, I—' She broke off and moved away from him. 'There's no one else here apart from Thanasis. He's been looking after the estate since my father had it.'

'Is that right?' Mavros said, shadowing her round the sofa. 'So Katia Tratsou isn't here?'

'Katia?' She looked surprised. 'But you said she was in Italy.'

'A white lie. No, Katia is still missing and I think your brother has taken her. You know he has a taste for young women.'

The actress closed her eyes and raised a hand to fend him off. 'Please. I'm not responsible for Ricardo.'

'You're responsible for yourself. If you know he's been breaking the law, you're as guilty as he is. I'm going to search this house.'

'You're welcome to,' she said, her voice stronger.

'Really?' That wasn't the response he expected.

'But you'll be wasting your time. Ricardo hasn't been here for months. Thanasis would have told me. And Katia has never been here. I invited her for Easter, but I didn't hear from her again.'

Mavros remembered the diary extract he'd found in Katia's room in the Pink Palace. The information that the actress had volunteered squared with it. 'And as far as you know, Ricardo doesn't have her?'

'As far as I know.'

'But you don't discount the possibility?'

She reached for a packet of cigarettes. 'My brother has certain . . . certain problems. I've always tried to help him.' She blew out smoke and sat down.

'You know he runs a night club called the Silver Lady?' Mavros said, joining her on the sofa. 'I think he's involved in the gang war that's going on in the city. He also arranged for my girlfriend and me to be met by a hail of bullets outside my apartment block last night.'

'Oh my God,' the actress said, her hand at her mouth. 'I haven't seen the news. Is she all right?'

'It seems so. You do know that Ricardo works for the city's biggest crime family?'

She drew on her cigarette. 'I know about the club, yes.'

He waved the smoke away. 'That isn't all you know, is it?'

'I . . . I've had suspicions.'

'Has he ever taken one of your protégées before?'

'No.'

'You don't look very sure.'

She glanced up at him, her eyes damp. 'He . . . he raped a young woman on set once.'

'She was a fourteen-year-old girl,' Mavros said sharply, remembering what his mother had told him. 'Is there anything else you know that might help me find Katia?'

The actress kept silent.

'Nothing at all?'

'He's my brother, for God's sake.'

Mavros stood up and went to the ornate fireplace. There was a photograph in a gold frame showing two children, the dark-haired girl with her arms wrapped around a younger boy. 'What about *my* brother?' he said, glancing round at her. 'You told me you'd never met Andonis.'

'That's right,' she said, stubbing out her cigarette.

'But it's not. I've learned that you were at an end-of-term party with him in the early years of the dictatorship.' He went back to the sofa and leaned over her. 'Manos Floros, Roza Arseni and Era Bala were there as well. You do remember them, don't you?'

The actress gasped. Her face was pale and her breath was suddenly short.

'Here,' Mavros said, pouring her a glass of water from the carafe on the table. He waited till she'd drunk it down. 'Why didn't you tell me? I've been looking for Andonis since I was a kid.'

'Forgive me,' she said, grasping his forearm. 'I don't know what happened to your brother. It's true, I did meet him at youth party gatherings. I'm sorry I didn't tell you. I'm not comfortable with that part of my life.'

Mavros wasn't giving up. 'What about when you were arrested? Did you ever encounter a torturer known as the Father?'

She was staring at him, tears flowing freely. 'How do you know that I was arrested? I . . . I wasn't tortured. I told them everything they wanted to know the first day.' She started to sob. 'I . . . I betrayed my friends and . . . and then my father got me out. Manos . . . Manos died because of me.'

He put a hand on her shoulder. 'How long has Era Bala been here?'

'You recognised her?'

'No, I've never seen her before. I think she might have seen something of Andonis in me, though.'

Jenny Ikonomou dabbed her eyes with a tissue. 'It took me over ten years. After she was discharged from hospital, she just disappeared. I employed a man, an investigator like you. For months he couldn't find a thing, but I kept paying him. Finally, he traced her to a mental hospital in Thessaloniki. They didn't know her name. She'd been found in rags on the street, begging for food. She had no papers or ID. And, of course, she doesn't speak.'

Mavros looked at her in surprise. 'She doesn't speak?'

'The doctors said she was traumatised so badly that she lost her voice.'

'Can I talk to her?'

'What's the point? She can't tell you anything. Often she doesn't even recognise me.'

'Why do you keep her here?' he asked, twisting the knife. 'To make yourself feel good? Or to wallow in the guilt you say you feel?'

Jenny Ikonomou's eyes sprang open. 'You've no right to talk to me like that.'

'I'm sorry,' he said, relenting. 'I thought Era might react to Andonis's name.'

'I doubt it.' She walked to the table and picked up her cigarettes. 'You can try, but in the morning. She'll need some time to calm down now.'

'In the morning? I've got to get back to Athens.'

'You're welcome to stay the night. I'm sorry I lied to you about your brother. Thinking back to those times is very difficult for me.'

'All right. Thanks for the invitation.' He smiled at her coldly. 'Now you can tell me about Roza Arseni.' He watched as the actress struggled with herself. Eventually she began to speak. It wasn't long before he was the one struggling to contain his astonishment.

The woman at the window watched as the early-morning light spread over the mountains across the water. She didn't see the bars behind the glass, only the contours of the mainland. In the first grey of dawn the wall of rock had been two-dimensional, but now it was filling out. The watercourses and cliffs were visible despite the distance, and the ridge was clear. Its lines and undulations had taken on human form. They called it the Sleeping Woman, she remembered that now. It was true, it did resemble a full-length profile – the nose and chin, the breast, the hands folded beneath, and the raised knees. The Sleeping Woman. Like her, she was silent. A witness in stone to the deeds of men. And women.

The man's face, she thought. She knew the face that had appeared at the window. The eyes, she'd recognised them, even though one of them caught the light in a strange way. Who was he? Why had he gone so quickly, disappearing into the darkness? She'd been awake all night, pretending to the nurse that she was asleep. Awake, living the years of her stolen youth again. The party when she thought she'd achieved happiness – yes, he was there . . .

'. . . and the music's very loud,' she said, pushing through the crowd of students in the basement flat. 'The police will come.'

'Let them,' Manos Floros said, smiling beneath his moustache. 'There are enough of us to put up a fight.' Shouts came from the far side of the room and he raised an arm. 'Keep the volume down, comrades. There may be informers in the block.'

She smiled at him. 'Thank you. I have to live with my neighbours.'

He nodded and squeezed her arm. She felt the nerves tingle even more than they did when she'd brushed against a jellyfish on the island the previous summer. They'd only gone as far as Aegina during the long vacation. There was too much to do in the city now that the Colonels' iron hand had closed round the people. They slept on a remote beach, a group of them lined up in sleeping bags like larvae waiting to turn into butterflies. That had been Manos's simile and she loved it. He had the soul of a poet, even though the Party didn't encourage what one of the leaders had called 'flighty language'. They didn't encourage romantic involvement between comrades either, seeing it as an unnecessary distraction.

'Can I play this?' The young man with the shining eyes held up a recording of Theodhorakis's songs. The composer's work had been banned.

'Ask Era,' Manos said. 'It's her flat, Andoni.'

She looked at the handsome comrade. He was the son of the much-mourned Central Committee member Spyros Mavros, who'd died shortly before the coup. 'All right, but not too loud. And no singing along.' She felt the young man's blue eyes on her. They were powerful, they seemed to see deep inside. She watched him as he went to the record player. He was younger than most of them, but already he was showing leadership qualities. Most of the female comrades were in love with brave Andonis. Not her, though. She wanted Manos and she thought he wanted her. She thought, but she wasn't sure. The doubt was killing her.

'I know the words,' said Jenny Zanni, one of the young man's admirers.

'No singing along,' Andonis said, winking at Era.

'How about a dance, then?' Jenny demanded. Her thick dark hair was crushed into Andonis's face as she clamped her arms around him. He didn't struggle.

'Shall we?' Manos said in her ear, his arms slipping around Era. 'We're young. We deserve some recompense for the risks we're taking. Come, Era. Soon we'll be free.'

It was at that moment that her uncertainties vanished and she began to believe that she and Manos could have a future together. Not just in the glorious days when the party triumphed but soon, maybe even that night. Manos turned her round and looked into her eyes, his breath playing on her face. It was sweet, despite the unfiltered cigarettes he smoked. She felt a wave of heat course through her, the hairs rising on her neck and arms. Could it really be that her dream was coming true?

'I'll never leave you,' Manos said, pressing her against him. His voice was tender, but there was strength in it, as if he meant that they would outlast the regime and live forever. 'You know that, don't you, my Era? We were born to be together.'

She felt her knees buckle. His powerful arms held her upright. 'I always knew it,' she whispered. 'But I wasn't sure that you did.' She held him tight, no longer concerned if the others saw them.

'Are you feeling faint, Era? Don't let her fall.'

She looked round as the mocking voice cut in. Roza Arseni. She was sharp, she was very active in the youth party, but Era had doubts about her. Roza always looked at Manos with barely concealed lust.

'Go away,' he said firmly.

Era watched as the young woman's expression hardened. Roza didn't dare to answer Manos back. He was trusted by the senior comrades. Era thought there was something twisted about Roza. She'd mentioned it to Manos, but he hadn't shown any concern. Instead he quoted his father, a famous resistance fighter. 'The struggle brings out the best in most people, but the worst in a few. Until the heat of battle rises, you won't know who will crack.'

As the music played and they began to dance, she looked across the room, her heart bursting with joy. Andonis was still in a clinch with Jenny. There was no sign of Roza. Era smiled.

She came back to herself in the chill of dawn, blinking away tears, and looked out across the grey sea. The salt element was a source of pain to her. Manos had met his end in the water, not in her arms. She lowered her gaze. Andonis Mavros, what had happened to him? Could that have been him outside her window?

Era felt her jaws moving, her mouth forming the shapes of words, but there was no sound apart from her rapid breathing. What was it her grandmother had said?

'Speech is silver, my child, but silence is golden.'

It wasn't true. Silence was a prison far worse than a room with barred windows.

# 15

Mavros woke early and went down to the ground floor of the villa. He found Jenny Ikonomou in the large and well-appointed kitchen. She was making coffee.

'Good morning,' she said. Her eyes were puffy.

He returned the greeting.

'How do you take your coffee?'

'No sugar.'

She filled a small cup. 'Same as me,' she said, handing it to him. 'I'll make another.'

Mavros sat down and thought back to what she had said the previous evening. Roza Arseni, her comrade in the youth party, had become Rea Chioti. It was so unlikely that he'd been instantly convinced. The woman had undergone extensive plastic surgery. That was standard practice for wives of wealthy businessmen, even ones who had nothing in their past to hide. Jenny Ikonomou had met her at receptions and hadn't been fooled – after all, she had professional knowledge of how to change one's appearance. The women hadn't acknowledged that they knew each other when they were young. The actress had put her dalliance with Communism behind her and the gang boss's wife had obviously moved on too.

'Do you think Roza who's now Rea knows that you know?' Mavros asked when she sat down opposite him.

'Definitely.' Jenny lit a cigarette.

'It seems strange that she hasn't admitted it, given that your brother works for the family. You know she's been running it since her husband became incapable?'

She met his eyes and then looked down. 'I don't follow that world.'

Mavros was inclined to believe her. She'd spoken of Rea Chioti without much feeling. 'You don't keep in touch with the comrades either?'

Jenny Ikonomou blew out smoke. 'A few. My generation of so-called idealists have sold out in all sorts of ways. They've become centre-left socialists, businessmen, media personalities.'

'And actors,' Mavros said, with a smile that she didn't return. 'I was wondering if you'd heard anything about what she did when she was in security headquarters.'

The actress put her cigarette out nervously. 'I wasn't interested, Mr Mavro.'

'Maybe you should have been.' He'd checked his notes before he went to bed. 'Roza Arseni was arrested five days before the others in Manos Floros's group.'

'So?'

'It didn't occur to you that *she* betrayed you?'

'No,' she said firmly. 'I betrayed Manos and Era. I told the police everything I knew.'

'You're blaming yourself needlessly. Once you'd been arrested, all of you would have talked sooner or later.'

'Not Manos.' She caught his gaze. 'Not Era.'

Mavros realised that she needed her guilt to sustain her. 'Can I see her now?'

'If you insist.' She stood up. 'But we'll have to leave if she becomes agitated. The nurse will insist on it.'

He followed her into the walled compound. Despite the early hour the old man Thanasis was filling a wheelbarrow, his shotgun propped against a hedge. He gave Mavros a suspicious look before going on with his work.

Jenny Ikonomou knocked at the door of the outhouse. There was the sound of a key turning several times. They were admitted by a dour woman in a white tunic.

'Please don't stay long, Mrs Ikonomou,' the nurse said, eyeing Mavros dubiously. 'You know she doesn't like strangers.'

The actress led him through another door that was locked behind them. 'Good morning, Era,' she said in a clear voice. 'I've brought someone to see you.'

The haggard woman was sitting at the window that looked on to the sea and the mountains. She turned her head slowly and took in Mavros. Before either of them could move, she darted across the room and wrapped her thin arms around him. He gave Jenny Ikonomou a wide-eyed look and then held the sobbing woman in a gentle embrace. After a while, she raised her head and took in his face. Then she smiled and her ruined features were transformed.

'I told you,' Mavros said. 'She sees something of Andonis in me.'

When she heard the name, the woman let out a gasp that could almost have been a word.

'I'm *Alex* Mavros,' he said, smiling back at her. 'My brother was Andonis. Do you remember him?'

There were more sobs and mouthed words, but no intelligible sounds.

'Come, Era,' the actress said, taking her arm. 'Let's sit down.'

The woman only moved with her when she saw that Mavros was going with them to the chairs at the window. When they sat down, Era took his hand in hers, her gaze fixed on his face.

'This may be painful,' he said, hoping she could follow his words. 'I'm going to ask you some questions about the time that you were arrested.'

Era's eyes remained on him.

'Did you ever meet a man called the Father?'

There was no reaction.

'He was one of the torturers.'

She blinked hard, her eyes glazing over with a film of tears, but she made no attempt to move her mouth.

Mavros looked at Jenny Ikonomou. 'Does she ever write things down?'

'No. The psychiatrists say there's a general block on her ability to communicate.' The actress shrugged. 'And on her desire to communicate.'

'Do you remember the names of any policemen?'

Era's face remained blank.

'What about Roza Arseni?'

There was an instant change, her eyes screwing up, and her jaws opening and closing. She started to hit her thighs with her hands.

Jenny Ikonomou leaned over and held them. 'What's the point of this?' she demanded. 'These memories are painful for her, as they are for me.'

Mavros would have liked to know why the woman was so disturbed by the mention of Roza's name, but he saw he had little time. 'What about my brother Andonis? He disappeared in late-1972. Did you ever hear anything about him?' He knew it was a long shot. Era had been in and out of hospital by then.

The woman squeezed his hand and then took her own away. She composed herself and looked out of the window, her mouth ceasing to move. A last tear rolled down her wrinkled cheek.

The actress signalled to him to get up. They left the silent woman to the spectacular view.

Mavros took a deep breath when they were outside. 'I have to get back to the city,' he said, extending his hand. 'Thank you for the bed.'

She clasped his hand briefly, then walked towards the house. As he was passing the old man's wheelbarrow, she called out. 'Alex!'

He turned, surprised that she'd used his first name.

'My brother has a house in the hills above Lavrion. Thanasis has a map for you.'

Mavros took the folded paper the old man held out, then raised an arm to her.

Jenny Ikonomou didn't return the gesture. Her face was a mask of suffering.

The Son bought a cheap mobile phone from a black man on a street corner. He walked into the market area in the opposite direction from the hotel. A sultry whore, her face plastered in make-up, gave him an inquisitive look but he ignored her. Maybe later. First he had an important call to make. He went into an alley where scrawny cats were sniffing around for food and pressed out the number he'd committed to memory.

'You know who this is,' the Son said when he got through.

There was a pause. 'What do you want? I thought you only spoke to the head of the family.'

'Not any more. Listen, Ricardo—'

'No names.'

The Son grimaced. 'Sorry. Listen, the old man has lost it. He can hardly hold a cup this morning, never mind anything sharper.'

'What do you want me to do about it?'

'Can't you talk to—'

'No, I fucking can't. I've got problems of my own.'

The Son had expected a response like that. 'All right, how about this? We do a job independently to show the boss how good we are.'

'What's this "we"? She already knows how good I am.'

'Does she? That Damis guy seems to be in favour now.'

'Fuck you!' Ricardo went quiet for a while. 'What kind of job were you thinking about?'

The Son smiled. He knew he could hook him. 'Well, the Russians seem to have learned their lesson.' He lowered his voice and told Ricardo his plan.

'Jesus Christ, you've got a lot of imagination for a butcher.' There was another pause. 'Let me think about it. I'll call you later.'

'No, my friend, I'll call you. This evening. Six o'clock.' The Son cut the connection, then opened up the handset and prised out the SIM card. He threw the former at a cat that scuttled away and crushed the latter under his heel.

As he walked back on to the street, casting a glance in each direction, he considered going back to the whore he'd seen. Tonight, he thought. After the job that Ricardo wouldn't be able to resist setting up. The bald man needed to prove himself to his boss again. Maybe he'd bring that tosser Damis with him. He could go the same way as the Father. The Son shivered as he remembered what the old man had done to him, raising a hand to the plaster on his neck.

The Father had humiliated him for the last time.

Mavros made the ferry by seconds, the sailor on the ramp frantically waving him across the quay. He watched as the ship reversed away from the mole and turned northwards. To his left, the mountains of the Peloponnese stretched away. The famous Sleeping Woman looked as peaceful as ever. He thought of Era Bala, her eyes on the ridge from the barred window. She was another sleeping woman, her past locked away, but he'd got through to her. If only she'd been able to talk about Andonis. And about the Father.

He went up to the top deck, telling himself to concentrate on Katia. The house that Jenny Ikonomou had told him about was a good lead, but he'd have to be careful. If the missing girl was there, it would be a big risk to turn up and break the door down. An experienced operator like Ricardo would have taken precautions.

He rang the hospital. A nurse told him that the doctors were with Niki and that she'd had a good night. He told her to say that he'd be there by midday. Before he could make his next call, the phone rang.

'You're still alive.'

'I'm sorry I didn't get back to you, Lambi.' The reporter had left a couple of messages when he was on the island. 'I was about to call.'

'Sure you were. I was beginning to think you were in a sack at the bottom of the sea.'

Mavros looked over the side. 'Not yet. What's going on?'

'Surprisingly little. It looks like the Russians have decided to keep their heads down.'

'Very funny,' Mavros said, remembering what had happened to the last victim.

'I like to keep my spirits up. Got anything for me, then?'

Mavros thought about it. If he let the journalist in on Rea Chioti's previous identity, it would appear in the next day's paper. That might send more than a shiver through her. But even if going public put the head of the Chiotis family in a spot, he didn't think it would push Ricardo into losing his cool.

'No, I've been wasting my time.'

'You bastard!' Bitsos shouted. 'You're on to something, aren't you? You're clamming up on me again.'

'I swear you'll be the first to know.'

'Excuse me if I don't hold my breath.' The reporter rang off.

The ferry was passing between a pair of tankers, the rust-streaked leviathans riding high in the water, when the phone rang again.

'Do you recognise my voice?'

It took Mavros only a couple of seconds. 'The gorilla called Damis.'

There was a laugh. 'The gorilla? Thanks a lot.'

'How did you get this number?'

'Your client gave me it.'

Mavros felt his stomach flip. 'You've spoken to Dmitri?' The suspicions about the Russian-Greek that he'd laid to rest came to life again. Then a worse thought struck him. 'What have you done to him?'

'Calm down,' Damis said smoothly. 'Your client is fine. Call him if you don't believe me.'

'I will,' Mavros said, moving away from an elderly couple who had appeared on the upper deck, pointing towards the Sleeping Woman. 'In the meantime, what do you want?'

'To meet. We need to talk.'

'Is that right? The last time I encountered you people, there were bullets flying. My girlfriend's still in hospital.'

'I'm sorry about that. It was nothing to do with me. Listen, this is important. It won't wait.'

Mavros looked ahead. There was a pollution cloud over the city, reaching down as far as the port. 'Can you get to Piraeus in half an hour? The quay for the Aegina boats.' He reckoned he would be safe enough in the busy port area.

'I'll be there.'

Mavros put his phone in his pocket and considered his options. He could call Kriaras and arrange for Damis to be arrested. His presence in the Audi with Ricardo and the man who turned up dead on the mountainside was ample grounds. But he was reluctant to do that. The guy had pulled his punch and there was something about him that suggested he wasn't the average hard man.

When the ferry cut through the dirty water of the inner harbour, Mavros went down to the deck above the cars. Through the bustle on the quay he could see the tall man, sunglasses covering his eyes. He was leaning on the bonnet of a large four-by-four, a short-sleeved white shirt displaying his muscular arms. Mavros wasn't sure he was doing the right thing. He got into the hire car and waited for the ramp to drop.

A space appeared beside Damis as Mavros drove out. He pulled in and opened his window.

'Get in,' he said, his eyes on the other man's waist. He didn't appear to be armed.

'What took you to Aegina?' Damis said, taking off his sunglasses.

'Why do you want to know?'

'I saw you on Ricardo's tail last night,' he said with an easy smile. 'You decided to stick with his sister.'

'Who were you following? Me or Ricardo?'

'Both.' Damis laughed. 'Don't look so surprised. You're not the only one who's suspicious of him.'

Mavros was kicking himself that he'd failed to check his mirror. 'What's this all about, Dami?'

The tall man looked around. People were boarding a ferry next to the one Mavros had come in on, men in white jackets selling bread rings to the travellers. 'Listen, I can't stay long. This girl you're looking for, why do you think Ricardo has her?'

Mavros told him about Katia's stay in Jenny Ikonomou's house. 'I'm pretty sure he grabbed her there. He's been warning me off ever since.'

Damis looked at him thoughtfully. 'That doesn't mean much. Ricardo spends his life warning people off. There must be more.'

Mavros was on dangerous ground. 'The Father and Son,' he said, watching Damis's face.

'The Father and Son? What is this? A prayer meeting?'

'Very funny. You know them, don't you?'

'Do I?'

'At least, you know who I mean.' Mavros leaned closer. 'They worked on the guy you and Ricardo had in the Audi the other night. I was on your tail.'

'Until we shook you off, Alex. You don't mind if I call you Alex?'

Mavros knew he was changing the subject. 'Call me what you like. You're tied to that killing, my friend. Is that why you're looking for a way out of the Chiotis operation?'

'Is that what I'm doing?'

'Why are you talking to me?'

'Because I don't like Ricardo and I don't want an innocent young woman to get hurt.'

Mavros took in the resolute set of his face. The eyes gave Damis away. They were sensitive, not those of a callous criminal. 'What are you going to do about it?'

'Look, it may be in the family's interest to cut Ricardo loose. He isn't as reliable as he used to be.'

'You're going to set him up?'

Damis raised his shoulders. 'If that's what I'm ordered to do. At this stage I'm just exploring possibilities.'

'Explore a bit further,' Mavros said, giving him an encouraging smile.

The tall man remained silent for a while, then began to speak.

Rea Chioti put down the phone and got up from her desk. The urge to open the safe and look into the gold mask's unseeing eyes was overwhelming. She broke away and went to her husband's room. The nurse sitting by the bed left quickly when Rea pointed to the door.

Standing by the twisted body, she looked into the damp eyes. She assumed they registered little, although the doctors hadn't mentioned blindness. They were milky, the irises obscured, and they didn't react to movement or changes in the light. It would be better if he'd lost his senses. She wanted a confessor who couldn't answer back.

'I think I'm losing control, Strato,' she said in an undertone. 'We're winning the war with the Russians. Fyodor has sent a message saying he wants a truce. He's taken enough losses. But the victory is compromised. Ricardo's plotting, I'm sure of it. He's never liked taking orders from a woman and, though he didn't betray me to the Russians, he's been busy building up his power. I thought the young man who saved me from the assassin's bullets was the answer, but now I'm not so sure. We ran a check on the area he claims to be from and there's no trace of any Damis Naskos. You'd say he changed it, many people in our business do, but until recently he was nothing more than a bouncer. How could he have obtained a false identity? We didn't give him one.'

Rea looked away from her husband's motionless form. The shutters were partially open, the cypresses beyond the bullet-proof windows swaying back and forwards in the breeze. 'Perhaps I'm being too wary. If I ask Damis, I'm sure he'll tell me his real name. Anyway, he isn't the most serious problem.' She ran her tongue over her lips. 'The most serious problem is the Son. The Father's trying to control him, but how long will he have the strength? The Father's getting old, he's . . .'

Suddenly she found herself back in the cells, her breathing shallow. The interrogator was leaning over her, his hand in her groin, searching, probing.

'You expect me to believe all that, you red bitch?' he said, his eyes dark pools of hatred. 'You expect me to arrest Manos Floros and his band of whores and queers on your say-so?' He gave her a cold smile. 'Without any coercion?'

'You should do,' she said, trying to smile back at him. 'It's all true.'

There was a hint of uncertainty in his expression. 'Why are you doing this, Roza Arseni? What's in it for you?'

'That's my affair,' she said, holding his gaze. 'But I want one favour in exchange.'

'I don't give favours to Communist traitors,' the interrogator said disdainfully, but curiosity got the better of him. 'What is it?'

'I want to watch when you torture them.'

'Why?'

'Because I loved him, but he preferred her,' she said, the last words burning her mouth.

The man who became the Father nodded with what looked like approval. 'You're hard, I can see that.' He laughed coarsely. 'Let's see how hard.'

Rea came back to herself. He'd hurt her, he'd violated her, but she didn't care. It bound him to her. Not with anything as weak or sentimental as love. What she felt for the man who'd tortured her, then Manos Floros and then Era, raping the simpering fool in front of them, was cast in the fires of pain. It was founded on respect for his abilities. When she encountered him years later with Stratos, it was a validation of her life – the torturer and his victim working to the same ends. Not that Manos and Era had talked, the fools. They kept their mouths shut, betrayed no one, said nothing of the plans that only they'd known about. Manos paid for that with his life, while the woman he'd chosen disappeared into the void.

'Mavros,' she said, the name springing into her mind. 'Andonis Mavros. He went missing too, though it was later in the dictatorship. And now his brother is looking for a lost girl with a connection to Ricardo.' She touched her husband's veined hand. 'Strato, you told me often enough that there are no coincidences in our business. Have I lost my wits completely? I authorised Damis Naskos, the man with a false name, to make contact with Alex Mavros.'

Rea walked away without looking back at her husband. She

called Damis and told him to report to her immediately. To her satisfaction, the young man sounded alarmed.

Mavros called his client as soon as Damis left.

'No, Alex, I have not plans for tonight.'

'Good. There's somewhere we have to go.'

The Russian-Greek's voice rose. 'You find Katia?'

'Maybe.'

'What you mean, maybe?'

'Look, I have a lead. We'll follow it up when it's dark.'

'I see. What time?'

'I'll pick you up at nine. And, Dmitri? Don't get your hopes up. This may not work out.'

'You see the boy Damis?' Tratsou sounded enthusiastic. 'He help me, you know?'

'So I heard. Listen, Dmitri, call me if he gets in touch with you again.'

'Okay, okay.'

As Mavros drove up to Athens, he tried to make sense of what was going on. Damis had reacted to the call he'd received like a soldier to an order from a very superior officer. Mavros wondered if it had been Rea Chioti. He'd told Damis about Ricardo's house near Lavrion. They'd agreed to meet in the town at ten o'clock that night. The bald man was usually at the Silver Lady then. As for Damis's denial that he knew the Father and Son, Mavros wasn't convinced. Although the pair's existence was an underworld secret, Damis had surely come into contact with them the night he was in the Audi with the victim. Then there was Ricardo. Damis said the family was suspicious of him. What if Damis was setting the bald man up to advance his own cause?

The lorry in front stopped suddenly, forcing him to stamp on the brakes. A gypsy boy in a torn vest was on the traffic island, bunches of roses in his arms. Mavros opened his window and bought one, winking at the gap-toothed kid. Niki would appreciate the fact that the roses were red. As he continued towards the city, he thought about Damis again. Had he made a mistake in telling him about Ricardo's hide-away? Maybe all he'd done was set himself and Dmitri up. He considered going straight out to Ricardo's house, but decided against it. The bald man might have gone there when the Silver Lady was closed. If he was with Katia when they arrived, she'd be in even greater danger. He found himself trusting Damis, and he needed him if he was going to track down the Father. Katia was the first priority, though. He owed his client that.

Mavros parked on the pavement behind the hospital. He cursed himself for a hypocrite, having kicked hundreds of cars that had obstructed his passage over the years, but there were no other spaces. The hospital was as crowded as ever, patients and their extended families spilling out into the corridors. He was surprised to see no policeman outside Niki's room.

'There you are.' She stood up unsteadily, her expression anxious. 'My phone battery's dead and the public phone's out of order. I was worried.'

'Sorry. I left a message when the doctors were with you.' He gave her the roses.

'Thank you, Alex,' she said, kissing him. 'I'm sorry. I'm a bit jittery this morning. I've remembered what happened outside your place.'

'Oh, shit,' he said, putting his arms around her. 'I suppose that's good from one point of view.'

'That's what the doctors said.' She swallowed a sob. 'I'm frightened, Alex. Why did those men fire at us?'

Mavros tried to comfort her, stroking her shoulder. Her lips were less swollen and there was some colour in her face. 'They were assholes trying to scare me off.'

'To do with Katia?'

'Sort of.'

'What do you mean?'

'It's a complicated case,' he said, looking away. 'Don't worry, I'm being careful. Where's the policeman?'

'I haven't seen him today. Am I in danger?'

'No, it was only a precaution. Are you feeling all right?'

'I'm a bit dizzy. Help me back to bed.'

Mavros pulled the sheet over her. 'Do you want anything?'

'No. I'm going to sleep.' She closed her eyes. 'Find Katia, Alex,' she said faintly. 'Find her and come back to me in one piece.'

Mavros waited until her breathing was regular, then went to the nurses' office. The woman in charge hadn't seen any policemen either. She told him that Niki would probably be able to go home tomorrow. Mavros walked away and called Kriaras.

'Why have you taken the guard off Niki?'

'Because there are other priorities,' the commander said drily. 'Have you got anything for me?'

Mavros knew he should tell him about Damis and about Ricardo's house, but he didn't. The last thing that would help Katia was the police turning up in force. 'No,' he said abruptly.

Back in his flat, he spent the afternoon writing a report on the search for Katia and what he'd learned of the Chiotis operation. He left the file, entitled 'For Commander N. Kriaras', on the desktop, and then copied it on to a diskette. He addressed an envelope to his sister, enclosing a note with the diskette saying that she could decide what to do with the story if anything happened to him. He smiled when he thought how un-impressed Lambis Bitsos would be by that. Then he went to the post office and sent the package.

He was ready.


'Are you sure this is a good idea, Mrs Jenny?' Thanasis watched as the nurse led the woman who never spoke to the Mercedes.

'Yes,' the actress said, smiling at Era. 'I've waited too long.'

'Is that long-haired snoop making you do this? I knew he was a bad one the minute I saw him.'

'No, no,' Jenny said, putting her hand on the old man's sinewy arm. 'This is something I've decided to do myself. But you're wrong. Alex Mavros isn't a bad one.' She got in behind the steering wheel. 'Don't bother telling my brother I'm coming. We should be back tomorrow.' She nodded to him, then checked that Era and the nurse were strapped in behind.

Driving down the mountain, she was aware of the sun sinking behind the ridge to the west. 'Look, Era,' she said, lifting a hand from the wheel. 'The Sleeping Woman. Do you see her?' She glanced in the mirror. 'It's all right, there's nothing to be frightened about. We're going to visit someone. It'll do you good.'

Era's head dropped and the nurse took her hand.

Jenny drove to the port. She'd convinced herself that what she was doing was for the benefit of poor Era, that her old comrade deserved the chance to put the past behind her. But now doubt was gnawing at her. Was she simply doing it for her own benefit, using the silent woman to assuage her own guilt? What if Alex Mavros was right and she wasn't responsible for Manos's death? Would confirmation of that change her life and Era's for the better?

The actress tightened her hands on the wheel. This was no time to be turning back. Tonight she would free herself from the past – or put an end to the worthless performances she'd been giving ever since she escaped the torturers.

The Father was staring out of the hotel-room window at the people below. They were like ants, passing endlessly up and down the streets in lines, their heads bowed and their limbs loose; filling buses, going down the steps to the underground railway station, hurrying to work, returning home like defeated soldiers. Was this what he and his brothers-in-arms had fought for? The country had become a hive full of drones. There was no love of the fatherland, no respect, no faith. The young were empty-eyed and heartless. He thought of the Son. He was going to have to take action. The Son was weak, rotten inside like the woman who bore him. The Father remembered how she'd ended – the push, the tumble down the stairs and the crack of her head on the stone floor. After that there was no chance she would betray him. When he'd seen the Son watching from the landing, the Father had been glad. He'd thought his heir would be like him, that he could take over the business, but now he knew differently. The Son was weak.

The phone buzzed.

'Yes,' the Father answered, expecting to hear the woman's voice.

'We have work tonight.' Ricardo spoke so quietly that he could hardly hear.

'What do you mean? I don't take orders from you.'

'This time you do. The boss is otherwise engaged.' There was a pause. 'She told me to say that this is the last round in the current hostilities and that she's relying on you.'

The Father was suspicious. It was the first time this had happened. Was it a trick? Did the Son have the balls to set something up with Ricardo? He found that hard to believe. The worm had been whimpering like a child ever since he held the knife to his throat. No, the woman really must be busy. It was understandable. Her husband was dying, she was in charge of the family in time of war. He felt his lips curve into a smile. What a woman she was, what courage and ruthless self-interest she possessed! She'd had those virtues before she met him, but he'd built on them. He was the one who'd made her.

'Are you still there?' Ricardo said impatiently.

'Silence!' the Father ordered. Should he go along with it? He had nothing to lose. He wasn't frightened of those fools. He might be old, but he could take them. Hadn't he just proved that with the Son? He'd do what the woman wanted, even if the order came indirectly. 'Very well. What time?'

'Nine o'clock.' Ricardo told him the meeting-point.

The Father put the phone back in his pocket and started to unwrap his equipment. He'd bought a new stock of hooks, as well as additional probes from a dental supplier. He'd tell the Son about the job later. He had other preparations to make first.

# 16

Mavros drove the hire-car up the sloping streets and found a space opposite Dmitri's flat. The noise from the bar was less noticeable than the last time he'd been in the neighbourhood. As he was about to cross the road, a long-haired young man on a motorbike came round the corner and drove on to the pavement. It was Zak, the guy who'd told him where Katia's boyfriend lived.

'You again,' he said, recognising Mavros. 'Did you hear about Sifis?'

'I did.'

The young man's face was grim. 'Bastards.'

'You know who did it?'

'It's obvious enough, isn't it? The people who supplied him with the dope. Here, did you ever find his girl?'

'Still working on it. Why's the bar so quiet?'

Zak shrugged. 'Apparently the locals have hired a lawyer.' He looked across the road. 'Oh-oh, here comes the Russian bear.' He went inside rapidly.

'You talk to those drug-takers, Alex?'

'I talk to them because they tell me things, Dmitri.' He led his client to the car. 'How do you think I got the lead we're following tonight?'

'Okay, sorry,' the Russian-Greek said gruffly. 'Where we go?'

Mavros pulled away from the kerb. 'To Lavrion.'

'I know this place. Many camps there. I visit friends. Stinking hole.'

'It isn't the most attractive town in Greece. But Katia may be nearby.' He told Dmitri about the house the actress had disclosed.

'You really think my Katia is there?'

'It's the best chance we've got,' Mavros said, not mentioning that it was also the only one. 'We're meeting Damis in Lavrion.' He glanced at the bearded man. 'Do you trust him?'

The Russian-Greek raised his shoulders. 'I learn to trust no one, Alex.'

'Not even me?'

Dmitri laughed. 'I pay you, so I trust you a little.'

'I hope you haven't brought that automatic pistol,' Mavros said, with a frown.

Dmitri opened his jacket. 'Look, nothing here.'

'All right.'

'You trust me now?'

Mavros turned on to the avenue that led towards the new airport. 'I suppose so.'

Once he cleared the traffic in the city centre, he was able to move quickly down the motorway heading south-east. The wide prong of Attica had only been accessible by single-lane roads until recently, but now Athenians were able to speed to their weekend retreats. Mavros remembered coming out to the country when he was a child, Andonis driving the ancient Fiat that their father had bought from a friend in the Party. They used to go to deserted beaches. Dorothy was always engrossed in a book and Anna dressed her dolls in clothes she'd made, while Mavros and his brother scrambled up rocks or played football. He saw the sign to Paiania and blinked hard. It was there that Andonis was last seen, back in '72. Was there really a chance he could pick up the trail after all those years?

They came into Lavrion. The lights on the power station were flashing in the darkness, the main street filled with people engaged on the evening walk. Many of them were immigrants in cheap clothes.

'Where we meet Damis?' Dmitri asked, looking around the crowd with distaste. 'Lavrion is like Lebanon, not Greece.'

Mavros wasn't going to let the Russian-Greek's prejudice pass. 'These people just want a better life,' he said, looking at his client pointedly. 'Like you.'

Dmitri ignored that. 'There he is,' he said, pointing to the dark blue four-by-four.

Mavros drove over and lowered his window. 'Good evening, Dami.' The tall man looked uneasy. 'What's the matter?'

'Ricardo left the Silver Lady an hour ago. I tailed him to the city centre, but I lost him.'

'Was he alone?' Mavros asked.

'He was driving the Audi. You remember Yannis and Panos? They were behind him in the Merc we picked you two up in.'

'You've no idea where they went?'

Damis's face was blank. 'There's something else,' he said, looking at Mavros. 'Mrs Chioti wants me to take you to her.'

Mavros felt a jolt of surprise. 'Why?'

'She didn't say. I don't think it's a social call.'

'Shit.' Mavros wanted to talk to the woman who'd been in the youth party with his brother, but Katia had priority.

'You think they come here?' Dmitri asked.

'I don't know,' Damis said, glancing at his watch. 'It's possible. Ricardo sometimes takes his victims to out-of-the-way places.'

'With the Father and Son?' Mavros said, leaning over to the back seat for the map he'd brought.

Damis didn't answer.

'Who's the Father and—'

'Don't ask,' Mavros interrupted his client. 'We'd better get going.' He pointed to a road marked in yellow on the map. 'We follow this for three kilometres, then we turn on to the track here. The house is at the end of it. Okay?'

Damis nodded. 'You lead.'

Mavros headed out of the town, to the west. The road began to rise into hills that he knew from previous visits were bare, the trees burned to clear the land for building. They passed a picnic area called Chaos and then signs to the ancient silver mines that had provided the wealth of Athens. They'd been worked by slaves. He thought of the Chiotis family and the Silver Lady. Foreign women were no better than slaves there. Was that to be Katia's fate?

'Here,' Dmitri said, pointing to the right.

Mavros signalled and saw Damis's lights flash in the mirror. They headed up a rough track, stones clattering against the bodywork. There were no lights ahead, the flank of the hill an inky mass. Then the moon, almost full, came out from a patch of cloud and lit up the ground. It was uncultivated, the spring flowers and vegetation thick. Through his partially open window Mavros could smell a mixture of scents. They reminded him of nights when he was young. A girlfriend had a car and they used to come out to the hills and lie on a blanket, crushing the vegetation. He tightened his grip on the wheel and wondered what they were going to find in the house on the hill.

'Switch off headlights, I think,' the Russian-Greek said.

Mavros did so, looking up at the moon. It was casting enough light on the stony way ahead. Damis followed suit. They went on slowly, grinding up a steep section past a rocky outcrop that brought them on to a plateau. To the rear, about a hundred metres away, stood a two-storey white building. It was unlit. Mavros stopped and got out. Damis met him between the vehicles.

'There's no sign of anyone,' Mavros said, peering ahead. 'We'll head over and see if we can park behind the house. Turn round so that we can make a rapid exit if necessary.'

'Okay, but we'd better be quick. Christ knows where Ricardo is.' Damis gave Mavros a tight smile. 'And don't forget – we have a date with Mrs Chioti.'

They got back into the cars and approached the house. The track led round the back. They managed to park in a location that was obscured from the approach road.

Dmitri was first out. He stepped up to the house, a small torch in his hand. All the shutters were closed and there was a heavy padlock on the back door. 'Katia!' he shouted. 'Katia!' A burst of Russian followed.

Mavros took his arm. 'Keep the noise down, Dmitri,' he said, leading him round to the front. A bare terrace was enclosed by a low wall, an untended vine hanging from a pergola.

'Doesn't look lived in,' Damis said, going up to the front door. There was another padlock on it, a heavy-duty chain protruding from holes that had been drilled through the door and frame.

Mavros took his client's torch and shone it on the lock. 'There are scratches around the keyhole. I think they're recent.' He glanced round at Damis. 'Any ideas how to get in?'

'Sure,' he said, pulling a matt black automatic from his belt. 'Stand back.'

'I don't suppose you've got a silencer,' Mavros said, looking round the moonlit hills.

'Sorry.' Damis pushed them back and aimed at the padlock. He loosed off a shot and knocked the shattered mechanism away. 'Now for the door lock.'

'Let me,' Dmitri said, lowering his shoulder. On his second charge the wood splintered and the door gave way. He pushed it aside, shouting his daughter's name again.

Mavros caught up with him and put a hand on his shoulder. 'Quiet,' he said, cocking an ear. There was no sound in the house.

Suddenly the lights came on.

'That's better,' Damis said, one hand on the switch. He was still holding the pistol in his other hand.

Mavros checked the ground-floor rooms. It was a standard design, a large sitting-room to the left and a dining-room with cheap table and chairs to the right. The kitchen at the back was long and narrow.

'Ricardo hasn't spent much on this place,' Damis said, going over to an old-fashioned fridge in the corner that was emitting a loud hum. He opened the door and gagged. 'Christ.'

Mavros stepped over quickly. 'What is it?'

'You tell me.'

Bending down, Mavros saw a clear plastic bowl. It was half-full of pale, spongy objects floating in liquid. He took a deep breath and opened the lid. It took him a few seconds to identify the contents. 'Tripe,' he said, with a relieved smile.

Damis gave a grimace. 'I can't stand that stuff.'

'It isn't rotten,' Mavros said, putting the lid back on. 'Someone's been here recently.'

The Russian-Greek came in and looked at them. 'Nothing upstairs. Three bedrooms, one bathroom. I don't think anyone sleeps in this house for long time.'

Mavros and Damis exchanged glances.

'Something bad here,' Dmitri said. He pushed his head back and sniffed the air. 'Maybe septic tank full.'

'Did you smell it in the bathroom?' Mavros asked.

His client looked at him thoughtfully. 'No.'

'You would have done if the tank was backing up.' Mavros inhaled again. 'You're right, something does stink.' He went to the sink. 'Not here, though.'

Damis opened the door of a ceiling-high cupboard. The three of them gagged at the wave of fetid air that rolled over them.

'Shit,' Mavros said, taking in the empty shelves.

'I think so.' Dmitri went closer. 'There is handle on panel at back.' He turned to them. 'And lock. Is door.' He started to heave at the wood. 'Katia?' he shouted.

There was a loud creak and then the Russian-Greek's body came back so rapidly that he almost fell to the floor. Recovering his balance, he ripped away the panelling to reveal a dark space. The stench was worse.

Mavros looked down past his client. He could see the uneven surface of a wall that seemed to have been hacked out of the bedrock. Dmitri clambered through and shone the torch down. 'There are steps in stone,' he said, his hand over his nose and mouth. 'Katia?'

The three of them listened for a reply. At first, there was no noise apart from the fridge humming and the breath catching in their throats. Then they heard it, a weak and muffled sound that could have been a human voice.

'Katia?' Dmitri shouted again, his eyes wide. Then he disappeared into the reeking hole.


When the Audi pulled up, the Son came out of the ring of light around the kiosk and strode to the front passenger door.

'In the back with me,' ordered the Father, as he stepped out of the shadows.

The Son managed a smile. 'If that's what you want.'

'That's what I want.' The old man put his hold-all on the seat and got in.

'Everything all right?' Ricardo asked, looking over his shoulder from the driver's seat.

'It is as far as I'm concerned,' the Father said curtly. 'Now drive.'

The bald man did what he was told without comment.

The Son sat staring out of the window at the traffic. He was telling himself to keep calm. The old bastard suspected something. He had a look in his eye that the Son remembered from his childhood – the look that said 'I know what you've been

doing, worm'. But he couldn't know. The Son had called
Ricardo earlier, as arranged. The bald man wasn't stupid.
He'd realised how unreliable the old man had become and he
agreed they had to do something. When the Son asked how
Ricardo would explain it to Mrs Chioti, he laughed and said
she'd be so shaken that she wouldn't be able to function. It
wouldn't be long till he was running the Chiotis family's
criminal operations. The Son wasn't concerned by that prospect. All that mattered to him was that the Father was out of
the game.

The Audi approached the flank of the Parliament building
and turned left. Soon they'd be on the road out of the city to the
north, then on the motorway past the airport. Ricardo had a
place above Lavrion, he'd told the Son. That was where they'd
do it. The bald man had sent two of his men on ahead. One of
them would pretend to be the next victim. That way the old fool
would start salivating and wouldn't notice that the fish spear
was pointed at him.

'What's the matter with you, boy?' the Father demanded.
'You're panting like a dog chasing a bitch.'

The Son got his breathing under control. 'It's nothing,' he
said in a submissive voice, seeing Ricardo's eyes on him in the
mirror. 'The pollution, it sometimes—'

'For God's sake,' the old man groaned. 'I've spawned a
pathetic weakling.'

The Son gave no reaction. He'd mastered his doubts. He
knew he could do it. Soon he would be free of the Father at last.

'Is there a light switch down there?' Mavros called from the top
of the steps, swallowing the bitter liquid that the stench had
brought to his mouth.

'Wait!' Dmitri yelled. 'Yes, here it is.'

The roughly cut steps were flooded in yellow light. Mavros
followed Damis down.

The Russian-Greek was on his knees by a mattress in the far corner. 'Katia,' he moaned. 'My Katia.'

Mavros went closer. The stone walls were unplastered and damp. Over his client's shoulder he could see a thin figure in a filthy night-dress. The blonde hair was knotted and grimy, but her face, though dirty, bore no marks. His client was struggling to undo a gag with his thick fingers.

'Here,' Damis said, handing over a switchblade.

The material fell away and the young woman gasped to fill her lungs, her eyes wide. She clung to her father like a small child, staring at Mavros and Damis in terror.

'It's all right,' Mavros said, kneeling down. 'We're with your father.'

She watched as Dmitri nodded, then she started to speak in Russian. Eventually she stopped, the words replaced by a long series of sobs.

The Russian-Greek stood up, his arms wrapped around her. As he turned, Mavros saw that his beard was drenched with tears.

'My Katia,' he said, his voice shaking. 'You find her, Alex. Thank you, thank you.' He moved towards the steps, taking care that his daughter wasn't knocked against the walls.

Damis went ahead, shining the torch on the steps. Mavros stayed in the basement that had been Katia's cell. Apart from the mattress, there was only a bucket on the floor in the opposite corner. There were faeces along the bottom of the wall. Although the food in the fridge suggested there had been someone in the house recently, the captive had been forced to empty her bucket around the cell. What kind of bastard would do that to a young woman? Fighting his anger, Mavros went up to the ground floor.

He found Damis outside the open front door. He was looking down the track. The moon had disappeared behind clouds. The glow from the town was in the sky to the east, but there were no other lights to be seen.

'I needed some fresh air,' Damis said.

'Me too. Dmitri's taken Katia upstairs?'

'He's going to clean her up.' Damis dropped his gaze. 'It makes you ashamed to be a human being.'

'Certainly should make you ashamed to be associated with the fucker who did this.'

Damis raised his eyes. 'I'm doing what I can to nail Ricardo.'

'That's big of you. Do you really think the next scumbag to take over the Silver Lady will be any better?'

'Probably not.' Damis looked away. 'We should go. Mrs Chioti's expecting us.'

'Give Dmitri some time.' Mavros went upstairs slowly, hearing low voices from the bathroom. His client was speaking tenderly, Katia answering between sobs.

Mavros knocked on the door. 'It isn't safe to stay here.'

'Can you find clothes, Alex?' his client asked.

Going into the front bedroom, Mavros pulled open the wardrobe. There were a couple of men's shirts and a pair of jeans. He hoped that Katia wouldn't mind wearing what were probably Ricardo's clothes.

After he handed them in, the Russian-Greek came out.

'She wants to dress herself.'

'We have to take her to a doctor, Dmitri. Has she been eating?'

'Every two or three days they give her some muck. And a little water. She drink now, but she can't eat.' He clenched his fists. 'The animals. I kill them all.'

Mavros stepped closer. 'Was she . . . did they . . .'

'No,' Dmitri said, shaking his head. 'This Ricardo, he is pig. He give her lift, saying he take her home. Then he knock her out and bring her here. But he didn't touch her. He told her he wanted her to . . . to go with him willingly. He said the girls in his club, they do it because they have to. With Katia, he wanted her to choose. When she say yes, she get out of that hole.' He gave a weak smile. 'My Katia, she is very brave. She not say yes. But she suffer so much.'

The door opened and Katia came out. She looked better, her face clean and her hair tied back, but there was an emptiness in her eyes that Mavros knew would take a long time to disappear.

'My father told me you're the one who found me,' she said in fluent Greek, giving Mavros a shy look. 'Thank you.'

'It's my pleasure,' he said. 'Come on, we have to get out of here.' He led them to the stairs. Dmitri watched over his daughter as she walked awkwardly, both hands on the walls.

As they reached the bottom, Damis came inside quickly and turned off the light. 'There's someone coming. I saw headlights on the hillside.'

Mavros went to the kitchen to extinguish the light there. Before he did so, he saw Dmitri pull an automatic pistol from behind his back.

'Sorry, Alex,' the Russian-Greek said, catching his eye. 'I lie. Maybe now you are happy I did.'

'Take your daughter back upstairs,' Damis said. 'And don't fire unless you have to.'

In the torchlight Mavros saw that he had drawn his weapon too. 'What am I supposed to do?' he asked. 'Throw the tripe at them.'

'It'll be better than nothing,' Damis said, with a hollow laugh. 'I'm going outside. I'll take cover behind the wall round the terrace. You get under the dining-room table.'

Mavros did as he was told, his heart pounding. Was this how it was to end? As soon as Dmitri and Katia were reunited, Ricardo and his men rolled up to reclaim her? He knew his client wouldn't allow that without a fight. But what about Damis? How committed was he to taking on Ricardo? How far could he trust one of Rea Chioti's men? Then he thought of the

Father. Was there really a chance that he knew anything about Andonis? How likely was it that a notorious torturer would talk if he did? He crouched under the table, listening to the sound of a high-powered car come closer up the track. It didn't go round the back as they had done. Two doors opened and were slammed shut. He heard footsteps approach the terrace.

'Turn that torch on, Pano.'

Mavros recognised the voice of Yannis.

'Here, Yanni, the door's been—'

There was a heavy thud and the sound of a body hitting the terrace.

'Hands high, Yanni.'

'Dami? What the fuck are you playin' at?'

Mavros went to the front door. Turning on the light, he saw Damis take an automatic and a switchblade from Yannis's pockets. The gorilla called Panos was stretched out on the stone tiles.

'You!' Yannis said, his eyes darting from Mavros to Damis. 'You bastards are in this together?'

'Get inside, shithead.' Damis pushed him forward, the pistol still raised. 'Here,' he said, handing Mavros the gun he'd taken from Yannis. 'You know how to operate a Glock?'

Mavros took the weapon and racked the slide. 'I think I can manage.' He heard steps on the stair and looked round. Dmitri was standing there, his face flushed. He went up to Yannis and drove his fist into his belly.

'You do this to my daughter, pig?' he shouted, grabbing his hair. 'Fuck you!' He smashed the other man's head against the wall.

'Stop it!' Katia screamed from the staircase. 'Stop it, all of you! You're as bad as they are.'

Damis grabbed the unconscious Yannis. 'You're right.' He glanced at Mavros and his client. 'Come on, get them inside.'

They dragged the two men into the house and sat them on

chairs in the dining-room. Damis found some rope in the boot of the Mercedes and bound their wrists. 'Pity we knocked them both out,' he said. 'I wanted to ask where Ricardo was.'

'You may still be able to,' Mavros said, pointing at Panos. The muscleman was groaning, his head swinging to and fro.

Damis went into the kitchen and returned with a saucepan full of water. He dumped it over the captive's head. 'Pano, is Ricardo coming?' he said, pulling the groaning man's tie tight. 'Is Ricardo coming?'

'Dami? Is that you? What the—'

Dmitri pushed Damis aside and grabbed the captive's neck. 'I'll kill you, animal. You feel my fingers?'

Panos squealed and tried to push his chair back. His face reddened and his eyes were protruding. 'Yes,' he croaked. 'Soon.'

'On his own?' Mavros asked.

'No . . . no . . .' Panos slumped forward as the Russian-Greek loosened his grip. He looked up at them blearily. 'He's bringing the . . . the Father and . . . Son.'

Mavros looked at Damis. 'We wait, okay?'

The tall man pursed his lips and then smiled. 'Okay, we wait.'

Dmitri glanced at his daughter and stepped back from the chair. He had the look of a man who'd just won the New Year's Day lottery.

Rea Chioti was sitting in her private quarters, a cigarette in one hand and a glass of cognac in the other. She was wearing a black trouser suit, her high heels on the rug beside her stockinged feet. By this stage in the evening, she would normally have changed into something less formal, but she was expecting visitors. The first ones should have been Damis and the investigator Mavros. She'd asked the ex-bouncer why his name didn't appear on any register in his home island. He said he'd bought a false ID card from a friend. She was almost convinced. She wondered where they were, but then the thought of Jenny Ikonomou distracted her.

When the actress rang in the afternoon and asked if they could meet, Rea had been puzzled. Although she'd met her occasionally over the years, they'd never acknowledged their shared past. Nor had they mentioned Ricardo. Rea assumed that Jenny knew her brother worked for the family and wasn't interested. The actress was notorious for her autocratic manner. Rea admired that, though she had no time for people who wasted their talents on TV. What could her former comrade want? She hadn't responded when Rea asked the purpose of the visit. Maybe she'd fallen on hard times and was going to blackmail Rea about the old days. That would be a very bad idea.

Emptying her glass, Rea stood up and looked at herself in the mirror above the fireplace. The plastic surgery had changed her appearance. Perhaps the actress didn't realise she was Roza Arseni. Another thought struck her. What if Jenny Ikonomou was going to tell her something about Ricardo? Recently he'd been behaving strangely. She wondered if Damis was right. Was Ricardo no longer reliable? It would be difficult to cope without him, but that would be nothing compared with life without the Father. She considered calling the old man to find out if he was all right, then dismissed the idea. Their relationship didn't work on the level of common courtesies. If the Father had lost his grip, he wouldn't tell her. He'd simply disappear, like an elephant heading to the graveyard.

The intercom buzzed.

'The actress Jenny Ikonomou is at the lower checkpoint,' her assistant said. 'She has two women with her. According to the guards, one of them is a nurse and the other's . . . well, the other's a patient.'

'What do you mean?'

'A mental patient, it seems. She's calm enough.'

Rea felt a stir of disquiet. 'All right. Make sure they're searched.'

She pulled on her shoes and stood to her full height.

Ten minutes later the actress walked in like a queen at the head of a procession. She was dressed in a full-length dress with brightly coloured African motifs on it, her raven hair swept back in a chignon. She nodded to Rea, then turned to the two women behind.

'Come in, my dear,' she said to the one leaning on the nurse's arm.

Rea stood where she was, an icy finger running up her spine. The woman's face was ravaged, her grey-white hair lank and her eyes moving continuously. There was something about her that Rea recognised, something about the expression – a kindliness, despite the restless eyes and the tight mouth.

'Who is this, Jenny?' she asked. 'Are you doing some kind of charity work?'

The actress finished settling the woman into a chair and signalled to the nurse to sit by the window. 'Yes, you could say this is for charity. Don't you recognise our old comrade, Roza?'

Rea made no reaction to her former name. She was studying the ruined figure in the armchair. No, it couldn't be, she thought. It was impossible.

'You do, don't you?' Jenny said, walking up to her. 'Come on, think back to when you were a student. When you were in the youth party.'

'No,' Rea said, blinking back a cascade of images. 'No, I don't know this person.'

'Say her name,' the actress insisted. 'Say her name, Roza.'

'Era,' Rea said in a low voice. 'Can it really be Era Bala?'

The woman in the chair looked at her, a flash of recognition in her eyes.

'That's right,' Jenny said, taking Rea's arm. 'Come closer. She doesn't speak, I'm afraid. She lost that ability after she lost Manos.'

Rea's knees almost gave way, but she managed to stay upright. She pulled her arm away from the actress. 'Why have you brought her here?'

'It's time we all came to terms with what happened during the dictatorship, Roza.' Jenny put her hand on the sitting woman's shoulder. 'You see, until now I thought that I was responsible for Manos and Era's suffering. I told the interrogators everything, they didn't even need to touch me. Then my father got me out of the cells. I was so ashamed. All I wanted to do was forget the Party and make a new life.' She gave a bitter smile. 'But it wasn't a real life. It was empty, nothing more than a series of disguises.'

Rea shuddered as she thought of her golden mask. 'You said you felt guilty until now.'

The actress straightened her back. 'That's right. Now I see it differently. I learned something from the brother of a former comrade of ours. Remember Andonis Mavros? His brother Alex has turned up new information. It was you who betrayed us, wasn't it? You were eaten up with jealousy, you wanted Manos for yourself. But he felt nothing for you except as a comrade.' She pointed to Era. 'I took her in when I found her, but you took her life away. Have you the courage to admit that to her face?'

Rea stepped back, her hands shaking. The woman she'd watched on the table, the woman she'd laughed at when the Father mounted her, Manos screaming, trying to break free from his bonds – this was what remained of Era. She was a silent wreck, but worst of all was the expression of delight that transformed her cracked features as she stretched out her hands to Rea. After all she'd been through, it seemed she held no grudge.

. 'No,' Rea said, her voice hard. 'This is insane.' She went to the intercom and called her assistant in.

'A shame,' Jenny said, 'but I can't say I'm surprised. You've been in the Chiotis family too long to have a conscience. I remember when you were a brave comrade, Roza. Before you forgot what it means to be human.' She turned away.

Rea watched as the women left. Era gave her another beatific smile before she disappeared behind the door.

What was it like to forgive the person who betrayed you, who watched you in your bitterest humiliation, Rea wondered. Then she remembered what the actress had said. Alex Mavros was the one who'd unearthed her secrets. She'd told Damis to bring him to the house. When they came, she'd have to relive the shame again.

Rea shivered, her breath rasping in her throat. It came to her how her grandmother had comforted her when she was little, saying, 'My Roza, you're too pretty to be unhappy.' She started to cry like the innocent child she wished she could become again.

# 17

Mavros was with Damis at the window of one of the bedrooms upstairs in the house on the hill. They'd left the ground-floor lights on to give the impression that Yannis and Panos had opened up the house. Dmitri and Katia were in the back bedroom. The Russian-Greek had a frightening expression on his face. Mavros didn't even try to take the gun from him.

'Are you sure those guys can breathe with the gags you tied round their mouths?' Mavros asked in a low voice. They'd put Yannis in the cellar where they'd found Katia and left Panos tied to the chair in the dining-room to lure Ricardo and the others in.

'Yes,' Damis replied, his eyes on the moonlit track. 'You're too soft, Alex. They're heartless bastards.'

'They're your partners.'

'You think I'm like them?'

Mavros thought about the way he'd been behaving. 'No, I don't. I'm not sure what you are. Why are you putting your life on the line with Ricardo, let alone the Father and Son? Rea Chioti isn't going to be impressed if we take them out.'

Damis looked over his shoulder. He took in the Russian-Greek with an arm round his daughter, the automatic in his other hand. 'It isn't right what Ricardo did to that girl. As for the Father and Son, they're butchers. I've seen them at work.'

'So you admit you know them.' Mavros saw the pain on his face. 'What's eating you?'

Damis turned to him. 'The woman I loved. Martha. She . . .

the drugs took her. I tried to get her off them, but she didn't make it.'

'She died?'

'Worse. She lost her mind. She doesn't even know me.'

Mavros moved closer. 'What are you saying, Dami? You're in this to get back at the people who traffic the shit?'

'There's something wrong with that? The Chiotis family have ruined plenty of lives apart from Martha's.'

Things fell into place – the punch that Damis had pulled, the way he'd made contact with Mavros and his client, his easy familiarity with weapons. 'You're an undercover cop, aren't you?'

'I can't answer that,' Damis said, his eyes locked on the track and the rocky outcrop beyond.

'You just did.' Mavros felt a wave of relief wash over him. 'Why don't you call for back-up?'

Damis shrugged. 'You know what would happen. The idiots would send in an army. They'd blow my cover and I'm not ready for that. I want to do as much damage as I can. That means putting the squeeze on Rea Chioti.' He shook his head. 'I don't trust my own people. The Chiotis family has bought plenty of them.'

'Does Nikos Kriaras know about you?'

'The new commander?' Damis moved his face closer to the glass. 'I imagine so. I don't know him. Do you?'

'Yes.'

'Do you trust him?'

'Not really.'

'Let's hope he isn't one of the family's men.' Damis raised a hand. 'I can hear a car.'

Mavros could too. He watched as a double beam of light shone up into the sky above the rock. 'They're coming.'

Damis nodded. 'Let's get downstairs.'

'Remember what we agreed, Dmitri,' Mavros said to his client on the way to the stair. 'Whatever happens, you stay up here with Katia.' He took in the young woman's wan face and wished he could have got her out of the house. But Katia gave him an encouraging smile, her arm round her father's broad back. She looked exhausted, but there was no sign of fear in her eyes.

Mavros hoped the same could be said of his.

The Father looked at the Son as the Audi came round the corner and headed up the track to the house. Although his offspring had the usual loose smile on his lips, there was an air of tension about him that confirmed the Father's suspicions. The fool was planning something and Ricardo was in on it.

'They're here,' the bald man said from behind the wheel. 'That's the car. I don't know why Yannis hasn't been answering his phone.'

The Father took out his mobile. 'No signal up here.'

'Ah,' Ricardo said, his shoulders relaxing. 'I thought something had happened to them.' He pulled up behind the Mercedes and looked round. 'They'll have the Russian trussed up ready for you,' he said to the Father.

The old man took the bag with his tools in one hand. 'Let's proceed, then,' he said, opening his door.

The Son stood at the steps leading to the terrace. 'Nice place you've got here, Ricardo,' he said ironically. 'You didn't think of planting trees to make it a bit more homely?'

'I think you'll find it's homely enough inside.' The bald man moved round the car. 'After you,' he said to the Father, extending his arm.

'No, after you,' the old man replied, watching them. The look that passed between the Son and Ricardo was the final proof. The Father saw the guilt in their eyes. He put his right hand into his jacket pocket and felt the butt of his service revolver. It was a long time since he'd used it, but he kept it in perfect condition.

Ricardo and the Son crossed the terrace close together.

The bald man walked in the open door. 'Yanni? Pano? Where are you?'

'In here,' came a deep voice from the room to the right.

The Son looked over his shoulder and smiled nervously.

The Father waved him forward, his breathing controlled and his heartbeat no faster than usual. He could handle whatever the fools threw at him. He'd been up against better men than them, he'd brought down the people who tried to destroy the nation.

Going inside, he closed the door behind him. The moment he noticed the splintered wood around the lock, he heard a footstep in the room to his left. The Father pulled the gun from his pocket, slipped off the safety and thumbed back the hammer.

Mavros stood up from behind the chair where Panos sat bound and gagged. He pointed the Glock at Ricardo and the heavily built young man who had come into the room behind him.

'What the fuck?' the bald man said, staring at him. 'Mavros?'

The shot from the hallway made all the men in the room flinch. There was a shout, the slam of a door, and then the sound of footsteps outside.

'Stay where you are!' Mavros shouted, pointing the automatic at Ricardo. He heard a car start and then reverse away at speed. Ricardo and the other man had frozen, the former with his hand hovering above his chest and the latter still clutching a hold-all. 'Drop the bag and raise your arms.'

They complied, the hold-all landing with a thud on the wooden floor.

Damis came in. 'He got away,' he said, shaking his head. 'He almost hit me. Lucky I pulled back at the last moment.' He took in the two men. 'Ricardo and the Son,' he said, running a hand over the bald man and removing an automatic from his jacket pocket. He did the same with the younger man and came up with a folded knife. He kicked the bag away. 'Did you bring your fish spear tonight, asshole?'

The Son gave a slack smile. 'I never go anywhere without it.'

Damis smiled back at him and then punched him in the midriff. The Son dropped to one knee, his face creased. 'I've been wanting to do that since I first laid eyes on you.'

Mavros looked beyond them. Dmitri had appeared in the doorway, his expression savage. Katia was behind him.

'No, Papa!' the young woman said, trying to get past him. She was held back by his arm. 'No! We must call the police.'

The Russian-Greek looked at Ricardo. 'You and I are going down to the cellar where you kept my Katia.'

The bald man turned to Mavros. 'You . . . you can't let him do that.'

'Give me a reason.'

'I . . . I'll pay.' His eyes moved from Mavros to Dmitri, but they kept off Katia. 'I'll pay you all. For God's sake, stop him. You can't—'

There was the sound of breaking glass, immediately followed by a gunshot. Damis dropped like a stone. Mavros was immediately flattened by the weight of the Son, the Glock knocked away and a hand clawing at his throat. Katia screamed, her hands over her ears, as her father disappeared down the hallway. As more shots rang out, Ricardo grabbed Katia by the shoulders.

'Shut up, you bitch!' he screamed, his hand drawn back.

'Don't,' ordered the Father from the doorway as Dmitri backed into the room with his hands raised. 'You,' he said to the Son. 'Get up and find a weapon.'

Mavros felt the weight roll off him and he gasped for breath. He looked across at Damis and saw no movement. There was a splash of blood on the floor around his head.

'Who's he?' the Father asked, pointing at the bound man in the chair. 'A Russian?'

'No, he's one of mine.' Ricardo pushed Dmitri against the wall. 'Did you really think you could beat me, you piece of shit?'

'You'd better untie him,' the Father said, his eyes still on Panos.

'Screw him,' the bald man said, looking round at the Son. 'Get your spear out. I want you to use it on this fucker.' He laughed. 'You can use it on all of them.' He glanced at the Father. 'Unless, of course, you want to string them up with your hooks and lines first.' He grabbed Katia's arm. 'Not this one, though. She's mine.'

The Son put down the automatic and emptied the contents of his bag on to the table. Mavros flinched when he saw the gleaming steel spear.

'Wait,' the Father said, kicking his own bag across to the Son. 'There are things we need to find out from these people.' He looked at Mavros. 'Who are you?'

Mavros watched in horror as the Son took out a cluster of fish hooks and a spool of line from the second hold-all. He looked back at the old man. This was his chance. 'The name's Alex Mavros,' he said, his mouth dry. He thought he saw a hint of recognition in the Father's eyes. 'My brother was Andonis Mavros, the resistance leader during the dictatorship. Did you ever torture him?'

The old man licked his lips. 'You aren't in a position to ask me questions,' he said in a cold voice. He looked at the Son. 'Be careful with those probes, you fool. They're new.'

Everyone in the room looked at the pointed implements. Everyone except Damis, whose eyes were sticky with blood.

That didn't stop him loosing off a series of shots from the weapon he'd fallen on.

Rea was standing over her husband. She'd sent the nurse away, telling her that she would stay with him for the next two hours.

But she knew she wouldn't be in the bedroom for as long as that.

Everything was at an end, she thought. Stratos's life was ebbing away, but it had been for months. It was only tonight that she'd realised hers was over as well. It was built on a lie, deep down she'd always known that. She'd thought she was hard and unfeeling like the Father. But seeing the woman she'd betrayed, the woman whose life she'd ruined, whose degradation she'd taken pleasure from and whose voice she'd silenced, had made her see that she was weak.

She leaned closer and looked at her husband's milky eyes. The lids closed slowly and then opened again. She wondered if that was an attempt to communicate.

'You're ready, aren't you?' Rea said in a low voice. 'I am too. This is a world of pain. You taught me that the only way to escape pain was to hurt other people, to live from their misery. I knew that before I met you. It was in my character. I drank it in, growing up in the parts of the city where poor people slaved to stay alive. Then the Father showed me that pain was power. I understood that instinctively. You showed me that human weakness is the other part of the equation – weakness for drugs, for sex, for status, for anything that can be sold.' She touched his scrawny arm. 'But it's all a lie.' She felt tears on her cheeks. 'My old comrade Era lives in agony. She lost everything, but she hasn't become like us.' She saw her husband's eyes flicker and realised that she was gripping his arm hard. 'You and I are monsters. The Father's a monster. We don't deserve to live.'

Rea let her husband's arm go. She pulled back the sheet and ran her eyes over his twisted limbs. This deformed body was what he'd earned from a lifetime of cruelty and violence. As she put the pillow over his face and pressed down on it, she thought of his victims – the drug-addicts, the dancers and prostitutes, the assassinated gang-members, the politicians and policemen he'd corrupted, the civil servants he'd bribed, the families that mourned. At least she was making some recompense for the suffering he'd caused.

When her husband's feeble struggles stopped, Rea went out of the bedroom. She crossed the terrace to the main block, vaguely aware that there was moonlight on the flagstones. When she was young she'd loved the moon. She caught a glimpse of herself walking back from a youth party meeting with the silvery light on her face, her heart full of revolutionary dreams. That must have been before the agony had started, before the jealousy she felt for poor, innocent Era had poisoned her. She'd always carried a seed of guilt. Why else had she chosen to call herself Rea when she changed her identity? Something in the depths of her being had made her take the name that was an anagram of Era, though she'd never admitted it to herself. Rea and Era. They were the same ruined creatures.

She went into the study and locked the door. Kicking off her shoes, she took the phones off the hook and switched off her mobiles. Then she stepped over to the fireplace and opened the safe behind the painting.

Rea looked at the mask, the blood freezing in her veins as she took in the bulging eyes and the disfigured face. She'd taken the woman beneath the carefully worked surface to be an image of herself, lips sewn to keep the past secret. But now she understood that the golden silence was not hers. It belonged to Era and all the other strong souls who hadn't allowed the pain of life to defeat them.

The head of the Chiotis family took the mask from the safe and went to the centre of the room. After she'd lain down, she placed the cold metal over her face. Then, in a decisive movement, she drew her husband's razor across her throat.

The room resounded with the shots, and then with shouts and screams. Damis let go of the automatic when the clip was emptied, his head slumping to the floor again. Mavros reached for the Glock. The Son was staring at a spatter of red on his lower arm. The Father stood motionless, his revolver pointed at Katia and the automatic he'd taken from Dmitri pointing at Damis.

'I'll kill them all,' the old man said to Mavros, showing uneven teeth beneath the nicotine-stained moustache. He glanced at Ricardo. He was flat on the floor, his chest a basin of blood. He looked back at Mavros. 'Put the weapon down.'

Mavros stepped back, empty-handed.

'Which one shall I do first?' the Son said, lifting the spear with his good hand.

'Wait, fool,' the Father said. 'We need to find out what's going on here.' He was still looking at Mavros. 'You think I know something about your brother, do you?' He gave a bitter laugh. 'Have you any idea how many of those Communist scum I worked on?'

Mavros took a deep breath. 'Tell me if Andonis was one of them. Please.'

The Father held his gaze. 'No.'

'No, he wasn't one of them or no, you're not going to tell me?' Mavros asked, his voice breaking.

The Father glanced at Damis. 'Check that he's dead,' he said to the Son.

Mavros gave an agonised groan when he realised he wasn't going to get an answer. He watched as the Son knelt down and rolled Damis over. There was blood all over his face. What happened next was so quick that the Father couldn't react in time. There was a crash as the Son was pulled head first to the floor, then Damis manoeuvred him in front as a shield. He'd grabbed the spear and was holding it to the Son's throat.

The Father still had one gun on Katia. The other was now on Mavros. 'You took a risk, young man,' he said to Damis, his voice level. 'How did you know I wouldn't shoot?'

'Because you aren't a killer,' Damis said, breathing heavily. 'This bastard is, but you aren't. You prefer to watch people suffer.'

Mavros looked at Damis. The shot that had come in the window must only have grazed his scalp. He glanced at Dmitri. He'd got up and was clutching his daughter, eyes wide. 'Nobody do anything,' he said, raising his hands. 'There's been enough killing.'

'I agree,' the Father said, stepping backwards. 'Come here,' he said to Mavros. He was still holding the revolver on Dmitri and Katia. 'I'm going to leave with him,' he said, indicating the Son. 'I give you my word that I won't harm any of you once we're in the car.'

Mavros glanced at the small part of Damis that he could see behind the Son. 'What do you think?'

'Let's try it,' Damis said in a weak voice. 'I can hold the spear on this bastard.'

Dmitri's mouth was open, but no words came from it. He was pushing Katia gently along the wall.

Mavros got up and moved slowly towards the Father. 'All right,' he said. 'I'm in your hands.'

'Yes, you are.'

'And the Son's in mine,' Damis said. He walked his captive forward, the point of the spear touching the sticking-plaster on his throat. 'Don't try anything.'

The Father put his hand on Mavros's shoulder and pushed him out of the door. Mavros could hear the breath catching in the old man's throat and the heavy steps of the Son to the rear.

Outside, there was no sign of the Audi. The Father must have left it down the track before he doubled back. Mavros was forced round to the driver's seat of the Mercedes. He could see the keys in the ignition.

'We'll take this one,' the Father said to the Son. 'Get in.'

Mavros watched as Damis opened the passenger door and

sat the Son down, the spear still at his neck. The Father got in, the gun on Mavros, and turned the key. Damis pressed the window button and then shut the door, moving the spear quickly back to the Son's throat through the open space.

Mavros realised then that there was a chance they were going to make it. But that meant he would lose the trail to Andonis. 'Did you . . . did you work on my brother?' he asked.

The Father engaged first gear, the gun still pointing at Mavros's chest. 'No,' he said, letting out the clutch. 'I didn't.'

Mavros and Damis stood where they were as the Mercedes swung round and jerked to a halt. The gun was on them, but the Father was looking beyond. Out of the corner of his eye, Mavros saw Dmitri coming down the hallway, a weapon in his hand.

'No!' Mavros shouted, raising his arms. 'No!'

The Mercedes disappeared in a cloud of dust before the Russian-Greek got to the terrace.

The three of them listened as the engine noise faded behind the mass of rock.

Mavros felt the tension leave his body, his shoulders sagging.

Katia came out of the house. Her face lit up when she saw that the three of them were safe.

As far as Mavros was concerned, that made everything he'd been through worthwhile.

Jenny Ikonomou was at the window of her bedroom in the Pink Palace. She was sipping from a glass of cognac. It was after three a.m. and the street below was quiet. She could see the moon above the radio masts on the mountain to the east.

Since they'd got back from Rea Chioti's house, a feeling of well-being had spread through her. She'd done the right thing. Era hadn't been disturbed by the sight of her old comrade Roza Arseni. And, though Rea had been shocked, Jenny had no doubt that meeting Era again would have done her good. The three childless women had to acknowledge their past. Except, in Era's case, there had been no words. Jenny had a faint hope that the experience would shock Era out of her silence, but she wasn't expecting a miracle. This was real life, not one of her TV melodramas.

She lit a cigarette and blew smoke against the windowpane. There was no sign of her brother. It was too early for him to come home. Recently he'd taken to spending the whole night out. It was a long time since she'd asked him about his activities. It was obvious he was up to no good – anyone trusted by the Chiotis family would have crossed the line many times. In the past she hadn't cared, but meeting Alex Mavros had made her think again. She wondered if he'd gone out to Ricardo's house. She'd never been invited. He probably took his women there.

She drained her glass. The Mavros men. She'd tried to block them from her mind when she cut her ties with the Party. The father, Spyros, had been an inspiring speaker, a lawyer who fought against injustice and drove himself to an early grave. And Andonis, he was the most beautiful man she'd ever seen. She fell for him the first time he spoke at a youth party gathering. Even though he was distracted by the struggle against the dictators, he'd allowed her to pursue him and had finally given in to her advances. Why hadn't she admitted that to the younger Mavros? Despite his long hair and strange, imperfect eye, he reminded her of Andonis. That was probably why she'd kept quiet. She'd suppressed that part of her life so well that thinking of Andonis was agony. Their brief romance ended before she was arrested and she'd never seen him again. And Alex was still looking for him. She felt a dampness in her eyes.

There was a tap on her door. The nurse came in. 'Excuse me, Mrs Ikonomou. Era's agitated. I think you might be able to comfort her.'

Jenny walked to the guest room where she'd put her old comrade. It was only as she went in that she remembered it was the one Katia had occupied. She hoped she'd see the promising young woman again. Era was sitting on the bed, her bare feet on the rug. She extended her arms when she saw Jenny and for a moment the actress thought she was going to speak. Her mouth was opening and closing, her forehead lined in concentration.

'What is it, my dear?' Jenny said, sitting down and putting an arm round her. 'Don't worry, we'll be back on the island soon. I know you want your room and the view to the mountains across the water.' She watched as the shrunken woman next to her continued to work her mouth, but no sound came.

'Was it difficult to see Roza Arseni after so many years?' Jenny continued, after a pause. 'I know it must have been. But I think she understands the consequences of what she did to you and Manos now.'

Era leaned her head against the actress's shoulder and they

sat motionless for some time, the nurse watching them with a smile on her lips.

Then came the sound of the doorbell.

'Who can that be at this time of night?' Jenny said, smiling at Era and getting up. 'I'll be back in a minute.'

She looked at the screen by the lift.

Alex Mavros was at the door, his expression grave. 'I need to talk to you, Mrs Ikonomou,' he said. 'It's about your brother. And Rea Chioti.'

Shivering with apprehension, the actress let him in.

Before Mavros went to collect Niki from the hospital, he managed to sleep for a couple of hours. He'd insisted on breaking the news to Jenny Ikonomou in person. She was very emotional, as much over Rea Chioti's suicide as Ricardo's death, which puzzled him. After the Father and Son disappeared into the night, Damis had called a police unit to the house on the hill, as well as an ambulance to take Katia to hospital. As soon as they arrived, Mavros and he drove to the Chiotis villa to confront the head of the family. They found her in a pool of her own blood with what looked like a Mycenaean death mask over her face. According to the guards, she'd been visited by Jenny Ikonomou and two other women earlier in the evening. Damis called in more police. The family's men slipped away when they saw the line of cars coming up the hill. As Commander Kriaras walked on to the terrace a nurse appeared, screaming that Stratos Chiotis had been suffocated.

Niki's voice was tremulous. 'From what you're saying, you could have been killed more than once.' She was sitting on the sofa in his front room, a hand to her eyes. 'Why do you do these things, Alex? I don't know how much more of this I can take.'

'Not all my cases turn out like this one.'

'It's not the first that has,' she said reproachfully.

Mavros put his arm round her. 'I'm sorry you ended up in the middle of it. The doctors seem to think you'll be all right.'

'If I can get the sound of that machine-gun out of my head.' She turned to him. 'I'm glad you found Katia. I hope she'll recover from what she went through.'

'So do I.' He remembered the joyful look on the young woman's face. 'I think she will, with time. Fortunately, Dmitri came out in one piece. He came close to losing his cool more than once.'

Niki smiled. 'He's a good man, Alex.' Her expression darkened. 'But those awful torturers, they got away.'

'They did.' Mavros stood up. 'But I haven't finished with them yet.'

'Where are you going?'

'To talk to Nikos Kriaras. He owes me a favour after what's happened.' He bent down and kissed her. 'Get some rest. I'll see you later.'

'Take care, Alex. And don't be late. You know how bored I get when I'm not at work.' She raised an eyebrow. 'I need to be entertained.'

He laughed. 'I promise I'll entertain you, madam.'

Mavros spent most of the taxi-ride on the phone to his mother and his sister. A TV news bulletin had shown him in the background at the Chiotis villa.

Damis was waiting for him outside police headquarters. His head had been shaved around the bullet wound and a bandage patched on.

'Shouldn't you be lying down?'

'What, here?' Damis looked at the armed policemen on the doors. 'The doctor did recommend that, but I'm not going to miss wrapping this up.'

Mavros followed him in and went through the procedure of obtaining a visitor's ID card. They took the lift to the eleventh floor of the concrete and glass block. The head of the organised crime division's office was at the end of a long corridor. They were shown straight in.

Kriaras was sitting at a wide desk that was stacked with files. He stood up when they approached, but he didn't extend a hand to either of them.

'Cheer up, Niko,' Mavros said. 'This should be the happiest day of your life.'

The commander stared at him and then motioned them to sit down. 'Yes, yes, the Chiotis family's operations are in disarray.' He pursed his lips. 'What bothers me is that I was kept out of things until the last moment. I'd expect that from a self-centred private investigator like Alex Mavros, but not from an undercover operative like Officer Ganas.' He gave Damis an icy look. 'How do you explain your actions?'

Damis returned his gaze and smiled. 'Ganas. I'd almost forgotten that was my name.' The smile disappeared. 'Excuse me, Commander, but I've learned to be very careful about who I report to. The Chiotis family owns plenty of my colleagues.'

'I hope you aren't including me among them,' Kriaras said sharply.

'I don't know. It's too early to say.'

Mavros stifled a laugh. He admired Damis's spirit, but it wasn't likely to prolong his career. 'Aren't you being a bit hard on the officer who almost single-handedly disposed of the city's worst criminal gang?'

'It's too early to say that,' the commander said. 'Besides, the family has diversified in recent years. Many of its legitimate companies will survive. The Russian gangs will fill the gaps soon enough.'

'Give us some credit,' Mavros said angrily. 'Ricardo was a murdering bastard. He was involved in the Father and Son killings. He kidnapped and confined a young woman in horrific conditions. Your people did nothing to find her. Can you blame us for taking things into our own hands?'

'That's enough,' Kriaras said, slapping his hand on the desk-top. 'You're authorised to conduct missing persons investigations within the law, not take on heavily armed criminals.' He turned to Damis. 'And you weren't authorised to take any action concerning Ricardo Zannis or the two men we found tied up in his house.'

'The one called Yannis murdered the drug dealer Sifis Skourtis,' Mavros said. 'Damis can testify to that.'

'All right,' the commander said, raising a hand to placate him. 'We'll need a full statement from you, Alex. And I mean full.' He stood up. 'Please leave us now. I want to speak to this officer alone.'

'Just a minute,' Mavros said, staying where he was. 'We aren't finished. You know Lambis Bitsos?'

An expression of distaste passed across Kriaras's features at the mention of the crime reporter. 'I wish I didn't.'

'Well,' Mavros continued, 'he's a good friend of mine and I owe him a story. I'll give him everything on this, including plenty about police incompetence and collusion with the Chiotis family . . .'

The commander eyed him dubiously. 'Unless?'

'Unless you give me the Father's real name.'

There was a long silence.

'What makes you think I know the Father's name?' Kriaras asked, his gaze directed at the wall behind Mavros.

'Stop playing games, Niko. Either he kept his own name, in which case you'll have it on file. Or he got a new identity, in which case it'll be in another file.'

'He and the Son are animals,' Damis said. 'I saw them at work.'

'It's a pity you didn't call us in at the time,' Kriaras said coldly.

Damis returned his superior's glare.

'The name,' Mavros said. 'You don't have to do anything else. Damis and I will bring them in.'

Kriaras looked at him sceptically. 'Is this about your brother?'

Mavros didn't answer. The torturer had said he hadn't worked on Andonis and Mavros was inclined to believe him. That didn't mean he might not have other information from the time of the dictatorship that would help in the search.

The commander turned away. 'I'm sorry. Even if such information existed, it would be impossible for me to pass it to you, Alex.'

Mavros looked at Damis. 'That's it then,' he said, getting up. 'I'm late for an appointment with the press.'

'Where are you going, officer?' Kriaras demanded.

'With him,' Damis replied coolly. 'I'm finished with the service.'

They walked away together and took the lift down to the ground floor.

'Is Damis a false name too?' Mavros asked.

'No, I kept my own first name. Too confusing otherwise.'

'Come on, then, Dami. I'll buy you the best cup of coffee in Athens.'

The sunlight was beating down on the roofs of the cars and the orange trees at the roadside. It was a fine day. The streets would soon empty as Athenians headed for the mountains and islands to celebrate Easter.

Mavros wondered about taking Niki away to a deserted spot: somewhere the vultures in the media, maddened by the story he was about to give Bitsos, wouldn't be able to track them down. He twitched his head to dispel the idea. There weren't any such places.

It was evening when the Father drove along the lakeside towards the northern town. Its lights were shining out across the water. Under the bright moon, the surrounding mountains were drained of perspective. They looked like the walls of a cell, the old man thought. Or a coffin. He looked in the mirror. The

Son was curled up on the back seat of the BMW. They'd left the Mercedes in a side-street in Athens before picking their own car up from the underground garage. The Son's arm was giving him trouble, though the painkillers the Father got from a chemist had kept him quiet for most of the long journey.

As they entered the outskirts of Kastoria, the Father ran over the decisions he'd taken. They had to get out of the house without delay. He'd heard on the radio that Stratos Chiotis and the woman had been found dead. He hadn't given them much thought. They were only the latest in the long line of people he'd known to predecease him. But he was worried that the new identity Stratos had arranged for him might slip out into the open. There were senior policemen who knew it, though most of them were dead. The investigator Mavros was the kind who'd get on to that. The Son had whined that they should have killed him and the others. The fool. He'd already forgotten that his own spear was at his throat before they got away.

They had to leave the country. There was no shortage of destinations. The Father had a Swiss bank account, as well as a suitcase hidden away. It contained half-a-dozen gold bars and $200,000 US. They could drive into Albania, Macedonia or Bulgaria, sell the car, and vanish. He considered the Son. His arm needed treatment. The old man didn't want to use a Greek doctor. They could bribe one to keep quiet about the gunshot wound or they could do away with him, but that would take time. The Father thought about killing the Son – he was unreliable, he couldn't keep himself under control, and travelling with him would be a constant risk. No, he told himself finally. The fool had learned his lesson – but if he did anything to attract attention when they were on the road, that would be the end of him.

'Pack a suitcase,' the Father said, after he drove the BMW into the garage beneath the house. 'We'll be leaving in half-an-hour.'

The house was cold, but there was no point in turning on the heating. The Father threw a few clothes into a bag, listening as the Son staggered around in the bedroom above. Then he got down on his knees and eased up the floorboards in front of the fireplace. The case with his money and gold was intact. He'd wrapped it securely in plastic sheeting. He opened it and ran his fingers over the crisp notes and cold metal.

'Jesus,' came the Son's voice from behind him. 'You never told me you had so much.'

'I never told you a lot of things, boy. Are you ready?'

'Yes.' The Son put a hand to his forehead. 'My head hurts. I need some water.'

The Father followed him into the kitchen. A mist was rising over the lake. He thought of the time he'd spent in the boat out there. It must have amounted to months, maybe years. It was a pity to lose his fishing gear. The lake was the only place he'd been at peace with the world, the only place he'd felt a bond with the Son.

He turned to see what his offspring was doing – and took the carving-knife full in his chest. As his eyes flickered and the last darkness came down, he found himself back in the cell with the woman who became Rea Chioti – on top of her, her thighs pressing against his sides. She was laughing and crying at the same time. The Father died with that image in his eyes.

The Son waited until after midnight. He'd wrapped the Father in a tarpaulin, then lashed an anchor and chains round it. The quay was deserted. He got the bundle into the boat without difficulty. His arm gave him no pain now. He was exultant. It was the start of a new life. He rowed out into the middle of the mist-covered water and edged the old man over the side.

'To hell with you,' he said, as the Father disappeared into the chill water. The ripples extended and soon all was silent again.

An hour later the Son was on the road to Albania, the money and gold hidden in various places around the BMW. As he approached the customs post, bribe folded in his wallet, he wondered when he would return to Greece. Two faces flashed up before him: the tall man called Damis and the long-haired investigator Mavros.

Sooner or later he'd be back for them.

It was nearly midday when Mavros led Damis into the Fat Man's.

'Nice place, Alex,' Damis said, looking round the café. The only other customers were a pair of wolfish men smoking at a table.

'No media stars in here,' Yiorgos called from behind the chill cabinet. 'I mean it, Alex. You're a disgrace.' He held up a copy of *The Free News*. 'According to that arsehole Bitsos you're responsible for smashing the Chiotis family operations. And the tossers in the police did precious little to help.' He screwed his eyes up at Damis. 'Who's your friend?'

'This is Damis Ganas,' Mavros said, with a smile. 'He's a policeman.'

Two chairs creaked as they were pushed back rapidly. The men who'd been sitting on them made for the door.

'You're doing wonders for my trade,' the Fat Man said, scowling. 'You know how much market traders like the law.'

'Don't worry,' Mavros said, sitting down at his usual table and beckoning Damis to join him. 'We'll buy everything you've got.' He gave Yiorgos an inquisitive look. 'Is there any *galaktoboureko*? I was just telling Damis how good your mother's pastries are.'

The Fat Man looked dejected. 'I was keeping the last two pieces for myself.'

'Paying customers take priority,' Damis said. 'That's what I learned at the police academy.'

'Where did you find this smartarse?' the café owner asked as he unwrapped the custard pie.

'On the case. Do you want hear about it?' Mavros always told him about his jobs when they were over. It was a kind of confession. Even though Yiorgos was a Communist and an atheist, he would never break the confidence.

'I've read the paper.'

Mavros laughed. 'You think that's everything? Damis here wanted to keep his name out of it.'

The Fat Man came over, an avid expression on his sagging features. 'Come on, then. Tell me what really happened. It says you're a hero because you never gave up looking for that girl.' He turned to Damis. 'Tell me that isn't true. I couldn't live with a hero coming in here every morning.'

'It's true all right,' Damis replied. 'Of course, he wasn't the only one.'

Yiorgos stared at them and lumbered away from the table. 'And what kind of coffee do you take, second hero?' he asked sarcastically.

'*Sketo.*'

'Sugar-free like the other one,' the Fat Man said. 'Why aren't there any overweight heroes?'

Mavros leaned towards Damis while the coffee was being made. 'Were you serious about quitting the job?'

'Why do you doubt it?'

'It's a big decision. You could shoot up the promotion ladder after this.'

'No, I've had enough. I did what I had to.'

'What are you planning next?'

Damis watched the Fat Man stirring the coffee over the gas. 'I'm going to visit Martha,' he said in a low voice.

'The woman the drugs took?'

'Yes.' Damis picked up his fork and took a mouthful. 'Christ, this is amazing.'

'The coffee isn't bad either,' Mavros said as Yiorgos came towards the table with his tray.

'Then what?'

Damis shrugged. 'I don't know. Any ideas?'

Mavros took the hint. 'You mean work? With me?'

'We were reasonably effective together this time.'

'I don't know. A lot of the time I don't have enough work to keep myself going, never mind two of us.'

'Maybe I could help you find more.'

'Maybe you could.' Mavros stuck out his right hand. 'All right. Let's give it a try.'

The café owner put the tray down with a crash. 'Now he's shaking hands with the policeman,' he said in disgust.

'Ex-policeman,' said Mavros and Damis in unison.

The Fat Man still wasn't impressed.

Paul Johnston

A Deeper Shade of Blue

When Alex Mavros is asked to track down a missing woman, he jumps at the chance to leave the stifling heat of Athens. Travelling to the small island of Trigono, he soon realises that there is more than one mystery to be solved. How did a young couple drown in the nets of a fishing boat? Why did a British journalist leave without telling her friends? Why is the millionaire Theocharis so nervous and whose bones does old Maro keep beneath her bed?

The answers lie in events that took place during the Second World War, events that tie in with the island's most ancient history. In a race to prevent a terrible crime being repeated, Alex Mavros is pitted against a ruthless and depraved killer . . .

'A sensual portrait of modern Greece, as well as a great page-turner: taste the salt, feel the heat as you follow the dramatic story . . . offers much more than the crime fiction genre usually encompasses: a rich and intelligent story, with fascinating characters'                    *Scotland on Sunday*

HODDER

Paul Johnston

The Last Red Death

IRAKLIS – a mysterious Greek terrorist group. A rogue off-shoot of the communist party. At its head, a man with many names. An elusive master assassin who has been in exile for ten years.

ALEX MAVROS – half-Greek, half-Scottish investigator. A man driven by the desire to find his missing brother, last heard of at an underground resistance meeting during the dictatorship.

GRACE HELMER – an American who saw her father murdered when she was a child. Iraklis was responsible.

Two businessmen are murdered in Athens. The trademark piece of olive wood is found with the victims' bodies.

Iraklis is back. And Grace Helmer employs Mavros to track down her father's killer.

'The character of Mavros and the portrait of Greece make *The Last Red Death* stand out from the crowd'
*Times Literary Supplement*

'*The Last Red Death* is that rare breed of thriller: a ripping page-turner that is also stylish and intelligent. The heart, passions and politics of Greece come absolutely alive under Johnston's masterful touch'
Jeffery Deaver

HODDER

Paul Johnston

Body Politic

Winner of the Crime Writers' Association John Creasey Memorial Dagger

'First rate crime fiction with an original twist'
*Sunday Telegraph*

An independent city where television, private cars and popular music are banned, where the citizens are dedicated to the tourists attending the year-round Festival, and where crime is virtually non-existent, Edinburgh in the year 2020 has its drawbacks for blues-haunted private investigator Quintilian Dalrymple.

But the brutal killing of a guardswoman – the first murder in five years – is enough to scare the Council of City Guardians out of complacency. It looks like the Ear, Nose and Throat Man has returned. And they are forced to turn to the many they demoted to uncover a conspiracy of violence and sexual intrigue that reaches into a dark heart of corruption and threatens to dismember the body politic.

'Fascinating and thought-provoking'          Val McDermid

HODDER

Paul Johnston

House of Dust

'Johnston's plotting is consummate and his characterisation deft. He is also a very funny political satirist'   *Observer*

It's April 2028. Youth gangs roam the streets of independent Edinburgh, forcing the ruling Council of City Guardians to seek advice. Experts from the utopian university-state of New Oxford recommend an extreme deterrent – a maximum security prison alongside the central tourist zone. But at the prison opening ceremony an Edinburgh guardian is shot.

Quint gathers evidence linking New Oxford to the assassination. Sent there to close the case, he finds a ruthless administration beneath the glossy hi-tech veneer. And a conspiracy which leads from New Oxford's mysterious heart, the place known only as the House of Dust, to his home city.

Quint Dalrymple's first investigation outside the former Scotland combines a taut and highly original thriller with pungent political comment.

'Hugely entertaining . . . engagingly imagined'   *The Times*

HODDER